THE HERO WE'VE ALL BEEN WAITING FOR
Julia Quinn

ELIZABETH BOYLE

USA Today Bestselling Author of
One Night of Passion

Stealing the Bride

A WORLD OF ROMANTIC
ENCHANTMENT AWAITS YOU IN
IRRESISTIBLE LOVE STORIES
FROM RITA AWARD-WINNING,
USA TODAY BESTSELLING AUTHOR
ELIZABETH BOYLE

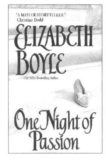

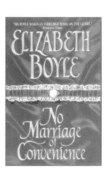

"ELIZABETH BOYLE IS
SURE TO LEAVE YOU SMILING."
Stephanie Laurens

"WIT, PASSION, AND
ADVENTURE,
ELIZABETH BOYLE
HAS IT ALL."
Julia Quinn

A SCANDALOUS ELOPEMENT

The Marquis of Templeton has faced every sort of danger in his work for the King, but chasing after a wayward spinster who's had the effrontery to run off with the wrong man hardly seems worth his considerable talents. But when the heiress in question is none other than Lady Diana Fordham, Temple is about to meet his match. Tempestuous and passionate, headstrong and opinionated, the lady is everything a man should avoid . . .

A DANGEROUS PLAN

Diana has no intention of making Temple's assignment easy. In fact she has every reason to turn his life upside down—just as he did to hers when he broke her heart years ago. Now it's Diana's turn to give Temple a lesson in love, from a teasing glance to a scandalous embrace. However, as she leads him on a merry chase from London to Gretna Green, they soon realize that a kiss once given is hard to forget, and a rekindled passion is impossible to deny.

ELIZABETH BOYLE

Stealing the Bride

An Avon Romantic Treasure

AVON BOOKS
An Imprint of HarperCollinsPublishers

This is a work of fiction. Names, characters, places, and incidents are products of the author's imagination or are used fictitiously and are not to be construed as real. Any resemblance to actual events, locales, organizations, or persons, living or dead, is entirely coincidental.

AVON BOOKS
An Imprint of HarperCollins*Publishers*
10 East 53rd Street
New York, New York 10022-5299

Copyright © 2003 by Elizabeth Boyle
ISBN: 0-380-82090-0
www.avonromance.com

First Avon Books paperback printing: July 2003

Avon Trademark Reg. U.S. Pat. Off. and in Other Countries, Marca Registrada, Hecho en U.S.A.
HarperCollins® is a registered trademark of HarperCollins Publishers Inc.

Printed in the U.S.A.

10 9 8 7 6 5 4 3 2 1

To my ever delightful and loving aunt,
Darlene Green.
Thank you for your endless kindness and generosity.
You live in my heart as your spirit
will live always in these pages.

Prologue

London, 1799

The Fates have a funny way of changing one's life in the blink of an eye, or in the case of Lady Diana Fordham, a moment spent pondering a bright blue bonnet in the window of Madame Renard's millinery shop.

In truth, she'd only paused before the confection of lace and feathers, ducking her head just so, to avoid being seen by her betrothed's cousin, the Marquis of Templeton, who happened to be strolling up the street, gold-tipped walking stick in one hand, his ever-present lorgnette in the other.

The pompous oaf was taking great pains to ensure that everyone noticed him as he paraded along the boulevard. Behind him staggered his ever present valet and driver, Elton, the poor beleaguered servant buried beneath a tower of packages from yet another of the marquis' notorious shopping forays.

Now, it wasn't that Lady Diana wanted to be impolite, for surely it made little sense to snub one's almost relation, as well as the heir to the Setchfield dukedom, but the marquis had a way of mincing about that grated on Diana's nerves.

Oh, there were Corinthians and gallants enough in London, their antics and exaggerated mannerisms hardly noteworthy, but Temple, as the marquis was known about town, made them all pale in comparison. While the *ton* awaited his pronouncements on fashions and seating arrangements with bated breath, Diana thought him nothing more than an arrogant, ridiculous waste of nobility.

For in her estimation, a true man, the type of man Diana admired, was one so honorable, so noble, he was only too willing to lay down his life for his King and country.

Just like her betrothed, Captain Colin Danvers.

Yes, she told herself, Colin was a true hero—not some frippery fellow who'd most likely faint at the first sign of an enemy flag—and probably from the mere fact that the colors weren't adequately coordinated.

Besides, Colin was also a sensible, dependable man. Not the type who made you want to hurl a salver at his head, or bribe a hackney driver to run over him—well, maybe not run over—just graze him a bit or splash a good measure of mud on his new boots and buff trousers.

No, Diana decided, it was better to risk being rude to the socially preeminent marquis than to spend the rest of the afternoon in vexation over the witty and cutting reply that would come to her hours later and would have been perfect for sending Colin's cousin packing.

But since this was an afternoon ordained by the Fates, Diana's attempt at avoidance was for naught.

Even as she took another feigned gander at the bonnet, a tall shadow darkened the afternoon light, while an arm reached over her shoulder, a telltale lorgnette in hand. The silver-framed glasses tapped twice on the glass and its bearer made a *tsk tsk* noise that was nothing less than mocking disapproval.

Diana wanted to groan.

Temple.

Dash it all, he'd spotted her.

"Oh, that shade of blue should be outlawed," he said, shuddering as if he were about to be consumed by his death rails.

Diana wished he would. Draw his last breath, that was.

"Really, my dear, robin's egg blue? Don't you think it's a tad youthful for someone of your advanced years, even if you are about to become a blushing bride?"

His voice, so full of affectation and superiority, rattled down Diana's spine, through her limbs, leaving her fingers knotted into a tight fist around the strings of her reticule.

How very Templish of him to comment on the fact that she wasn't the youngest bride of the Season, as if being nineteen and unmarried was a crime. Never mind that he was right, the shade would be terrible on her.

Was there nothing the man forgot?

Well, there were some things he had . . .

"You needn't worry, my lord," she began to say, "I didn't intend—"

"No, no, don't rush to thank me from saving you from such a disastrous choice," he said, stepping back like a preening rooster, walking stick placed at a jaunty tilt and his other hand on his hip. "Why, I wouldn't be able to look my cousin in the eye if I knew that he'd spent the last three years battling the Spanish or the Russians or whoever it is he's been bedeviling with Lord Nelson, only to sail home to find you standing before the parson wearing that dreadful thing."

Diana struggled to remind herself that she was the daughter of a highly respected nobleman, as well as an almost-graduate of Miss Emery's Establishment for the Education of Genteel Young Ladies—and, as such, cursing at this oaf would not be to her credit.

Still, Diana found herself clenching her teeth to keep from sputtering a very unladylike oath.

Oh, botheration, she thought instead as she gathered her best manners back into place.

Forcing a smile on her lips, she turned ever so slowly around and gave the marquis a polite nod.

"My lord, how lovely it has been to see you again. But alas, I see Mrs. Foston coming and I must—" she said, as she went to sidestep out of his shadow.

Temple stuck his arm out to block her escape, then with the handle of his walking stick, he tipped back his tall beaver hat so he could look her directly in the eye. "There now, Lady Diana, you needn't try to bamboozle me with your fancy Bath manners. While I'm sure your father spent a fortune to see you well schooled, it is obvious his money was ill-spent. Why, I can see from your expression you'd like nothing more than to pluck the ribbons from that hat and strangle me with them. But then again, you've never been like the rest of these ordinary girls they try to pass off as Originals, now have you?"

Diana's gaze flew up, fully expecting to find the marquis' mocking glance staring down at her, but there was something altogether different glimmering behind his dark, mysterious eyes.

A light daring her to contradict him. To disprove his words, and just be ordinary.

Or even, she found herself thinking, an offer to be more than just a well-mannered miss.

An offer she'd accepted from him once before . . .

Yet whatever was alight there beneath the wicked tilt of his dark brows, it was hastily doused when, from behind him, Elton let out a low cough.

"Uh-hmm, milord," the man said. He made a jerking nod

toward a nondescript doorway tucked between two shops across the street, where an elegantly dressed young woman paced back and forth.

Despite the fact that her face was all but hidden in the depths of her bonnet, Diana instantly recognized the other woman as Mademoiselle Lucette de Vessay, the only child of the Comte and Comtesse Sandre. The girl's émigré status and lack of funds had not diminished her good standing in the Marriage Mart. Having come out a year earlier, she'd taken the staid *ton* by storm with her coy French manners.

And much to the annoyance of the other young ladies seeking husbands, what Miss de Vessay lacked in dowry was more than made up for by her ravishing good looks and her lofty connections to the House of Bourbon. Her father had died at the Place de la Révolution on the same day as the King, serving his ruler to the bloody end. As for the comtesse and her daughter, it was rumored they'd been rescued from their tumbrel by a heroic, yet unnamed Englishman.

Not even London's best gossips had been able to elicit their benefactor's identity from the grateful ladies.

But why Miss de Vessay was on Bond Street, unescorted and hidden beneath such a poor disguise, Diana could only guess.

And from the look on Temple's face, she suspected he knew the answer.

"Oh yes, how right you are, Elton," the marquis was saying, slanting a haphazard glance across the street. "I'll be late for my appointment with my, uh, tailor. I fear I must leave you to your own devices, Lady Diana," he added hastily, reaching to take her hand and make a quick bow over her gloved fingers. He lingered for a moment longer than appropriate, his dark, fathomless eyes meeting her gaze with a flash of something that caught her breath in her throat.

Once again Diana felt that he had something else to say.

What surprised her even more was that she longed to hear it.

After all these years, damn the man, he still had the power to leave her heart trembling.

But all he said was, "To the tailor's, it is. Lawk, if I don't get there early for my fittings, he starts on his own and makes the most dreadful mistakes." And with that, Temple took off in that great ambling stride of his that Diana would have recognized anywhere.

"Yes, go," she said after him. "I would hate to keep you from such an important task." And she would have left it at that and gone into Madame Renard's just to buy the hideous bonnet, if only to prove Temple wrong that the shade wasn't dreadful on her, when she heard a scuffle behind her.

She turned to discover Mademoiselle de Vessay caught in the arms of two ruffians. In a flash, they dragged the helpless girl through the now open door, plucking her from the street before anyone noticed.

That is, except Diana.

She spoke before she even thought about it. "Temple!" she cried out. "Temple, help! Miss de Vessay has been—" Diana stopped before she could even finish when she realized her pleas were falling on deaf ears.

Temple paused for a moment, glancing at the empty spot where the French lady had once stood, then with an apparent shrug of his shoulders, continued around the corner as if his only care in the world was whether to choose gold or green for his next waistcoat.

Why, of all the henhearted, inconsiderate . . . Diana fumed.

She glanced around for her companion, but Mrs. Foston was still in the ribbon shop next door.

Not that the widow would be of much help. Diana glanced up and down Bond Street, only to find it deserted. Of all the times to be shopping, she'd chosen this unfashionable hour when there was no one else about except a few harried ladies' maids.

And since Diana had taken a hired carriage, there was no capable and burly Lamden footman to call to action.

She drew a deep breath, and realized there was only one thing she could do.

Go to Miss de Vessay's aid herself. Though she barely knew the girl, and what she did know, she didn't overly care for, she couldn't let her fall prey to this evil mischief.

Without glancing left or right, she dashed straight into the street and was almost run over by a fast-moving carriage. In a flash the gilded crest of the Setchfield duchy blazed past her eyes.

Temple, in his grandfather's elegantly appointed carriage, was fleeing in the face of adversity.

Her hands went to her hips, her mouth set in a hard line. The strange fleeting feelings he'd ignited in her moments before vanished as she resolved herself to the truth about the marquis.

Not only was he a vapid fool, but an undeniable coward.

Diana was of half a mind to go after the useless nit and give him a thrashing herself.

But that would have to wait, she knew, as a hapless cry of protest came issuing out of the doorway ahead. She girded her resolve for battle and tried to open the door. She pulled and turned at the handle, but it held fast to her attempts. Somewhere beyond the portal, there was another cry for help and a great commotion erupting, and Diana knew she had little time to lose.

Ignoring the fact that she had on her best pelisse, she

rammed her shoulder into the door again and again until it finally gave way. Without hesitating, she dashed inside.

Darkness greeted her, and she blinked and swiped at her eyes in hopes of gaining any sign of what was before her. Then she spied a bit of light coming from the end of the corridor, a beacon guiding her further into this fool's folly.

She pressed on despite her better judgment.

When she got to the end of the hallway, there was a partially open doorway that led to the alleyway behind the shops. As she looked outside, the sight that met her eyes wasn't the one she had prepared herself to witness.

On the ground lay one of Miss de Vessay's assailants. His lifeless eyes stared directly at her, while a pool of blood bubbled around the hilt of a knife buried in his chest.

Diana's throat went dry, her knees buckling despite her best efforts to remain stalwart. She dropped to the floor, her hand catching hold of the latch to steady herself. Beyond the dead man lay the crumpled form of Miss de Vessay, but to Diana's relief, the lady still lived, for her shoulders shook with the ragged shudders of weeping.

And then to Diana's shock and amazement, she realized there was a man standing over the dead villain. And not just any man.

Temple.

His once jaunty beaver hat was gone, his immaculate and perfectly cut jacket torn. Blood poured from a split lip. His chest rose and fell in great heaving rails as he stared down at his vanquished foe.

Diana saw her entire world topple. Temple hadn't fled from the scene, but raced around the corner and into the alley, with an uncanny intuition as to Miss de Vessay's terrible fate.

Gone was the fop, the fussy Corinthian, the man of precise manners and witless jests. And standing in his place was a man transformed, a hero in its noblest definition.

Diana reeled back into the shadows, her heart hammering at the sight of him—the man she'd thought lost forever. The man she'd once loved with all her heart.

And even as she found him, he was almost lost anew. For the second assailant rose from a hiding spot amidst a pile of refuse, deep in the shadows, a pistol in one hand and a deadly gleam in his eye.

"Temple, behind you," she shouted.

With instincts she didn't know any man possessed, he dropped to the cobbles of the alley and rolled, even as the report of the pistol shattered the muffled silence around them.

The bullet meant for Temple's heart ripped into the doorway above her, sending shards of wood showering down. Diana fell face first to the floor, her eyes screwed shut, her hands over her ears, as another pistol fired.

As quickly as the alleyway had exploded in violence, a deafening silence filled the void. It claimed every sound she thought possible, even the pounding of her terrified heart. Yet nothing could hold back the inevitable and unending sounds of London, which very soon started to reclaim their hold. After what felt like hours, but was most likely only a few moments, she willed herself to open at least one eye and see what had happened.

She didn't know if she dared. Having seen the face of death on a stranger was one thing, but seeing Temple thusly, she didn't know if she could bear it.

Yet she had to look.

Peering through the smoke and haze, she spied the other man still standing in the rubble, smoldering pistol in hand.

The curse that she'd held back earlier, the one meant for

the marquis, sprang from her lips, followed by an anguished "*Temple*."

As she said his name, it was as if the wind carried her cry forth, the heart-wrenching grief behind it sending his dangerous foe teetering and wavering, until he toppled over. He hit the ground with the kind of thud that left Diana no doubts that he was dead.

Still she couldn't see Temple.

She scrambled to her hands and knees.

As she was about to call for him again, Miss de Vessay found both her feet and her voice.

"Monsieur! Oh, *mon chèr* Temple!"

The girl's dress was torn in two places and spattered in mud. But her dirty gown hardly mattered. Her hood had fallen back, and her hair fell free in a halo of tangled dark curls. Her face paled by her experience, still claimed a delicate rose hue which colored her cheeks and lips. She looked like an angel rising to take him to heaven.

Diana wondered how a woman, any woman, could look so beautiful in such a state of dishabille? She took one look down at her own dirty and ruined costume and knew she resembled a tattered scarecrow in comparison.

"Oh, monsieur, are you well?" Miss de Vessay asked, taking a few measured, yet tentative steps forward.

It was then that Diana spied him rising from the ground, holding a small pistol, his jaw set in a line of fierce determination.

He lived.

Her heart lurched into a wild tattoo of celebration. Temple was alive.

And Diana realized something else.

He'd lied. He'd lied to the *ton* with his pandering masquerade, his light quips, and his foolhardy antics as the town fool. Yet of all his sins, the one that scorched her short-lived happiness into a livid anger was that he'd lied to *her*.

Temple shot a brief glance at one opponent, then the other, before turning his attention to Mademoiselle de Vessay. "Are you hurt? Have you been harmed, Lucette?"

Lucette? He was on such intimate terms with the lady that he called her by her given name?

Diana's anger started to boil over.

"*Non. Oh! Chic alors*, you have saved me yet again, Temple." She reached up, a lacy handkerchief in her hand, and dabbed ever so gently at his mouth, her gaze locked on the curve of his lips.

Diana had the urge to reach out and give the flirtatious French girl a good shaking. Why, the saucy minx was all but begging Temple to kiss her!

Something Diana knew a little bit about.

"And now you have saved me," he said softly, his fingers twining around Lucette's hand before he took the handkerchief from her and finished the task of cleaning his bloodied face without her overly attentive assistance. "Thank you, mademoiselle, for your warning. If you hadn't cried out, I fear I would not be here."

Lucette shook her dark head. "Monsieur, it was not—" Then she glanced up where Diana stood hidden in the shadows of the doorway and stopped, her eyes widening. If she saw Diana, she gave no indication to Temple, for she quickly returned her adoring gaze to him. "It was really nothing, monsieur, considering all you have done for me and my mother. You have saved my life twice now, and my small act today is nothing in comparison to your endless and selfless bravery." She paused, so utterly poignant in her emotion, as only the French could be before she finished with a simpering, tear-laden declaration, "I will remain forever in your debt."

Diana's hand covered her mouth to stifle a gasp. The de Vessays' savior was Temple? Temple in Paris? During the Reign of Terror? *Impossible.*

And yet . . . perhaps not. From what she had seen today, it was possible to believe that Temple was capable of anything.

Including deceiving her into thinking he wasn't the man she'd loved.

Temple began straightening his waistcoat, then smoothed back his hair into some semblance of order, the fop starting to replace the hero. "Lucette, I have never thought of our past as a debt to be repaid. I did what was necessary—what any honorable man would have done that day."

They stared at each other for a moment, as if both reliving an experience that neither of them was likely ever to forget, and Diana felt a pang of jealousy run through her.

That Temple had shared so much of his life with this . . . this . . . other woman, while she had been led to believe otherwise about him, left out of his life, his secrets . . . well it stung Diana to her very core.

"You have taken your last assignment, Lucette," Temple was saying. "Now that the French are aware of your work for Pymm and the Foreign Office, you will no longer be safe in London."

"But *mon cher*—"

Her words ended as he put his forefinger to her lips. "No protests. I shall not hear them. You can no longer be a part of this dangerous work." He nodded toward the end of the alley. "There is Elton with the carriage. He will see you safely to your apartment. Then you and your mother are to leave town. At once."

The lady took one glance down the alley, and then shook her head. "*Non, non.* I cannot do this thing you ask."

Diana was of a mind to offer to help the girl pack.

"Lucette, do not try your wiles with me," Temple said. "I know them too well."

I just bet you do, Diana seethed.

"Go to Lord Seaton," he said, continuing his instructions. "Tell him you have changed your mind. Marry him, Lucette. He will keep you safe."

"In Scotland," she pouted.

"Yes, in Scotland. But never fear, one day you'll convince him to bring you back to London. He loves you too much not to fall prey to your requests. Besides, I suspect you have more than just a fond regard for him as well."

Some regard, Diana thought, as she watched the girl practically throwing herself at Temple. If she were Lord Seaton, she'd toss the flirtatious baggage into the nearest loch and let her drown.

To his credit, Temple disengaged himself from his enthusiastic admirer, then escorted her down the alleyway to his waiting carriage.

Diana tried to breathe in and out in an even keel, as she sorted through the upheaval in her heart.

Temple hadn't deserted her three years earlier. He'd just joined the desperate struggle to save England from French tyranny. What had he said to Mademoiselle de Vessay?

It is too dangerous.

He probably thought he was saving her from a life of worry and heartache.

"Wretched fool," she muttered.

She would have waited for him—for a dozen years if that was what it would take. She wrung her hands together until she stopped at the recognition of one thing she'd forgotten in all the confusion.

The emerald and pearl betrothal ring on her finger.

The horror of her realization sent her bolting down the

hall, fleeing back to the civilized world of Bond Street until she stood once again in front of Madame Renard's millinery shop as if the last ten minutes had never happened. The crunch of carriage wheels caught her attention, and in a blinding flash, the Setchfield carriage sped past her, leaving her alone with the realization that she was engaged to the wrong man.

"Oh, Temple, why did you do this to us?" she whispered after his departing carriage.

Too dangerous . . . too dangerous . . .

Damn him, she thought. Damn his foolish sense of honor.

Well, if Temple could forsake her because his honor and nobility demanded as much, she would do what she suspected women had done since time immemorial. Find a way to persuade him otherwise . . . no matter how long it took or how many betrothals she had to break.

Chapter 1

London, 1809

It was, by all accounts, a rather typical night at White's. The men of London's social elite had gathered together for another evening of drinking and gambling and bragging to their hearts' content.

Who would have guessed that these rarefied members of the *ton* were about to witness the scandal of the Season?

As usual, the most crowded spot in the great room was around the Marquis of Templeton, or as most people called him, Temple. Not exactly the proper address for a man who by chance, or rather by birth, was the Duke of Setchfield's heir, but Temple he was, and, many suspected, Temple he would always be.

Cut off by his imperious grandfather from any family funds because of his wastrel ways and because he wouldn't bend to the duke's constant demands, he made do as he could, by being the perfect houseguest, the best of company. In short, he was invited everywhere.

There were advantages to having the marquis as a part of one's social event. He knew all the gossip. He could spot an ill-tied cravat across a shadowy room faster than a Bow Street runner could collar a pickpocket. With the aid of his trusty lorgnette, he could tell whether a man's coat had been stitched by Weston or by a country tradesman copying the master tailor's latest trends for half the price.

If you needed to know what color was best to wear to Lady Brickton's fête, which young miss had the plumpest dowry, or from whom to obtain the finest, fittest, and best polished Hessians, then Temple was your most capable confidant.

So it was that the marquis moved through the *ton* like a blithe and welcome breeze, invited everywhere—for it would never do to snub a future duke—and laughed at for the follies, foibles, and bill collectors following in his wake. He lived his life without an apparent care in the world, as long as one discounted his agonizing search for a tailor who would overlook his continual lack of funds.

In truth, he was a man to be envied.

In truth, he was a man living a singularly calculated lie.

So while he stood in White's, the living example of all that was wastrel and foolish about the *ton*, his mind was far away on more pressing matters. Problems so urgent that few would have thought they'd find anyplace to lodge amongst all the wool and lint that most believed made up the interior workings behind the marquis' engaging smile.

Especially considering his current subject of discussion— a lecture to young Lord Harry Penham on how to select the perfect valet.

The jest lay in the fact that Penham, on his first Season in town and a greenling in every definition of the word, obviously knew nothing of the fact that Temple had never hired a valet, let alone that he couldn't afford the services of one.

Temple's only servant was a disreputable one-eyed man who drove the marquis' carriage and ran his errands. Elton was recognized by one and all, and most held him in fearful regard, for it was rumored that Temple had bought the man off a scaffold—if only to have a loyal servant who wouldn't mind an infrequent salary.

But obviously Penham knew none of this, for he hung on Temple's every word as if he were receiving Holy Scriptures.

"What agency are you using?" the marquis asked, his lorgnette tapping at his chin. "For you'll never find the right fellow without the help of a good agency." He eyed the disgraceful state of the younger man's cravat and made a *tut tut* noise that signaled his wholehearted disapproval. "Let me guess, you've retained Fogelmann's?"

When Penham nodded, Temple shuddered and clutched at his heart. "Upon my horror, you'll be sporting some Oriental tied piece of silk before the end of the week." He glanced at the gathering crowd. "Which I daresay might be an improvement on this." Temple took his lorgnette and swirled it through the mess of lace and silk that made up Penham's woeful attempt at a waterfall.

Several in the crowd began to chuckle.

"Well, I-I-I-" Penham sputtered, quite flustered at being put in the spotlight by the infamous marquis. "I-I-I didn't know."

"Obviously." Temple sighed again and eyed the man from head to toe. "A Cambridge man, I suppose."

Penham nodded again, this time a little more warily.

"Whatever are they teaching there these days?" Temple stalked around the young man, tapping his lorgnette in his palm like a riding crop. "A gentleman must be prepared for all sorts of calamities. Why, you never know when your valet may take ill," he advised. "Or for that matter, run off complaining about lack of wages or some other nonsense." This comment brought a hearty round of laughter. Temple winked at his audience over Penham's head. "It is imperative that you are able to do a respectable job yourself or you'll never catch the eye of that certain lady."

This brought Penham's attention up in an instant. "But I didn't think anyone knew that I—"

"Tut tut," Temple said. "Read the betting book, my good man. Or better yet, read the *Morning Post*. You and Nettlestone have caused quite a sensation with your competition for that lady's hand."

"My intentions toward her are quite honorable," Penham asserted. "Not that the same can be said for my rival." He nodded toward Aloysius, the seventeenth Baron of Nettlestone, who sat across the room playing *vingt-et-un*.

"Yes," Temple drawled, sparing a glance first at one man, then the other. "I daresay your heart and estate in Dorset could use the improvements her fortune will bring more so than that drafty pile of rocks Nettlestone calls home."

Penham tried to stammer out a response, but Temple stopped him with a shake of his head. "Now back to the matter at hand. The state of your cravat. One cannot call on such a discerning chit without displaying the utmost sense of fashion. Why, I can assure you, the lady in question will never respect you if you show up looking like a dustman." He tipped his head back to give everyone a better view of his own meticulously tied silk. "Penham, let this be your first lesson in courting. A correctly tied noose. It will prepare you for marriage better than anything else."

This brought another tide of laughter.

"Now, I've always said that a good heiress and her fortune are a terrible thing to let lie fallow, so let me be of assistance in your quest for her three thousand a year." Temple began removing his coat and nodded at the young man to serve as his valet. Penham bounded up from his seat, only too willing to give the marquis the assistance he needed. "This shall be a lesson to all of you on how to tie a proper cravat without the aid of a valet," he said, beginning to unwind the length of cloth from around his neck.

A ripple of awed whispers sped through the room. Some left their card games with a pile of markers in front of winning hands. Others left good friends mid-sentence, while some of the older dandies, who liked to ape the younger set, rattled and wheezed away from their brandies and boasts of past conquests to hear the marquis' secrets.

"Say here, Temple," Lord Nettlestone called out, barging across the room and pushing his way through the crowd. "The lady is very likely to be *my* wife. I'll not let Penham have such an obvious advantage."

"My dear Lord Nettlesome—" Temple began.

"Nettlestone," the man corrected.

"Right, right. Nettlestone. However do I always get that wrong?" He slanted a glance at his audience, his brows arched in wide-eyed innocence.

Most had the decency to stifle their laughter as best they could manage.

"Now there, Nettlesome," Temple said. "Take a seat next to young Penham here, and may the better man win the lady's favors."

The two rivals glared at each other.

Temple tapped his lorgnette against his chin. "Now, where was I? Ah, yes. How to tie one's cravat without the aid of a valet."

The baron waved over a waiter and haughtily demanded pen, ink, and paper be brought immediately—lest any detail of Temple's lesson be missed.

Once the writing implements arrived, Temple held up his neck cloth, about to begin his demonstration, when at that moment the door to White's opened.

An unusual chill, especially for June, rifled through the room, rustling newspapers and wigs alike, bringing a shiver down more than one spine.

There wasn't a pair of eyes in the room that didn't turn toward the entrance.

"She has been taken!" a frantic voice cried out. "Kidnapped by the veriest of scoundrels!"

The patrons of White's were well rewarded with the spectacle of the Earl of Lamden making a blustering and blazing entrance, brandishing his silver-tipped walking stick like a broadsword. He might have appeared like a fierce, mighty clansman of old, one of his Scottish forebears, if it hadn't been for his gaunt and yellowish features, giving evidence to the rumors that he was indeed ill and dying.

His frenzied lament, tinged as it was with a shocking madness, brought a stunned silence to White's. The London club had seen many an undignified display in its more than one hundred years of catering to the privileged males of England—angry curses over lost fortunes, or the drunken ramblings of a lovelorn young buck, but not this, this mindless, almost feral rage.

Lamden pressed farther into the room. "She is taken, I tell you! Can't any of you nitwits hear me? She has been stolen away!"

Penham stood up. For all his provincial manners, he was a decent sort. "Who, my lord? Who has been taken?"

"Diana, of course! She's been carried off to Gretna Green."

It took a moment for everyone in the room to digest the fact that Lamden was discussing his eccentric spinster of a daughter, Lady Diana Fordham. And once they realized the extent of what he was saying, that she had been spirited away like some lithesome and innocent beauty in the dewy blush of her first Season, most couldn't conceal their amusement.

The room pealed with a hilarious refrain of guffaws and hearty bellows.

But not so Temple. If the chilling breeze that had made its eerie way through the room had gone anywhere, it seemed to have settled in his gut.

Diana? Stolen away? It couldn't be, Temple told himself, before he even realized his heart had taken an unnatural skip at the shocking news.

Likewise, Penham and Nettlestone did not join the others' levity, for they stood watching the scene before them unfold, mirror images of disbelief etched across their faces.

For up until a few moments earlier, each had been of the opinion that Lady Diana would soon be his wife.

The rollicking laughter from the rest of White's patrons had yet to subside, but it did so with the utmost urgency when Lamden began pounding the floor with his walking stick.

Thump! Thump! Thump! The silver tip dug into the oaken floors with the same authority as a schoolmaster's switch.

"Enough of your disrespect! I have heard enough!" Lamden bellowed.

The earl, mad or not, was not one to be gainsaid for long. His English lineage was far too hallowed, going back, some said, to Arthur, while his Scottish titles were of royal blood. Besides, he was an elderly man who had served his King and country well, and if his daughter was indeed in peril, it was the duty of every respectable Englishman in the room to see that she was brought back safely to the bosom of her family.

It could, after all, be their own sister or daughter who was about to be the subject of one of the Season's best *on dits*.

Temple stepped forward, hauling a chair for the wavering old man, but stopped himself. It was one of the hardest things about posing as an idiot, one couldn't do the decent thing when it was so very necessary.

Fortunately, Penham took the cue and guided the earl into the comfortable confines of the richly appointed leather seat in the center of the room. "Tell us, sir, what has happened to Lady Diana?"

"Taken away, I tell you. By a most scurrilous fellow." Lamden bowed his head into his hands and let out a sigh that should have tugged at the hearts of all who heard it.

Instead, before Penham could ask who this knave might be, bets began circling the room as to this daring fellow's identity. It never took much to convince the patrons of White's to start tossing down wagers, and this was too rich an opportunity to allow it to pass without joining into the rampant speculation—propriety and respect aside.

Temple caught one of the waiters by the arm and whispered to him. "Go fetch the earl some whiskey. Glen Adich, if you have it." He slipped the man a coin, one he could ill-afford.

Moments later, the efficient servant returned, glass and bottle in hand, and served the earl a fortifying measure.

Lamden absently muttered his thanks, and then glanced at Penham. "I'd resigned myself that she would marry either you or Nettlestone. I wouldn't have been pleased, you being only a second son, and Nettlestone, well . . ." He fluttered his hand dismissively toward the man as one might wave off an errant fly. "Well, he's Nettlestone."

Many around the room nodded in understanding.

The earl's lament continued. "But this . . . this is kidnapping! A deed most foul!"

"Who, my lord?" Penham asked. "Who has done this to your daughter?"

Lamden held out his glass, and Nettlestone, who had also moved forward, poured another measure. The earl drank, wiped his mouth, and then closed his eyes.

White's hadn't been this silent since the time the Duke of Northrup had waged his best Kent properties on the single turn of a card. Every ear strained to hear the earl's next words.

"Cordell. She has been taken by Viscount Cordell."

The silence erupted into a collective gasp. Lady Diana might have run off with the devil himself and been in better company. A reckless gambler, caused in no small measure by his excessive drinking, Cordell had recently been involved in some shady mishap in the stews. He hadn't been seen around town of late, and there had been whispered conjecture that he'd gone to escape not only his creditors, but also the magistrate.

Obviously, he'd been around enough to convince Lady Diana to run off with him. In this gamble, he'd certainly cast his die into a rich pot. She was Lamden's only child and heiress. Money enough to keep even Cordell dicing and whoring for years.

Penham leaned over toward Temple. "Is this Cordell a bad sort?"

"Bad?" Temple snapped before he knew what he was doing, breaking out of his characteristic sunny disposition. "You haven't heard of *Cordell*?"

"I-I-I didn't know," Penham stammered, returning to the earl's side and looking as if he wished himself back at his poor country estate with only the adoring company of his hunting dogs and his ill-tempered mother, the Dowager Marchioness of Staverly.

"I admit I've been reluctant toward your suit, lad," Lamden said to the young man. "But if you will bring her back, stop this travesty before it is too late, I will gladly give her to you."

"But, my lord," Nettlestone protested. He straightened his bottle-green jacket and rose up on his toes so he looked the seated earl in the eyes. "What of my proposal? 'Tis well known the lady favors me over Penham here."

A tide of laughter trailed after this ridiculous boast.

And Nettlestone, never overly witty enough to realize that he was making himself appear ridiculous, glanced up, his bandy chest puffing out and stretching his yellow striped waistcoat to the point where the buttons threatened to burst their threads. "I say she does. She favors me over Penham. And I daresay I'm the better man for her." He turned back to Lamden. "I'll fetch her back for you, my lord. I've the best set of cattle in town and the fastest curricle. I'll be on the Manchester road before Penham here can even summon a hack."

Penham ruffled at this declaration. While he was only a second son and unlikely to inherit since his brother already had five sons to his lusty credit, Harry's Penham lineage made him as eminently qualified as a prospective son-in-law as Nettlestone.

But Nettlestone had the younger man on one point—the baron was a better horseman. Whereas he irritated all he met in Society, for some reason the hoof-and-cloven set found him irresistible. No one was his equal in getting an impossible amount of miles from even the worst set of nags.

It had once been bet that Nettlestone could get more miles out of a Jersey cow than Penham could his brother's best Barbary Arab.

As the two men began to argue the matter, Lamden's

walking stick once again brought order to the chaos, pounding on the floor thrice, then a fourth time, before the two men ceased their bickering.

"She must be saved. Someone must bring her back. Just return my dearest Diana. And the man who saves her shall have her as his bride." Lamden sighed and shook his head with a sad air of resignation. "Just get to her before Cordell steals her across the border. *Steals more than he deserves*."

Penham and Nettlestone nodded in complete understanding. The two rivals glowered one last time at each other before they shot toward the door, tripping and scrambling their way like a pair of terrier pups. Well-wishers and compatriots tossed their coats and hats forward, then followed them into the street, cheering encouragement.

The noise and excitement brought patrons from Brook's, as well as Boodle's, outside. Soon St. James looked like a Monday afternoon at Tattersall's.

Temple stood at the window and watched as the two suitors shot hasty orders to their drivers before setting off for Highgate and then on to the Manchester road.

A long unheard voice nagged at him. *Do something.*

Unconsciously he shook his head, ignoring the need to follow its unwanted advice.

Demmit, Diana. You're a headstrong, willful bit of baggage. What trouble have you found your way into now?

Nothing that was any of his business, he decided, turning from the raucous display. To his surprise, he spied his cousin, Colin, Baron Danvers, stepping out of the shadows from across the room.

Of all his relations, Colin was his favorite, so he grinned at the sight of him, having thought him well out to sea on another of his clandestine voyages for the Admiralty.

At that moment Lord Oxham stopped by Temple's side.

The tall, narrow man sniffed and shook his head as he glanced in Colin's direction. "I say, it's a fine turn of events when a man who should be swinging from the end of rope is as rich as Midas just because he has a talent for piracy and thievery." He turned his back to Colin, giving him the cut direct.

"Piracy and thievery, well, I never!" Lord Bethel, another of Temple's set, added in agreement.

"I fear I will have to extend Lord Danvers the courtesy of my company," Temple told them. "One may choose his friends and companions, but I fear family is another matter."

"Bah," Lord Bethel spat out. "I don't see how he dare show his face here. Dirty business and its cowardly ilk have no place at White's."

"Yes, perhaps," Temple agreed, all the while casting a discerning glance at the cup in Bethel's hand—filled to the rim with illegal French brandy. It was good to know the man knew where to draw the line on not associating with "dirty business."

"Besides," Oxham muttered. "You were about to share with us your secret for tying that infamous cravat of yours."

Temple took a preening stance. "I wish I could, my friends. But my cousin's money has a way of coming in handy when I am short on blunt. So if you'll excuse me, I'll see if he is inclined to buy me a drink or two . . . and perhaps loan me something for my tailor. Elton informs me the man is becoming rather insistent about my bill, despite the fact that I am a walking advertisement for his services."

The gentlemen all laughed, but once Colin stepped into their midst, their good humor ended and en masse they moved away without so much as a word.

Other men might have taken such a slight to heart, but Colin's court martial and subsequent disgrace nine years earlier had made such occurrences commonplace, and he barely spared the departing fops a glance.

Instead, he caught Temple by the arm and steered him to a quiet and secluded corner. "Are you going after her?" he demanded.

Temple smoothed his wrinkled sleeve. "After whom?"

"Diana, you witless lout. How can you stand idly by and watch her be married off to one of those . . . those . . ."

"Idiots?" Temple offered.

"Yes, idiots." Colin frowned. "How can you?"

Once again that needling little spark of conscience prodded him. He ignored it, just as he intended to ignore his cousin. "Might I remind you, the lady wouldn't be in this spot if you hadn't allowed your betrothal to her to go awry."

Colin had the decency to flinch at this accusation, but any guilt he might have felt didn't last very long. "You know that isn't what happened." On the eve of the baron's wedding to Lady Diana, Colin's conviction for treason had been made public. The lady had cried off—quite vehemently—not that anyone had questioned her hasty decision.

However, Colin had always maintained that there was another reason for her sudden reversion of affections . . .

Temple groaned. "Don't start down this path again, cousin. The lady is not suited for me, and I am certainly not suited for her."

"But—"

Temple held up a hand to stave off any arguments. "Diana has the luck of the devil. She'll land on her feet like a tabby cat. We both know her only too well. She'll probably have Cordell sober and knitting socks for orphans before they reach Northamptonshire."

Colin gave a grudging nod to that notion. There was no arguing the lady had bottom and nerve to spare. The scandal at Almack's and her escapades in Hyde Park were proof of that.

"So enough of this," Temple said, pulling up a chair for Colin and then one for himself. "Tell me what brings you back to town so soon."

Colin remained standing. "I don't believe this. You aren't going after her?"

"No." He let his tone ring with a firm measure of finality to convince Colin of his resolve not to get involved where Lady Diana Fordham was concerned.

Reluctantly, Colin took his seat, and Temple changed the subject immediately. "Now tell me what has you back in port so soon. I thought you were bound for Spain again." He waved for a bottle to be brought over, then leaned back, stretching out his legs in front of him and folding his arms over his chest. "Let me guess—you discovered your devious wife stowed away again and had to bring her back. Now there is a task for the stout of heart."

"No, Georgie is safely home. Actually, I was in France and happened upon some disturbing information. I came home immediately to—"

Temple sat up in his seat. "Is this about Orlando's murder?"

Colin's youngest brother, Orlando, had been murdered two years earlier, and there were still more questions than answers surrounding the circumstances.

His cousin shook his head. "No, it is something entirely different. In fact, I asked Pymm to meet me here."

Temple's brow arched at the impending arrival of the Foreign Office's disreputable spymaster. "Pymm? Here? It must be dire indeed. Especially if you got him to come to the hallowed halls of White's rather than meet him in that wretched hellhole he loves so much in Seven Dials."

Colin shuddered. "So you've been to the Rose and Lion, have you?"

"Only once when I was green and foolish," Temple confessed, grimacing at the memory. "I still can't believe you enticed Pymm to come *here*. You know he never mixes with the *ton* unless it is an absolute necessity."

"Actually, I suspected I'd find you here as well. I wanted to ask if either of you had heard rumors about—"

"There you are." A sharp voice interrupted Colin's question.

Temple spared a glance over his shoulder. There was no mistaking that dirty, ill-tied cravat, or the rumpled and stained coat. "Pymm, my good man, would it hurt you to simply find a decent tailor?"

Already several of the members were casting disparaging glances in their direction at this latest unwanted addition to Temple's coveted table. Given his shabby appearance, they probably assumed Pymm was a bill collector who'd managed to slip past the watchful eye of White's imperious doorman and was even now dunning the marquis for his long unpaid tailor's or greengrocer's bill. As a courtesy to Temple, they edged away from his table, staying a respectful distance from his unwanted guest—besides, most of them had their own credit problems, and they might well be next on this man's list of those up the River Tick.

"Tailors! Bah," Pymm said, waving a hand at his favorite, and at times most exasperating, agent.

For if the truth were told, it wasn't Temple's gadding about town that the Duke of Setchfield found so objectionable. What galled him to the core and had been the bane of their relationship for over a decade was that Temple chose to risk his life and limb, as well as the continuation of the Setchfield dukedom, in the secret service of his King and country.

Instead of basking in the luxury his grandfather's goodwill could provide, the marquis took assignments that had sent him into the battlefields of Spain and the very dark and oh-so-dangerous heart of Paris.

"I daresay I didn't know you held membership at White's," Temple said, "for if I had I would have invited you down here more often."

Pymm glanced around and shuddered. "My membership was a gift some time back from the prime minister. Hardly something I sought out. In truth, I've never been here. Don't like to make myself a familiar sight, if you know what I mean."

Temple wasn't surprised at his superior's lofty connections. "Well, you should drop in more often. Why, if you'd been here just a half an hour earlier, you would have witnessed the spectacle of the Season."

Pymm nodded at a passing waiter. Before telling the man what he wanted, he asked, "Who's buying?"

Colin raised his hand.

The man grinned and ordered a rare and expensive bottle of port.

"As I was saying, you'll never believe what happened," Temple continued.

Pymm's gaze rolled upward, as if he doubted that any excitement at White's could offer something of interest to him. "Sir, I have neither the time nor the interest in the falderal that makes up the wasted hours in this place," he said, as the waiter arrived with a tumbler and the bottle. Pymm filled his glass to the very rim and made no offer to share.

Not that Temple expected him to. "You wouldn't be saying that if you'd seen the state Lamden was in."

"*Lamden?*" Pymm sputtered. "Here?"

"Thought that might interest you. Him being one of your

old cronies and all. In quite a lather too." Temple leaned back, enjoying the rarity of relaying a piece of information to Pymm that the man did not already know . . . or suspect. "Apparently his daughter has run off with Cordell."

"This is a disaster," Pymm wheezed, struggling to catch his breath. He grappled for his glass, and hastily brought the drink to his lips and took a long, deliberate draught, as if he hoped it were an elixir to make some nightmare fade into oblivion.

"Oh, it gets worse," Temple told him. "Lamden sent Pins and Needles after the happy bridal couple. Pins and Needles? Can you imagine two more useless fellows to send after your errant daughter?"

"He did wh-a-a-at?"

Pymm looked about to be overcome with apoplexy, but that didn't stop Temple. He grinned and leaned forward. "He sent Lord Nettlestone and Lord Harry Penham after Diana and Cordell. What a lark!"

Temple's superior turned positively bilious.

Colin crossed his arms over his chest, glaring daggers at his cousin as if he were a child caught stealing tarts.

Ignoring the censure aimed in his direction, Temple instead relished the rarity of besting Pymm. However, his joy at the other man's discomfiture didn't last very long. For after a few moments, Pymm's eyes narrowed, a look of pure intent erasing the man's queasy appearance.

As he turned his sharp gaze on Temple, the marquis knew he was about to pay the piper for thinking he could best the Foreign Office's legendary spymaster.

"Damn Lamden!" Pymm said, his voice low and full of anger. "He always was a hotheaded fool. 'Tis why he spent most of his career here in London and not in the field. Especially after . . . after . . . well, never mind that." Pymm's nose twitched and he took a quick, nervous sip from his glass, and then frowned when he realized the tumbler was empty. "I had hoped to see this matter handled with some delicacy. See the girl fetched home, quietly, discreetly," he said as he reached for the bottle.

This caught Colin's attention. "You knew about Lady Diana's kidnapping?"

Pymm shot him a withering stare, and it was enough to settle Colin back in his seat and keep his questions to himself.

"Since when did you meddle in the affairs of ladies?" Temple dared, winking at his cousin. "Perhaps Pymm here thought to court the heiress himself."

But Colin didn't appear to share in his amusement over the situation. "Oh, do shut up, Temple. You of all people should be as upset about this as Lamden."

Temple's gaze cast upward and he shook his head. *Not again.*

"What's all this about?" Pymm asked.

Before Colin could explain, Temple jumped in. "My brine-soaked cousin here is of the opinion that the lady holds some secret tendre for me, and I for her." He shot Colin a withering glance. "Which I do not."

Colin snorted, but said nothing further.

"*Tendre* or not," Pymm said, "what is of importance here is that the lady be returned to London posthaste. Or if it can be arranged, given over to Nettlestone or Penham so she can be married. Immediately."

Temple tapped the side of his head. "Did I hear you correctly, Pymm? You advocating marriage? Why, the world must be coming to an end." He laughed loud and hard.

His superior was not amused. "Stifle it, Templeton. You're in deep enough as it is. Best not add to your problems by casting your ill-timed humor on the situation." Thus said,

Pymm sat up straight in his seat. "I'll remind you that the Lamden earldom was loyally serving this country long before your orange-selling ancestress started her ignoble rise into the peerage."

Temple had the audacity to smirk. He was one of few members of his family who found it highly amusing that the family's elevation was the result of a saucy redheaded chit who'd got her start selling a variety of wares to London's groundlings, before by chance she caught Charles Stuart's roving eye.

His eye and other things . . .

Yet Pymm was right. The Lamden lineage was royal in far more impressive ways and with far more noble service than the descendants of some upstart, enterprising little wench from Dover. And the current earl was no exception to his family's illustrious past.

Lamden did deserve a hefty measure of respect, and his daughter the same consideration. Even if she was a bit of an eccentric and slightly long in the tooth.

Yet despite his own convictions that the lady could very well take care of herself, no small measure of guilt tugged at Temple's heart. He told himself it was simply a matter of honor, for King and country, a feeling he would have had over any honorable lady led astray.

Certainly not for the reasons Colin continued to put forth.

That Diana cared for him. An unlikely tale. Not after . . . Temple shook away the memory. No, there was no doubt in his mind she despised him. Why, the spiteful little minx's carriage had nearly run him down in Mayfair not a fortnight earlier. Oh, she'd apologized profusely and very prettily for her driver's wayward course, then sighed just so, that really she didn't see any need for a fuss since he was merely grazed and not truly run over.

No, Lady Diana did not carry any devoted regard for him. Not in the least.

As for him, carrying a *tendre* for her? Indeed! He'd as soon take Elton's toothless mother to bride.

"So what would you have me do, Pymm?" Temple asked. "Fetch Diana home for you?" He laughed at such a notion. He who had slipped in and out of Paris prisons, had infiltrated Napoleon's court. As if he even had the time. He knew full well he was about to be sent on a mission to the Ottoman Empire, a posting he'd been nagging and plaguing Pymm to secure for him for years.

Pymm removed his spectacles and wiped them with what once might have been a white handkerchief. "Actually, that is exactly what I want you to do," he said as he put his eye-glasses back on. "And not just me. This comes directly from the Secretary."

Temple's smug levity deflated. "You can't be serious. You said not a fortnight ago to keep a bag at the ready, for I was going to Constantinople."

"Your assignment to the Ottoman Empire is being delayed."

"Delayed? Because some chit had the effrontery, and dare I say it, poor judgment to run off with the likes of Cordell? Why, just last week you were ranting and complaining about your need for an agent at the sultan's court."

"You are not going." The finality of Pymm's words hit Temple like a slap in the face.

"Not going?" He'd spent twelve years angling for this assignment. "You know damned well finding Diana is an errand for some greenling recruit," he argued. "Send that smug, wet-behind-the-ears Denby. I hear he's itching to go about on some great task. Trotting up to the border and back after Lamden's daughter will be a good start for him." Temple leaned forward. "I'm your best agent, Pymm, not some lad to be sent on errands. I should be where I am needed most—and you know that is at the sultan's court."

Pymm took another swallow from his glass, probably a little too hastily, for Temple's sharp gaze became wary in an instant.

"You've already sent someone to Constantinople," the marquis said, pointing an accusing finger. "Oh, don't tell me, you sent Denby?"

"Now, I hardly think whom I sent matters at this point," Pymm began.

"You did! You sent Denby. He's a veritable child. He'll be discovered before he's been there outside of a week, that is if he can find his way across the bloody Channel."

Pymm smirked, cupping his drink in his hands. "You could take some lessons from him. He doesn't take unnecessary risks."

"Dammit, Pymm, this is the final straw," Temple said, rising to his feet. "You promised me that assignment, and now you've gone and sent some . . . some . . ."

"I believe the words you are looking for are 'promising young replacement.'"

At this Colin grinned.

Temple knew damned well what his cousin was thinking, and he didn't like it one bit. "If you think I am going to be replaced by—"

Pymm rocked forward, and any sign of amusement on his features disappeared. "By a better man, if you must know. Now sit down and not another word, sir, or this interview is over, and there will be no more assignments. Not to Constantinople, not even to Scotland." He sighed and shook his head. "You know as well as I do, this isn't of my making. But you've become reckless, Temple. You've taken too many risks over the last year. And to say there are those who are greatly displeased would be an understatement."

"Risks?" Temple retook his seat, then shook his head as if he were dismissing some idle report in the *Post*. "What risks?"

"Need I mention Hapsburg?"

Temple shifted.

"Or the countess in Vienna?"

The marquis almost smiled at that one, but Pymm's serious expression canceled such a notion.

"I'm still trying to write a report that won't have my head being posted outside the Tower regarding your exploits in Paris this past winter. Passing yourself off as Josephine's cousin. Why not just march yourself into an audience with Napoleon and offer him your services?"

Temple glanced down at his fingernails with an air of disinterest.

Pymm groaned. "I had hoped *that* rumor was just another Banbury tale made up by the clerks at Whitehall, but I can see it is not."

He shrugged. "Boney had need of a Persian interpreter and I thought I might be of assistance." He leaned forward, his eyes alight with mischief and delight. "The conceited fool nearly hired me. Can you imagine if I had gotten the post? I would have had access to information not even you could presume."

Pymm's eyes narrowed, momentarily enticed by the idea of such a treasure trove. Yet even as Temple could see that man's mind began to whirl with the possibilities of having an agent on Napoleon's personal staff, he shook it off.

"Enough!" Pymm said. "Did it ever occur to you that Napoleon might have wanted you to actually perform the job of a translator? Dammit, man, you don't even speak Persian."

Temple dismissed this accusation with a nonchalant shake of his head. "A minor inconvenience. I could have mastered the language quickly enough. In fact, I've taken that into consideration." He dug around in his jacket and pulled out a small slim volume, which he laid down in front of Pymm.

The Persian Language and Dialects, by Sir John Sutton.

"You are the most arrogant, irresponsible agent I have, and I won't tolerate your antics anymore." Pymm pushed aside the primer, his voice lowering to a deadly whisper. "Temple, I cannot make excuses for you any longer. Time is running out. The Secretary wants your resignation. And he has support from the King. I don't think I need tell you who is pressuring His Majesty."

His Grace. Only the Duke of Setchfield would be so shameless.

Even in the face of these odds, Temple was, by no means, about to give up. "You can't mean this, Pymm. Not my resignation."

"I fear it is so. If you don't take some steps to temper your recklessness, I won't be able to get you an assignment checking rumors in Bath."

Temple let out a long sigh. "Do I have any choice?"

Pymm shook his head. Then began fishing around in his coat. In moments he handed two pieces of paper to Temple. "These should smooth any problems you encounter."

Temple glanced at the documents, shocked at what he held. *"A special license*! You don't expect me to wed her?" He immediately shot a glance at Colin. "Not one word from you."

Pymm shook his head. "If you cannot get her back to London without any mishaps, find one of her bumbleheaded suitors and press him into duty."

Temple glanced again at the document. It was signed by

the Archbishop of England himself, and allowed for every ir-regularity that Diana's hasty marriage might necessitate.

He could only guess what dark secret Pymm held over that dignified and proper man's head to obtain such unprece-dented carte blanche.

And the second document was just as bad. "A writ for Cordell's arrest?"

"In case the viscount proves reluctant to hand her over." Pymm took the papers, folded them back up, and pressed them once again into Temple's unwilling grasp. "Give that writ to any magistrate or constable and he'll hold Cordell for at least thirty days. That ought to be enough time to see all this undone."

"You want me to have a man arrested for running off with a spinster? Oh, that's rather shady, even for you, Pymm."

Pymm's weaselly eyes gleamed with unabashed pride.

Temple rose and stuffed the papers into his jacket pocket.

"Anything else you aren't telling me?" Temple asked, his years of experience dealing with Pymm leaving him suspi-cious when the man started extending a helping hand to a friend. Pymm had gone to great lengths in a short period of time just to see Lady Diana's reputation saved—something about the entire situation didn't add up. "This seems like quite a bit of bother for a runaway spinster."

Pymm's brow furrowed. "Whatever do you mean? There is nothing more to this than a favor to one of the King's most loyal subjects." His flinty gaze held firm, not a flicker of de-ception, not a waver to be found.

"And there is no other way?"

The man shook his head.

Temple shrugged, then leaned down and fetched his Per-sian lesson book. "I am going to Constantinople."

"Fetch that gel home, Temple, and you will be well rewarded."

Colin rose as well. "Temple, wait. I think you should—"

"Not one word," he replied, "I don't want to hear another word from you on this subject. The matter is closed. Mark my words, gentlemen, I'll be back by the morrow with Lamden's errant daughter." His gaze locked with Pymm's. "Then I'll hold you to your word, sir." With that said, he caught up his hat and coat and stalked out of White's as if he were on a mission for the devil.

Pymm hastily gathered up his own shabby belongings, catching up the bottle of port, and started for the door, but Colin snagged him by the arm and held him fast. "There is more to this than just a simple favor to Lord Lamden, isn't there?"

"There is nothing of the sort," Pymm ruffled, trying to shake loose Colin's iron grasp. "You are getting as suspicious as that wife of yours."

At this, Colin smiled. "If Georgie were here, she'd have your head for not telling Temple the truth." Colin released him.

Pymm staggered free, paling at the notion of Georgie's wrath, but only momentarily. He brushed Colin's warning aside by smoothing his rumpled coat with all the air of a wounded dandy. "You've been at sea too long, Danvers. You're seeing mermaids where there are none."

"No, sir, I have made enough runs of late between England and France to know there are rumors aplenty afloat."

"And what would they have to do with Lamden's foolish chit of a daughter?" When Colin had no response, Pymm harrumphed, and caught up his hat and walking stick. "You know better than to listen to idle gossip and fish tales. Good day, my lord."

Colin stood for a few moments and tried to make the connections between the reports he'd heard of late and Lady Diana.

But it was as Pymm said, all an unlikely tangle. Not that Colin was ready to give up. He served his country with the same determination as Pymm and Temple, and what he suspected could mean tyranny and more war for all of them.

As he started for the door, one of the young bucks called out, "Eh, Danvers. Where is your cousin off to in a pig's whisker?" The man glanced to his friends and grinned. "He isn't considering joining Penham and Nettlesome, is he? Perhaps thinking of stealing the bride for himself?"

This question was followed by a round of hearty laughter, as if there had never been such a joke.

"Temple? Leg-shackled to Lamden's daughter?" Lord Oxham said. "Never."

Heads nodded sagely from Temple's brethren of confirmed bachelors and rakes.

Colin paused only for a second before he asked, "Would you care to wager on that?"

Chapter 2

The fate of Lady Diana Fordham was hardly as dire as her father would have had the patrons of White's believe. She hadn't been kidnapped or taken against her will, or carted away in the dead of night.

For earlier that same day, at precisely half past noon, she and her companion, Mrs. Foston, met Viscount Cordell in front of Madame Renard's millinery shop and got into his hired coach to begin their journey north.

She knew what she was doing was going to once again cast her name into the scandal pot, but she had no other choice.

If anything, her earlier brushes with dishonor, when she'd thrown over Lord Danvers at the time of his court-martial, the Almack's debacle, and the foolishness over her early morning appearances in the park, would be nothing to the tempest she was currently embarking upon.

She wouldn't have even been in this muddle if it hadn't been for . . .

Shaking her head, she let that thought fall away. Ten long

years of waiting. Well, she was done with waiting for the suitor who never arrived.

Oh, there had been men who'd called, men seeking her fortune, but she'd sent them packing, their ears ringing with the peal she'd rung over their greedy heads.

Then after all these years of waiting and hoping for the one man she'd marry, something else had happened. Diana found herself cast amongst those poor oddities who sit against the walls at dances. Hapless ladies who have their hostess desperately searching for an escort to guide them to the supper table.

She didn't even want to say the word.

Yet on the day that Lord Nettlestone came to call, she saw only too clearly in the drawing room mirror what the rest of London already knew: she'd become a spinster.

At nine-and-twenty, she could hardly be counted as one of the dewy-eyed, properly innocent debutantes who flooded the city each spring.

Instead, she was just another curiosity to be pitied—and most definitely not emulated.

If that wasn't bad enough, it was well known that Nettlestone had vowed to marry before the end of the Season and had spent the entire spring courting every eligible daughter and young lady in London in search of his baroness. Thus far, he'd been refused thirty-two times. By every miss, lady, and even a few widows. It had taken him to mid-June to find his way to the front door of Lamden House.

Diana knew all this because Mrs. Foston, her companion for the last thirteen years, had a remarkable skill at uncovering every bit of gossip pattering its way through the London drawing rooms. According to the widowed lady, even Miss Tilden had refused him. And that lady had always been London's premier old maid, an eccentric of the first order.

Why, she wore breeches and had named her six pugs after the Royal Dukes!

So if Lord Nettlestone had called on Miss Tilden *before* he'd considered calling on Diana, that could mean only one thing.

Diana had become a spinster. The last spinster.

Oh, the very notion was too terrible even to consider.

Though not as terrible as being the next Lady Nettlesome, a proposition her father had suddenly taken great interest in.

It was as if he had finally looked up from his newspapers and endless correspondence and decided to take an immediate course of action to deal with the problem of her unmarried state. And so he had amended his promise of years earlier that she could pick her own bridegroom.

Now she could choose between Nettlestone and Penham.

Choose between Needles and Pins? She'd rather start collecting pugs with royal names.

Diana shuddered and glanced across at the seat where the viscount lounged, a deck of cards in his hands. He was playing a game of chance with only himself—and losing.

So much for knights in shining armor and her girlhood dreams of valor.

But sometimes, just sometimes, things could work out the way they should, she told herself, as Lord Cordell's hired carriage rolled past the last of London's gray scenery and out into the countryside. The green hills and valleys brought her a measure of comfort—for she knew only too well that back at Lamden House, her disappearance would be causing no end of havoc.

I'm so sorry, Papa. But this is *the only way,* she thought, clinging to her conviction that her elopement with Lord

Cordell was the right decision. It was the only one she could make to secure the future she wanted so desperately.

And the one she would do anything to avoid.

Finding Diana wasn't as easy as Temple had boasted. He and Elton followed the lovebirds' trail along the Manchester road as far as Broughton, but then it was as if they had disappeared.

"I wonder if . . ." Elton muttered as yet another innkeeper swore not to have seen them.

"Wonder what?" Temple asked, willing to try anything to find the errant bride and her worthless groom. Seated beside his driver atop the Duke of Setchfield's second-best berline—one liberated from the Setchfield liveries during the dead of night—Temple scanned the empty countryside hoping to catch a glimpse of his quarry. The duke would be livid that Temple had taken such a liberty without his express permission, but they'd needed a vehicle large enough to carry Diana and Mrs. Foston back to town.

As for Cordell, Temple intended to let him rot in the nearest gaol.

"Well, if I were heading north," Elton was saying, "and weren't looking to be caught, I might take a less conspicuous route."

"Such as?" Temple prodded, glad for the day he'd hired Elton.

Flipping the ribbons and steering the horses out of the inn's yard and onto the road, Elton said, "I wouldn't be taking the Manchester road, like those two young fools from White's were headed."

"Wouldn't that be the best route?" Temple asked. "More posting houses and better road, I'd think."

"The Manchester road is the obvious choice," Elton said, with a smug smile and his one eye glittering. "With the right driver and fresh changes of horses, you could make Gretna Green in about two and a half days." He made the pronouncement as if traveling such a distance was but a hop across a lane. "But the shortest road ain't always the best route, milord. Especially if you don't want to be caught by an irate father or a pack of fortune hunters bent on stealing the bride for themselves."

Temple nodded. "So which way would you go?"

"This way," Elton said, nodding at the road onto which they were turning.

"And this way is?"

Elton grinned. "Running parallel to the main road. The towns are little more spread out, but there's change enough of horses along the way to make the journey in good time."

"How can you be certain?"

"I know."

When Elton used that tone, Temple didn't bother questioning him. He knew a good deal about Elton's past, but there were some unaccounted years in the man's history. The few things he had said over the years left Temple with the suspicion that his manservant had been on more than his fair share of country roads and lonely highways . . . and not always with the best of intentions.

Still, Elton's instincts—ill-gained or not—served them well. They got lucky about ten miles up the road.

The innkeeper glanced down at his shoes and shuffled his feet as they made their inquiries concerning Lord Cordell and Lady Diana. From the man's wary expression, Temple knew the innkeeper had seen them, though it might take some convincing to get the man to be a bit forthcoming.

Temple pulled out his money pouch and gave it a jangle. As he'd suspected, it was just the right incentive to unhinge the man's memory. The fellow didn't need to know it contained only a collection of nails, since Temple never had enough money to make up a good bribe.

Still, the deception worked, as it had for years.

"Now that you mention it, there was a coach came by here some hours ago that might be who you are looking for."

"And they went . . . ?" Temple continued to prod. Lawd, it was like getting an extra hundred pounds out of his grandfather.

The man scratched his chin and gave Temple a long, long look. "Are you the aggrieved *parti*?" The man winked and leaned over to nudge Elton. "That's French you know. I've always wanted to say that, ever since I read it in one of those lovey-dovey novels my wife likes to read. She was a vicar's daughter, learnt all her letters and more."

"How lucky for you, sir," Elton said, as if that was the most interesting thing he'd heard all day.

Temple wasn't so patient. "Yes, yes, that's very nice, but which way did this coach go?"

"Hmm," the man said. "You never did say, are you the aggrieved *parti* or not?" he repeated, mangling the poor French language enough that it should have been a crime.

In France, it most likely was.

"No, I'm not."

The innkeeper tipped his head and studied Temple. "Don't see why you care then."

"I don't care. The lady is of no interest to me."

"I think he doth protest too much," the man joked, nudging Elton once again. "That's from some famous playwright. Me wife likes to say it when I tell her I haven't been drinking too much ale. Which I usually have been." He glanced once again at Temple. "So you protest all you doth, milord. But I'm thinking a man doesn't come all this way to fetch back a wayward lady unless he's got a stake in the matter."

Demmit if Elton didn't smirk at the innkeeper's assessment. If it hadn't been for his years of immeasurable loyalty, Temple would have strangled his servant.

"I assure you, sir, I am not the aggrieved *parti*."

The man chuckled. "Turned you down flat, did she? Oh, women, they do like to put us men in a lather, don't they? I daresay you know that, milord, coming all this way to set her straight."

Instead Temple took a deep breath and tapped down the urge to issue another denial concerning Diana. "Does it truly matter, sir?" he said through gritted teeth. "Her father is an honorable man and would like her returned. I have been asked to see the task done in his stead."

The innkeeper's jaw worked back and forth. "Hate to see a young couple thwarted in love." He glanced over at Elton. "Thwarted—that means they'd get caught."

"Is that so?" Elton replied.

"Right it does," the innkeeper said, slanting a glance over at Temple. "So, milord, are you of a mind to thwart young love?"

"Hardly, sir, if I thought the couple was in love. I can assure you that is not the case."

"Actually it does rather surprise me to see anyone chasing after the likes of *her*."

So he had seen Diana. Anyone who referred to her in that tone had most definitely met the lady.

"If you don't mind me saying," the innkeeper said, leaning forward, "you being the rejected one and all, she's got a right sharp tongue." He glanced over at Elton and shuddered ever so slightly.

Elton, disreputable fellow that he was, nodded in sympathetic agreement.

"Like one of them London fishwives you hear tell about," the innkeeper said. "Arguing with him over which way to go and the like. She had this map and a book she was reading from, telling him they were off course." He paused again, wiping his meaty hands on his apron. "Right she was, this isn't the quickest of routes to the border, but who likes to tell them that?"

Temple didn't need to hear another word. They'd found Diana. He turned on one heel and started striding back to his carriage.

"Mind my advice, never marry a smart one," the innkeeper called after him. "You'll never know peace in your house if they've got a head stuffed with ideas."

"Jonas? Are they staying to eat or just wasting your time with a lot of gossip?" The shrill voice pierced the dark common room of the inn, stopping Temple in his tracks and sending the horses into a nervous prance in their traces.

"Ah, there she is, gentlemen. The fair flower of my life." The man grinned as his wife came barreling out the door, a rolling pin in one hand and her other balled up in a tight fist.

"She was a rare find, I imagine," Temple said, meaning every word of it.

"Aye, that she was," the man agreed, beaming with pride. "Still quite a sight to look at, wouldn't you agree?"

Temple and Elton had the good sense just to nod.

"I had quite a devilish bit of competition when I went courting her. But I won her heart with my fine prospects." The innkeeper jerked his thumb back at his ramshackle establishment. "Prospects, sir, will win you a bride every time."

"Well, are they eating or not?" his particular bride called

out, sending the horses to whinnying and stomping their feet at her strident notes.

"Not, my good lady," Temple told her, bowing low, before he continued his hasty retreat toward the carriage.

Elton was already in his perch and calling to the horses, when Temple climbed up beside him.

For a time, they rode in silence, Temple ignoring the way Elton was still chuckling about the innkeeper's assertion that he was after Diana for himself.

Instead he enjoyed the warmth of the sun on his face and the sight of England in the summertime. There was no other place like it. The smell of the new grass, flowers bursting up from the corners of hedges, fruit trees blowsy with flowers. It was heaven.

And he knew with a certainty that was born from the experience of seeing hell.

The Terror in France. The battles for the Peninsula. The treacherous murder of his young cousin Orlando. He'd spent so many years walking amid death that being surrounded by the ripe, lush landscape of England, his beloved country, comforted him like a mother's arms, her summer breezes like a tender kiss on his forehead, welcoming him home.

They rounded another curve, and before them the old Roman road lay straight and seemingly endless . . . and empty.

Temple let out an exasperated sigh.

"Why are we going after this gel?" Elton asked, breaking the silence between them.

"As a favor to Pymm," Temple told him.

"Harrumph," Elton said, settling into his seat. "Don't see why you don't just marry her yerself. It's not like you couldn't use the money. Be nice to be paid regular-like."

Temple stared openmouthed at the man. All the years

they'd traveled together, he'd never heard Elton utter a word about their lack of funds or the dangerous paths they trod.

"I have no intention of getting married. To Lady Diana or otherwise."

Elton just shrugged. "Seems a shame to see a good fortune go to waste. Either way, let's hope Lord Cordell sticks to his guns and stays on this road so we can find them right quick."

"Why wouldn't he?"

"Given what I've heard about Lady Diana, she's as likely to take the ribbons herself if she doesn't fancy his choice of route."

Temple glanced over at the man. He didn't realize Elton was so familiar with the lady. "What makes you say that?"

"Well, it being Lady Diana and all. Everyone knows she's a brassy bit of baggage. Got more gall than my aunt's tabby cat."

Temple couldn't argue with that. Diana had sent quite a few suitors packing through the years and wasn't known to do it with any measure of female delicacy or care.

Elton shrugged. "If you ask me, she's lived too long without a man. Makes a woman short a sheet, as me mum likes to say."

"Ah, your mother's fabled eloquence," Temple said. "And what would her remedy be for the lady's malady?"

"Marriage." Elton nodded with an alarming assurance. "That'll set her back on the straight and narrow. Once she's wedded and well bedded, she'll be right as rain. You mark my words."

First grumbles about his infrequent salary and now this ode to wedded bliss.

"What do you know about marriage?" Temple crossed his arms over his chest and eyed his fellow crabbed bachelor.

"I know enough that the right woman only comes once . . . hmm . . . mayhap twice in yer life. Only a fool lets her go." Elton spit over the side of carriage.

"I highly doubt marriage to the likes of Cordell will improve Lady Diana's mental capacity."

Elton shrugged, a sort of time-will-tell gesture that left Temple all the more uncomfortable with Diana's most recent escapade.

To be honest, he'd always felt some measure of responsibility whenever he heard Diana's name bandied about. It was foolish, truly, for he hadn't been the cause of her broken engagement to Colin.

So she was known to be a little eccentric, but dash it all, it wasn't like she was a traitor to her country.

Just a bit headstrong.

Make that far too headstrong.

He took a deep breath. Really, Diana's problems weren't anything that couldn't be brought in line by the—

Right man.

Temple shifted in his seat, not at all comfortable with the direction of his thoughts. He was starting to sound like his cousin Colin. And Elton.

Or worse yet, Elton's harridan mother.

"I just don't know why she'd run off with the likes of Cordell," he said aloud, without even thinking.

The carriage rounded a curve, and Elton nodded at the sight before them.

A coach sat haphazardly beside the road. A broken wheel lay to one side, and the horses were unhitched.

"Looks like you can ask her yerself, my lord."

For just then, out from the shade of the carriage stepped a woman, her blond hair glinting in the sunshine like the golden hue of the cowslip blooming alongside the roadway.

Diana.

Lithe and lovely, she stepped into their path, a chip bonnet in her hand, the blue ribbons fluttering in the breeze. The London wits could laugh at her spinster state, but the sight of her sent an odd thrill racing through Temple's blood.

Gad's sakes, she was a tempting minx. The rest of Society could have their mincing, fresh-faced, and doe-eyed beauties. In his estimation, there was something all too very tempting about Lady Diana Fordham, and even more so at nine-and-twenty than when she'd been one of those impressionable young ladies standing in the wings at Almack's.

Seeing her again, for the first time in months he reckoned, he didn't know whether to celebrate at finding her safe and apparently unharmed, or to offer to stand as Cordell's best man in the wedding—just to see her wed and out of his life.

And most importantly, out of his heart.

Diana peered down the road at the carriage headed toward her, being driven along at a perilous pace. And here she'd been about to give up on their ever gaining help.

She looked again and recognized the one-eyed driver. *Elton.* Which meant they'd sent Temple to fetch her home.

Well, she'd expected no less.

But as Elton continued to drive the horses along, he did so without any indication of slowing them down.

And then it hit her.

Temple had no intention of stopping.

The wretched man was going to leave her on the side of the road with the likes of . . . She took a glance over at Lord Cordell, who lay on the carriage's only blanket, on the only grassy spot, a moistened handkerchief draped over his face.

She took a deep breath and reminded herself that this man was her fiancé.

Her beloved intended, she thought with a barely repressed shudder.

Now Temple meant to leave her with the likes of Cordell?

"Not likely," she muttered, as she stepped out into the middle of the road in front of Temple's speeding horses.

It was all Elton could do to stop the carriage from cartwheeling into the same state of disrepair as Cordell's.

But Diana hadn't come this far to balk at a few thousand pounds of horseflesh, metal, leather, and wood hurtling at her with the same deadly intent that spinsterhood carried.

"Lord Templeton. We won't be interfered with," Diana said, her hands now set on her hips as Temple climbed down from his still shuddering berline. "We are on the path of true love and intend to marry."

Cordell rose from his shady patch and eyed Temple with a mixture of disgust and amusement. His lemon-yellow coat nearly matched the color of his hair, which lay curled about his head à la Brutus. But for his penchant for dissolute living he might have been handsome; however, drink and wild company had left him with the florid features and droopy eyes of a much older man.

The marquis laughed. "La! Milady, aren't you droll. Who said anything about a rescue? And my dear Lord Cordell, stop contemplating a second, for I'm hardly the bride-stealing type." He nodded toward Elton, who was even now consulting with Cordell's driver over the state of the viscount's carriage. "This is all my jarvey's doing. Elton has a soft spot for true love."

Cordell took one more bemused glance at Temple, then settled back down to his game of flipping cards into his over-turned hat.

As much as he would like to smash his fist into the man's

face, as Temple, *ton* fool and Society darling, he could hardly behave like a hero from some French novel.

Though what Diana saw in this dissolute excuse for a man, he couldn't fathom. Women! Perhaps Pymm had the right idea. The fairer sex was an unfathomable, untrustworthy lot.

Elton returned and with a shake of his head, announced that the other carriage was useless.

"Then I insist you all ride with us," Temple said, opening the door of the duke's roomy berline. "We were on our way to a house party, but I would be remiss if I didn't lend you a hand to the next town where you can find the assistance you need."

"Right kind of you, Templeton," Cordell said, getting into the berline without a glance back at his bride-to-be, her companion, or their luggage.

Temple smiled at Lady Diana as she stomped past him, her traveling case in hand. He took her hand to help her up, and for a moment their gazes met.

How had he forgotten how blue her eyes were on a summer day? Or the way they sparkled in the sunshine . . .

And how they made him forget to breathe.

She looked at him, almost expectantly, as if she wanted him to decry her actions, demand an explanation. Claim her for himself.

Words he wouldn't utter. Words she, of all people, knew he'd never say.

The spell broke as Cordell called from inside. "Got anything to drink in here, Templeton? It's nigh on past noon and I'm parched."

"Sorry, sir," Temple said. "I never partake before evening."

"Some help this," Cordell grumbled.

"My hand, my lord?" she said, plucking her fingers free

from Temple's grasp and getting into the carriage without his help.

He let her go and, ignoring Cordell's complaints, went to assist the final passenger, Mrs. Foston, Diana's ever-patient hired companion, who was pointing her cane at which bags she wanted Elton to tie onto the Setchfield berline.

"Madame," he said. "A moment of your time."

"Yes?" Mrs. Foston was a tall, angular woman whose sharp gaze missed nothing. The perfect hired companion for a willful young lady. Perfect, that is, until she'd let such a travesty befall her charge.

"Why didn't you prevent this?" Temple asked. "How could you let Diana run away with the likes of that sot?"

She shook her head. "What would you have me do, my lord? Let her run off alone? She was quite determined. No, I thought it best that at least she have me along."

Temple ran a hand through his hair. This was hardly the answer he'd been seeking. "I would have thought you, madame, would have had more sense than to allow this."

Mrs. Foston drew herself up to her full height. "And what about you, my lord?" she asked. "Some might say the same about you." With that, the lady stomped over to the carriage and got in beside Diana, wielding her cane like a veritable staff.

Temple stood there openmouthed. Why did the entire world think Diana was his obligation?

"Not for very much longer," he muttered under his breath.

And somewhere in the back of his mind a quirky little voice chanted back at him.

You doth protest too much.

After an hour or so on the road, Temple glanced up from the book he was reading. "Is something wrong, sir?" he asked, holding up his lorgnette to send a speculative glance in Cordell's direction.

The other man sat slumped heavily against the wall of the carriage, his face a ghastly shade of gray.

"Why, you look positively ill," Temple said.

"I am fine," Cordell responded through clenched teeth.

"No, I think not. You have all the appearances of a man about to cast up his accounts."

"Traveling doesn't agree with him," Diana said irritably. "Just leave him be." She snapped her book shut and glared at Temple.

"Perhaps it's the company he's been keeping," Temple noted, returning his gaze to his studies and ignoring the way Diana's eyes blazed with a murderous intent.

He could just see her mind awhirl as she considered and rejected one perfectly blistering rebuttal after another. He was saved from her tongue lashing by her companion.

"What is that you are reading, my lord?" Mrs. Foston asked, trying to return the party to some semblance of well-bred order.

He held the book up. "I am studying Persian."

"Is that Sir John's work?" Diana asked.

Temple nodded. "Yes, Sir John Sutton."

"Sutton?" Cordell asked. "Sutton, you say? Isn't he the fellow who turned traitor and hanged himself?"

Mrs. Foston gasped.

"Yes,'tis the same man. But despite his dishonorable end his work remains highly regarded."

"Harrumph," Cordell snorted. "Seems to me you like the company of traitors, Templeton. This here Sutton fellow and that turncoat cousin of yours, Danvers. Cowardly ilk, I say."

Diana coughed at the mention of her former fiancé.

Cordell snorted. "Oh, right. You were betrothed to Danvers, weren't you? Sorry business, that. Well rid of him, I'd say."

Temple thought she'd be better rid of her latest choice of groom.

"Still," Cordell was saying, "what nonsense is this, Templeton? Learning Persian. Turning into a bluestocking, are you?" The man chuckled.

Temple shook his head. "Me? I think not. But Elton is getting on in years, and I'm thinking of hiring a Persian servant to replace him. I hear they are quite loyal. Thought I'd get a head start on learning how to tell the poor fellow that his wages will be late."

Cordell chortled, then went back to staring at the scenery.

Temple glanced at Diana. "And what of you, my lady? What are you reading?"

The viscount groaned. "You'll regret asking her that one."

Diana ignored her betrothed. "This is a book my father had commissioned. *Antiquities of England: A Traveler's Guide.* It's by Mr. Theonius T. Billingsworth, a historian of some renown. Perhaps you've heard of him?"

"Can't say that I have," Temple admitted.

"Deuced lucky on that account," Cordell muttered, crossing his arms over his chest and laying his head against the side of the carriage before closing his eyes.

Even Mrs. Foston didn't look overly enthusiastic.

Diana ignored them. "He's quite witty, and he lists all the perfectly interesting monuments and sights along the various roads in England. Why, he even lists your grandfather's grand estate in Sussex as well as smaller estates . . ." She paused for a moment, thumbing through the little book. "Ah, yes, here it is, even Lord Nettlestone's castle merits a mention."

Temple tapped his lorgnette against the window on which

Cordell's head rested. The *rat-a-tat-tat* set the viscount's mouth into a pained frown.

"Funny you should mention Nettlestone," Temple said. "I saw him the other night at White's. Along with your father, my lady."

"My father?" Diana asked.

At this, Cordell opened one eye, his florid color paling.

"The earl created quite a stir," Temple said, continuing to tap his lorgnette against the window.

"He did?" The question that should have come from Diana actually came from her intended. Now both eyes were open and Cordell sat up a little straighter. "Was he overly distraught? Angry, perhaps? Didn't make any threats, did he?"

And this was Diana's choice for a husband? Temple mused. Perhaps she was as addled as the old London cats liked to speculate.

"There was so much commotion, I couldn't quite tell," Temple said, glancing down at his fingernails and examining them as if suddenly they were the most important things he'd ever observed.

This didn't set well with Cordell. "What was his remedy, sir? That is, if you recall. I need to know." The man's left eye started to tic with a nervous flutter.

"His remedy, you ask? His remedy. Hmm." Temple tapped his lorgnette against the wall of the carriage, each *thwack* making Cordell twitch that much more. "I believe he sent some likely fellows after you. Now if I can just recall their names."

Cordell leaned forward, while Diana sat poised in her seat, her only sign of distress a slight furrow across her fair brow.

"Their names," Temple said, continuing his thrumming beat. "I believe they were your latest conquests, Diana. What the devil are their names? Hmm . . ."

She closed her eyes and shook her head. "Do you mean Lord Harry and Baron Nettlesome?"

"Nettlestone," Temple corrected.

"Yes . . . yes," she said testily. "Nettlestone."

"Well, I just thought that since he was a favorite of yours, you would at least know his name."

"Believe me, my lord, I had it correct the first time."

Temple grinned. "That you did. Pins and Needles it is. I do like young Penham."

Diana's eyes narrowed, and Temple was glad he was on the inside of the carriage and not outside on the road. Elton was loyal, but Diana had enough money to bribe even his stalwart heart to run him down.

"Good lad, that, Penham," he continued. "So fresh-faced and full of honor. And Nettlestone. Now he's a rare one as well. And good with the cattle and those of an obstinate temperament. I can't imagine how we found you first, for he's a dab hand with the ribbons." Temple sat back, his gaze directed at Cordell. "Now the real question is: Which one of them do you want to be found by? Mark my words, they are both determined to discover you, for Lamden has promised Diana's hand to whichever one brings her back to London."

"He what?" Diana rocketed forward in her seat.

"He promised your hand in marriage to the man who saved you from Cordell." He spared a glance at the viscount. "No offense, sir."

"None taken," the man muttered, his eyes now wavering like the Union Jack in a stiff breeze.

Meanwhile, Diana's mouth fell open in a wide, indignant O.

Temple reached across and with one finger under her chin, pushed it closed. "You'll have a mouth full of dust gaping like that." Then he winked at her.

She brushed his hand aside, and glanced over at Cordell to see if he was going to protest Temple's taking such liberties.

Cordell was too busy muttering to himself.

Temple swore he heard the man say, "Hadn't expected this."

Seeing his opportunity, he forged ahead. "Now, if I were you, my dear viscount, I think I would prefer to be found by Nettlestone than Penham."

"You would," Diana said, her arms crossed over her chest.

"Not for the reasons you might suspect, my lady. For you see, Penham is a crack shot. And when he challenges Cordell here, as any honorable man would do, he'll shoot him dead. One shot, straight through the heart."

Temple drew a deep, wheezy breath, and then placed his hand dramatically over his chest.

"Oh my goodness, no!" Mrs. Foston said, clutching her cane until her knuckles turned white. "Why, that's horrible. Such a wretched, awful way to die. And so painful, from what I hear."

Cordell paled further.

Diana's gaze rolled upward as if beseeching the heavens, though Temple doubted she was saying a prayer for her intended's life. "And what about Lord Nettlesome?" She finally asked in a tone that hinted that she really didn't want to hear the answer.

"Nettlestone," Temple corrected.

"Yes, yes," she said. "You don't think Nettlestone will challenge Lord Cordell to a duel?"

"Of course he will," Temple said. "And he's a crack shot as well. But Nettlestone still has enough blunt to afford a nice headstone, a real bang up job of marble and such. Yes, the baron will see you credibly buried, Cordell, whereas Penham appeared rather hotheaded about the matter. Quite out of character for Lord Harry, but I fear he's a man thwarted in love. Likely to shoot you like a dog and toss you into the ditch." He punctuated his last sentence with a few more taps of his lorgnette.

Like you deserve, you bastard, he thought.

That was enough to send Cordell's breakfast racing forth. He turned to his bride-to-be and proceeded to toss his accounts all over her gown.

Temple drew back his immaculately polished boots. "Tsk, tsk," he mused, tapping his lorgnette once again on Cordell's shoulder. "I say, my good man, are you unwell?"

Diana snatched the silver-framed eyeglass out of Temple's hand and tossed it out the window.

"Good riddance," she said, before turning her attention to Cordell and her ruined gown.

"Ah yes, true love," Temple commented, as he knocked on the roof for Elton to stop the carriage.

As it pulled to a halt, Cordell's hand shot for the latch, flinging open the door and then falling face-first into the ditch. Without even trying to stand, he began retching anew.

Temple sighed, and then extended his hand to Diana to help her out. "True love," he mused again. "What was it you were saying about its course earlier, my lady? It seems for you it has hit a bit of a rough patch."

Chapter 3

They passed through three small villages before they came to Geddington. A quaint, medieval-style town, it would probably have slipped into obscurity if it had not been for the fact that one night, some five hundred years earlier, the body of Eleanor of Castile, Queen of England, had lain in rest in the tiny hamlet during her long funeral procession back to London. For this moment in history, it proudly bore one of the legendary crosses raised by her grieving King and husband as monument to her selflessness and bravery.

Beyond the historical significance that put the town in Billingsworth's learned tome, the village also boasted a wheelwright . . . and as luck would have it, a magistrate.

The wheelwright promised he would have the viscount's coach fixed by morning. The magistrate was another matter.

They had all settled at an inn, aptly named The Queen's Respite, where the innkeeper greeted them smartly, obviously seeing a tidy sum to be had from a lady, her companion, a viscount, *and* a marquis.

"Yes," Temple said, looking around the common room. "I

do believe I will stay the night with your party, Lady Diana."

Just as long as it takes me to engage the magistrate and his constable in securing your betrothed in the nearest cell.

Diana frowned. "But you don't have to stay on my account, my lord," she said, her Bath manners coming to the forefront. "I couldn't live with myself if *I* was the reason you delayed your attendance at this house party." Her gaze narrowed. "I don't recall hearing about any house parties being formed. Just where is it that you said you are going?"

"I don't recall that I said," he told her in a blithe, breezy manner. "Besides, you need someone here to safeguard your reputation, my lady. I would be remiss as a gentleman if I didn't add my protection to your fair and unblemished virtue." He bowed low.

She snorted, in that so very eccentric manner of hers. "At nine-and-twenty I don't think I need worry about that."

Temple rose and leaned toward her ear. "I wouldn't go announcing your age so loudly. Cordell is lousy at numbers, and probably still thinks you are but in your third or fourth Season." He grinned and left the room whistling a saucy tune.

Looking back, Temple wagered she was trying to decide which of the innkeeper's tankards she could afford to break over his head. Before she counted out her coins, he continued out of the yard and into the town to discover where the magistrate lived.

Unfortunately for Temple, the town official was gone, away on business until the next morning, along with the constable and the constable's assistant. All that was left standing between Geddington and lawlessness was the magistrate's pimpled clerk, a lad who appeared too nervous and flustered even to read the writ Temple carried, let alone execute it. Instead, he offered his assurances that his employer would be back in Geddington first thing in the morning.

Temple muttered and cursed at this turn of luck, for there was nothing left to do but return to the inn and keep an eye on his quarry.

Cordell proved easy to find. The viscount was settled at a table in the common room playing vingt-et-un with a florid-faced wine merchant and a traveling vicar—who looked more dissolute than holy. The stakes were already starting to pile up, and not in front of the viscount.

Diana was nowhere in sight.

"Where is your bride, Cordell?" Temple asked, wondering if the man even remembered that he was supposed to be traveling swiftly for the Scottish border.

"Dunno. Went for a walk, I believe. Her and that wretched book of hers." The viscount glanced up from his hand. "Thought tonight was going to be a dead bore, but as you can see I've found a fine set of company. I'd invite you to play, but as I recall you don't."

Temple tapped his forehead with his finger. "Haven't the wit to keep my cards straight, I fear."

Cordell's companions looked up and eyed him as if he'd suddenly turned into a Christmas goose, stuffed with gold.

"That, and I've never had the extra money to toss about. I do so hate to disappoint you, gentlemen, but I'm a man without means."

In an instant, the goose that had looked so fat and tasty suddenly became as appealing as week-old mutton in July.

"Yes, that is a problem, Templeton. No property you'd care to offer or family heirlooms to pawn off?" Cordell asked.

Temple had a feeling the man knew both means of funding only too well. "No, all entailed and still in my grandfather's thrifty hands."

"Hmm. Too bad. Perhaps the old boy will cock up his toes soon and you'll be your own man." The viscount chuckled and smirked at his companions.

Temple gritted his teeth, once again reminding himself that killing Cordell outright, while a favor to Society, would only turn this already ridiculous assignment into months and months of reports and paperwork, upon which he suspected Pymm would insist.

Not to mention the requisite duel with Cordell's hotheaded and equally worthless brothers. He could hardly dispatch the entire lot of them because they had a horse's ass for a sibling.

"Be a sport," Cordell was saying, as he eyed the cards in his hand. "Go look for her, would you? I've almost run out of funds, and I believe she has a tidy little purse tucked away—for emergencies or some other foolishness. God knows where it is hidden because it isn't in her traveling bag." He turned back to his game, and nodded to the vicar to add another card to his already precarious hand.

So dismissed, Temple wondered if Elton was as good at forgery as he was at finding his way about the countryside on a moonless night. He'd have his adept servant add a few charges to Pymm's writ to ensure the contemptible viscount spent the next few years cooling his heels in this little hamlet.

Temple strode out of the inn, something niggling at the back of his spine that warned him Diana shouldn't be left to her own devices.

Though truly, he told himself, what ill fate could await her in Geddington? Then he saw her and wondered at the wry joke the Fates had in store for him.

Diana meandered around the triangular base of the town's Eleanor Cross, her gaze never leaving the trio of statues that made up the middle section of the tall, stately monument.

He stood back for a few moments and just watched her, comparing her profile to that of the long-dead queen known for her determination and resolute heart.

Diana and the lady had a lot in common. And that was what had his chest hammering, his gut in knots.

Never one for conventions, she held her beribboned bonnet in one hand, and in the other, her guidebook. Her honey-blond hair sparkled in the last vestiges of sunlight. And as she tipped her head once more to gaze up at the long-lost queen, her mouth turned in a sad, lonely smile that prodded at Temple's heart.

There is something not right here, he told himself. If he'd run away with Diana, he certainly wouldn't be spending the evening playing cards in some lonely inn.

No, indeed. Why, he'd have her unbound and undressed and . . .

"So you found me, Temple," she said without even turning around.

Her words held a second meaning that he wasn't about to acknowledge. Any more than he wanted to continue his own silent reverie into the dangerous environs that she usually stirred inside him.

All he could manage to say was a tongue-tied, "Aye, Diana."

She walked once again in a circle around the monument, her hand reaching out every so often to trail over the stone.

Temple crossed the distance between them, putting his arm up against the statue to block her path.

She came to a stop, her face set in an annoyed display, her blue eyes flashing in challenge. "My lord, if you are here to rescue me, you are sadly mistaken. As I said before, I'm of no mind to return to London."

"As I said before, I have no intention of returning you to your father."

Because my orders are to see you wedded.

Perhaps it was here in her company, he realized the enormity of what that meant.

It had been an easy promise to make in London, but now, as he stood before her, something inside him quaked at the notion of handing Diana over to another man.

Temple took a step back from her.

She cocked her head and stared at him. "Temple, why did you come after me?"

He knew what she wanted to hear—that he'd come after her for all the right reasons. That he'd come after her because he cared. And he knew damn well that if he said that, there would be no turning back.

So instead he told her, "I didn't."

She only smiled, and then continued circling around the steps.

"I didn't, I tell you," he said, following her like a rapid mummer. When she just shrugged her shoulders as if she knew better, he stepped around her. "Demmit, Diana. This isn't a game. I didn't come after you to stop you from being wed."

One brow arched delicately and then she went back to her tour around the statue, Billingsworth in hand.

Temple ran his hand through his hair and let out an exasperated sigh. "Can we just discuss something else?"

She came up behind him and ducked around him. "Fine. According to Mr. Billingsworth, Eleanor bore Edward eleven children."

Relieved for a change of subject, Temple said, "And you would like to have eleven children?" Suddenly he saw the roundabout track of her conversation.

She grimaced. "I think not." Her hand reached out to

touch the timeworn stone, her fingers trailing over the granite in a wistful brush. "A few would be nice."

Her words held a touch of dreamy magic, for suddenly he saw her wish come into being.

There would be Diana, her shining hair braided and twisted in a glorious crown around her head. And at her feet, happy, laughing children played.

For a moment, Temple believed that such a world could exist. A place of love and happiness. Of honor and trust. Of family and hearth and home.

And then he blinked again, and there was nothing before him but an eccentric spinster and her flights of fancy.

By all that was holy, he needed to stay out of Diana's dreams.

They weren't his.

He went to reach for his lorgnette, to use it as he did in town, as a prop to distance himself from his heart. But then he remembered, she'd tossed it out the window.

So he resorted to the sly wit that made him so popular. "I imagine your Billingsworth forgot to add that Edward was a rather practical bastard. He used Eleanor's dowry to pay for these crosses." Temple regretted the words the moment he said them. Gads, he sounded as cynical and delighted as his grandfather would be to burst her romantic bubble.

Diana cast him an annoyed glance, then let out an exasperated sigh. "What a surprise! I should have known that *you* would find the crass version of such a romantic story."

He shifted from one foot to the other. "I didn't mean—"

"No, don't say another word." She held up her hand to stave off his feeble excuses. "You just proved my theory that men can't bare their hearts with any measure of honesty."

Temple thought that was interesting. Here was a lady running off with the *ton*'s most disreputable bounder and she wanted honesty? "Ah, my lady, you wound me to the quick. To my very heart."

She glanced at him, a sly, quick movement that caught him unaware. "But Temple, the last time we were alone, you swore quite vehemently that you no longer possessed one."

His gaze met hers. "You remember that?"

She glanced away and began to circle the monument anew. "Yes, Temple. How could I forget the day you broke my heart?"

He groaned. She would have to bring that up.

When he caught up with her, trailing behind her as she went around the statue again, her gaze remained fixed on the woman above her, as if she were trying to learn some lesson from the serene face gazing down at her.

"According to Mr. Billingsworth, Edward wept for his queen for five days after her death, refusing to see anyone or leave his room." Diana tipped her head this way and that as if gauging the other woman's mettle. "I think they must have shared a rare and special love."

"Hardly that romantic," he said, feeling more than uncomfortable with the witchery she was spinning around him.

Diana had always had that ability to leave him feeling unbalanced. It was the precise reason he always avoided her in town. Better to pretend that Lady Diana Fordham never existed than to spend his evenings watching her from across a crowded room.

He did his best to undo her magic. "Does your Billingsworth also say that her brother brokered the marriage as part of a trade deal with Edward's father? A rather commonplace arrangement, I gather, and not exactly simmering with romance."

"Oh, but that's what makes them so special," she enthused. "'Tis rare enough when two people marry for love, but when two people are tossed together for all the wrong reasons and discover they love each other so very deeply, that is indeed a very rare gift."

Temple shook his head. "How unfortunate that love can't be like that now."

Diana glanced up from her book where she was probably digging for more facts. "You don't think two people can simply fall in love and marry?"

"Perhaps. But for us—in our situations, in our station, we marry for other reasons. Property, lineage . . ."

"Trade agreements?" Diana teased.

Temple laughed. "Still, I don't think you can hope for love. You'll just be disappointed. And love itself isn't any guarantee of happiness." His parents' marriage was a perfect example of that.

"I don't believe that for a minute," Diana said. "Besides, I haven't waited this long not to have love."

"And you love Cordell?"

Diana closed her book. "That is none of your concern."

"I think it is. At least it is now." Temple caught her by the arm. "Cordell? What can you be thinking? Why, I'd rather see you married to Penham or even Nettlestone than see you saddled to that wastrel. Who, by the way, is gambling away your dowry. Money he hasn't got. You wouldn't catch him erecting monuments to a loyal and devoted wife—unless it was a pile of coins piled high on green baize, and being offered in loving memory because he holds a handful of queens."

"Perhaps romance isn't as important to me as it once was."

It was almost on Temple's lips to argue the point, but what right did he have to decide the lady's heart?

Or the loss of one.

"I wouldn't think you cared a whit whom I married," she

said, pulling herself free of his grasp and setting off once again.

"Well, certainly not Cordell," he argued, following her. "Come now, if you insist on being married, surely Penham wouldn't have been a bad choice." He paused for a moment, watching her. "A bit young for you—"

She swung around, her brow arched sharply.

Temple was a man familiar with war, which meant he knew when to beat a hasty retreat. "Not that young," he offered, then changed his mind and waded into the bloody field. "Well, yes, demmit, he is too young for you. He's a veritable pup. And you are . . . you are . . . a woman grown."

"Thank you for noticing." She sauntered away.

Noticing? How could he help but notice? No man in his right mind wouldn't be tempted by the delicate curve of her hips, her lithe form, the soft swell of her breasts. And those blue eyes that sparkled with a mixture of mischief and something else . . . enticement and innocence.

Gads, she was a walking minx. One he studiously avoided for just those reasons.

And to his chagrin, she'd stopped her tourist's ramble, and he nearly bumped into her. She glanced over her shoulder and right into his eyes. "Tell me, Temple, would you truly let me marry Cordell? Let the viscount take me as his wife?"

This close to her, he could smell the rosewater she favored, drown in the depths of her blue eyes, nearly touch the silk of her skin.

She turned ever so slowly, until they were face-to-face. "You'd let Cordell take me to his bed?"

While his breath seemed to have left his lungs, one vehement thought came erupting out of his gut so hard it was all he could do not to say it out loud.

Over my dead body.

She smiled at him again, as if she could see the conflict in his eyes. "I thought not." With that, she stepped down from the base of the monument and started walking across the square.

Damn you, Lady Diana Fordham, he wanted to curse, as she poked her nose back into her book, pretending she didn't care that he stood there gaping after her like the village idiot.

"You should be inside," he called after her. "It will be dark soon and it wouldn't be safe for you to be wandering about."

"Oh aye," she said, looking at the upstanding townspeople who were taking advantage of the late light and pleasant evening by strolling about the town. "I suppose there are villains lurking about those woods yonder just waiting for a likely lady."

"There may be," he said, feeling hard-pressed to find anyone looking slightly villainous or even mildly odd. In truth, the only people in Geddington who fit that bill were seated at a table in The Queen's Respite playing vingt-et-un. "Why don't you just go inside. Mrs. Foston is probably worried about you."

"I doubt it," Diana said. "She was asleep on my bed when I left. I'll probably end up in her room tonight, for she's terribly difficult to wake. Not that I relish spending the night in a room above the stable yard." She paused and smiled at him. "No, I prefer to stay out here for a bit longer."

Temple came to stand before her. "Do you ever do what you are told?"

"Never. Do you?"

He wished he'd said no to Pymm back at White's. Then he certainly wouldn't be in this tangle. "You'd be amazed," he told her.

"I would be," she said. "Besides, I have my reasons for not going in just yet. I'm waiting for something."

"And what pray tell might that be?"

She nodded up at the sky, already dimming. "The first star."

"The first star?"

"Yes." She scanned the darkening dome overhead. "I always like to watch for the first star of the evening. You can rarely see them in London, but when I am in the countryside, I always look for it."

He knew he shouldn't, but he had to ask, "And why do you do that?"

"To make a wish, of course." She looked at him as if he had just grown another head. "Oh, Temple, sometimes you can be such an old wigsby. You weren't always such a curmudgeon, you know." She nudged him in the ribs and went back to gazing up at the sky.

He rubbed his side and wished she were a little more conventional. A little more missish. A little less Diana. "Once you've seen this star, you'll go inside?"

"If that is what you wish."

They stood there for some time in the quiet of the dusk.

He couldn't take the silence for very long. It jangled at his nerves. "What are you going to wish for?"

"I can't tell you that. It would spoil the wish."

"I doubt that telling me your wish is going to jeopardize its likelihood one jot."

She didn't appear convinced.

"If you won't tell me, then I will guess." He tapped his chin with his finger. "I believe your wish will run something like this: I wish that Cordell will not find my emergency funds."

She shook her head. "I wouldn't waste such a precious commodity on something like that." She paused. "Besides, he'll not find my money."

The way she said it with such finality made Temple smile.

Perhaps he would have no need for Pymm's writ. He could just wait and let Cordell squander Diana's stashed coins, and then she'd be the one answering challenges over the viscount's murdered body.

"Any other guesses?" she asked.

Around them, the birds were offering their final songs before heading to their nests. The soft sweet trills, the light wind ruffling through the town, and the glorious sky overhead offered more romance. Something Temple hardly needed in Diana's company.

She looked first up at the sky, and then at him, her head tipped just so, her lips parted, her eyes glittering with a beguiling challenge.

As he looked into her eyes, watched her tongue moisten her lips, he knew exactly what her wish was.

The demmed little minx was trying to seduce him.

"Diana—" he started to say in warning, but even to his own ears he didn't hear the refrain that needed to be said.

Don't do this, Temple. Remember Constantinople. Remember your vow not to marry. Remember her betrothed just across the street . . .

It couldn't have been staged better in Haymarket. All of it. The damned statue and its romantic past. The lanterns offering their flickering challenge to the coming darkness. The birds lulling them together.

And Diana. She was made for kissing. Her lush mouth, the fair silk of her skin, those glorious blue eyes.

She could lure a man halfway across the world with those eyes.

Perhaps she already has, an impish voice whispered in his ear.

Try as he might to remember she was nothing but troublesome baggage, he found himself bending his head to hers.

The moment he made this tiny movement, gave her any inclination that he was wavering, she melded into him.

No, he shouldn't be doing this, he told himself, even as his arms pulled her close. He knew only too well what mayhem those lips could wield, what trouble lay in their wake.

For this wasn't the first time he'd ever kissed Lady Diana Fordham.

But as his mouth crashed down over hers, claiming her lips in a kiss he couldn't resist, he swore, by God, it would be his last.

Temple could deny all he wanted that he hadn't come after her, but Diana knew the truth the moment he kissed her.

Until then, she'd had her fair share of doubts.

It wasn't every day that a woman went to such great lengths to stage an elopement scandalous enough to catch the man she really loved.

Whatever his excuse, Temple was here now, and he was kissing her.

Kissing her exactly as she remembered.

His lips pressed against hers, demanding them to open beneath his touch. She did so only too willingly, inviting him to invade her with a teasing whisper of her tongue.

Come back to me, Temple, she wished, as the first star sparkled its magic overhead. Rising up on her toes, she threw herself against him in a wanton embrace.

As if he heard her silent wish, he answered her entreaty. His tongue swept inside her, daring her to follow him onto the path of scandal and ruin, as he had so many years ago.

If his kiss had almost ruined her then, it was undoing her now.

He groaned and pressed against her, his arms wound around her, pulling her so close she could feel the pounding of his heart, the heat of his body, the length and hardness of his . . .

Diana knew she should be shocked by the intimacy of his embrace, but it only made her purr in contentment, in satisfaction, in a desire to know more.

Feel more.

His tongue still teased hers, and she grew bolder, teasing him back, reveling in the heated glory of being in his arms.

"Oh dear God, Diana," he murmured into her ear. "What you do to me."

She tried to keep from grinning. She failed utterly. With her head on his chest, she said, "Temple, I knew you would come for me. Come back to me."

The moment the words tumbled from her lips, her world tilted. She heard the skip in his heart, his chest tightening beneath her cheek, felt that horrible wall of indifference start cutting her off from him.

"No, Diana," he said, his voice full of a resolute determination she knew only too well. "You're mistaken. I haven't come back. And you know I never will."

Chapter 4

Temple remained outside the inn, still in a daze from Diana's kiss and the stinging retort she'd flung at him when he'd told her that he would never come back to her.

He didn't know what was worse, the way his body still thrummed to her tempting passion, or that she considered him a heartless old goat.

Of course, Diana had chosen a more cutting phrase.

Never one to mince words, he supposed she was right. He was nothing more than a heartless bastard. Give him another few years and he'd put his grandfather's stodgy reputation to shame.

I am not Setchfield, he told himself. But in truth, he knew one day he would be, in name and deed . . . and stony heart.

Yet what could he do? Offer for Diana? Let her live in his impoverished state? Leave her for months on end, unprotected and in a state of uncertainty, while he trotted off on another dangerous mission for Pymm?

No, it was too much to ask of her. He'd been right to disavow her all those years ago, and he was still right to do so now.

Yet in the back of his mind, the part untouched by his grandfather's scorn and wrath, he knew those were a coward's answers, obvious and safe. For if he was of a mind to delve deeper into his soul, he knew he'd find the real reasons he'd refused Diana tonight.

And it was a place he would not go. Not even for her.

Indeed, if he was half the man he should be, he would not have stopped at that kiss. No, if he had a heart, if he was willing to ignore every bit of common sense he possessed, he'd have tossed her in the back of the Setchfield berline, ordered Elton to drive like the devil to the border, and started their wedding night before the horses hit their stride.

Leaning against the wall of the inn, he let the cool stone invade his heated body while his mind drifted over what Lady Diana's reaction might be to such a wild ride. That is, until he spied Cordell come out the door.

Out of blunt, eh, old man?

The viscount looked one way and then the other across the inn's small yard. Satisfied that no one else was about, he tucked his hat low on his brow before reaching up and snatching down the lantern hanging in the eaves. With the light in hand, he strode quickly across the yard, turning down the street and out of sight.

As the other man rounded the corner, Temple spied something else that brought him out of his shadows.

Cordell carried a saddlebag.

The man was leaving. Abandoning Diana.

At first glance, Temple considered this a boon bit of business. Certainly it would make the morning easier, not having to face Diana as the magistrate hauled her betrothed off to jail. And despite the fact that Temple was glad to see such a welcome event, suspicion filled his mind as he watched the other man flee like a criminal.

Why the devil would Cordell leave in the dead of night? In a matter of days he could have an heiress bride, and possess more money than whatever he'd probably stolen from the inn.

Temple hadn't been in Pymm's employ all these years not to have his every instinct stand on edge, and before he knew what he was doing, he started after Cordell.

Even as he pushed off the stone wall, he let out an exasperated sigh. What the hell was he going to say to the fellow when he did catch up with him?

Oh say there, Cordell, lost your way? One usually travels to Gretna with his bride.

Temple shook his head.

This entire errand was so far beneath him. Pymm had better been telling the truth about the assignment to the sultan's court. Then he could get far away from London, his grandfather, and especially Diana and her wishful kisses.

As it was, Temple had no problem following Cordell through the sleepy village. Actually it was quite boring, for Cordell had no idea how to skulk about, his saddlebag slapping against his leg and the lantern rattling like a church bell as he traveled across the city's famed medieval bridge and out into the darkness.

Temple had to do little more than follow the glow of the lantern and listen to his fumbling gait.

Where the devil is he going? he thought, about the same time he heard the viscount come to a faltering stop, cursing and complaining.

Ducking behind a tree, Temple waited for the man to get his bearings.

"Not worth it," Cordell muttered to himself, leaning heavily against a tree as he caught his breath. "Steady there, old man. You're holding a handful of aces."

If he was trying to be discreet, he was doing a wretched job of it. At this rate they would end up being shot by the magistrate's pimpled clerk.

After a few more mumbled complaints, Cordell set off again, leading Temple across a clearing and tramping through a patch of thick hedges.

The man finally headed into a meadow and Temple came to a stop, still concealed in the thick trees ringing the glen.

The moment Cordell got to the middle, out of the shadows came a trio of riders. The viscount squawked in protest, nearly dropping his lantern.

"What the—" Temple muttered beneath his breath as he reached for his pistol, the one concealed in his coat, thinking he was about to have to save Diana's worthless betrothed from a robbery. But as he patted his empty pocket, he realized his weapon was still back in the berline.

But it was no matter. Apparently the viscount didn't need his assistance.

Cordell's protests ended with a telling question.

"Where the devil is my money?"

Diana closed the door to her room, leaning against it as if she could bar the world from intruding on her thoughts.

Oh dearest heavens, how could she have forgotten what it was like to kiss Temple?

Her hand went to her lips, still tingling from where his mouth had covered hers in a kiss that had nothing to do with chivalry and everything to do with passion.

Passion. The very word left her knees trembling with the notion that he hadn't wanted to stop kissing her, that he would have . . .

"Oh, botheration," she muttered. At this rate she'd die a spinster.

It wasn't as if Temple hadn't been tempted. Oh, he could make every denial he wanted to, but his kiss told her everything she needed to know.

Temple still held feelings for her. At least his body did.

She smiled at this, taking a deep breath as she recalled the way he'd claimed her—with his lips, with his arms, with his hands—and with a steely determination that belied the foppish man most took him for. She sighed.

How could the *ton* not see the hero beneath the fool?

For to touch Temple was to feel the strength of his will, the depth his honor, even if it was buried beneath a charade, languished in the forgotten part of his soul.

She'd suspected as much, that the man she'd fallen in love with still resided inside the foppish lace and fine tailoring encasing his masculine form. Oh, he hid it well, Temple did, he'd even fooled her long enough to almost see her wed to Colin.

Luckily she'd learned the truth before she'd made that disastrous mistake. Not that there hadn't been times since her broken betrothal when even she'd wondered at her own sanity, languishing in her Mayfair tower for Temple like some sad medieval heroine.

Then just when she'd find herself on the verge of giving up her lonely vigil, something always happened to renew her faith, replenish the vow she'd made.

From across a crowded room, she'd catch Temple watching her, a dark, smoldering passion burning in his gaze, like a silent plea to her heart not to forsake him.

Not to forget what they once shared.

The heart-wrenching flash would be there for only an instant, but it was enough to ignite her hope for months.

And then there were the rumors that floated about the *ton* amidst the flotsam and jetsam of gossip—of a hero who'd stolen plans from Napoleon's couriers and saved an entire brigade . . . of a man who'd stopped foreign agents from infiltrating Whitehall . . . of a gentleman spy who crisscrossed the Continent carrying English interests far and wide, braving all manner of personal dangers.

Those whispered tales had warmed her heart, thrilled her spirit, for she knew with a certainty who that man was and why he'd disavowed her.

Tonight, his kiss had revealed something he could never hide from her again—that Temple, *her Temple*, still lived. Especially when she'd dared him to let her marry Cordell, let the viscount take her to his bed.

Why, he'd looked positively capable of murder. Hardly the town fool or the *ton*'s able jester, but a man of deep passion and a determined heart.

So now it was up to her to set that man free, the man of strength and masculine power who sent her heart racing, her blood afire.

A hero to save her from her own folly before his penchant for heroics destroyed him.

Diana knew now that it was only a matter of chipping away at the thick walls he'd built around himself—his indifference, his Corinthian manners, his whimsical antics.

At least she'd gotten rid of that accursed lorgnette. At this Diana grinned. That was a first step, a chink in his fortress, a handhold to start tearing it down.

But would that be enough? she wondered. What if she broke through his stony façade and he still denied her? Denied them a chance at happiness. At all the starry wishes they could discover in a lifetime together.

Diana sighed and crossed the room to her lonely, narrow bed.

Something held Temple in check, and until she discovered

he truth behind his denials, she wouldn't rest. She'd been a
ool to lose him all those years ago. But all these years of
vatching and waiting had taught her patience and persever-
nce.

And she was done with patience.

Temple drew as close as he dared to Cordell's meeting
lace.

"My money," Cordell whined, his hand outstretched. "I
vill have my money. And it had better be in gold. I was
romised gold if I brought *her* here."

Her? This caught Temple's attention. Diana?

One of the riders nudged his horse forward, until it stood
ye to eye with Cordell. "We have your gold, monsieur."

"You came a long way to get the chit, and you're welcome
o her," the viscount said, obviously more inclined to be
riendly now that he was about to gain payment for his ser-
ices. "Mind me asking what you want to take her to Paris
or?"

The leader sat up straight in his saddle. "*Oui,* I do mind. It
s none of your business."

Cordell shrugged. Apparently his curiosity could be
uelled with gold.

But not so Temple's. If he didn't know better, the man
peaking was none other than Jean-Marc Marden. One of
Napoleon's most trusted agents.

Temple shook his head. French agents in Geddington?
Doing business with Cordell?

Marden held a heavy-looking purse over Cordell's head.
You will be paid when we have the bride. Not before. Those
vere the agreed upon terms. The bride, Monsieur Cordell,
hen your money."

The bride? What was going on here? Cordell was selling

Diana to a pack of French agents? Temple didn't know wha
was more unbelievable—that Cordell was working with the
French or that the French were willing to pay gold for tha
muslin-draped bit of trouble.

And gold, for that matter.

For one scandalous moment, Temple thought perhaps he
should have brokered a better deal with Pymm.

Obviously there was more to this than Pymm's false as
surances that it was a mere favor for one of the King's most
loyal subjects.

Why that cagey, lying son of a—

The rattle of coins as the pouch hit the ground at Cordell's
feet yanked Temple's attention back to the matter at hand
The pouch had split and the tempting sparkle of gold spilled
out at the viscount's feet.

"How do I know it is all there?" Cordell complained. "I'l
not be cheated after all the trouble I've gone to."

Temple cringed. He had always considered Cordell a bi
of a lobcock, but now he revised that assessment. The mar
was an outright idiot. To practically call three mounted, and
most likely well-armed men thieves was as close to getting
one's throat cut as one should ever dare.

"Your gold is all there, monsieur. I am a man of my word."

The thick, oily sneer behind Marden's words ran down
Temple's spine.

"You'd better be," Cordell replied, sounding all the more
like the arrogant and overbearing lout that he was.

The Frenchman appeared unimpressed. He straightened
in his saddle, a tall, imposing figure cloaked in black. Hi
words were filled with deadly calm. "Then we are all wel
satisfied. You have enough to settle your debts with some left
over. And we have our bride."

Temple watched the exchange but couldn't see the sense of it. Why would Cordell be willing to take this small fortune in gold when back at the inn his bride-to-be offered him riches that would put this French offering to shame?

Cordell's avaricious gaze had yet to waver from the pouch. "And the girl? She will be silenced? I won't have that little bitch showing up and yapping a pack of lies at the inquiry. It would be demmed inconvenient."

"That problem is well in hand." Marden nodded to one of his cohorts. "She will not be available to testify for quite some time. If ever, that is." The three men laughed.

"Hmm. Glad to hear it," Cordell said, adding his own chuckle to their coarse laughter. "I never did anything wrong, mind you, but that gel thought she could get a fine bit of blunt from her lies about how that whore died. It was all just a misunderstanding gone afoul. If you know what I mean."

His stomach churning at this revelation, Temple realized he'd found his answer. So the rumors about Cordell's run-in at a Seven Dials brothel hadn't been just malicious gossip.

From what Temple knew, the viscount, well in his cups, had badly beaten one of the girls. Bad enough that the poor chit had died the next day from her injuries. Of course he'd denied being with her, but apparently the girl had a partner who'd witnessed his violence—and been too frightened to stop the viscount's vicious attack.

Her testimony was said to be the basis for murder charges to be filed against Cordell.

Temple muttered a vow upon the lost girl's soul, for he knew that if Marden had dealt with her, her inability to testify was permanent. She deserved more for her courage to bear witness against a member of the *ton* than to be murdered by this evil trio.

"Satisfied, monsieur? Your reputation is safe and you've been well compensated for your troubles."

Another one of the riders urged his horse forward. He blocked Cordell from Temple's view, but his words were clear enough to be heard.

"Is she untouched? Does she remain a virgin?"

"Yes . . . Yes . . ." Cordell told him, casting an annoyed glance in that direction. "To tell the truth, I don't see what your Emperor wants with her. She's got a shrew's tongue and a temper to match."

Marden leaned over. "She is no longer your concern."

"And good riddance, I might add. Another day cooped up with her and that wretched travel book of hers would have sent me—"

"Enough, monsieur," Marden said. "Now where is she?"

Temple's mouth opened in shock. Up until this point it had all seemed so unreal that he hadn't really considered the consequences before him—Cordell was selling Diana to a pack of French agents.

But now the peril of the situation sent Temple's blood pounding. The moment Cordell opened his mouth and told them where Diana was, she was in danger. Grave danger, if his instincts were telling him true.

And they'd never wronged him before.

He muttered a curse under his breath. *Oh, how the devil did I ever get involved in all this?*

Cordell nodded toward the village. "She's at the inn. The Queen's Respite, near the center of town."

"Which room?" Marden pressed, his hand loosening his grip on his reins and running beneath his cloak.

No, Temple wanted to shout. *Don't tell them, you fool.* He patted his coat again, hoping he'd just missed his pistol the last time he'd checked. He knew only too well what was about to befall Cordell.

And there wasn't anything Temple could do if he wanted to live to save Diana.

"The last room down the hall," Cordell said impatiently, not paying attention to the shifting movements above him, too intent on gathering the last of the coins into his greedy hands and stuffing them back into the pouch and into his pockets. He rose and faced his conspirators. "To the left when you get to the head of the stairs." He gave the bag an appreciative shake. "Give her my love."

"We'll give her more than that, monsieur," Marden said, pulling out a pistol and firing a shot straight into Cordell's heart. "We'll give her your condolences."

The viscount staggered back several steps, his mouth open and moving, but no words came forth.

Temple stood rooted in place, impotent rage seething through him at his own inability to come to the man's aid. What could he do with his pistol back at the inn and Diana's destiny so uncertain?

In truth, the viscount had sealed his own fate the moment he'd become embroiled in this treacherous affair.

Now it was his undoing.

The man clutched at his coat, where already a red stain spilled across the pale yellow wool. He looked down at his own ruin and then back at his murderer. "You dirty, conniving—" His strangled words ended as he fell over dead.

Marden shrugged. "*Adieu,* monsieur." He tucked his pistol back inside his cloak, then said to one of his henchmen, "Retrieve the gold before we go fetch our bride. He has no use for it now."

There followed some low, rough laughter.

The bride. Temple glanced over his shoulder, where he could barely discern the lights of Geddington. Diana! Her name shot through his shocked thoughts like a howling wind.

In the meadow, a French curse tainted the air. "He won't let go of the pouch."

Temple wanted to smile. Even in death, Cordell remained a greedy, grasping bastard.

"Then cut off his hand, you fool. Just get the money," Marden ordered.

Backing away from the horrific scene and the complaints of the horseman, Temple made his way out of the woods as quickly and silently as he could. If the French discovered him, there would be no one to protect Diana from whatever they had planned for her—since he knew only too well what they were capable of.

But before he cleared the trees and could hit the road in a dead run, the horsemen thundered past him and into Geddington.

His heart sank. He'd never reach her in time.

Oh dear God, Diana. I've failed you yet again.

Elton sat in the peace and quiet of the empty stable yard, smoking his pipe and glancing occasionally at the sky. The moon hung far overhead, just a faint silver whisper that offered little in the way of light or guidance through the darkness. Stars, taking advantage of the reluctant moon, sparkled and twinkled, radiating their own glory without the competing light from their brighter, much larger sister.

Ah, he mused, puffing on his pipe, it was a night made for the roads. He could almost hear the sound of a coming carriage, feel the restless movements of his horse beneath him as it too sensed the coming fray. Then he'd dash out in front of the driver, pistols in both hands, and say . . . say . . .

By gads, he couldn't remember what it was he used to say.

"Get a good night's rest, you old fool," he muttered to himself. He sighed and tapped out his pipe. He'd given up that profession the day the hangman had put a noose around his neck and pronounced his final punishment.

If it hadn't been for the marquis' intervention . . . well, he owed Lord Templeton his life, and he certainly couldn't start indulging in old ways just because a perfect night tempted him to ride the roads again.

Yet . . . it was as if he could hear the pounding hooves calling him, coming closer.

"Ye're getting batty," he said, wondering at the lure the road still held over him. He should go inside and seek his bed, for it was a warm and rare one indeed, but he couldn't just yet. His lordship had gone and wandered off, and until he was back, safe and sound, Elton was going to maintain his vigil.

Then he heard it again. The thick, enticing sound of hoofbeats coming closer. He wasn't off his knocker. It was horses. Four of them, coming at a breakneck speed.

And it wasn't a carriage. He knew that just from the sound. *Riders.* He frowned and ducked behind a bale of hay. Some instincts never died.

Riders rarely brought good news. He knew that much, and so he concealed himself to see what scurvy business they were about.

Not that it surprised him that trouble was descending around the quiet inn. Wherever his lordship went, trouble was sure to follow.

And that's why he didn't mind so much being in his debt and all.

Life with his nibs was never dull.

The riders thundered into the yard, their horses clattering to a stop.

The innkeeper came out almost immediately. "Gentle-men, what can I do for you? Rooms? Meals? A hot drink to chase away the chill of the evening?"

A brute of a fellow jumped down from his mount and pushed past the innkeeper, sending the poor fellow onto his backside.

"Oh aye, trouble," Elton muttered under his breath. He shook his head and glanced toward the inn. And Lady Diana and her Mrs. Foston were in there without his lordship around.

Elton didn't like this one bit.

The innkeeper rose from the ground. "I'll call the magistrate! I'll get the constable! I'll not have trouble in my—" He fell silent from a knock on the head by one of the other riders. The assailant and his partner stormed inside, following the first fellow.

Muttering a rather obscene curse, Elton considered his options.

Then came the answer to his problems.

"Elton?" the only too familiar voice of his lordship hissed through the dark stable yard. "Elton, where the devil are you?"

"Here, sir," he said, relieved for the marquis' timely arrival. He stepped into the light only to find himself facing a disheveled Temple. His normally meticulous employer looked as if he'd been chased by the hounds.

"Where are they?" the marquis asked.

Elton didn't need to ask who. "Inside," he said, jerking his thumb at the doorway.

"All of them?"

Elton nodded. "Aye."

Temple stalked across the yard to the berline and reached up and under Elton's seat, where they each kept a brace of pistols stashed, just in case.

Obviously this was one of those instances.

While his lordship checked the pistols, Elton began leading their mounts out of their stalls. He could put the horses in their traces and have them ready for traveling quicker than the best postboy.

"This is going to be just like Amsterdam," Temple shot over his shoulder. "We've got to get out of here. *Now*."

"Aye, sir," Elton said, his hands running through the leather lines and guiding the beasts into their places. Then he paused, realizing exactly what his nibs had just said. "Like Amsterdam?" He glanced at the horses the riders had come in on. "Not that!"

"Yes, just like that. Consider our experience with the Dutch a dress rehearsal for tonight. But this time our enemy is French."

"French!" Elton spat, as Temple dashed toward the inn. He didn't know whom he hated more, excise men or the French. As far as he was concerned, they probably shared the same devilish sire. His hand went first to his missing eye, then to the knife in his belt.

"Hope they enjoy their walk back to the coast," he said, as he started toward the four waiting mounts.

Temple dashed inside and went up the stairs, ignoring the overturned tables and the few patrons cowering beneath them. Down the hall, Marden and his companions were trying to break into Diana's room. The old inn had weathered many a change, but the doors to the room, built at time when sturdy meant just that, was not about to give way.

Inside the chamber, Mrs. Foston screamed and rallied on. "Murderers! Thieves! Oh, somebody help me!"

Temple hung back, remembering what Diana had said about switching rooms with the lady because she was so hard to wake.

Not that I relish spending the night in a room above the stable yard.

With the French well occupied trying to gain their prize, Temple stole down the hall in the opposite direction. When he got to the end, he turned down a short corridor that led to a back staircase. There at the head of the stairs was a door that he gauged led to the only room that looked down on the stable yard.

He put his ear to the sturdy oak, but heard nothing within. He tried the latch and thankfully found it opened. Considering a trio of Frenchmen hadn't been able to bash in the other door, he had been afraid he was going to have to go search for a cannon. He said a word of thanks to the thrifty innkeeper who hadn't wasted money on a lock for a servant's room.

He slipped inside and closed the door behind him. Once he did so, the ruckus down the hall was muffled and barely discernable. In fact, the room was almost peaceful, except for the soft snores rising from the sleeping form on the narrow cot situated beneath a small pair mullioned windows.

"Diana?" Her name whispered from his lips.

There was a rustling in the sheets, and a long bare leg poked out from beneath one of the blankets.

"Diana, is that you?" he choked out, unwilling to move too close. Gads, didn't the chit have the decency to wear *something* to bed?

"Aye, Temple. 'Tis me." She rolled over, the sheets falling away, revealing the lithe limbs and soft, beguiling curves that so belied the determined woman they contained. She wore only a chemise, so white and fine that it did little to hide the bounty beneath. The rosy hue of her nipples shone through, as well as every other glorious secret she kept so well hidden during the day.

Suddenly the threat of the French was nothing to what the

sight of Diana was doing to his senses. Her tousled hair and come hither glances were enough to drive a man to forget all his convictions and lose himself in the silken embrace of her arms, the downy depths of her thighs.

She smiled, the one which drove him to distraction. So knowing, so victorious, so enticing. "You've changed your mind, I see."

Changed his mind? The commotion from down the hall grew louder. Recalling the real reason for his moonlight visit, he swung around, pistol pointed at the door.

"Trouble, Temple?" she asked, her delicate brow arching. "And here I thought you'd come to steal me away from Cordell." She sat with her knees tucked to her chest, the sheet pulled up to her chin so very modestly. Yet there was nothing modest about the enticing sparkle in her blue eyes.

The light glowing there twinkled and teased him to steal more than another man's bride. To carry her to some time-forgotten place and make love to her forever. The seductive notion bewitched him only for a moment before another streak of French curses came racing down the hall, leaving the air blue with their vehement pronouncement.

Even Diana had the decency to blush at what she was hearing.

"Demmit, Diana, this isn't the time," he said.

He glanced around the room and spied a traveling valise beside the bed. He hoped it contained a change of clothes. He didn't bother to ask, but caught it up with one hand, while the other reached over and threw open the window.

"What are you doing?" Diana demanded, scrambling up from the bed, thankfully with the sheet in hand. "Close that window at once. I won't catch my death."

"You'd be surprised what you could catch tonight," he told her, leaning out the window.

Blessings on you, Elton, he thought, as he waved to his servant. The man had their carriage and horses harnessed and ready.

Down the hall a great crash sounded, and a piercing shriek rent the night.

"That's Mrs. Foston," Diana said, heading toward the door. "We must do something! Why, it sounds like she is being murdered!"

Temple caught her by the arm. "Oh no, we don't," he said, as a loud *thwack* and then a yelp echoed down the hall.

"Take this, you scoundrel." *Thwack! Thwack!* "I'll not let you take my virtue!" *Thwack! Thwack!*

"From the sounds of it, the lady has the situation well in hand," he said, as he turned toward the window, dragging Diana with him.

"Let me go!" she protested, now starting to fight him in earnest. "This is madness. This is insane. Botheration, if you wanted me to go with you, all you had to do was ask."

Temple spun around, shaking a finger under her nose. "Listen, I didn't want any part of this. None, mind you. But now I haven't got a choice. You're coming with me, but just until I can get you to safety, so don't get any ideas about what it means, because I'm only doing this just this once."

Mrs. Foston screamed again, but this time there were no telling protests from her infamous and well-used cane. Then her protests ended in a muffled bevy of complaints.

Temple heaved a sigh of relief and then added a few curses. They'd finally found a way past the lady, but hadn't harmed her. Yet. At least Marden possessed some morals. Still, if they'd apprehended Mrs. Foston, that could only mean they now knew Diana wasn't in the chamber.

He hadn't the time to be standing around just waiting for them to come looking for her.

His gaze shot across the room, taking in the meager furnishings, hoping to find something that could help slow down their pursuit, but the landlord's thrifty sense went beyond a lack of locks for the serving classes. Just the low cot, a poor excuse for a chair, the woven seat more hole than weave, and a tattered set of curtains hanging on a cord across the windows.

Nothing! Not even a small trunk or wardrobe to shove against the door, for there were just hooks on either side of the door for hanging up clothes.

He glanced once more at the window, then the door.

"It'll have to do," he muttered, reaching up and wrenching the curtains from the wall.

"Temple! What are you doing? I'll not pay for damages because you've gone mad." When he began yanking the cord free from the draperies, and then tested its strength with a tug between his hands, she stumbled away from him until her back hit the wall. "Wha-a-a-t do you intend to do with that? Temple, I told you I'd go quite willingly."

At first her words made no sense, until he realized what she was thinking.

He almost grinned. Serve the chit right to be trussed up and tossed out the window like a stolen Christmas goose.

Lord knows, she tied him up in knots at every chance she got.

He considered explaining what he intended to do, but discarded the notion. It wouldn't hurt her to be a little afraid of him.

He tied a quick loop in one end of the rope and hung it over the first hook. Pulling it taut, he twisted the middle portion around the door latch and finished by tying the end of the rope to the hook on the other side of the door.

Taking a step back from his handiwork, he eyed it and

hoped it would buy them enough time to get ahead of the French.

Out in the hall, the commotion was coming closer. The French agents were going room by room searching for their prize. Since the inn was all but empty, they weren't meeting with much resistance to slow their progress, or finding any success.

"Who are these men?" she asked. "Friends of yours?"

He shook his head. "Hardly. Business associates of your betrothed."

"What? Did he lose again?"

"In a manner of speaking," Temple told her. The pounding of boots continued to grow louder. "We haven't much time," he said, crossing the room and throwing open the other shutter. Thankfully the innkeeper was also rather lenient in keeping his stable yard cleaned up, affording them the perfect means of escape.

Without a second glance, he tossed her bag into the yard.

"What are you doing?" Diana protested. "Those were my clothes!"

"Good," Temple told her. "I'd hate to have to travel tonight with you in just that sheet."

"Travel? Just where do you think I am going?"

"At present," he said, taking a deep breath and steeling his nerves as he caught her up in his arms, sheet and all, "you are going out the window."

She stared at him, her eyes wide, her mouth falling open.

He'd never thought he'd see the day that Lady Diana Fordham found herself speechless. Yet here she was gaping and sputtering as if there were no words to be found.

For a moment she stared into his eyes, her gaze a mix of confusion, fear, and anger.

The first would subside when she realized what he was

going to do with her. The last might well be his undoing.

"How are we to get out if you've barricaded the door?" she asked. "Fly?"

"Exactly," he said, tossing her out the window. The sheet rippled in the air, and then there was a soft *thump*.

Her sputtered complaint told him she'd landed safely.

"Temple!" she howled. "You fiend. You tossed me into a pile of sh—"

She finished her protest with a word he highly doubted she'd learned at Miss Emery's.

Chapter 5

By the time Temple landed beside her, Diana was ready for him.

"How dare you toss me out a window . . . into this . . . this . . . this pile of . . ." Her mouth pursed, for she wasn't about to repeat the word again. "I could have been killed," she finally managed to say.

"What awaited you inside was far more dangerous than this, my lady," Temple said in a manner so singularly unapologetic that one might have supposed he had purposely forgotten to claim her for an unwanted dance at Almack's. Before she could sputter another complaint, he caught her by the hand and yanked her free from the mire in which she'd landed, pausing only long enough to stoop over and retrieve her valise as they went headlong across the yard.

His grip closed around her wrist with an unforgiving resolve. She wagered that she could fight him all she wanted, but in the end, Temple was going to have his way.

He'd just tossed her out a window, for goodness' sakes.

Loose stones and cobbles bit in revenge against her bare

feet—feet that wore only the finest slippers, boots of the softest leather, and stockings of the most whisper-smooth silk.

She could imagine what they looked like now gauging from the foul matter squishing between her toes.

Elton sat in his perch, the reins in his hands, the horses prancing about, looking ready and willing for a wild flight, as if all part of some madcap rescue Temple had decided to stage just for her benefit.

The marquis marched to the carriage, hauling her along, until he got to the open door, then he swung around to catch her once more in his arms.

Oh no, she thought. Not into his arms. When he'd cradled her moments earlier in her room, she would have offered him anything. Her lips, her touch, her heart, her body—though certainly not if it meant being tossed out a window.

Then again, even that might be worth it to feel him catch her up one more time.

Just then, there was a huge crash from her former chamber.

"What was that?" she asked.

Temple didn't reply. He swung her up into his arms and then tossed her inside the berline.

Scrambling to right herself, she shoved her chemise down over her knees and looked up only in time to catch her valise, which came flying in behind her.

Really, she was going to have to talk to him about his manners when it came to stealing ladies.

"What about Mrs. Foston?" Elton was saying. "We can't leave her, milord."

"There isn't time," Temple said. "Besides, the last I heard of the lady, she had matters well in hand." There was another crash inside the inn, followed by shouts and cursing.

Diana stuck her head out the door. "We can't leave Mrs. Foston behind. It wouldn't be proper."

Temple just looked at her as if he wondered if she truly knew the meaning of the word.

She did. When it mattered, that was.

"Mrs. Foston is in danger," she pointed out.

"Aye, sir," Elton chimed in. "Couldn't we just—"

At the door of the inn, Marden came thundering out, a pistol in hand.

Temple let out a shrill, sharp whistle that sent the horses bolting in their traces. He dove headfirst into the berline, directly into Diana's lap.

The wild start sent her reeling back, and for a moment, unable to issue any more protests as the carriage careened out of the stable yard and into the street, leaving her teeth chattering almost as loudly as the horses' frantic hooves.

She tried to rise, but Temple held her pinned to the floor.

"Get off of me!" she said, struggling to get up. "I can solve all this by just giving these ruffians the money Cordell owes them. He obviously played too deep tonight."

"About six feet, I'd say," Temple muttered, holding her down, even as a shot rang out after them.

The carriage careened again, swaying dangerously from one side to the other.

She changed her mind about getting Temple off her and clung to him like an anchor.

What had Cordell been thinking, playing with such ruffians? *The fool.* Couldn't he have waited just a few hours more before gambling away the money she'd promised him? Apparently not, as the report of another pistol echoed after them.

"Oh, this is ridiculous," she said. "Tell Elton to stop and I'll give them the money they are owed."

Temple bounded up, pulling a pistol out of his jacket and

leaning out the window. "They don't want your money, Diana," he said over his shoulder.

Not want her money? "Then whatever are they tearing about the inn searching for?"

He said nothing for a moment, then said in a tight voice that sent shivers down her spine. "*You.*"

"Me? Cordell wagered me?"

"In a matter of speaking."

"What sort of man would wager a woman?"

Temple snorted, as if the answer was obvious.

She flinched, for she'd known what kind of man Cordell was when she agreed to this business with him. The bastard would probably wager away her virginity if he thought he had a willing taker.

"So who are these men?" she asked.

"They aren't just men. They're French agents."

French agents. In Geddington? Now it was Diana's turn to snort. Why, it was ludicrous.

"Temple, are you in your cups? Because if this is some jest of yours, some prank for those jinglebrained mullets you call friends back at White's, I'll not let you sully my name for the sake of your gadabout reputation."

Temple's mouth set in a hard line that belied any evidence of his foppish fame. "You sealed that matter, my lady, when you decided to parade about the countryside with the likes of Cordell."

Her hands balled up into fists. "I wouldn't have had to if . . . if . . ."

If you hadn't held me at arm's length all these years.

She huffed and sat back on the floor, clinging to the seat as Elton continued to drive as if the entire militia was after them, not just Cordell's angry creditors. *French agents, in-*

deed! What did Temple take her for? Some green girl straight out of the schoolroom dreaming of romantic adventure?

Honestly, she'd always dreamt of a knight-errant carrying her off in some gallant rescue, vowing his undying love, while fighting off her thwarted suitors.

But the hard-edged man across from her didn't leave her breathless. He frightened her.

Elton had given the horses their heads, and they ran down the pitch-dark road at a reckless pace.

"Temple, tell him to slow down. I doubt Cordell will pursue us this far."

"You're right about that," Temple said, once again in that vexing manner of his, as if he knew far more about her life than she did. He turned back and leaned out the window, but she tugged his jacket hard enough to spin him around.

"You tell me what is going on! I don't believe for a minute these ruffians are some nefarious agents of Boney out to stop my elopement. Besides, what do you know about continental intrigues and spies?"

"Never mind what I know. Believe me, they are French and they want you for something," he said, shaking himself free and peering into the darkness, aiming his pistol down the road.

"Temple, you *are* in your cups. I think these men are just some of Elton's former associates you hired for the evening to give me a good scare." She shook her head. He was just testing her, to see how much she knew of his life. "Quite a fine jest, but enough is enough. If you wanted to carry me off, you could have saved your money and just knocked on the door."

"I certainly didn't ask for *this*," he said.

"Then you shouldn't have come after me," she said, crossing her arms over her chest.

"I didn't have any choice," he said. "And furthermore—"

The report of a pistol ended his harangue.

Temple cursed and shoved her back down on the floor. "Stay down. If Elton followed orders, they won't be after us for long."

She ignored him and poked her head up anyway. "Temple, really, this is starting to be ridiculous. Would you just tell Elton to stop? I will pay these men the money Cordell owes them, and they will stop shooting at us."

"I told you, they don't want your money."

"Not want money? That is all the viscount has ever wanted."

"No longer, Diana. Cordell has no use for your money."

"Are you telling me he's given up gambling?" She shook her head. "Not even I'm so innocent as to believe such a reversal will ever happen."

"Oh, believe me, Cordell made his last wager tonight."

"I suppose he lost," she muttered.

"As a matter of fact, he did."

"How much this time?" Really, she had been very specific when she had entered into this arrangement as to how much she would reimburse him for his services, and if he thought he could chisel her out of a few hundred pounds more, he could go straight to the devil. Still, she had to ask, "How much did the viscount lose?"

"Everything, Diana." Temple turned and looked at her. Even in the meager light of the carriage, she could see the stern set of his jaw, the determined line drawn across his forehead. "Cordell lost everything tonight."

A frisson of worry niggled down her spine. This was no jest. No lark Temple had arranged merely to frighten her, to punish her for dragging him out of his comfortable London confines.

"Everything? I hardly promised him everything . . . why,

I was quite specific when we reached our agreement that I would—"

Another shot rang out; this time it hit the side of the carriage, sending a shower of splinters down around them.

Diana yelped and ducked back down. When she peeked up, Temple was taking aim and firing a shot at their pursuers.

She scrambled up and caught his arm, sending his shot wild. "What are you doing? You could kill someone!"

"I believe that is the point." He aimed again.

"Temple, this is all just a misunderstanding, just a—"

Another shot rang out, and it found its mark right over her head, covering her in bits of wood and upholstery.

"Botheration," she sputtered. "That one was just far too close for comfort. What is Cordell thinking? When I get my hands on him, I'm going to wring his wretched neck . . . I'm going to—"

"Diana, you'll do no such thing," Temple said, firing another shot and ducking back inside to reload.

"And why not? Is this one of those honorable things that only men can settle over a grassy meadow at dawn? Forgive me, but a lady has her honor as well, and I intend to see mine avenged."

"Then you can thank the men behind us for taking care of your honor."

His icy tone sent another flurry of concern down her spine. "What are you saying, Temple? What are you *not* telling me?"

"Do you really want to know?" he growled out at her.

"Yes!" What she wanted was to get to the end of this miserable ride and go back to the inn. If Temple wanted to make a point, he'd done so. She didn't need to be shot at any longer to understand that her association with the viscount was foolhardy.

"That is not Cordell back there," he told her.

"How can you be so sure?"

"Because he's dead. He's lying facedown in a meadow outside that village with a bullet through his heart."

Diana shrank back. *Dead?* Temple had to be wrong. The viscount had a reputation for playing deep, but she would have paid his debts. Well, up to their agreed-upon amount.

Now he was dead? How could that be? She shook her head, trying to find something to say.

"What, no tears for your lost bridegroom?" Temple asked.

She shook her head.

"Good girl. Don't bother wasting a drop on the man. He was in the process of selling you when he went to his reward."

First one saddle gave way, sending its rider toppling into the dust, and after the second one came flying loose, Marden brought his own mount under control with a sharp tug of the reins, then looked back at his fallen comrades.

Fargues and Dorat rose from where they'd landed, shaky but unharmed.

"They've gotten away," Fargues, the younger of his compatriots, complained.

"I can fix these saddles," Dorat offered. "We can be after them in no time."

Shaking his head, Marden dismissed the suggestion. If he guessed correctly, their saddles were useless. No amount of repairs would save them.

For it was how he would have disabled his enemies if he wanted to make a quick and clean escape. Instead, he considered what to do next, his nimble, treacherous mind discarding one option after another.

"Who of our enemies, monsieur, would be so bold as to take the lady from us?" Fargues asked.

Marden had been pondering the same question since they'd left the inn and begun chasing the fleeing carriage. "No one," he said. "At least, no one from France. No one knows of our quest." He'd made sure of that before they'd left.

"I think our thief must be English," he said slowly, as if trying to convince himself. "Another fortune hunter like Cordell has stolen our bride."

The others nodded. It was the only likely explanation.

"And if he is English, he might be useful," Marden said, a plan unfolding before him even as he spoke. Turning his horse around, he gave his orders. "We go back."

"Back?" Fargues echoed. "But we cannot."

"And why not?" Marden asked.

The man glanced uneasily at his compatriot and then at his leader. "Monsieur Cordell is still there," he said in a tone that suggested perhaps their leader had forgotten the viscount.

"Ah, *oui*," Marden said. "Monsieur Cordell. I think you will find he is going to be as much use to us dead as he was alive."

Diana didn't know how long she sat on the floor in stunned silence after hearing Temple's news about Cordell, but obviously her grief had been overcome by exhaustion and she'd fallen asleep. When she awoke, the carriage was still moving, and she was curled up on the seat, a thick horse blanket thrown over her for warmth.

Someone had seen to her comfort, though she didn't know why. She'd as likely get them all killed.

Just as she had Cordell.

Diana shuddered. Oh dear, what had she done?

She knew exactly what she'd done. Used gold to entice a man into helping her and then led him to his death.

Still, could it have been as Temple said, that the viscount had been using her as well? She didn't believe for a minute that French agents killed the viscount. In all likelihood the man met his fate from cheating at cards.

And what of Mrs. Foston? Diana prayed her dear companion was well and safe. Though, knowing the lady and her indomitable spirit, the villains who'd attacked her were probably still licking their wounds.

It was odd not to look across the carriage and see her frowning visage, and it was a contingency that Mrs. Foston had feared—that they would become separated. Diana could only hope that Letty wouldn't make good her threat and now return to London . . . and to Diana's father with a full accounting of their plans.

Wiping her hair out of her eyes, she blinked a couple of times and then focused on her surroundings, setting aside the suspicions that had haunted her ever since Temple had claimed they were being chased by French agents.

A ridiculous notion, that . . .

She blinked again, and this time the sight of a basket on the floor caught her eye. Leaning over, she pulled back the cloth covering it, only to find within a sturdy loaf, slices of cheese, and a flagon of . . . She tugged the cork free and sniffed.

Tea.

Diana sighed. Her clamoring guilt over Cordell's fate subsided in the wake of the growling from her even noisier stomach.

Besides, as her father always said, there was nothing that couldn't be pondered with better clarity on a full stomach.

Though she didn't know whom she had to thank for this bounty, Temple or Elton, right now she could kiss them both as she dove happily into her first meal in what seemed like ages.

While Miss Emery would be appalled at her manners, Diana tore off a hunk of bread and stuffed it, along with a large piece of cheese, into her mouth.

Overhead, she could hear Temple and Elton talking, their words drifting like manna to her curious ears, as welcome as the thick slices of bread were to her complaining stomach.

"Why not go back to London?" Elton was saying. "I could slip into Geddington and find her Mrs. Foston. I know of a road that is hardly ever used."

Diana smiled. She'd always liked Elton

"No, London will be the first place they look for her," Temple said. "She's not safe until we learn *why* they want her."

She sighed. Why did any man want her? *Her dowry.* Cordell had probably wagered all of it, so it was no wonder his fellow gamesters had set out after them. It made much more sense than Temple's suggestion of some evil foreign plot.

"Pymm might be able to help," Elton suggested.

"I have a feeling Pymm would know more about this than he'd ever let on." Temple blew out a loud breath.

Biting into another piece of bread, Diana glanced up at the roof of the berline and frowned. Oh, the last person she wanted sticking his nose into her plans for Temple was Mr. Pymm. Not that it wouldn't surprise her to see her father's old friend offering his assistance. Pymm loved to meddle.

She could well imagine what advice he'd give Temple.

"Harrumph," she snorted between bites of bread. Pymm's involvement would only make the task ahead that much more difficult.

"If you want to be rid of the gel, why not marry her off to Pins or Needles? You could wash your hands of her right smart. Let one of them fend off these blokes."

Diana nearly choked. What was Elton doing suggesting

such a stupid notion? The last thing she needed was another person urging Temple not to marry her.

She'd have to set his driver straight the first chance she got.

Of course, there was one large problem with Elton's course of action. They'd have to drag her kicking and screaming to the altar before she'd ever marry Penham or Nettlestone.

Temple had been right the night before. Lord Harry was too young for her. That, and the idea of living with Lady Staverly for the rest of the dowager's natural days, was enough to send any woman begging for sanctuary from the nearest convent.

As for Lord Nettlesome, besides the fact that he was just that—nettlesome—she didn't care to spend her life with a husband who looked her directly in her breasts. The least she wanted in a groom was a man she could look up to, literally, that was.

No, Elton's plan lacked one essential element: a willing bride. Besides the fact that neither Temple, Penham, nor Nettlestone had the necessary funds to obtain a special license, a hasty marriage was a moot issue.

Lost in her own musings, she now strained to hear what Temple was saying to Elton's suggestion, but they hit a rough patch of road, and from the clattering of the berline and the bouncing track, she couldn't hear a thing until the last of his words.

"—then I'll be well and done with this."

Well and done, how?

"Oh, botheration," she muttered, shivering from nothing that had to do with the temperature outside, rather the cold, uncertain fate awaiting her. She tugged the blanket more tightly around her, then looked down and realized she still wore nothing but her chemise.

The same chemise she'd donned with the foolish hope of seducing Temple.

Had it been just last night that he'd kissed her? Just a few hours since she'd heard him come stealing into her room, and she'd thought that finally, just finally, he'd come to his senses.

Oh, drat it all. She'd turned what had seemed such a brilliant plan back in London into a wretched muddle.

Still, she wasn't under the hatches yet. She had Temple's kiss to her credit. A passionate, heart-stopping moment that held more promise than she could have hoped for in years.

Now all she had to do was find a way to convince Temple that one kiss wasn't enough—for either of them.

And never would be.

Chapter 6

⌒⌒∞⌒⌒

They arrived in the bustling town of Nottingham late in the evening. Their progress had slowed considerably as they neared the town because the roads were clogged with farmers' wagons and carts. Apparently the town was hosting a large market the next morning and was filled with merchants and their customers.

This, Temple explained to Diana, was best under the circumstances. They could take rooms at some nondescript inn and leave at first light without drawing much notice.

Yet finding lodging turned out to be more difficult than they thought. The town was bursting with visitors, and all the inns were full.

Diana looked out the window and frowned as he came back from yet another lodging house that hadn't a spare bed to be let.

"Tell them who you are," Diana said, tired, dirty, and ready for a good meal and a well-drawn bath. "If that doesn't work, tell them who *I* am."

He shook his head. "I can't do that. I don't want anyone to know we've come this way."

Diana groaned. "Not that nonsense again about French agents, Temple? It wasn't that good of a story last night, and since I know for certain you are well and sober now, I'm starting to fear your hinges are coming loose." She glanced back at the comfortable looking inn with the enticing scent of roasting beef wafting across the yard. "Why don't we just go out to Harwith House? I went to school with Lady Harwith, and I am sure she and the earl would be more than willing to offer us an entire suite of rooms."

Temple folded his arms over his chest. "No. I don't want anyone to know we are here." He climbed in beside her and gave Elton the orders to continue to another establishment. "And my hinges are in perfect working order, thank you. You, on the other hand, would do well to believe me. You are in danger. Mortal danger."

She snorted. "From French agents?"

"Yes," he said.

If he wanted to continue this charade that he was indeed rescuing her from some terrible fate, so be it. Diana smiled indulgently at him.

His brow furrowed into a deep line as he crossed his arms over his chest. He hadn't shaved, and his coat was dusty from riding up with Elton. That this rumpled, disreputable rake had replaced that fussy popinjay she hated so wholeheartedly only made her grin that much more.

She couldn't imagine Temple looking more handsome than he did at this moment.

"I don't see that there is anything to smile about," he said, sticking his scuffed up boots out in front of him.

"You wouldn't, but if you are correct and I'm wanted by

agents of Napoleon, that means I must be infamous." She paused for a second, letting a wicked gleam glow in her mischievous gaze. "Do you think I'm a danger to my country?"

"You're a danger, all right," he muttered.

She laughed aloud. "If you feel you need to persist in this charade, be my guest. As I said before, all you had to do was ask and I'd . . ." The carriage hit a hole in the road, jolting her mouth shut before she once again confessed her true feelings.

. . . I'd follow you anywhere.

Temple didn't know what was worse, her blithe refusal to believe they were running for their lives, or her unflagging confidence that he was going to come to his senses and declare his heart.

Declare his heart, indeed! If anyone should know he didn't possess one, it was Diana. Yet she still persisted. Clung to her faith in him. Faith he'd hardly earned and, more importantly, didn't deserve.

She was a vexing mix of contradictions. Innocence and tenacity. Bold manners and soft glances.

Somehow during the course of the day, she'd managed to change into a green muslin gown and dress her hair in a simple braided coronet. At one of their stops, she'd picked a small nosegay of wild roses, which sat in her hands bound in a green ribbon she'd probably foraged from her bag. A hint of sun kissed her cheeks and nose, compliments of the afternoon she'd spent riding atop with Elton—a great lark she'd begged to be indulged in and Temple only too willingly allowed, if only to avoid listening to any more passages read aloud from the erudite Billingsworth.

Let Elton listen to the history of England. The last thing Temple needed was to be cooped up with Diana. Even reading from her boring book, she was a tempting minx.

A temptation he needed to avoid.

Oh, she might consider this all a great lark, but the world he lived in had no place for someone like Diana.

Someone who believed that love could conquer any hardship.

Didn't she know how that very perilous emotion was what caused a fair share of the troubles in the world?

No, to look at her now, sitting across from him looking like a perfect example of what was good and innocent in English womanhood, one might be tempted to believe in poetry and the joy of love.

Rather than consider that road to misery, he deliberately turned his thoughts to more pressing matters. Like what the French would want with her.

Perhaps she was right and his hinges were coming loose.

Cordell dead in a meadow at the hand of one of Bonaparte's top agents?

It made no sense.

And the other part of the night, something one of the men had asked Cordell, stuck out as odd.

Is she untouched? Does she remain a virgin?

He suspected Diana was still a virgin, but where had she learned to kiss like that? Her lips had left him breathless with their passionate, fiery blaze, the kind of kiss that marked a man's memory forever.

He glanced over at her. Who the hell else had she been kissing? He shifted in his seat, and when she glanced up at him, one brow arching like a question mark, he frowned again and wrenched his gaze out the window to the busy streets.

What the devil did he care if Diana was kissing other men? Her indiscretions were the least of his concerns. She could kiss half the *ton*, and a good measure of Napoleon's court for that matter, and he wouldn't care.

Oh, but he did.

Temple held back a desperate groan. Truly, this was all Colin's fault. Him and his theories about *tendres.*

Tendres indeed! He was merely a man assigned to do a job. Find the lady and return her to her father. Then he'd urge Lord Lamden to see his wayward daughter locked up in a convent with twelve-foot walls.

Safe from harm. Safe from causing any more damage to his already failing, fallible heart.

How was it that he'd faced countless enemies, stared death in the face, but no one had ever shaken his faith, had the power to upend him like Diana?

He knew the answer only too well. Because Diana was the only woman he'd ever met who touched his heart with just the merest glance of her fair blue eyes. She conquered his heart in a way that left him defenseless to common sense and good reason.

No, to fall prey to Diana would tumble the walls of his carefully constructed world.

What was it Elton had said?

. . . marry her off to Pins or Needles. You could wash your hands of her right smart.

And he had just the piece of paper that would see the job done in no time.

Pymm's special license.

Yes, that would be the perfect solution. Temple could marry Diana off to Penham or Nettlestone and then let that fool deal with her headstrong ways and deceptive wiles.

Yes, that solution buoyed his spirits immensely.

Yet as he turned to shoot a triumphant glance in her direction, he didn't see a simply dressed woman who needed to be packed off and gotten rid off. No, all he could see as he looked across the interior of the carriage was the soft glow of her skin, the pink of her lips, the swell of her breasts.

Memories of her kiss from the night before flooded his thoughts, sent his blood pounding southward.

No. No. No, he told himself. Don't give in to temptation. But he knew damned well she could steal his soul with her kisses. So that meant all he had to do was to avoid kissing her. That shouldn't be so hard.

Then he'd marry her off. Let that man be branded by her lips, revel in her passions, explore every inch of her lithesome, delectable form until . . .

Temple shuddered. *Demmit, that wouldn't do at all.*

This entire muddle was enough to drive a man to . . . to . . . He didn't want to think what he would do.

Should do. Wanted so much to do.

Closing his eyes, Temple feigned sleep. Blessed, peaceful sleep. Only there he knew he'd find her invading his dreams, his hopes of solitude. He let out an exasperated sigh.

"Are you well, Temple?" Diana asked.

"Fine, perfectly well, never been better," he grumbled, shying a glance in her direction.

The cheeky minx had the nerve to grin triumphantly at him. Well, that did it. So she thought she could get the better of him? Not so.

He'd plucked her affections from his heart once, he could do so again. Marrying her off to Penham or Nettlestone would certainly settle the matter, once and for all.

Yes, he'd even offer to give her away. If only to convince himself that she was truly gone from his life.

Elton turned the horses into the yard of a small inn already crowded with carts and people. Temple didn't hold out much hope of their finding a room, but in a few moments Elton returned with a bit of good news.

"They've got one room, but it's expensive," Elton told Temple. "Ten quid."

"For a room?" Temple whistled at the exorbitant amount. If not for the rush for lodgings, the chamber probably went for naught but a few shillings.

"I don't care if it's beneath a manure pile," Diana said, "I intend to take this boon." She started to push Temple aside in an attempt to get out, but he held her fast.

"I haven't the money for it," Temple told her.

"Yes, but I do," she shot back, holding up her reticule and giving it a good shake to prove her point.

The jangle even widened Elton's eyes, and if Temple knew his driver, the man probably knew the amount the purse held down to the last Brown.

As much as it went against his grain to take her offering, what choice did they have? The horses needed rest.

How the devil was he ever going to repay her? Perhaps he should find out how much gold Marden was offering for her.

He might well need every coin the Frenchman was willing to exchange just to keep her in lodgings. Then again, Temple thought with a smile, he'd send the entire bill to Pymm.

Let the old curmudgeon pay for this errand of mercy.

"Fine, you can pay tonight," he told her, "but just remember our story. I am a wool merchant and you are my sister. We are traveling from Norwich to visit our sick mother in Manchester. Be discreet and circumspect as much as possible and try not to draw undue attention to yourself."

Diana nodded like an obedient schoolgirl, then proceeded to elbow him aside in a scramble to get out of the carriage.

To his ever-growing chagrin, she immediately set to work ignoring everything he'd just said.

"You there," she called out to one of the boys lolling about the yard. Reaching into her reticule, she drew out a gold coin.

The glitter of such a princely sum attracted the boy to her side in a flash.

"Please see that my bag is taken to my room," she said to him. "And if there is a tub of hot water up there before the hour, that knavish-looking gentleman over there will give you another of these for your troubles."

Temple nearly choked. A guinea just for bringing up water? With that sort of largesse she'd attract the attention of every urchin and beggar within twenty miles. Worse yet, she wasn't tossing just her money around, but his as well.

And he had naught but a bag of nails and a few spare shillings.

"I'll have it done in half the time, milady," the boy said, a wide grin spilling across his freckled features.

She smiled over her shoulder at Temple and sailed into the inn with all the regal bearing her forebears were entitled to claim.

"Some merchant's sister," Elton huffed. "Next she'll be ordering up oranges and duck for supper, and expecting you to pay for all of it."

By the time he recovered his outraged wits, she'd disappeared inside. Temple went after her, but found she'd wreaked a swatch of havoc in her wake wider than Napoleon could have, backed by his entire army.

If Pymm thought the paperwork on Temple's little ventures in Paris the previous winter had been difficult to report, what he was about to do to Lady Diana Fordham would take a Covent Garden scribe ten years to compose a suitable fiction that wouldn't see them both dancing at Tyburn.

The previously indifferent innkeeper came bustling forward. "Lord Hood, my apologies for not coming out personally."

Temple looked over his shoulder to see if the man was

talking to someone else. But the innkeeper had his greedy gaze fixed only on him.

Lord Hood? When had they agreed he'd have a new name and title?

"Her ladyship requested that you be seated and have a drink down here while she takes a few moments to refresh herself." He held out a chair at a wide, empty table near the window. "By chance I have a bottle of St. Laurent in my cellar."

St. Laurent? How did the minx know that was his favorite wine?

Elton. He should never have let her ride up with him, though at the time it had seemed a good idea. She'd probably used those hours to wheedle and ply every secret Temple held dear out of his servant.

The innkeeper was still holding out the chair for him, into which he gratefully dropped. The man hurried away, only to return a few minutes later with a dusty bottle and a large glass. "Here you go, milord. A nice year, this. Hard to come by, iffin you know what I mean." The man leaned forward. "Could we call it a favor amongst gentlemen iffin we don't mention this particular vintage to the sheriff? He's right particular about Frog goods."

"Am I to suppose that would be the Sheriff of Nottingham?" Temple said with a bemused chuckle.

The innkeeper didn't look at all amused, rather he lowered his voice in an awed whisper. "Oh, aye. And he takes his job quite seriously, he does. Considers it his duty to the good name of Nottingham."

Temple suspected Diana would take great joy in knowing that they were under the jurisdiction of the Sheriff of Nottingham. Then it hit him. Lord Hood. She'd christened him quite deliberately, and probably from her never-ending wealth of information from the now infamous Billingsworth.

If he didn't know better, she was most likely upstairs or-
ganizing a tour of the notorious robber's haunts.

A few moments later, a tall, red-faced woman, her graying
hair tied back in a tight knot, came out of the kitchen carrying
a large plate and set it in front of Temple.

"There you are, milord. Chicken pie."

He stared down at the plate, the enticing aroma curling
around his nose and setting his mouth to watering. He couldn't
remember the last time he'd smelled anything so enticing.

He grabbed the fork and took a toothsome bite. The aroma
hadn't even begun to do the delicious dish justice. He took
another bite as quickly as he could.

The cook chuckled. "Her ladyship said you'd like that.
Said it was yer favorite."

"Aye, it is. I just didn't know she knew." Temple took another bite, reveling in the thick chunks of chicken and sweet
carrots.

The cook nodded, a sly grin on her face. "A wife always
knows those things."

Temple choked and stammered. "A wha-a-at?"

"A wife," she said, nodding to the stairs leading up to the
rooms. "She also saw to it that your man had a nice plate of
ham and cabbage sent out to him."

"She did all that?"

"Of course she did. She's a right good one, looking out after you and your manservant. You picked out a fine wife."

"My wife?" Temple ground out, setting down his fork.

"Yes, yer wife." The lady shook her head. "An April gentleman, are you? Still not used to hearing her called that, I
suppose. Me husband over there," she said, nodding at the
man behind the bar, "he still has a bit of a turn over the idea
of being married. And him being twenty-three years past the
parson." She chuckled and went back to her kitchen.

His wife. Oh, Diana had been busy all right. And he was going to put an end to it right now. She'd gone from slanted glances and come hither kisses to chicken pie.

He'd completely underestimated her resourcefulness.

Temple started to get up, but his stomach protested heartily, growling and complaining at leaving behind the flaky crust and a small river of hot, thick gravy. He stood for just a few seconds before settling back down and digging into his supper.

It wasn't as if Diana was going anywhere. And it was his favorite meal.

As he took another heavenly bite, he wondered what other little lies she'd been telling the staff. If he didn't put a stop to her immediately, by morning he'd be saddled with a fictitious brood of moderately well-behaved children, a manor house with a leaky roof, and a mother-in-law who vexed him entirely, all courtesy of one Lady Diana.

Not if he could help it. He'd put a stop to her shenanigans immediately. This wasn't a game.

But as he ate the best pot pie he'd had in ages, washed down with his favorite French wine, Temple found himself imagining the quaint manor house and the clutch of children Diana was most likely describing to the enthralled upstairs maids.

Before he knew what he was doing, he found himself once again caught by her spell. For there on the well-manicured lawn of Hood Hall, he saw himself in that fine picture, playing with the two boys and a fair-haired little girl with bright blue eyes and a penchant for mischief.

Even as he tried to shake himself from such foolish musings, he couldn't help wondering what names she'd given their children.

*   *   *

Temple went upstairs to find her right after dinner. He rapped on the door and steeled himself not to let any further fanciful musings steer him from his course.

"Come in," Diana called out sweetly as a new bride might.

Hardly the anxious groom, he opened the door cautiously. "Are you decent?"

"Always," she answered.

The door remained cracked only the barest of inches. "Diana, are you dressed?"

"Of course," she said. "Come in and see our room." She stood in the middle of the large, airy chamber. "Isn't this a splendid place. I can't believe we found it."

He glanced around at the elegantly appointed chamber— fit for two with its large bed, tasteful furnishings, and large fireplace—and did his best not to view it as she did, a romantic hideaway, but as an expenditure he could ill-afford.

"*We* are not staying in it." He glanced around again, his gaze sweeping only momentarily over the great, big, comfortable-looking bed. "You are. Alone."

"Alone? I hardly see how that will lend any credence to our story." She plopped down on the bed and patted the spot next to her.

"Your story, madame. Not mine." His felt his brow crease into a hard line. That wasn't the only thing getting hard at the sight of Diana on the splendid bed. "The reason I came up here is to discuss the matter of your elopement. Or should I say staged elopement?"

"Staged?" she said, acting the veriest of innocence. "I had every intention of marrying the viscount." She sniffed a little. "At least until his unfortunate demise." Sighing, she looked up at him. "That is, unless I can find someone else."

Temple ground his teeth. "Don't look at me, Lady Hood. I have no intention of being your next victim."

She flinched, and he knew as lightly as she might dispense with Cordell's fate, she carried the guilt of it. She blamed herself for the man's death.

"I need to know the details of your agreement with Cordell. How long have you been in league with the man? Was there anyone else who helped him secure the carriage or who he mentioned would aid your plans?"

Diana cocked her head and stared at him. "Why, Temple? Why does any of that matter to you, of all people?'

"Because the viscount was involved in some very shady business, and I mean to get to the bottom of it."

"Cordell played too deep. He probably cheated. You practically said as much last night." Her eyes narrowed, and she said, "What more do you want me to tell you? That he was part of some great French conspiracy?" She edged off the bed and walked over to where he stood. "Temple, tell me, what do you know of French intrigues? French fashions, yes, but Boney's plans? I daresay that hardly seems in *your* realm."

Temple shifted. She might know about chicken pies and wines, but she didn't know all his secrets. She couldn't.

"While we're discussing mysteries, do you mind if I ask where were you last winter?" She pressed her finger to her lips. "I don't recall seeing you for two, perhaps three months."

He'd come up here to confront her, to set her straight on who was in charge, but she was pulling the rug from beneath him and launching a swift counterattack that left him grappling for answers.

"My bills got a little tedious," he said, backing away. It was his favorite excuse for why he went missing for months at a time, and one everyone readily believed.

"Hmm," she mused. "Is that so?"

For the first time he saw someone doubt one of his lies and

knew that he was facing his most dangerous enemy. If anyone could unravel his house of deception, it was Diana.

What he needed to do was get this conversation back on track.

"Of course it is so. I often have to leave town quickly."

"So I've noticed."

"Lady Diana, this isn't about my travels, it's about yours," he said, wresting control of their discussion. "And until we know the lengths to which those men who chased us last night are willing to go, I believe discretion is the better part of valor."

"And you know this based upon your experiences of, shall we say, running from your bill collectors?"

Temple grasped onto her offering with both hands. "Exactly!"

She crossed her arms over her chest. "Then I'll defer to your superior cowardice and skill at prevarication and play along for now."

Temple bowed and left her, and as he closed the door to her room he realized she'd just called him a coward and a liar.

And she'd been right on both counts.

"Oh, bother," Diana muttered as she watched Temple flee. That hadn't gone well at all. Perhaps she shouldn't have told everyone they were married. But it was a fine sight better story than some dreary tale about a merchant and his spinster sister.

Why did she always have to be cast into the role of the pitiable spinster?

No longer. Never again, she vowed, even as she recalled his stony insistence that he would not stand in Cordell's shoes. Not that she blamed him. Her betrothal to the viscount certainly hadn't ended as she'd planned.

She went over to the door and considered seeking Temple out. But in truth, she knew him well enough to surmise that she'd only drive him higher into the hills, deeper into his own stony resolve.

His resolve she knew only too intimately. Like an old friend.

Ever since that day on Bond Street, when she'd discovered Temple's deception, she'd made it her mission to learn everything she could about him.

She'd taken to noting his comings and goings from Society. Enlisting Mrs. Foston's aid, the lady having always had a fond regard for the marquis, the two women had discreetly followed his travels from the gossipy sidelines of London's fashionable ballrooms and salons.

From her vantage point, Diana marveled at Temple's skill. She'd even gained an unlikely ally in her mission, someone who cared for Temple like a son and shared her fears that some harm might befall the marquis. As she learned the depth of Temple's commitment to his cause and missions, she fell in love with him all over again.

Then last year, he'd gone missing for over seven months and Diana nearly went mad with worry. She'd all but ordered her carriage to Whitehall and demanded an accounting of Temple's whereabouts, if only to discover if he still lived. Then to her delight and chagrin, he'd reappeared a fortnight later at a ball, the same gadfly Temple the *ton* loved.

Yet to her critical and well-trained eye, he looked thinner, strained and worn out from whatever dangerous task he'd undertaken. Oh, how she'd ached at the sight of him—and it was all she could do not to race across the crowded room and launch herself into his arms.

The reasons that had restrained her then seemed only too foolish now.

Ladies, Miss Emery would have admonished, never make a public display of their emotions. Propriety, especially when it concerns a gentleman, must always be observed. A lady is never forward in an effort to gain the attention of a man.

Bah! Diana thought. She'd spent too many years bound and frightened by what would happen if she crossed that ridiculous line. Bound as well by her own fears of what would happen if she did declare herself to Temple—that he would reject her once again.

Oh, the sting of his denial, one horrid night during her first Season, had been enough to keep her properly seated and waiting for him to make the first declaration all these years. Despite it, there had been times when she'd spotted him glancing in her direction, as if he were reconsidering his own course of action—a dark, fleeting hint of passion, of the love they'd shared so long ago.

Those fires still burned in his heart as they did in hers. And all she needed to do was to discover how to get them to blaze to life once again.

She flounced down on a chair, crossing her arms over her chest and kicking her feet out in front of her in a most unladylike manner.

Her slippers met something solid, and when she tried to kick it out of her way, it would not budge. Absently, she glanced down to see what was in her way.

Temple's valise.

The boy, in his enthusiasm, must have brought up all the bags in the carriage, not just hers.

She smiled and scrambled out of her chair to kneel before the bag.

Her fingers went to the buckle but stopped. Ladies do not

pry into concerns that are not their own, she could hear Miss Emery say.

Diana doubted Miss Emery had ever been kidnapped and taken to an inn by a man trying very hard not to seduce her.

Convinced that her sins weren't that grievous, she freed the latch holding the leather bag closed and opened up the sum of Temple's life.

At first there wasn't much of interest. A spare neck cloth, the small volume on Persian he'd been reading the day before.

Persian servant, indeed, she thought as she thumbed through the pages. *Temple, you can barely afford Elton, let alone some exotic servant.* She tossed aside Sir John's learned tome and dug deeper into the bag. A piece of thick vellum rustled beneath her inquiring fingers.

Hmmm, she mused. *This might prove interesting.* Unfolding the paper, she glanced at the first line emblazoned across the top and felt as if the very floor had dropped out from beneath her.

A Special License for Marriage . . .

Dear God, he had come to marry her. Quickly, she began to scan the lines below, but found her joy short lived. There under the description of bride was her full name and age, but the same couldn't be said of her groom.

That space was blank.

No groom . . . Why, that meant . . .

She gasped, Elton's words from earlier in the day tolling through her thoughts.

Marry her off to Pins or Needles . . .

Elton hadn't spoken out of turn. With this paper, Temple could marry her off to Boney, with the blessing and approval of the archbishop himself.

How could he? Diana swiped back the tears threatening to

spill down her cheeks. He hadn't come after her to save her from herself. He'd come after her to see the job done. But not the one she'd thought.

Oh, this was terrible.

Drat you, Temple, she thought, glancing up at the candle and at the paper in her hand. *I'll not let you do this to me. To us.* She'd burn this wretched piece of paper and thwart his idiotic plans.

Yet even as she went to touch the corner to the flame, something stopped her. *He'll not do it. He'll not marry you to Penham or Nettlesome or any other man, for that matter.*

He couldn't. He wouldn't.

She plucked it back from the candle even as the corner started to pucker and darken.

She had to believe that the man she'd known all those years ago, the man she'd loved since she was barely out of the schoolroom, would never let her marry another man.

But he had before. *He would have let you marry Lord Danvers. He would have let you marry a hundred others.*

No. There was a reason for Temple's indifference. An explanation for why he'd changed so utterly and completely, beyond the ones that she already knew.

As she began to pull her hand out of the bag, her fingers brushed against something else. Another book.

The careworn edges and soft leather spoke of a possession most beloved.

She caught hold of it and pulled it out.

The plain, thin volume was not unlike what many people used as a journal or record book.

A journal? At this Diana grinned. Temple's diary. Now that should prove interesting.

She pushed aside his valise and scrambled over to the fireplace, settling on the rug before the hearth.

She looked down at the volume in her hands and wondered what clues it might hold.

An account of his mistresses? Hardly, Elton said he didn't have the time or the money.

A record of expenses? She shook her head. She had a feeling Temple didn't keep track of his debts, leaving that vexing job to his grandfather's beleaguered secretary.

She closed her eyes and said a small prayer that this book would help her discover the truth in Temple's heart. With that said, she opened to a random page.

When she peeked down at the secrets it held, she was stunned at what she read.

> *In the light of the moon,*
> *I beheld a goddess.*
> *She captured me in her glory,*
> *Enraptured me by her grace.*

Poetry?

She leafed through the yellow, well-thumbed pages. Lyrical words, words of longing, lines that brought a tear to her eye with their simple, touching beauty. That he loved someone, with such deeply held passion, didn't surprise her. But now she was left with only one question.

Is it me?

It was well past midnight when Temple found himself standing before Diana's door, wondering at his own sanity.

Desperate to find a peaceful and comfortable place to sleep, he'd come to this. With this being the only room available for him in the entire inn.

Since she'd informed everyone that they were husband and wife on a much belated wedding trip, he could hardly insist on separate chambers. It would appear odd. Put a chink in their already tenuous story. Not that there were any rooms as it was.

So he'd intended to sleep in the carriage, slipping outside when no one was looking. Not a comfortable solution, but the most available.

Only by the time he'd gotten to the carriage, he discovered that his ever-resourceful Elton had already nabbed the space. And was snoring happily away inside the comforts of the Setchfield berline.

Now, Elton didn't just snore, he created an unearthly din. Temple often wondered if that had been the man's Achilles heel, the deafening peal having delivered the once crafty gentleman into the hands of the law. Not that it mattered now. There wouldn't be any possibility of finding sleep within fifty yards of the carriage.

Even the stable boys were fleeing, carrying their blankets and shooting sleepy darts at the dreadful racket coming from the carriage. Yet before he thought to ask where they were going, the boys were gone, sliding into the night like a pack of displaced alley cats, leaving Temple no choice but to return to the inn.

Besides, despite the calendar's assurance that it was June, the night was cold. Not really a night to decide if he had a gypsy's fortitude.

Certainly he could manage a few hours in the same room as Diana without being driven to some rash mistake? He was a sensible man, used to deception and subterfuge.

Diana was just another adversary to outwit.

Staring at the oaken panel that separated him from his enemy, he decided that his foray last winter into Napoleon's court had been about as dangerous as one of his aunt's card parties compared to the hazards Diana posed to his traitorous heart.

Taking a deep breath, he slid the key into the lock and opened the door, pausing a few breathless seconds to listen. Inside the chamber there wasn't a sound.

Satisfied that she was well and good in the land of Queen Mab, he took the direct route across the room, making for the fireplace, where a thick, cozy rug lay. As he went, he shrugged his coat onto a chair and settled his boots, which he'd taken the precaution of removing out in the hall, down beside it. His cravat and waistcoat followed.

Then, ignoring the soft, rounded shape curled up in the middle of the enormous bed, he made his way as silently as a housebreaker to the rug before the hearth.

It wasn't his feather bed in his London town house, it wasn't even the leather-covered, well-sprung seat of the berline, but it was better than the common room, where he would be putting himself on display for all types of gossipy speculation.

Settling down on the rug, he breathed a sigh of relief, then closed his eyes and awaited blessed sleep.

His reprieve didn't last very long.

There was a rustle of sheets, and then the swoosh of the bed's silken counterpane being turned back.

"Temple," Diana said in a whisper-quiet voice full of invitation and mischief. "Don't you think you'd be more comfortable up here?"

Chapter 7

❦❦❦

"Excuse me?" Temple sputtered.

"You heard what I said," Diana whispered in that silken, enticing voice of hers. "It would be far more comfortable to sleep in this bed than on that floor." The sheets rustled once again, and he could see the flash of white muslin as she turned the coverings further back in invitation.

"I beg to differ," he said, recalling how much her kiss had put him into knots. The idea of sharing a bed with her . . . now, that was enough to put him into an early grave. "Besides, it would be completely beyond the pale for me to take your bed and ask you to sleep on the floor. I'll be fine right here."

He made a great show of stretching and settling onto his makeshift bed.

"Oh, you misunderstood me. I've no intention of sleeping on the floor."

Temple hadn't misunderstood her. He was merely doing his best to ignore the alluring notes in her voice, the soft swish of sheets. Even now her rose-scented perfume, which

he hadn't noticed when he entered the room, started to en-
snare his senses. "Diana, go to sleep. I've slept in far worse
places than this."

He rolled over on the narrow rug, his feet clanging into
the fire tongs, sending them tumbling atop him. Temple
cursed and kicked the clattering piece aside.

Ignoring the muffled giggles rising from the bed, he
stretched again and tried to find some measure of comfort.

His silence only seemed to spur her efforts. "Oh, don't be so
foolish," she said. "It's a cold night." She paused for a second
and then sweetened her offer. "I can't believe you prefer an oak
floor over a feather mattress and a thick, warm coverlet."

He didn't. But the floor didn't conjure all kinds of notions
that would end up having him facing the parson.

Notions that had nothing to do with feather mattresses and
coverlets, but rather the passionate vixen they held between
them.

"Diana, you know as well as I that sharing a bed is the
worst sort of idea. It's just not done. Why, you'd be ruined."

A rather unladylike snort came from the bed. "Any worse
than I am now? I hardly think so. Now stop being such a
ninny and get in."

"No."

"Oh Temple, you can be so ridiculous. You made your intentions, or rather lack of intentions, quite clear last night. I'm
not inviting you into this bed with some grand plan of seducing you. You don't find me to your liking, and I've accepted
that. Now just get in. It's not like I haven't been in a bed with
you before, and I survived that experience unscathed."

She had to bring that up, he thought. "I was hardly in any
condition to seduce you then."

The sheets rustled anew as she rolled over. "Oh, you were
capable."

Temple didn't need the candle lit to know the minx was grinning. "Diana! What the devil do you know about a man's capability?"

"Only what you taught me," she said. "I suppose I should thank you. Miss Emery never included anything of that nature in her class on marriage and wifely obligations. But then again perhaps it is all different when a man and woman are married. But I don't think I'd prefer it differently, I rather liked the idea of a man being—"

"Enough!" Temple sat bolt upright. If he'd had the coverlet she was so generously offering to share, he'd have stuffed both ends into his ears. "Diana, this conversation has gone too far. Can we just get some sleep?"

"If we must." She rolled again, the whisper of the sheets as inviting as her soft sighs as she tossed this way, then that. "This is such a large bed. I hardly think there is any impropriety in sharing it. Why, if you stay on your side, and I stay on mine, you'll never know I'm here."

Oh, he'd know. Only too well.

And that was the problem.

"Diana, if you haven't a care for your own reputation, what about mine? I don't think your fiancés would be overjoyed to discover their future bride sleeping alongside another man." Temple rolled over so he faced the bed.

One enormous, comfortable, made-for-hours-of-lovemaking bed.

He shook his head and continued, reminding himself and her of the consequences of what she sought. "Would you really want me to face Penham over pistols?"

"No. Nor Nettlesome," she said.

"Nettlestone," he corrected.

"Yes, right." She paused. "I imagine the baron *would* kill you."

Temple sat up despite his better judgment. "I think not—" Even as he began his defense, he realized the trap he was falling into. One of her devising. "That's not the point," he told her instead.

She sighed, as if mourning his lost life. "Well, if not Nettlestone, I fear Lord Harry would dispatch you quite easily."

"Madame, I do have some prowess with a pistol."

"How is that, Temple? When did you gain this reputation as a crack shot?"

He ground his teeth together. "Just suffice it to say that once I was done dispatching them—"

"That is, if you lived," she interjected.

"Yes, if I lived," he said, annoyed that she held even the slightest doubt he wouldn't. "Then there would be your father. I'm sure he would demand satisfaction as well."

She rose up in the bed, hugging her arms around her knees. "Oh, my father wouldn't have any qualms about you sharing my bed. He thinks you are a complete imbecile, incapable of—"

"Demmit, that's quite enough!" he said, scrambling up from the floor. "A man can only take so many slings against his honor before he . . . he . . ."

"Gives in?" she suggested. She threw back the sheets again and moved over, patting the space she'd just vacated. "There's plenty of room, and it's far more comfortable than that rug."

If Temple had been a man of principle, he would have refused her right there and then. But he wasn't. Principles left one stranded beside a snoring servant or attempting to sleep on a hard floor.

Besides, it was a glorious-looking bed.

He took a step closer and felt his resolve weakening. He'd come this far in life resisting the temptation of Lady Diana Fordham, he told himself, he could do so for one more night.

He paused before the bed. The crisp sheets smelled slightly of lavender and a good soap. "If I decide to take you up on your offer," he said, "it is on the condition that you roll over and go to sleep."

"Oh yes, certainly," she said, opening her mouth in a wide yawn and patting her lips with the palm of her hand. "I fear all that fresh air today has made me terribly weary."

She could feign sleepiness all she wanted, but Temple saw quite clearly the saucy glint in her eyes.

Go ahead and celebrate, you little minx, but I am not falling prey to your wiles. Not when the East beckons. Not when all I've worked for is so close at hand.

Freedom from his charade with the *ton*. Freedom from his grandfather's machinations. A chance to be someone other than Setchfield's wastrel heir.

A chance to escape that nagging feeling that dogged his lonely heart, taunting him that there was more to life than the daily challenge of living one tremendous lie, living a double life.

Just as the sparkle of her blue eyes teased him into believing that passion and love could conquer all his long-held misgivings and fears.

Diana was already well settled on her side. She glanced up at him. "Change of heart, or am I sleeping alone?"

"No," he said, climbing into the bed. "But let me remind you, I'm only doing this so you will let me get some sleep. And nothing else."

"Of course, Temple. As you wish."

Wishes, Temple wanted to tell her, *had nothing to do with it*.

Diana turned her head to hide the smile that was surely turning her lips.

Oh, Temple could be the most stubborn, exasperating man she'd ever met. Still, she was relieved he'd finally given in. She'd been starting to run out of arguments.

She snuggled into the bed and marveled at the strangeness of having another person beside her.

Oh yes, she had shared a bed with Temple once before, but that hardly counted. He was conscious and able-bodied this time.

"Quite nice, I say. Don't you agree?" she asked, deliberately forgetting her promise to cease her chatter.

There was a long moment of silence from the other side of the bed. Then, "Do I dare ask, what is 'quite nice'?"

She patted the space between them. "This. Sharing a bed. I've always wondered what it would be like to sleep with someone. A man, I mean." She snuggled closer to the middle. Closer to Temple.

"I wouldn't know. I don't make a habit of sleeping with men."

To her chagrin, he moved farther away. It was a huge bed, and at this rate, she could well find herself spending the entire night chasing him across the sheets.

"Oh, very funny. But you've had mistresses. I imagine you've spent the night with them, haven't you?"

Temple sat upright. "Diana! How I spend my nights is hardly a fit subject to be discussing with a lady."

Diana rolled over. "Well, I think it is patently unfair that a man can sleep with whom he pleases before he is wed, while we women are forced to sleep alone."

"Perhaps men and woman don't sleep together so men can get some sleep." He flopped back down and turned away from her.

"I hardly think so. Men always seem to want to sleep with women." *And women with men.*

Diana stared at his broad shoulders, her fingers itching to reach out and run feverishly beneath his white linen shirt, to explore the muscled contours so close at hand.

Temple let out a loud sigh. "Well, you seem to be the expert on the subject. Is that your experience with Penham and Nettlesome, that they want only to share your bed?"

She laughed. "Heavens no. They just want my money."

Temple rolled over. "Let me assure you, not every man who calls on you is merely interested in your money."

There was a smoky tenor to his words that sent a shiver racing down her spine. It reminded her of the way he kissed, so passionately, so confidently, so full of promise. She looked up from his lips to his eyes, his so very dark eyes, the ones that held so many mysteries, and realized they were giving away one right now.

"You aren't, are you?"

"Aren't what?"

"Interested in my money." No, when Temple looked at her like that, she knew her fortune wasn't what he was contemplating.

"Diana, if I were interested in your money, you wouldn't have any."

She shook her head. "I hardly think that even you, spendthrift that you are, could squander *my* dowry."

"If I were to marry you, there wouldn't be any dowry. Your father would disinherit you."

She sighed. "I suppose you're right. He'd be rather vexed at the idea of having you for a son-in-law."

" 'Vexed' wouldn't be the word I'd use."

"Still, I doubt he'd cut me off without anything."

"He would." Temple sounded rather confident on the matter, as if he had considered the subject on more than one occasion.

"That would be rather inconvenient," she said. "We wouldn't have any money."

Temple nodded. "Not a penny between us."

Diana hardly liked the idea of that. She shared Temple's love of fine things, and the idea of living in the streets or begging didn't suit her at all. Then the obvious occurred to her. "We wouldn't be without assistance. Your grandfather would be thrilled. He's always wanted to see you wed, and I believe he has a certain fondness for me, even if I did refuse Colin twice."

"His grace would be in alt over the notion. And that would be the problem."

Diana sat up on one elbow. "Are you telling me, Temple, that the reason you won't have me is because your grandfather would be well pleased?"

"His feelings have nothing to do with my decisions. Besides, I've gone this long without his money. I intend to continue doing so."

Diana considered arguing the point, but his tight, cold tone suggested that further inquiry would only send him fleeing back to the sanctity of the rug.

Or worse, the stables, where she imagined he'd come from to begin with.

She rolled on her back, her arms crossed over her chest. "Then I suppose if we were to wed," she said, "we wouldn't be able to afford a room as fine as this."

"That depends on how much gold you have stashed away in that valise of yours."

Diana laughed. "Now you sound like Cordell." Once she said the viscount's name, her humor faded into an awkward silence.

"Temple," she finally whispered. "How did he die?"

Though it wasn't a subject fit for a lady's ears, she knew Temple would tell her.

"He was shot." Temple shifted and rolled toward her. "Straight through the heart. He barely had time to know what hit him, so I doubt he suffered overly much."

To her shame, she hadn't even considered such a sympathetic line of thought. She'd chosen Cordell because of his ruinous reputation. He was the worst sort of man, and his end, tragic though it might be, had been, in many ways, inevitable.

"Do you think he murdered that girl?" She turned her head and gazed in his direction. "The one from the stews?"

Temple's brow arched. "What do you know about that?"

She shrugged. "That he beat a girl to death, then disavowed the entire tragedy."

He shuddered, a rising tide of anger washing over his features.

"She was a young girl, wasn't she?"

Temple glanced away at her question, his silence all the answer she needed.

Though she didn't consider herself naïve, Diana still had a hard time believing that men could be so evil, or that they could intentionally harm one so young and unprotected.

"You shouldn't have—" he started to say, his mouth closing in a firm, hard line, as if the words caught in his throat.

She knew exactly what he was thinking.

If she knew Cordell's nature, whatever had possessed her to willingly put herself in his company?

Of course, he was right. And she deserved whatever fury he was about to unleash at her. Cringing, she waited for the explosion.

It didn't come.

"Diana," he said, reaching out to cup her face. "What would have become of you if I hadn't found you?"

The warmth of his fingers curled from her cheek to her heart. "It matters not," she told him. "Because you did."

She would have run off with that monstrous Corsican himself if she believed it would have wrought this . . . this miracle.

She snuggled toward his side of the bed. "I'm safe now."

He groaned, the earthy kind that spoke of barely restrained need trying to claw its way to freedom. "Hardly safe," he said, his fingers sliding behind her neck and into her hair.

She inched closer, and still he did not release her, his gaze holding her in its smoky grasp. "I've never felt more secure in my life."

It was the truth. Where once his kisses left her trembling with unknown fears, now they only tempted her into that unknown abyss of passion and release.

His fingers slid down her neck, over her shoulders, leaving irresistible tendrils of desire in their wake.

Diana shivered. "Temple—"

"Sssh," he told her. "Sometimes you talk too much." He silenced her with a heady, hungry kiss.

Diana's mouth opened under his bidding without a moment's hesitation. His tongue challenged hers, drawing her into a sweet duel as they danced and tangled.

Aching desire awakened and blossomed within her, stretching and stirring in places so long asleep. Diana wanted to cry out in elation, but instead let her joy run through her fingers as they splayed over his chest, ran wild over his shoulders.

The muscled strength beneath her fevered touch left her breathless, while his lips bedeviled her, whispering kisses over her face, the nape of her neck, her ear, teasing her into believing anything was possible.

That a man could feel so dangerous, so hard and unforgiving to touch, yet devour her with such delicious sensations, amazed her. Left her craving so much more.

"Diana," he breathed into her ear. "My goddess."

Her entire body stilled. Had she heard him true? Goddess? *His goddess*. Once again.

His kiss deepened with a savage hunger, and she responded in kind. She hadn't waited all these years to bow to some ridiculous notion of maidenly fears.

When his fingers curled around one of her breasts, she let out a deep, throaty sigh of pleasure. It was a tantalizing feeling, but only to be overrun moments later when his thumb began to rub over her nipple until it tightened into an aching, pebbled tip. A frenzied intoxication overtook her, leaving her gasping for air, her wits fleeing in the face of a torrent of desire that sprang to life under his masterful touch.

"Oh, oh, Temple," she gasped, as his lips replaced his fingers and he began to suckle her. Instinctively, she arched toward him, her body not satisfied with just the touch of his hand, the heat of his mouth.

She wanted to feel him. All of him. She closed the distance between them, pressing herself up against him.

And the moment their bodies collided, in the instant that her hips met his, her legs tangled with his strong thighs, as her arms twined around his neck, a blazing heat ignited between them.

A recognition, an awareness of how well they matched and kindled.

Wrenching his mouth from hers, Temple stared into her eyes as if he was seeing her for the first time. Then he caught her in his grasp, and in one breathless motion, rolled her on her back, covering and pinning her to the mattress with his body.

Diana gasped at his sudden claiming, but the sound was cut off when his mouth swooped back over hers and he continued to devour her as if he'd never find his fill.

* * *

Temple considered himself a man of careful reason. But with Diana in his arms, his yearning for her swept aside any resolve his mind claimed.

He shouldn't have kissed her the night before. It had only whetted his appetite. And now he reveled in her kiss, the feel of her silken skin, the taste of her lips, like a man starving.

This wasn't the tempestuous, curious girl he'd once loved, but a woman grown, with needs that met his with an insistence, with a power, that left him unable to resist her.

As he covered her with his body, there was now only her thin chemise and his breeches between them.

His manhood throbbed for freedom, ached to be buried in the sweet, tight channel between her thighs.

Her hips rose to meet his, brushing their invitation in a swaying dance, as if she knew the struggle he was waging.

He shouldn't be doing this. He'd been sent on an honorable mission, and this . . . this insanity wasn't going to make his job any easier.

She was tugging at his shirt, pushing the linen aside. Her chemise had ridden up to her thighs, letting her bare legs rub against his breeches.

His breeches. Her chemise.

They were both an insurmountable wall and a flimsy prison.

For if he tore down the wall, he knew for certain he'd encase them both in a prison from which there would be no escape. Diana would hate him for what he would have to do, and he didn't know if he had the strength of will to do it—to set her aside as he had years ago, and keep her safely out of his life.

Her hips once again pressed against him, and he felt his resolve crumbling.

Like her kiss, his need for her tried to convince his reason that just once, just this one night would be enough to sate his desire. To forever end his longing for her.

But like her kiss, Temple knew in his heart that once would never be enough. Once tasted, Diana would forever be the only woman he would desire.

And so he did the only thing he knew how to do.

He wrenched his lips from hers and scrambled out of the bed.

"Temple?" she said, her throaty voice anxious with need, her hand reaching out to catch hold of him again.

Oh, he knew what she was feeling, only too well, for the cold of the room hit him like a slap in the face.

"No, I can't do this."

"I beg to differ," she said.

"No, I won't do this," he said, backing away from her. "It isn't right. It isn't honorable."

She groaned and edged toward him. "Temple, would you just forget your wretched honor for one demmed night?"

He shook his head and turned from her before the tears in her eyes washed away the tenuous thread of resolve to which he clung.

Diana awoke early the next morning, just as the sun started to find its way through the curtains. She stretched and rolled over and realized there was someone else in her room.

Someone in her room?

She nearly flew out from beneath the sheets in a state of shock. Then she remembered.

Temple. She'd spent the night with him.

Well, almost.

And what a glorious night it might have been, if not for his insufferable honor. Despite that, it had been like a dream come true to have him kiss her again. To have him claim her as if she were his goddess.

Now if she could just get him to . . .

Diana sighed. Obviously she still had her work cut out for her. Woe be it to her plans if Penham or Nettlestone were to catch up with them. Temple might just make good on Elton's suggestion and give her to one of them to marry.

She clung to the hope that she'd found in his valise. That some battered and worn book of verse could hold the key to her future seemed so unlikely, and yet . . .

> *Stolen moments, caught in her kiss,*
> *I devour, I perish, but on thoughts of her.*

The lyrical words floated into her thoughts, like the dust motes swirling in the morning rays of light. She'd read his book of verse from cover to cover and had never before felt so moved by mere words.

That Temple held such rare, raw emotions gave her hope that she could rediscover the man she loved. He was there, his kiss promised her that much.

So no, she told herself. He wouldn't do it. He would never let her go. She had to believe that. Whatever held his heart in check, whatever had changed his mind all those years ago, she knew she had but this one last chance to wrench him free from his self-imposed prison.

Better to break her own heart trying to find his than to continue to watch him from the lonely walls where spinsters sat at Almack's or through opera glasses from the dark corner of her father's box.

Yet whatever the key to his heart was, she wasn't going to

find it lolling about in bed. Though she considered waking him up, she recalled Elton's warning about the marquis' morning demeanor.

A regular baited bear, he is, miss. Pay him no mind. He'll be right as rain once he gets a bit of that awful coffee he likes.

Diana hardly needed to put Temple in a foul mood first thing. He might marry her off to one of the stable lads and be done with her. Especially given the pained expression he'd gone to bed with and the bruises he'd wake up with after spending a stubborn night on a hard floor.

Yes, perhaps it was better just to let him sleep.

She slipped from her bed, her toes curling in displeasure as they hit the cold floor.

Diana frowned and hurried over to where she'd left her clothes. She pulled on her bodice and then her skirt, sighing at the state of them, and wondering if perhaps she could get them spotted and brushed before she had to don them again.

Glancing at the mirror, she shuddered.

Her hair stuck out in several different directions, and her eyes were puffy. Mrs. Foston would have apoplexy if could see her charge in such a state. Grabbing up her brush, Diana made the best of a bad situation and wondered how anyone ever survived without the assistance of a maid.

Would that be her future with Temple? Penniless, and having to make do for herself? She might even have to learn how to cook.

Dear Lord, that would be a wretched kettle.

She sighed, then brightened. Mayhap Elton knew how to brew a decent pot of tea.

Temple hadn't gone this long in his grandfather's poor graces without learning how to make do, and she would too, if it came to that.

An impoverished future with Temple was a fine sight better than all the servants in the world. Or worse yet, than spending her remaining days being called Lady Nettlesome.

No, she'd take to begging for alms before she'd let that happen.

She shivered again, and considered that perhaps Temple wasn't the only one who required his morning ritual to arise fresh and ready for the day.

A spot of tea was just what she needed.

Sneaking out the door, she made her way down the hall. Below, the kitchen staff could be heard hurrying about their duties. She passed by a window, and outside the lads from the stable and the postboys were dashing about, getting ready for another day's hard labor.

She paused at the head of the stairs, for below her the common room was already bursting with customers breaking their fast and discussing business matters with their neighbors.

Diana didn't quite know what she was supposed to do. She'd never been alone in an inn before. She'd always traveled in the company of her father and Mrs. Foston, and either of them handled these matters, or there was the usual legion of maids or other help who scurried back and forth to do her bidding.

No one even seemed to notice her, a rather disconcerting feeling, since she wasn't too sure what she should do next.

"Ooof," she stammered as someone barreled into her from behind.

"Oh aye, sorry, milady. I dinna see you," a maid said as she peeked around the mountain of sheets piled in her arms. "Are you going down for breakfast then?"

"I suppose so," Diana said.

"Well, settle down at that empty table over there and the master will see to you right quick. Once he gets done talking with the sheriff, that is."

"The sheriff?" Diana asked.

"Aye," the girl said. "Came around a little bit ago, looking for a deadly pair." She nodded below, where the innkeeper stood talking to a tall, dark-haired man. The maid leaned closer. "Murderers," she confided. "Murdered a gentleman in Geddington, night afore last. Heard the sheriff tell the master that the dead man was a real fancy toff. A viscount."

A viscount. In Geddington. Murdered.

The maid continued her gossipy tale. "They say it was another gentleman who did the task. The witnesses said the pair argued over a lady and this here gentleman shot the poor viscount dead away."

Witnesses? They'd seen Temple? Seen him . . . It was too terrible to consider. Oh, what had she done? Provoked him to commit murder?

Her legs began to wobble, leaving her feeling that the floor beneath her feet was going to give way. "Did you say *murder*?"

The wide-eyed maid nodded. "Aye. Fighting over a woman. Can you imagine? A man wanting you so much, he'd kill another for you?" The girl shivered. "Makes me blood run cold. I wouldn't want to be sleepin' next to a man who done murder, would you?"

"No, indeed," Diana managed to stammer. Oh dear! What had Temple done? When he'd said that Cordell had been killed by French agents, while it was a flimsy story at best, she'd never supposed that he'd killed the viscount!

No, it couldn't be. Temple would never commit murder. There had to be some mistake.

"Miss, are you well?" the maid asked. "If you don't mind me saying, you look right ill."

Diana shook her head. "No, I'm fine. Thank you."

The sheriff continued to hold the innkeeper's rapt attention as he started describing their party, first by holding his hands up to about her height, then putting one hand over his eye—which could only mean Elton.

And from the dismay on the innkeeper's face, he was coming to the same conclusion as well. Though to his credit, he didn't give away his guests. Diana guessed the man was trying to figure out how he was going to get paid for her extravagances if he turned his lucrative customers into the sheriff's custody.

"Is there something I can do for you, milady?" the maid asked.

Diana shook her head, then looked at the girl as if she were peering through a fog. "I'm sorry, what were you saying?"

"Wait, aren't you that newlywed pair?" The girl smiled broadly as she broke once again into Diana's shocked reverie. "Me sister had the same thing happen. She was sick right from the start. From the looks of yer color, I'd say you'll have a nice little bundle by Easter next."

"Whatever do you mean?" Diana asked, her attention still riveted on the innkeeper and the sheriff. From the wide-eyed look on their host's face, it appeared his fears were about to outweigh his greed.

"A babe, miss," the maid said. She shifted her armload again and winked. "That husband of yers has that randy look to him. Got you with child before the parson said his blessing, didn't he? Well, I won't tell no one, but you'd be best to go back to yer room and lie down a spell till yer color comes around. If I didn't know you were having a baby, I'd swear you'd just seen a ghost."

* * *

The door to the room flew open, rattling it nearly off the hinges.

Temple scrambled upright from the slab of hard floor that had been his bed. He fumbled for the pistol he usually kept under his pillow, but found only the thin blanket Diana had tossed at his head before she rolled over in a huff and buried herself deep in her goose-down haven.

A whirl of muslin dashed across his sleep-crusted gaze.

"Good morning," he muttered, as she began grabbing up her belongings and stuffing them willy-nilly into her valise.

"Hardly that," she spat out. She reached up on the chair where he'd left his waistcoat and cravat. She threw them at him. "Get dressed. You've been discovered. That is, we've been discovered." She paused for only a moment before she darted back to him and snatched his clothing out of his hands and stuffed both pieces into his traveling case. "No time for those. You'll have to make do as you are."

Crossing the room, he caught her by the shoulders. "Diana, be still. Whatever are you going on about?"

"He's downstairs. I mean, they're downstairs. We haven't a minute to spare." She shook free and headed to the window, throwing open the drapes, then shoving open the sash. She threw her leg over the edge, but a glance downward stopped her. "Oh, the devil take us. We're too high up. How will we ever escape now?"

Temple felt as if he were watching a Haymarket comedy. He didn't know whether to applaud or cringe at her well-played bout of madness. "Diana, come off that window." He took her by the arm and led her away from the ledge and into the solid safety of the middle of the room.

In her state there was no telling what she might do.

"Now who has come? Is it Pins and Needles who've got you in this state?" he asked.

"No! No! Neither of them." She paced a couple of steps, then whirled around. "Oh, how could you, Temple?" she asked, shaking a finger at him. "You've gone and ruined everything. Everything, I tell you. Whatever would possess you to do such a *thing*?"

"What is this tragedy you think I've supposedly committed?" he asked.

She gazed upward as if she were the sane one seeking patience. "Murder, my lord. What were you thinking when you killed Cordell?"

Chapter 8

❝**K**illed Cordell?" Temple shook his head. "I did no such thing. Where did you hear such nonsense?"

"The sheriff. He's down below with a writ for your arrest."

Temple shook his head. "The Sheriff of Nottingham is downstairs looking for me?" There was no way on earth he'd heard her correctly.

She nodded emphatically.

He swore under his breath. He could hear Pymm now *tsk*-ing and muttering over his report.

Lady Diana was allowed to slip from my grasp when the Sheriff of Nottingham arrested me for the murder of Viscount Cordell.

"Diana, this is all a mistake. I didn't kill Cordell."

"They think you did. Why would they think that, if it weren't true?" Diana's eyes began to well up.

The sight of those starry tears lighting her blue eyes tore at his common sense. Against his better judgment, he gathered her into his arms. "Believe me, I didn't kill Cordell."

Though I would have liked to, he mused.

"So why does the sheriff think you did? According to the maid, he's got a writ for your arrest."

"Listen to me, Diana. I did not kill the man. The French agents who followed us the other night killed him."

Diana pushed out of his grasp and took two steps back from him. "Temple! Not this ridiculous nonsense about French agents again."

"But it's the truth. I followed Cordell out into a meadow and saw him meet with three men. When their business was done, the leader shot Cordell and retrieved the gold they'd paid him."

Diana threw up her hands. "This is the best you can do? Oh, Temple, you need to work on your fictions. First that rubbish about you being a merchant and me your sister, now again with this ludicrous tale of French agents in Geddington. You'll never save your neck from the rope if that is the best defense you can offer."

"Diana, it's the truth," he told her.

She put her hands on either side of her head and groaned. "Oh, botheration, you are around the bend." Then her eyes lit up. "That's it! You could claim it happened in a moment of jealous insanity. I'll even testify for you, tell the judges you're utterly mad."

"Diana—" Temple's protest was cut off by a pounding at the door.

"Open up, in the name of the Sheriff of Nottingham."

"Dear Lord, they've found us!" She darted again for the window, but he caught her by the back of her skirt and held her fast.

The sheriff, in his eagerness to arrest a dangerous felon, didn't wait for a reply, instead laid his shoulder to the door and broke it open.

Diana let out a short squawk of dismay.

"Lord Templeton?" the sheriff asked.

"Don't answer him," she said, stepping in front of Temple, as if she could shield him with her lithe form.

He pushed her back behind him. "Yes, sir. I am the Marquis of Templeton. How may I be of service?"

The man appeared taken aback. Almost, one might say, disappointed at such a forthright answer.

Diana supposed the local tyrant was hoping for a pleading denial, followed by a desperate fight. She glanced around the room seeking another route of escape, a weapon of some kind.

Holding up his hand, the sheriff revealed a piece of paper. "My lord, I have a writ for your arrest, signed by the magistrate of Geddington."

From the doorway, the innkeeper stood watching the proceedings in wide-eyed horror.

"And what crime did I supposedly commit?" Temple asked.

"Don't play coy with me, my lord. You know 'twas murder. There were witnesses."

Now it was Temple's turn to be surprised. *Witnesses?* How could there be witnesses when there had been no one else about but . . .

Then he saw with only too much clarity the brilliance of it. Marden had returned to Geddington and presented the magistrate with a more convenient version of the murder.

What better way to flush out one's quarry than to use the law? With Temple arrested for the crime, and out of his way, Marden would have a clear path to Lady Diana.

Damn the man's cunning.

"Sir, I fear there is more to this than meets the eye. I believe—" he began.

"Are you Templeton?" the man said, interrupting.

"Well, yes, but—"

"And were you in Geddington night before last?"

"Yes, but—"

"Then there is no mistake, my lord. In the name of the King, I hereby arrest you for the murder of Viscount Cordell. Now if you will come along with me—" He reached out to take Temple by the arm but froze before moving another step. "What the—" he sputtered, the man's face going white as a sheet.

And when Temple glanced over at Diana, he realized why the sheriff looked as if he'd seen his own end.

The poor man was staring down Temple's pistol held in Diana's wavering grasp.

"Bloody hell! Diana, what are you doing?" Temple took a step toward her, but she knew what he intended and so she turned the weapon in his direction.

That brought him to a quick halt.

"I'll not let them arrest you," she said.

"Now, miss," the sheriff stammered, waving his hands out in front of him. "Don't make this any worse than it has to be." He took a hesitant step toward her.

Temple had to give the man his due; he was either brave of heart or a demmed idiot.

She swung the pistol back toward the sheriff. "Not another move, sir."

Temple cringed as her hand trembled. "Gentlemen, I'd suggest doing as the lady says. That's my pistol, and the trigger is very sensitive."

The innkeeper made a strangled, gulping sound as he shook like an autumn leaf in a tempest. The sheriff showed a modicum of sense and stopped swaggering.

Temple turned to his would-be rescuer, caught by both his

dismay at her course of action and the sheer audacity by which she lived.

Gads, she was an amazing woman. She looked like a veritable Amazon with her fiery eyes sparkling with deadly intent. In truth, she struck fear in his heart, and she was on his side.

"Diana, put that pistol down."

"No! I don't care if you did kill Cordell. I'll not let them arrest you."

"Would you listen to me? I did not kill Cordell!" Then he turned to the innkeeper and the sheriff. "I didn't kill the man."

Disbelief marked all their faces. Including Diana's.

Temple groaned. "Now I'm going to ask this one more time. Put that pistol down before someone gets hurt," he told her. The way her hand trembled under the weight of the piece, she'd as likely shoot him as the sheriff.

"No! I won't let them hang you," she declared.

"Miss, we won't be hanging his lordship," the sheriff told her.

"At least not until after the inquest," the innkeeper added hastily.

Temple and the sheriff shot the man equal looks of irritation.

Diana wasn't listening to any of them. "Temple, get your cravat." She waved the pistol at his open valise.

"My cravat? What, you want me to show these gentleman the correct way to tie a neckerchief?"

She glanced upward and shook her head. "No, you ninnyhammer, I want you to use it to bind their hands." Smiling at the sheriff, she said, "My apologies, sir, but I fear it is the only way."

"Miss, you don't want to do this," the sheriff told her, taking a tentative step forward. Temple was now convinced that man took his namesake as the scourge of Nottingham far too seriously. The fool was going to get himself shot. "You'll be in as much trouble, if not more than the marquis if you persist in this course of action."

"He's right, Diana," Temple told her. "Are you sure you want to do this?"

She gazed into his eyes and nodded. Her conviction, her faith in him even when she thought him capable of murder, astounded him.

Temple's heart constricted. She'd follow him anywhere. He knew that with every certainty he possessed. The damned foolish chit would follow him to the ends of the earth.

She was mad . . . and so was he.

If he wasn't willing to bet his last breath that Marden was behind this warrant, and that the wily Frenchman was most likely close at hand, Temple would never have considered going along with her foolhardy attempt to flee the law.

Then again, if Marden hadn't murdered Cordell, he wouldn't be in this muddle.

He did his best as well to ignore the fact that if Diana hadn't run off with Cordell to begin with, none of this would ever have been cast into motion.

Still, the problem remained that if he were in the Nottingham gaol, he'd have no way to protect her from whatever nefarious plans the determined French agent had for the lady.

And it was obvious from these trumped-up charges that Marden was willing to go to great extremes to gain his "bride."

Diana caught his attention with a long, exasperated sigh. "Temple, are you going to stand there all day woolgathering or are you going to tie these men up?"

Always the sharp-tongued little minx, he thought, grinning at her. "You're asking me to ruin my best cravat, I'll have you know," he told her as he rummaged through his valise.

"I dare say you can withstand the loss," she shot back. "After all, I am saving you from having a different sort of noose."

He approached the sheriff, cravat in hand. "My apologies, sir."

The Sheriff of Nottingham, obviously as concerned about his reputation as the innkeeper had said the night before, wasn't about to be tied up—not willingly.

He cocked back a fist and swung it at Temple, apparently thinking he was dealing with nothing more than another idle member of the nobility.

Temple was hardly that. He'd met far more ruthless opponents during his years of service than this earnest sheriff. He dodged out of the man's path, and landed a facer in the wink of an eye, knocking the man cold and sending him flying.

Right into Diana.

To his horror, the pistol in her hand fired, followed by a horrific shriek from the innkeeper. He spun around to find the pasty-faced man sinking face-first to the floor.

Meanwhile, Diana lay on her back, arms swinging wildly in the air, with the unconscious form of the Sheriff of Nottingham sprawled over her. She paused for a second and peered over his shoulder. Her eyes were wide with horror, her mouth trying to move to form the question that Temple didn't know if he wanted to answer.

Nodding at the innkeeper, she finally managed to ask, "Did I kill him?" She closed her eyes and started to sob. "Oh, what if I killed him? I didn't mean to."

Temple dashed to the man's side. Without hesitating, he

rolled the innkeeper over. Thankfully, there was no sign of blood anywhere. And the man's chest rose and fell in regular fashion. Before he could check him over completely, there was the thump of boots down the hall.

He glanced up to find Elton coming to a fumbling halt in the doorway. And then he saw the real damage of Diana's erratic shot.

A gaping hole in the plaster right over where the innkeeper had been standing. The bullet had likely whistled past his ear and given the man a good fright. Enough to have him faint dead away.

"What the devil?" Elton said, looking first at the innkeeper's body, then at the unconscious sheriff draped inelegantly over Lady Diana. He shook his head in dismay. "Can't a man even get a decent breakfast down before you two start causing all sorts of trouble?"

They rode from Nottingham, first driving southward for over an hour at a deadly pace, leaving the city far behind them. Elton had already seen to having the horses ready, and all that had been left to do was assure themselves that both the innkeeper and the sheriff were well, then bind them up and lock them in the wardrobe. Diana had hastily finished packing before making their excuses and tossing coins to the gaping staff.

If they were being pursued, no one had caught up with them, but Diana wagered that not even Lord Nettlestone and his legendary prowess as a whip could catch Elton once Temple's servant got his hands on the reins and a wellmatched set before him.

They finally stopped at a crossroads, and Diana peeked out the window to spy Temple muttering something to Elton about getting to bottom of this business. After the two men conferred, Elton climbed back up into the driver's seat and Temple got in the carriage with Diana.

The carriage bolted to a start again, and then veered hard to the right and off on another of Elton's shortcuts.

An old, straight track, used mostly by locals, she guessed. And headed in the wrong direction.

"Why are we going north?" she asked. "Shouldn't we be off for London? Surely between my father and your grandfather, they can get to the bottom of all this nonsense."

"If by nonsense, you mean Cordell's murder, that is not my problem, since I didn't kill the man."

"Fine, Temple, if you say so," she shot back. "But unfortunately, not everyone is as understanding as I am."

He snorted and crossed his arms over his chest.

Though her words had come out a tad more sarcastic than she'd meant, she had been telling the truth when she said she didn't think him capable of murder.

Oh, there had been a wild romantic moment in the Nottingham inn when she'd envisioned him standing across a field of grass, facing Cordell for her hand, but that in itself was a ridiculous notion.

For one thing, Cordell wouldn't have had the wherewithal or courage to stand up and face his enemy without pissing himself, let alone show up.

And besides, Temple was many things, but a cold-blooded murderer he was not. No, there was a mistake in all this, and time would sort it out.

That is, if the sheriff didn't catch and hang them first. What they truly needed was a more convincing fiction to prove Temple's innocence.

"Really, Temple, I'm to believe that French agents killed

the man? The only things remotely French that Cordell
would have been involved with were illegal brandy or some
imported tart he promised to marry before he swindled her
out of her last remaining family heirlooms."

"That is precisely why we aren't going to London,"
Temple told her. "I can't go back until I know why he was
killed."

Diana could offer half a dozen reasons why someone
would have wanted to kill Cordell, but judging from the deep
crease in Temple's brow and the firm set of his jaw, she
doubted he wanted to hear her theories.

And when he stuck out his feet until they sat on the seat
beside her, and closed his eyes, she knew he wasn't in the
mood to discuss the matter.

And so she let him brood in his dour silence, while she
watched the countryside pass by.

There was more to this than Temple was letting on.

Could he be right that there were French agents chasing
them?

She shook her head. It was utter nonsense. It had to be.

But then again . . .

"Ho there! I do say, ho there!"

The urgent cry brought Diana jolting awake.

Her hand lay on something firm and muscled, and she realized it was Temple's thigh.

She'd been asleep on his lap, and he'd been holding her as
she napped.

When she looked up at him, he looked like an alley cat
cornered by a stray dog—all points and ready to fight to his
last breath.

Some foppish Corinthian, indeed!

She scrambled out of his arms and into the seat opposite him. "Have we been discovered?"

Hoofbeats echoed in the road behind them. "I do say, Templeton, is that you? Hold up there."

"Demmit," Temple cursed.

"Who is it?" she asked.

"Stewie."

Diana cringed. Of all Temple's London set, Lord Stewart Hodges, Stewie to his friends, was perhaps the most inquisitive and persistent of fellows. Confident that everyone found him fascinating, an unending source of gossip, he made his way through the *ton*, inviting himself everywhere and oblivious to the fact that everyone found his ingratiating attempts at charm and his overstated claims of personal glory utterly annoying.

Elton opened the trapdoor. "Do I stop, milord?"

"Aye, Elton, or else he'll run that poor animal into the ground trying to catch us."

Elton muttered something that Diana, despite her better manners, smiled at, and the carriage slowed to a stop.

"Can't have Stewie seeing you," Temple said, and he caught her by the arm and upended her onto the floor. Before she could protest, he tossed a blanket over her.

"Stay put and don't breathe a word," he warned. "If Stewie knows you are with me, mark my words, you'll be Lady Nettlestone before nightfall."

Diana bit back the protest rising in her throat. Temple certainly knew how to leave her mute as a fish.

Not to mention the fact that he was right. Stewie was more efficient in spreading gossip than the *Morning Post*.

Diana heard the door open and felt the carriage sway as Temple got down.

Though the idea of marrying Nettlestone was enough to

keep her cowering beneath the blanket, she couldn't resist taking a small peek.

"Stewie? Zounds, is that you?" Temple was saying, once again the London dandy. "Why, I'd all but given up seeing civilization today, and here you are to remind me that good taste is alive and well."

Wherein most people when they went rusticating chose to wear their less than fashionable togs, Stewie eschewed such common sense. The gentleman wore a bright blue coat and an orange waistcoat, the color of which was so bright, Diana suspected it could be seen all the way in London on a dark night. Piled up around his neck was a cravat arranged in some extravagant display of silk and lace, while down below his boots glowed with a remarkable sheen. He might as well have been in Hyde Park making the afternoon rounds, rather than gallivanting about the countryside.

The foolish nit grinned at Temple, as if he'd just found some long-lost and well-to-do relative, jumping off his lathered horse, and greeting his friend with a great handshake, then a loud slap on the back.

The pair might have just bumped into each other at White's instead of standing on a deserted country road.

"I thought that was your carriage going by, Temple," Stewie said. "No one can drive like the devil is at his heels better than Elton." He doffed his great hat in the man's direction. "Ho there, Elton. Good to see you again."

"And you, milord," Elton said with a loud snort, then a spat of something.

Stewie leaned toward Temple. "You might consider getting a new driver, old man. I fear Elton isn't only missing an eye, but his hearing is nigh gone. I was calling after you for the last mile and a half before he had the good sense to pull to a stop."

Temple's brow arched. "Shocking!"

"Yes, well, one can't expect good manners from the lower classes. It ain't in their breeding."

Diana heard Elton muttering a rather descriptive oath about Stewie's likely lineage.

Unaware of the way his forebears were being disparaged, the man continued on unabashedly. "So do tell, what are you doing out *here*?"

Diana closed her eyes. She could well imagine the choice tale Temple was about to spin.

"Lost, my good man," he said. "Utterly and completely."

Lost? That was the best he could come up with? What kind of nobcock would believe that?

Then she remembered his audience.

Temple continued. "If you hadn't happened upon us, I fear we would have been driving in circles all night."

There was more grumbling from the driver's seat.

"Been that way myself a time or two," Stewie confided. "Damned poor roads up here. That, and this wretched horse can never tell what direction I'm going. As it is, I was headed back to town. Least I thought I was. Buxton, you know. Wife wanted to try the waters, compare them to Bath and all, so we've taken a house for the month."

Stewie paused long enough to draw a breath and continued on, barely missing a beat. "Now what brings you up to these parts? House party? Shooting? Say, you aren't here to take the waters as well? Getting on in the years, you know, Templeton. Quite restorative, them waters. At least the wife claims they are. Not that I need them." He slapped his ample belly and let out a great wheezy breath. "Fit as I was the day I married her," he chuckled, then nudged Temple. "And her five thousand a year."

Diana grimaced and held her tongue.

That well could be her name and fortune being bandied about in such a mercantile manner.

And given Stewie's penchant for gossip, it soon was.

"Now hold on, just a minute," the man exclaimed. "I know what you are about. Why, you sly dog!"

"Never have been one to keep anything from you, Stewie," Temple said in that droll, bored London manner that made Diana shudder. "You've always possessed a remarkable mind."

Remarkable was a word for Stewie, all right, Diana thought.

"Oh, you are a rare one," Temple's friend exclaimed. "Pretending to be lost, when all the time you are capering about like all the rest of them!"

"The rest of who?" Temple asked. "Pray tell, what exactly is it that I am about?"

"Why, the bride! Lamden's chit. The entire countryside is looking for her. Pins and Needles were through just yesterday rabid to find her. Her and her eight thousand."

He chuckled anew, and Diana pulled the blanket more tightly over her head so she didn't have to hear it.

"I fear you're mistaken," Temple was saying. "*I'm not looking to be leg-shackled.*"

Diana couldn't help wondering if he was saying that with so much emphasis for Stewie's benefit or for hers.

For once in his life, Stewie wasn't so easily misled. "There now, you can be as coy as you want with the others, eh, Temple. This is your good friend here. The chit is worth a fortune. And until your grandfather sticks his spoon in the wall, that kind of blunt would come in rather handy for a man like yourself. Can't go on dodging the tailor and your landlady forever, now can you?" He sighed and elbowed Temple again. "Take it from a dab hand at these matters, a well-dowered wife is the best kind. Why, if you were to find the bride and get her over the border first, think of it, we could come up here to Buxton every summer together, you and your wife, and me and my Alice. The ladies could take the waters together and whatever else it is that they do during the day, and we could take the town by storm. Bit of riding, bit of gambling, bit of sport, if you know what I mean."

Diana couldn't help but crack the blanket a bit and peer out, if only to catch a glimpse of Temple going green at the prospect of such a future.

To her delight, Temple looked positively ready to throw himself under the wheels. Then again, perhaps Stewie was doing more harm to her plans than she could hope to repair.

"Now never fear about Penham, he's too young to worry about. Why, what is Lady Diana? Thirty-four? Thirty-five?"

Now it was Temple's turn to smile. She saw him shoot a quick grin in her direction before he answered. "I believe the lady is just thirty."

Thirty? How dare he? He knew damned well she was nine-and-twenty. And barely that, if one were truly interested.

Thirty-five, indeed!

And to make matters worse, she heard Elton chortling away from his perch.

Oh, botheration! The devil take all three of them. She crossed her arms over her chest and brooded, while Stewie continued his outrageous conjectures.

"Nettlesome's your real worry. He's determined to have her."

"Nettlestone," Temple corrected.

"Right you are there. Annoying man, really. Can't see how anyone can tolerate him. Not like us, eh, Temple? Men of the world. Men about town."

"Right as always, Stewie," Temple replied.

"Now we're getting somewhere. If you've a mind to steal

the bride for yourself, rest assured I'll never tell a soul. Your secret is safe with me. You have my word on it as a man of honor."

Diana snorted.

Temple coughed to cover the sound and shot a glare in her direction.

She smirked at him, then put the blanket back in place. The only reason Stewie would hold his tongue was that there was probably no one in Buxton who cared to listen to his prattle.

Yet she soon found she was going to have to change her opinion of the unswayable man. For now that he'd stumbled onto what he assumed were Temple's plans, he would move heaven and earth to see his friend succeed, never mind if Temple wanted his help or not.

"I would invite you to come and stay the night with us, but the house we took is fair to bursting at the seams as it is. The girls are with us, and they brought friends along, so I wouldn't ask you to set foot inside. A veritable female den, it is." Stewie shuddered.

"It's too kind of you to even consider such an offer, but I fear I must be pushing on," Temple said.

"Bah! You'll stay the night, I insist. I'll show Elton the way into town and see you well settled at the hotel. Fine place it is. And then tonight you can join me at the Assembly Rooms. We'll come up with a strategy to find your bride before those other chaps get their greedy hands on her fortune. Besides, tonight is a masked ball. I love a good masquerade, don't you? Perhaps your bride will show her face." He laughed at his own bad joke.

Diana noted Temple didn't find it the least amusing.

She knew, as well as he did, that Stewie wasn't going to be naysaid. Now that he had devised their agenda, he wouldn't relent until Temple acquiesced.

"The horses could use the rest, milord," Elton called down. "Wouldn't hurt to consider the gentleman's kind offer."

Diana wanted to laugh. That was probably his driver's way of repaying Temple for making them stop in the first place.

"I don't know—" he began.

"It's settled then," Stewie said, slapping Temple on the back once more and bringing his protests to a sputtering halt. "We're off to Buxton. Ah, it will be a memorable night."

Diana hoped so.

Chapter 9

❦❦❦

"**A**ccording to Mr. Billingsworth, the waters of Buxton have been providing restorative cures since the time of the Romans." Diana glanced up from where she sat in the middle of the bed reading.

Temple tried not to groan. He didn't know what was worse, having to listen to that wretched Theonius T. Billingsworth or being trapped by Stewie into spending the night in Buxton.

True to his word, the dogged man had escorted Temple to the town's famous hotel, where he averred to all that the Marquis of Templeton must be afforded every luxury. By the time Stewie had bored the manager into a glassy-eyed stupor with an unending recitation of all Temple's lofty connections and social superiority, every gaze in the lobby was fixed in their direction.

Temple had little doubt that by nightfall there wouldn't be a man, woman, or child in the surrounding population who would not know of his arrival and that he was to be Stewie's personal guest at the Assembly Rooms that evening.

Including the local magistrate.

It would be only a matter of time before the officials in Geddington and Nottingham realized they hadn't fled south to London, but rather turned and headed north.

Also adding to his troubles was the room Stewie insisted he be given. Not just any room, but an elegant suite placed at his disposal.

One he could ill-afford.

Diana, on the other hand, had taken their good fortune to heart. Elton had smuggled her in through the servants' entrance and she was happily ensconced on his bed making the most of all the hotel had to offer, including a tray of fruit and cakes the manager had sent up.

"Perhaps," Diana was saying, "you should consider taking the waters first thing in the morning. They may well rid you of whatever it is that is ailing you." She studied the tray, then selected a plump strawberry, popping it into her mouth.

Temple glanced out from the dressing room, in which he was changing into his evening clothes. "Nothing is ailing me."

Except being wanted for a murder I didn't commit. And being chased by Boney's top agent, who wants to kidnap an English spinster.

"I don't know," she said. "You look a bit choleric."

Temple added one more item to his list: a spinster bent on bedeviling him into an early grave.

If he was choleric, she should look no further than the nearest mirror to see the source of his troubles.

Oh, why couldn't Diana have possessed the good sense just to take the first man who offered for her and be happy for that small favor?

Because that man was you.

He was still muttering under his breath when he glanced up and spied the skeptical arch of Diana's fair brow. When he caught her staring at him, she went back to reading her travelogue . . . aloud.

"Oh, listen to this—"

"No!" he said, stumbling out of the dressing room. "No more from that wretched travelogue. It was probably written by some bluestocking who's never left her lonely London attic."

Diana sniffed, but thankfully closed the book and tossed it to one side.

Temple soon regretted having disparaged her reading material. At least it had kept her diverted from their previous discussion, the one to which Diana now returned.

"I don't see why I can't accompany you tonight." She glanced at his state of undress and smiled. "You obviously need the help."

He ducked back into the dressing room and yanked his breeches on. At least his shirttails were long enough to keep her from having something else upon which to express her opinion.

"Leaving me here alone is a bad idea," she was saying. "I think you would be better off taking me with you so that you can be assured I'm in no danger from your nefarious French foes." She chuckled, and he knew it was because she still regarded his tale of dangerous foreign adversaries as the worst sort of invention.

He stepped back into the main room, and she flashed a smile at him—one he knew was meant to charm and entice him.

She scooted across the bed until her legs swung over the edge. "Take me with you, Temple. I promise to be on my best behavior." Having kicked off her shoes, she wiggled her toes enticingly inside a pair of pink silk stockings. The toes gave way to a narrow foot that led to a curved, delicate ankle, which led up to her . . .

Temple shook his head.

"How can you just say no?" she said, misunderstanding the direction of his thoughts. " 'Tis a masked ball. You heard Stewie say everyone would be wearing a costume. No one would even know I was there."

Yes, that is true, he wanted to tell her. *No one but me.* And that was the problem. He'd spend the better half of the evening distracted with the knowledge that she was somewhere nearby and probably attracting trouble.

For a spinster who was considered by most as well past her last prayers, Diana was certainly determined to cut one final scandalous swath through Society.

But there was no way Temple was letting her out of this room.

For if the tale Stewie had regaled him with, and for the most part the man's long-winded accounts were usually true, half the countryside was hunting for Diana. Word had spread that her father would find most any man other than Cordell acceptable as a son-in-law.

Such rumors had flushed out every fortune hunter and would-be bridegroom in the race to find and steal the bride.

While Temple's common sense should be telling him to hand her, along with Pymm's special license, over to the first taker and be done with the entire situation, he couldn't do that. Despite it being the most sensible and expedient solution.

Not as long as Marden remained a part of the puzzle. And Pymm's involvement as well. Pymm never did a favor for anyone unless it aided Britain's interests.

So how could the fate of Lady Diana Fordham have any bearing on England? Or France, for that matter?

None of it made sense, and until it did, he'd keep Diana well concealed.

"Please, Temple," she pleaded. "Let me go with you."

This time he shook his head in earnest. "Impossible. No one knows you are with me and I want to keep it that way. Besides, if you need anything, Elton will be close at hand." He went over to a chair where his efficient servant had left his pressed neck cloth.

"But what if something happens to you?" she said, rising up from the bed, her balled hands resting on her hips. "What if someone tries to arrest you again?"

"I hardly think you need any more charges of impeding justice."

She tossed her head, as if such an inconsequential concern really could matter.

"Diana, I won't have you in any further danger. Don't you see the harm that may befall you if you insist on accompanying me? If I am caught, who will see you safely away?"

She glanced up. A flicker of interest blazed in her eyes.

You care, it said. *You care about me*.

Demmit, this wasn't at all what he needed. He didn't care. *He didn't*. She needed to understand that.

He measured the silk in his hands and then began the intricate job of tying it around his neck.

Come to think of it, it might be of more use tying up the minx just to ensure she didn't try to follow him.

His fingers fumbled, and the intricate and perfect silk folds shot out in different directions.

Temple glanced down at the rumpled mess around his neck and cursed.

Reaching for the tray on the bed, Diana popped another

strawberry in her mouth before crossing the room in that easy, languid manner of hers. Standing before him, her eyes, so blue and pure, glittered with amusement.

"Let me," she said softly, smoothing the wrinkles with her hands by pressing the cloth onto his chest.

He stared down at the top of her head, her blond hair shimmering in the candlelight. There was a slight stain of strawberries on one corner of her lips—one that could easily be wiped away with his handkerchief, or his finger, or better still, his lips.

Gut-wrenching desire, the same hot-blooded fire that had almost been his downfall the night before, raced through his veins.

Yet it wasn't just her proximity that sent Temple's senses reeling. Nor her perfume, so light and airy it teased him into remembering the day before as she'd picked roses from the hedges.

No, it was her touch, so sure and confident. So damned familiar, as if she'd done this for him for years. This intimate, personal ministration, her own way of soothing his ruffled nerves.

It left him shaken and hungry—longing for what he'd almost had the night before. Aching to catch her up in his arms, toss her into the downy confines of the room's magnificent bed, and finish what he'd so honorably declined the night before.

"I can do this," he said, trying to shoo her hands away.

"Yes, I know you can," she said, standing firm and unwilling to relinquish the cloth. "So can I."

To his amazement, she did. Her nimble fingers folded the cloth anew and then proceeded to secure it into a perfect mail coach knot.

She patted it into place. "That should do."

"Thank you," he whispered, almost afraid to say anything. He'd never had anyone help him with such care. He'd always managed to fend for himself.

Until now.

"Temple?"

"Yes?"

"Do you ever grow weary of your life?"

The truth slipped from his lips before he could stop himself. "Aye, goddess, I do."

"I could help." Her soft assurance rocked his precarious grip on common sense almost as much as her touch.

"Diana, if I am to make an appearance, then I must be going." He tried to leave. He failed completely. Her hand on his sleeve was all it took. It and the tremble that ran to his spine.

"Temple, I don't want you to go. I'm afraid for you."

"Contrary to what you believe, I am capable of taking care of myself." He adjusted his jacket and faced her.

"That's what I'm afraid of," she whispered, reaching up to cup his face with her warm, tender fingers.

He should never have let her get that close, for the moment she touched him, his resolve started to crumble.

Visions of her naked beneath him in that magnificent bed danced before his eyes.

"Take me with you," she pleaded.

But all he heard was the first part. *Take me*.

"Diana," he said, lowering his mouth to hers. "You are a goddess meant to tempt the hearts of men."

She sighed and leaned closer, but just before their lips touched, there came a great pounding at the door.

"The magistrate?" Diana whispered.

The answer came in a voice calling from the other side of the locked door.

"Hey ho, there! Templeton,'tis me, Stewie!"

"Worse," Temple told her as he propelled her into the dressing room. "Stay put," he warned her before he shut her in.

Diana waited until Lord Stewart and Temple had left before she willfully disobeyed him.

She was hardly going to allow him to endanger himself for her sake.

Not when all this was her doing.

Creeping from the wardrobe, she'd just opened the door and started out into the empty hall when Elton stepped from the shadows.

"Now, milady, where do you think you are going?"

"Where do you think, Elton? I am going after his lordship."

Elton shook his head. "You do as his nibs says, and stay put."

"Don't you start as well, Elton." She pasted on her sweetest smile. "We've come this far together, haven't we? Don't tell me you're going to renege now?"

"Well . . ."

"What about our agreement? Retirement? A fine farm? A stable of horses?" Diana could see her enticement was once again working to whittle down his defenses. She knew Elton cared as much as she did for Temple. The older man loved him like a son. "Elton, what if his lordship knew about Mrs. Foston?"

Elton cringed. "That's hardly fair to go and be dragging Letty into this pot of soup."

"Perhaps you should have told him that you married my companion last year."

"Now, milady . . ."

Diana sighed. "And Mrs. Foston is so fond of the country-side. Why, just the other day she was saying—"

"I don't need you telling me what my Letty likes. I know she's fond of them flowery things and hedges and pretty gardens. She's told me often enough." He sighed.

"And might I remind you, she only agreed to this plan on the grounds that you would be here with me, to aid me in any way possible."

Elton huffed and crossed his arms over his chest. "I'm worried about her, I am."

"I am too." Diana knew it had torn Elton's heart in two to leave his Letty behind. "But she's resourceful, and a dab hand with that cane of hers. From the sounds of it, she'd set those men on their heels."

He snorted and then smiled, but his fond regard for his wife wasn't in question.

It was her insistence on disobeying Temple's order to stay put.

And from the deep crease running across his brow, Diana knew he wasn't going to give in easily. She pressed her point further.

"This isn't just for you and Mrs. Foston, Elton, but for Temple. You know it as well as I do. Please, let me go."

He shook his head. "On this I think you should listen to his lordship. He's of the opinion that you are in some sort of danger, and he's as likely as not to be right about it."

"In danger? Botheration, Elton! Temple's half mad. You said it yourself when you came back with him from Paris in February."

"Well, I didn't mean—"

"Oh yes, you did. You've seen him of late. You know him. He's taking too many risks. He'll get himself killed if he continues." Her hands were once again on her hips. "I will not let that happen. Will you?"

Elton's jaw worked back and forth, as if chewing on her words.

She knew Temple's loyal servant agreed with her. If he hadn't, he would never have agreed to his starring part in her runaway engagement farce.

"So will you let me go?" she asked.

"I don't think Letty would approve of you going out unescorted. She made me promise you wouldn't come to no harm if we got separated from her."

"And I won't. You can see me to the Assembly Rooms, and once inside, I will go directly to Temple's side." She saw him starting to capitulate. "I promise, Elton. No harm will come to me."

Elton made a low groan, as if she were wrenching his disobedience out of him. He was entirely loyal to Temple, but his concern for his employer's reckless turn of late outweighed even his unswerving fealty.

"Oh aye. You can go. But I don't see how. It's a costume sort of party. And you don't have anything to wear."

She bit her lip. Dash it, he was right. She could hardly make an appearance in her wrinkled and dirty traveling dress.

Then she remembered Temple's words. *A goddess. Meant to tempt the hearts of men.*

A goddess. She glanced around the room, her gaze settling on the elegant bed.

She stalked over to it and began yanking away at the gauzy curtains and the coverings. "I most certainly do, Elton. I most certainly do."

* * *

Temple had planned on making only the briefest of appearances at the Assembly Rooms. Then he'd duck out and be away. He'd instructed Elton to have the horses and carriage ready to go just after midnight.

And most importantly, to make sure that Diana was well in hand.

For the hundredth time he glanced around the room, half expecting to see her sauntering through the crowd, a victorious grin on her face, and her eyes alight with mischief.

She'd acquiesced to his demand that she stay put for the night, but he didn't believe for a minute that she'd do as he bid her.

That only made his desire to leave all that much more pressing. And it had nothing to do with their unfinished kiss.

Stewie had probably saved him from disaster.

"Temple," the man said. "There you are. You are as difficult to keep track of as the highwayman you've chosen to portray."

Stewie stepped back and eyed him. "I think it was ingenious of you to choose to portray a highwayman. Taking a cue from Elton, eh? 'Tis brilliant, sir. Brilliant." He stepped back and struck a pose, obviously waiting for Temple to make the same observations about his costume.

The man had come as a Turkish vizier. He wore a great turban made of purple silk that teetered above his head. Atop the turban there sparkled an array of paste gems and feathers dyed in a rainbow of colors.

The dazzling, wavering display was enough to send one to the necessary with a bad case of nausea.

But if the turban wasn't homage enough to extravagant excess, Stewie had spared no expense on the remainder of his costume.

On his chin, he'd glued a horsehair beard that waggled down over his plump belly all the way to the wide belt wound around his robes.

And his robes! Why, they looked as if he'd purloined the wall hangings and bedsheets from a cheap Southwark brothel.

Temple cringed inwardly. This was what he'd come to? Pandering to society's misfits?

Before he wouldn't have minded the idea of being included in Society's collection of fools. But every moment with Diana made him despise his double life even more. There was something about the way Diana looked at him, how she regarded him, that made him long to be the man she saw, the man she'd once loved.

Loved still, despite his best efforts to the contrary.

"Uh-hmm." Stewie coughed again, spreading out his arms and turning back and forth to afford Temple a full display of his blinding splendor.

Temple blinked a few times to clear his vision and managed to sputter. "Outstanding! Beyond imagination!"

"Yes, yes," Stewie agreed, his hand going to the scimitar tucked into his belt. He leaned forward, then wiggled his fingers for Temple to come closer. "My wife thought this costume gaudy. Refused to come with me tonight, saying I looked a veritable horse's ass. Can you believe it?" he confided. "And perhaps it is, given our country company." He shot a significant glance around the room where the regular complement of King Henrys and Oberons strutted their ensembles. "But I thought it too fine a costume to save until next Season. Don't you agree?"

"Utterly," Temple said, nodding enthusiastically. "Such a display will have no equal, no matter the company."

Stewie's chest puffed out. "Always said you were a man of impeccable taste, Temple."

"Uh-uh," Temple told him, shaking a finger.

"Ah yes, I forgot. Dick Turpin, gentleman of the roads," Stewie grinned. "And when anyone asks you, you can tell them I am the Grand Vizzard."

"Vizier," Temple corrected.

"Oh no, my good man," Stewie said, shaking his head with such vehemence, it threatened to topple his entire head-dress. "I am quite sure it is vizzard. Like gizzard."

Temple nodded, and then scanned the crowd again, but the room had quickly filled to a horrible crush. As he was jostled yet again by another smiling milkmaid, he turned to Stewie and asked, "Is there always such a crowd?"

"Here?" Stewie laughed. "Why, usually there is enough room for a game of cricket." The man glanced around and then winked at Temple. " 'Tis all your doing. Why, the tickets for tonight sold out within an hour of your arrival in town. Dash it, we'd have been in a fine spot if I hadn't already secured a pair."

Yes, how lucky, Temple thought, as yet another sheep's crook bumped accidentally into his back. Obviously Stewie hadn't gone to the same great lengths to inform the marriage-minded mothers of the room that he was also up the River Tick when it came to funds.

They probably wouldn't be so ruthless in pitching their hapless daughters in his direction if they knew their future duchess would be living in a one-room apartment in St. Giles—shared for the most part with a former highwayman.

He saw a Juliet being steered in his direction and stepped back into the crowd and behind a column to avoid any more bruises.

Stewie had turned his attentions to entertaining a young fellow dressed as Lancelot with great stories of London, and therefore didn't realize Temple was no longer at his side, thereby affording him a chance to escape.

As he began to move deeper and deeper in the direction of the back wall and toward a garden door, he heard a conversation that stopped him cold.

Softly spoken words, said in French. But any beauty of the language was lost in the menacing tone with which they were uttered.

"They say he will be here tonight. Find him and you will find the bride."

Temple paused a few paces past the trio of men, reaching up to adjust his mask to feign a reason for his proximity.

"And how do we do this?" one of the men said, his voice almost too low to hear. "Look at this crowd. He could be any one of these . . . these . . . fools. And what of the bride? How will we ever find her?"

While Temple shared the man's opinion of the company, he had no doubt about whom they sought.

But why? What the devil would a trio of French agents want with a runaway spinster?

It made no sense. But their dangerous tenor only made him realize the urgency of the situation.

And of his need to get back to Diana. As quickly as possible. He wasn't about to let them find her. Not now. Not ever.

If it hadn't been for his years of training in the field, and the restraint that Pymm claimed he lacked, he would have bolted from the room in a blaze of heroic thunder to Diana's side. And most likely with Marden and his cohorts in his fiery wake.

But his London indifference carried him calmly through those agonizing moments as he finished adjusting his mask even as his heart raced at the notion of Diana back at the hotel, alone and unguarded, save for Elton. Though he knew his driver would stake his own life to save her, in Temple's heart that job was his.

Always had been.

That recognition startled him almost as much as Marden's next desperate utterance.

"I want her found. Tonight. Let nothing or no one stand in your way. Templeton is here, and so must our bride."

Then to his horror, he spied a trio of feathers coming in his direction.

Stewie.

"Eh, there, Turpin," he called out. "Thought I'd lost you. Come back out of there. You'll never believe who just arrived."

Temple had no choice but to push back into the crowd, back toward his tenaciously attentive friend, lest Stewie create a hullabaloo.

"Look there," the man said, pointing toward the entranceway.

Temple couldn't see anyone he recognized.

"Don't you see them?" Stewie asked, rising up on his toes and waggling his fingers in the direction of the double doors. "Pins and Needles. I told you they were about."

Sure enough, Stewie was right. The pair of adversaries were making their entrance into the room. Neither man wore a costume, rather they were still in the same evening clothes they'd been wearing at White's four days earlier.

Obviously their quest for the runaway heiress had become part of the local gossip mill, for two paths parted down opposite sides of the room, allowing them to make separate entrances.

Temple found it amusing that they were more inclined to

glare darts at each other than actually look for their intended bride in the crowded room.

Then to his own chagrin, he realized he too had been caught up in the spectacle. He twisted around to find Marden and his men, only to discover they'd melded into the crush of the Assembly Rooms.

He muttered a curse under his breath.

Stewie heard him and misunderstood his anger. "Never fear there, Temple. I'll help you out with these fellows. Between the two of us fine wits, we should be able to locate your heiress before those young pups."

Temple shuddered. First at Stewie's assertion that they were intellectually equal, and then the man's intimation that he wasn't counted amongst the younger set any longer.

When had he gotten old? Then again, when had he ever lost an adversary in a crowded room?

He was definitely losing his edge.

The blame lay, he knew without a doubt, on Diana's doorstep. The minx was enough to rattle any man's wits. If he was of a right mind, he'd march right over to the hotel, haul her back to this room, and hand her over to Penham or Nettlestone—whichever one he had the misfortune to bump into first.

Then she could be their difficulty.

But that ignoble problem was still his. At least for the time being.

"Oh, tonight is a rare one," Stewie was saying. The feathers on his turban began another twittering dance, sending the plumes fluttering into Temple's nose.

He swiped at them, trying to clear his vision.

"Do you see that fine bit of lace?" Stewie said, as he elbowed Temple in the ribs and pointed at the entrance. "Now, there's a chit who could make a man forget he's after a spinster's gold."

A collective gasp of shock rippled through the room, leaving in its wake a silence of stunned disbelief. Temple knew the origin of this calamity at the doorstep.

Diana.

Chapter 10

Slowly he turned his head, glancing over his shoulder at the entranceway where a lone woman stood.

A barely clad masked woman.

Temple's jaw dropped.

Now, he considered himself rather jaded. And there was little in the world capable of rendering him speechless. He'd seen too much in his career to be scandalized by the antics of Society. But the costume Diana wore, or rather didn't wear, stunned even him.

Gone was the fashionable, yet sensible, dress she usually wore.

A gauzy length of silk lay over her shoulders, falling to the floor in a mock Grecian shawl.

Mock in the sense that it concealed nothing.

Then he recognized the gossamer fabric as the draperies from the bed in his hotel room. She'd twined them around her body in imitation of one of those enticing marbles in the British Museum that anxious mothers hurried their impressionable children past, lest they be ruined by such a lewd display.

Diana's costume would probably give even the enthusiastic curators vapors for a week.

The wrapping wouldn't have been so dramatic, so scandalous if she'd chosen to wear something beneath it . . . something other than just her chemise. To make matters worse, she'd pushed the short sleeves off her shoulders, leaving them bare and her breasts nearly exposed beneath the shimmering drapes that had once fluttered in his room.

And his room wasn't all she'd ravished to obtain her outlandish costume.

Her hair sat piled atop her head in a flurry of blond curls, bound in place by a wreath of ivy. Torn, he suspected, from the walls of the hotel. Willful strands tumbled free from the greenery into a swaying path of temptation down to the fair prospect of her bare shoulders.

For a moment she stood perfectly still, as if she were sculpted of marble, gazing out from behind her mask at the gaping crowd. Then in a slow, precise movement, she turned ever so slightly toward the open door, as if she were waiting for someone to join her on her throne of steps.

It was a calculated move, Temple decided, for the silence erupted once again into a sea of gasps and whispered reactions from behind a bevy of fluttering fans as she revealed the other surprise of her costume.

From the men in her audience, Diana received an applause made up of a hundred or more sighs of longing. Even Stewie's never ending litany fell into an unearthly silence as the poor man's mouth gaped and flapped at words that couldn't get past his rattled wits.

Stewie wasn't alone in his wordless floundering. Temple's breath caught at the sight before him.

She'd torn the back of her chemise asunder, so it displayed her flawless skin from the nape of her neck all the way down to that small enticing plane at the bottom of a woman's back where a man's palm fits perfectly.

It was as if she'd bared herself in an open invitation for someone to claim that one spot . . . to put his hand on her, and pull her into his arms for an endless night of lovemaking.

As much as Temple wanted to curse her foolhardy audacity, his body had a completely different response. Her enticement challenged him to reconsider everything he'd ever known about her.

Yes, he'd always thought of her as beautiful. And he'd always known she was passionate. But this . . . this wanton display boldly declared her spirited sensuality, the desires of a woman grown offered brazenly to him, and only him.

He knew she was challenging his honor and resolve not to bend to the shared hunger and desires that inextricably bound them together. Nor would she tolerate being kissed and set aside any longer.

In her choice of costumes, she'd thrown down the gauntlet and declared war. Diana knew, as well as he did, that making love would be the only way to stop the raging battle of desire between them.

Just then, her searching gaze met his, and her sweet, rose-colored lips curved into a wickedly sly smile.

Dare to hide me away, will you? she seemed to be saying.

He knew now he'd only been trying to cork a genie back into her bottle. An impossible task, if ever there was one.

She began her descent down the steps, and young bucks and would-be gallants raced forward to offer their assistance.

She disdained them all with a wave of the impromptu bow she'd fashioned out of a branch and carried loosely in one hand.

Temple now added one shrubbery to her list of damages.

Notwithstanding his own aching need for her.

Her indifference did not slow down the hopeful, including her rival suitors, Lord Harry and the baron.

And he had to give it to her, when Penham and Nettlestone arrived at her side, she never missed a step. Rather than give herself away, she gave her faithless betrotheds the same cold greeting she bestowed on all the others and kept walking toward the only man in the room she seemed to see.

What had he said to her earlier this evening?

A goddess meant to tempt the hearts of men.

He put his hands on either side of his forehead and shook his head. She'd taken him at his word, and dressed as her namesake. Diana, the huntress.

God help him, he'd become the unwitting prey of one determined goddess.

Perhaps he should add his name to the long list of mortal men who at one time or another foolishly spurned a goddess.

The crowd parted in a wave of shocked disbelief at what their usually staid evening had become.

For those who forsook the evils of London, this flagrant display of decadence only affirmed their beliefs that the city had become nothing short of a modern Sodom and Gomorrah.

And now its wickedness and corruption had invaded Buxton, no less!

As Diana continued her slow, measured progress, Temple heard the beginnings of murmured rebellion forming in the ranks of the ladies in attendance.

Glancing around, he realized if he didn't get her out of the room and fast, she'd probably be the subject of the first witch burning in these parts in over a century.

Diana slowed before him only long enough to say, "Our dance, sir." Catching up his hand, she led him toward the musicians.

"Diana," he whispered into her ear. "We had an agreement. You were to stay in the hotel."

She glanced over her shoulder. "You presented your wishes, my lord," she replied. "I don't recall ever agreeing to them."

Temple dug in his heels and brought them both to a halt. He leaned over to her ear, the beguiling scent of her perfume filling his senses, pure and tempting as a rose in December. And, as with its forebear, he knew enough not to get too close.

Both the rosebush and Diana bristled with thorns.

Wary, but ready, he told her in no uncertain terms, "Hear this. We are not dancing. We are leaving. Now!"

She shook her head, her curls tossing in their own wave of disapproval. "Temple, how you've managed all these years without me, I simply don't understand. Can't you see that if you were to carry me out of here right now—which is what you would have to do, *carry me*—I fear that would only lead to more speculation than what is already running rampant through this room." She smiled and pulled him the two steps onto the floor, and then waved her hand in a regal acknowledgment of the musicians.

The poor quartet must have sensed the ugly mood growing in the room and started playing a lively romantic set. Most likely to drown out the ill wind of chatter rising around the now-infamous pair before them.

Temple had no choice but to dance with her. In an attempt to offer them some cover from the prying crowd, he grinned as amiably as he could and waved at the crowd to come and join the dance.

Those inclined to gossip and the busybodies of Buxton, citizens who didn't share their neighbors' righteous indignation, caught hold of a partner and entered the forming lines, if only to get close enough to speculate on the lady's identity.

Diana smiled blithely, as if she were wearing a perfectly elegant and proper gown, and this assembly was nothing more than a typical Wednesday evening at Almack's.

Temple did his best to continue the charade, but it was nearly impossible. This close to her outrageous costume he realized just how naked she truly was—why, he could almost discern the rosy hue of her nipples. He didn't dare look any further south for fear of what he might spy.

But he did, and much to his chagrin, he realized her pillaging hadn't been limited to just the hotel's property. The wretched little thief had gone through his valise.

"Is that girdle my best cravat?" he asked.

"Yes. Quite charming, if I do say so myself." She raised her hands and moved her hips back and forth to offer him a better view.

As if he needed any more of a vantage from which to observe her. What he should be doing was scanning the crowd for Marden. And Lord Harry. And Nettlestone. Any of whom could upset the delicate balance of this topsy-turvy evening.

"I believe that was packed in my valise when I left. What were you doing going through my belongings?"

She had the shameless audacity to blush beneath her white mask, but he didn't know why she bothered. He didn't believe for a second she had a shred of morals left in her possession.

"I didn't go through your valise," she shot back, just before stepping out of his grasp and into the grinning and appreciative care of a rather skinny Friar Tuck.

"Elton fetched it for me," she said when she rejoined him.

"He's still alive?" For from the first moment Temple had spotted her, he'd assumed that Elton was singing with the heavenly choir, because if he wasn't dead already, he would be when Temple returned to the hotel.

Then again, this was Diana he was dealing with. And dressed as she was, he wondered if there was a man alive capable of naysaying her wishes.

Including himself.

He decided to stop staring at her and concentrate on more practical matters. Such as how to get them away from the assembly, and how he was going to manage to pay for the damage she'd wreaked upon the hotel.

"What else did you manage to purloin for this illicit getup?" he asked.

She grinned. "You find me illicit?"

"I don't want to discuss how I find you," he shot back. She moved out of his grasp and down the line of dancers. Certainly not here. Not in public.

More like in a private room. Preferably one with sheets and a wide, cozy bed.

Temple cringed. There he went again. He needed to concentrate. They were in danger. Real danger, and all he could think about was despoiling another man's intended.

Whoever the lucky bastard might be.

"I want to hear what you think," she whispered when she returned to his side.

"I'm sure you don't want to hear what I am thinking right now?"

"That bad?"

"Yes. I should hand you over to Nettlestone this minute and be done with your troublesome ways."

"But you won't," she said with supreme confidence, her unflagging resolve annoying him to no end.

He tried to will himself to just do it. He should. Yet he couldn't decide who deserved her more—Nettlestone or Penham. Or whether there was more reward in seeing Diana live the rest of her life with the *ton* referring to her as Lady Nettlesome or Lady Harry?

He had to admit, the first title was rather appropos.

"Now, how do you propose that we elude my oh-so-dedicated fiancés?" she asked, glancing over his shoulder in the direction where Temple assumed Pins and Needles were still trying to outswagger each other.

"It isn't your bumbling betrotheds who have me over a fence. 'Tis someone else."

Even with her mask on, he could see her gaze roll upward.

"Oh, Temple, not this Banbury tale about nefarious Frenchmen seeking to steal me away."

She whirled out of his arms and to the edge of the dance floor. Temple made the steps to rejoin her, and was about to take her proffered hand when he spied a man stepping from the crowd behind her.

From behind the fellow's mask, his wide-eyed gaze nearly burst as it fixed on Diana's back. From his open mouth and slightly upraised hand, it was as if he saw something so unbelievable that he dared not breathe or touch it lest it disappear.

And then the man's lips formed two words.

La mariée.

The bride.

Before Diana knew what was happening, Temple caught her by the hand and cut a haphazard course through the carefully made lines of dancers.

He sent couples scattering in all directions.

"Oh, pardon me. So sorry. Please excuse us," she shot over her shoulder as he continued his madman's dash.

"Temple, slow down," she called after him. "Why, you nearly toppled that poor lady."

He didn't reply, but continued plowing through the room, stirring up a swath of chaos in their wake.

And it wasn't as if she could tug her hand free from his grasp—he had a hold on her that she doubted even an immortal could break.

He pushed between two matrons who had their heads bent together in companionable gossip, sending them cartwheeling apart in a flurry of lacy caps and cashmere shawls like two hens caught in a barnyard breeze.

Botheration, what was wrong with the man? Diana craned her head around to offer some sort of apology, but what she saw stopped her social niceties.

A trio of men floundered behind them, but their intent was obvious, as their gazes were fixed on one person.

Not Temple. *Her.*

These weren't penniless rakes out to snare her fortune from Cordell's grasp—or her father's, for that matter. They had a continental air of disdain and sophistication to them that no Englishman could ever manage, except perhaps Temple.

An odd shiver ran down her spine, a harbinger of something well beyond her ken.

Temple's Frenchmen.

He'd been telling her the truth.

And they weren't after her fortune. They wanted her.

She didn't know how she knew, she just did. But why they pursued her, she couldn't fathom. Whatever their reason, she wasn't of a mind to stay the evening and find out.

She stopped dragging her heels, forcing Temple to tow her, and instead started pedaling after him.

But just as fast as she caught up to his frantic pace, he came to an abrupt halt, leaving her to slam into his back. She peered over his shoulder to find a man dressed as a colorful caliphate in their way.

Stewie! No one else would have the sheer nerve to wear so many colors at once.

"Ah, Turpin. You rakish devil. The ladies can't resist your charm, now can they? Why, I remember once at Lord—"

"Your robe," Temple demanded, releasing Diana, and starting to rip the purple silk wrapper off the man's shoulders. "Give me your robe."

"I do say," Stewie complained. "This is highly irregular. Friendship is one thing, but to steal a man's clothes—"

Diana glanced back into the crowd and saw that their pursuers had had the misfortune of ruffling Lord Nettlestone's feathers. The small, imperious man stood blocking their path and demanding satisfaction for their rudeness.

Surprisingly, Lord Harry had dropped his animosity toward his rival and stood at the baron's shoulder, like a ready second.

Given Nettlestone's inflated opinion of his rank and due regard, the French might find themselves blocked for the remainder of the evening.

"Stewie, I haven't time for pleasantries, now give me your robe and be quick about it," Temple told him.

Diana suspected she knew what he was about. "Please, my lord, you must help us," she implored.

"Lady Diana?" Stewie ripped off his mask, his eyes bugged out wide.

"Aye," she told him.

He looked her up and down and then shook his head.

"Who would have known? Who would have ever suspected?" Then he glanced over at Temple and grinned. "You lucky devil. Should have known you'd be the one to uncover such a diamond."

"Yes, quite," Temple said. "Now will you help us?"

"Oh yes. Most delighted." He shrugged off his robe and handed it to Temple. Then he took another speculative glance at Diana as if he still couldn't quite reconcile that the creature before him was the same Lady Diana Fordham whom the rest of Society took for granted as that odd little spinster.

"Thank you, Lord Stewart," Diana said.

"Stewie, please my dear. I'd be honored if you'd call me Stewie. All my friends do."

"Thank you, Stewie," Diana told him, somewhat flattered at the man's tone of adulation. She had never made a conquest before, and she didn't realize how gratifying it was to have a man gaze at her with such open adoration and for reasons other than her bountiful dowry.

Now if only Temple would do so . . .

"Stewie, I need more than your robe." Temple was saying.

Stewie started to stammer out a protest, "Sir, I am barely decent as it is, would you have me as unclothed as some Cyprian?" He glanced again at Diana. "No insult intended, my lady."

"None taken," she replied.

Behind them, Nettlestone's voice raised in protest. "Sir, I will have your apology or I will have satisfaction."

"Out of my way, you dog," said one of the men, rising up to his full height and towering over the baron.

Nettlestone, thickheaded as ever, hadn't the sense to realize he was wading into dangerous waters.

"Dog, you say? You dare insult me again? Then it is satis-faction I demand."

While Diana had to admit she was thankful for the diver-sion Nettlestone was unwittingly providing, she worried that the man was about to meet someone who truly wasn't going to be bullied by a penniless baron.

The Frenchman let out an exasperated sigh and nodded quickly to his companions. Then in a flash, he cocked his fist and leveled it into Nettlestone's stunned face.

The man keeled over like a stone. But if the Frenchman thought he had subdued the bothersome man, he didn't know the mettle of a Nettlestone. The baron struggled to his knees, cursing and complaining and vowing vengeance that in-cluded the wrath of all his noble forebears.

The French were hardly impressed and began to step over his muttering form.

"Now see here," Lord Harry said, stepping forward like an honorable second. "That was hardly sporting." For all his worthy intentions, Penham landed in a heap atop his once sworn enemy.

With their path now clear, the men renewed their pursuit across the crowded and chaotic room.

"Temple," Diana squeaked. "They're coming."

Temple took only a quick glance at the situation in hand and said to Stewie, "Create a diversion."

"A diversion?" Stewie stammered. "I fear I'm not very good at playacting."

Temple yanked the gauzy length of fabric from Diana's shoulders spinning her like a top. He handed her Stewie's robe, which she gratefully donned, ducking behind him to hide herself. Meanwhile Temple steered their friend in an-other direction. "We need a false bride."

"A what?" Stewie asked.

He shoved the drapery into Stewie's hands. "Toss this over that chit over there." He nodded toward a lithesome young blond, dressed as Juliet, standing nearby. "Declare her Lady Diana, the missing heiress, and make sure everyone in the room hears you. *Everyone*, Stewie." He glanced in the direction of Penham and Nettlestone, who were now rising like a pair of phoenixes.

Neither man looked ready to bear their insult any longer.

"But she isn't Lady Diana," Stewie protested, as Temple prodded him in that direction. "I fear it will be a horrible faux pas."

Temple groaned, but Diana stepped in and came to his aid. "Stewie, don't you see what a boon this is to you and the young lady? Why, you'll both be famous. And it will give you such a fine tale for next Season. With your skills as a raconteur, you'll be in great demand for years to come to tell your heroic part in our escape."

Diana could see the wheels turning in Stewie's mind. The social advantage of being Temple's aide-de-camp, his Will Scarlet, the hero who aided true love, was too tempting, no matter the hot water it might land him in.

Besides, Diana knew Stewie saw the other side of the coin.

If Temple succeeded in carrying Diana across the border to Gretna first, his friend would be married to an heiress, his pockets once again plump.

A good friend to call upon in a pinch when his own wealthy wife held the purse strings a little too tightly.

In a flash, Stewie was off. He tossed the cloth over the unwitting girl's shoulders and said in a voice that could have carried his battle cry across the fields at Hastings, "Lady Diana! I have found you! I do say, the missing bride! Whatever are you doing here?"

Diana didn't get the chance to see what happened next, for Temple had her hand in his and yanked her through the crowd that now surged toward Stewie and his false bride.

Instead of going out the front door, they ducked out a side door, into the gardens.

Down a path and around the building they finally found themselves out on the crowded street before the Assembly Rooms.

Nearby, a lad stood beside two horses tied to a post.

"Whose cattle?" Temple asked, digging into his pockets.

Diana guessed he was searching for coins and pulled out a guinea she'd tucked into the hem of her chemise. She pressed it into his fingers. "Will that work?"

He glanced down. "I hope so." He turned back to the boy. "Whose animals are these?"

"Some toff from town. Needlesome, Nettlesomething—" the boy said, scratching his head as he searched for the correct name.

"Nettlestone," Diana and Temple said in unison.

"Aye, that's it," the boy said. "And the bay belongs to a younger fellow. Wasn't much of a rider. He nearly fell off when he was trying to dismount."

"Penham," Temple said.

"Yes," the boy agreed. "Them's the two that own these horses."

"Well, they're mine now," Temple said, catching the reins. He tossed the boy Diana's bounty. "This should keep you well out of their reach until I repay them."

"But sir . . ." the boy protested until he looked down and saw the gold in his hand. He'd probably never seen so much money at one time in his entire life.

"Do you know Lord Radcotte?" Temple asked.

The boy nodded. "Aye. He's the magistrate around here.

But I don't think he'd be all happy about me giving away horses."

"He won't mind if you tell him this: Temple said it was a matter of some expediency."

The boy frowned. "A matter of what?"

"Expediency." Temple nodded to Diana to take the other set of reins.

She did so, but could see the boy still working the word over on his tongue, chewing it like old mutton. "Oh, botheration, just tell him Temple needed the demmed nags," she said as she guided the animal, Penham's docile bay, toward the mounting block.

"That I can do," the boy said with a bob of his cap and his coin clenched in his hand.

Temple smiled back. "And tell him you haven't been paid and that I promised he'd be most generous."

Diana glanced over at him and tried to conceal her grin. The incorrigible devil. That was what he was. No wonder his grandfather despaired of his ever becoming a respectable member of the *ton*.

"Can you ride in that?" he asked, glancing again at her costume.

She didn't bother to respond, just shot him a dark glare, before she reached down and gave her chemise another good rip, this time splitting the gown up to her thighs. When she looked up, he was openmouthed with shock, so she knew she'd made her point.

Having ridden since she was a child, Diana climbed up and onto the horse and waited for Temple to do the same.

The crowd from the Assembly Rooms began spilling into the streets. Angry voices and calls for the constable shattered the peaceful night.

With a nod, Temple was off, and Diana dug in her heels and brought her mount around to follow him.

When she caught up she said, "What about Elton? We can't just leave him."

"He'll be along," Temple assured her.

"How will he know where we are?" They were moving through the city now at a fast clip, clattering through the streets and growing closer and closer to the outskirts of town.

"He'll know."

They continued to ride at a furious pace, and when they hit the wide, straight Roman road that headed out of town, Temple gave his horse its head, and the animal sprang to life.

Docile manners forgotten, Penham's horse sensed a capable rider on its back, and happily took off in a wild gallop matching stride for stride with the other animal.

Diana wondered if Temple actually knew where they were going, for he left the road almost immediately and struck out cross-country.

Without her guidebook, without a map, she'd have been lost, but Temple rode with such a steadfast determination that she had to believe he knew exactly where they were headed.

Then again, with Temple leading her, she'd have followed him to the moon.

Temple knew he had to put as much distance between him and Marden as possible. Even the horses' hooves seemed to be pounding out the refrain of the man's words.

The bride, the bride, the bride.

What the devil could Marden want with Diana? It was a question that would have to wait until they found a safe haven from which to solve this wretched puzzle.

They rode for as long as they dared push their mounts. To

his amazement, Diana never complained, never begged to rest, just matched his course with a dogged look on her tired face.

Finally, he realized she'd topple off her mount before she'd ask him to stop, so he slowed their pace and a few minutes later pulled to a stop beside a hayrick.

"We'll rest here," he said, climbing down. He held out a hand to help her. The fingers that wound around his were like ice. "You're freezing."

"It's not that bad," she said, her teeth chattering over the words.

Temple shucked off his coat and wrapped it around her shoulders. "Wait here for just a minute." He paused for a moment, listening, then grabbed the horses' reins and led them to one side of the field. Sure enough, a small brook babbled along the edge of the grass. The horses drank, and then he led them to a nearby hedge and tied them loosely to the thorny branches.

When he got back, he dug into the freshly mown hay and made a nest for the two of them.

"Your chamber awaits you, my lady," he said, bowing low before her.

She managed to smile and crawled into the bed he'd prepared. When he joined her, she didn't protest or complain—not that he'd expected her to—rather, without hesitation she curled into his arms, laying her head on his chest. A long sigh slipped from her lips, and it felt as if the weight of her worries fled her tense and strained body.

"Temple?" she whispered a few minutes later.

"Yes, Diana?"

"Were those men at the Assembly Rooms your French agents?"

"Yes."

She sighed again. "I fear I owe you an apology."

He glanced down at her, and then put his finger to her lips. "Sssh. No apology necessary."

Her hand caught his, and she brought it down to rest over her heart. "Whatever would they want with me?" She glanced up at him, her eyes full of questions he couldn't answer.

The Temple of London would have spouted a glib reply or made some jest in hopes of easing her anxieties, but he could see her fear as plainly as he felt his own coiling in his gut. There was only one thing he could be with her. Honest.

"I don't know," he said.

They sat in silence for so long, Temple suspected she might have fallen asleep, but then came the quiet, pleading question that changed his life.

"You won't let them capture me, will you?"

"Never, Diana. Never." He kissed the top of her head, sealing his vow.

She nodded with a trust born from a love he'd disavowed so long ago, he wondered how he could deserve her unwavering confidence. And when she curled deeper into his arms and finally did succumb to the peace of sleep, Temple held her against him, afraid to move lest he wake her.

Afraid to move lest he ruin this incredible moment.

Instead, he turned his gaze heavenward, searching for the answers that eluded him like the mysterious secrets of the stars themselves.

"Oh, goddess, what am I to do with you?" he whispered, before he placed another kiss on her brow.

The only reply was the words echoing through his mind, as if borne overhead on the hooves of Pegasus.

The bride. The bride. The bride.

Chapter 11

❦

The warm light of morning brought answers that the dark of night could never have offered.

Temple awoke to find Diana still cradled in his arms.

Their shared warmth held him spellbound. He gazed at the soft blush of her cheeks, the disarray of curls, and the content, easy smile on her lips. He could well imagine finding her thusly every morning—waking her with soft, teasing kisses that would grow more ardent and hungry as she stirred to life.

And if he knew Diana, a morning kiss would never satisfy her.

Or him.

Yet such dreams were not Temple's fate. They couldn't be as long as his life continued as a Gordian knot of obligations and entanglements.

Those fanciful dreams, those fleeting moments fled as she stirred. Temple knew only too well that dreams had no choice but to recede, chased and persecuted by the stark face of morning into the nether reaches from whence they'd come.

The aching need he'd felt the night before was now replaced with that familiar emptiness, a pit of loneliness he'd known all his life.

This was his choice? To live like his grandfather? To turn into a bitter and angry old man?

He let out a frustrated sigh. Diana deserved to be loved, loved with a mindless devotion.

As his father had loved his mother. Passionately. Unapologetically. And yet his father's love had been his undoing, his greatest weakness.

As Diana was his.

To love her, claim her, marry her would be like leaping into a great abyss. He shook his head, as if standing on that terrifying precipice staring into the black unknown, so very unwilling to take that leap into certain disaster.

At least, he told himself, the pangs of loneliness were familiar, their ache almost a comfort compared to the alternative.

Yet the feeling only worsened when Diana turned her head up and smiled at him.

Her tousled hair lay in a halo of ringlets around her face. This close he could see the tiny path of freckles on the bridge of her nose.

He'd forgotten she had freckles. Hadn't he once teased her about the delightful little spots, kissing his way across their path, comparing it to steering a course through the heavens?

Yes, when he'd been a young fool. A man who could believe in dreams.

He sighed and let go of those things one could never hold.

She rose and stretched, first his coat falling away, then Stewie's robes. Temple gazed up at the fair prospect of her back, until he came to a sight that stopped him cold.

There he saw quite plainly what had sent Marden into a state of shock.

He stood up and stared and tried to comprehend what it could mean.

"Temple?" Diana said, glancing over her shoulder. "What is it?" Her eyes were once again full of questions, but her lips held a smile, one for him and only him.

He shook his head. "Nothing. Nothing at all." It had to mean nothing. For it couldn't be what he thought it was.

And if it was, it meant Diana was in graver danger than even he could have imagined.

Glancing around the awakening countryside, he turned to her and said, "We should be away from here."

The smile on her face faded to that look of wretched resignation she'd worn for so many years.

The one he hated. The one he'd put there because he had no choice.

Diana hadn't come this far to give up on Temple yet. She'd seen only too clearly the battle behind his dark gaze.

He wanted her. Of that she had no doubt.

He could have handed her over to Nettlestone or Penham last night. Or even to the French, for that matter.

If she was honest, she'd given him more than enough cause to want to wash his hands of her. But he hadn't.

And while he'd thought her asleep, he'd stroked her hair and kissed the top of her head.

She'd almost rolled over in his arms at that very moment and begged him to admit the truth. That he loved her.

But something held him back. And until she could discover how to untangle whatever bound his feelings in check, find some way to cut him free, there was no use in forcing herself on him.

Kicking at a stone with the toe of her slipper, she cursed

when the darn thing turned out to be the tip of what felt like a boulder.

Perhaps that was just what she was trying to do by getting Temple to acknowledge that they belonged together.

Kicking a boulder.

They had ridden for several hours when they came to a small village. The bake shop was open, and Diana sniffed appreciatively at the smell of freshly baked raisin buns.

"Can we stop?" she asked, ignoring the pointed stares of the villagers they passed. Stewie's robe, decadent and glaring in the evening shadows, was positively bilious in the light of day.

Not to mention that since she was riding astride, her bare legs poked out in a rather indecent display.

"I would like something to eat," she said.

He glanced over his shoulder. "I gave Elton the last of my coins to pay for the hotel. I fear we are in dun territory until we get to Colin's."

"Lord Danvers'?" she sputtered, reining her horse to a halt. "That is where we are going?"

"Well, yes. Where else would we go?"

"I don't know. I assumed we'd make for some Setchfield stronghold."

Temple shook his head. "Sorry to disappoint you, but all the duke's holdings are in the south. The only hope we have is Colin. Now come along."

Diana held fast. "I cannot possibly go to Lord Danvers'. It wouldn't be proper."

Temple's brow arched. "Thus says the lady riding about the countryside in her chemise?"

At that moment, a matronly lady walked past them. She

spared only one brief glance at Diana's costume, then took a deep, outraged breath and muttered something about "the naked immorality of London" before she continued down the sidewalk.

"I'm hardly naked," Diana said to the matron's stiff back. She held out one edge of the purple silk. "This is a robe, I'll have you know."

"Is that what it is?" Temple said. "I defer to your wisdom, Grand Vizier Diana." He bowed and touched his forehead in an exaggerated salaam.

"Oh, do be serious, Temple. You know I can't possibly arrive on Lord Danvers' doorstep."

Temple straightened. "This is hardly a social call." He eased his horse beside hers and leaned closer. "Colin is the only one who can help us. Besides, it isn't as if you just tossed him over last week. It's been nine years since you two parted company. He's a married man with a passel of children." He paused and ran a hand through his dark hair. "And if I know Colin and Georgie, there is most likely another wretched little Danvers on the way."

Diana glanced down. Why couldn't he see that was exactly why she couldn't go to Colin's house? When his life was everything she wanted most in the world.

Temple reached over and caught her chin, tipping her face back to his. "It isn't Georgie, is it? For she's quite a gel and not likely to carry any resentments that you were engaged to Colin first. She's not one for all the manners and rules of Society, believe me."

"Oh no, it's not Lady Danvers," Diana said quickly. Hardly her. She'd seen Georgie a few times in town, in the park with one of her sons or shopping with her daughter. And while the *ton* as a whole shunned the Danverses because of Colin's treasonous past, Diana had secretly thought that

Lady Danvers appeared to be an engaging and interesting woman. One she would like to befriend.

"You don't still harbor feelings for Colin, do you?"

She bit back a smile at the almost angry tone of his question. "No, Temple. It's not that."

"Then I don't see what the trouble is."

He wouldn't understand. For she suspected he didn't know what it was to long for a hearth and home of one's own.

Another pair of matrons passed by, both of them sending outraged glances in Diana's direction.

Temple twisted in his saddle, glancing up and down the street. "You need to get out of those clothes."

"I hardly think that my performing a reenactment of Lady Godiva is going to endear me to these villagers."

"No, that's not it. You are rather . . ." He glanced her up and down and shook his head. "Noticeable. And we need to disappear." He sighed. "I doubt any of these tradesmen are going to give me credit. Even if I was inclined to tell them my name, I doubt they'd believe me. We look like a lost pair from a traveling show."

"We don't need credit," Diana said, unwinding his cravat from her waist. "I have money." She shook the cloth, and a wealth of coins fell into her hand.

"You never cease to amaze me, my lady," he said, bowing his head.

"I hope I always will," she said softly.

Half an hour later, they left the local seamstress's shop with Diana once again properly gowned.

This time her appearance on the village streets drew no more than the usual curious glances that strangers were apt to receive.

"I think that went well," Temple said.

"Yes, I daresay," Diana replied. "It cost you nothing."

He grinned. "And what is wrong with that?"

She shook her head.

"Do we have enough left over for breakfast?" he asked.

"Only if you promise not to tell everyone I am your sister. Or that we were set upon by robbers."

"Whyever not?" Temple glanced back at the dressmaker's shop where the dour woman stood in the window, her arms crossed over her slight bosom and a frown still dividing her pinched features.

"Lawd sakes, Temple. No one in their right mind would believe such a fiction. That mantua maker thought I was your doxy. She stuck me four times with pins to show her disapproval."

"Is that all it takes to get your cooperation?" he said. "I wondered what had made you go so still and quiet. Perhaps you could loan me a farthing or two so I can buy myself a card of pins."

She laughed and elbowed him good-naturedly.

He offered her the package containing Diana's costume that the seamstress had begrudgingly wrapped. "If you don't like your new dress, you could change back to your old ways, oh goddess of the east."

Shaking her head, Diana said, "No, I think not. But really, did I look like someone's poor, forlorn sister dressed in my chemise and Stewie's robe?"

"Let's just say you look more discreet in your current fashion choice than you did before. Now about breakfast," he said. "A night outside has left me famished. What say you?"

"Do you think we have the time?"

Temple nodded. "Yes, for once we eat, you'll find your carriage awaiting you, my lady."

Diana looked up at the sound of horses and the wheels of a carriage. To her delight, Elton pulled to a stop before them.

"Morning, milady," he said, doffing his hat to her. "Milord."

"No trouble finding us?" Temple asked.

Elton looked offended at such a question. "But I wouldn't suggest waiting around here too long. You left quite a ruckus back there."

Temple glanced over at Diana.

"I hardly think that was my fault," she said to both of them.

Elton coughed and sputtered. And then like any good servant, he glanced away and laughed.

Early the next morning, at his cousin's house, Temple found the answers he was seeking.

At least enough information to know that Pymm had sent him on more than just an honorable errand for an old friend.

"He called her '*La mariée*,'" Temple said. "The bride. What the devil does it mean?" He paced in front of the fireplace of Colin's study.

Colin, Baron Danvers, sat in a chair nearby, watching his cousin through narrowed eyes. "*La mariée*? He called Diana that?" He scratched his chin, his brow furrowed.

"You know what this is about, don't you?"

His cousin slowly nodded. "I've heard rumors. That's why I returned so early from my last trip." He paused for a moment. "Napoleon intends to set aside Josephine."

Temple waved his hand, scoffing at the gossip. "That rumor has been floating around diplomatic and less-than-diplomatic circles for almost two years now. 'Tis nothing but conjecture."

Colin shook his head. "No. The Emperor has sent out envoys to all the royal houses of Europe, in secret, of course. He wants a royal bride. Someone to lend him an air of nobility to secure his claim to the divine throne of France. Every one of these men knows that if he brings home the right chit, he'll have his choice of posts. There are rogue agents crawling all over the Continent looking for an impeccable bloodline and willing parents."

"That hardly explains what they are doing in England," Temple told him. "In his right mind or not, the King would never allow one of the royal princesses to marry that upstart."

Rising from behind his desk, Colin crossed the room and stood by the door, as if he expected spies in his own household. After a moment he crossed back to the fireplace and faced Temple. "They aren't here for one of George's daughters. They are here for Louis's daughter."

"That's impossible, Louis's daughter is—"

"Not that one," Colin said, interrupting Temple's argument. "Louis's illegitimate daughter. She's the one they are looking for."

"Diana," Temple whispered, the truth hitting him.

Colin tipped his head and gazed at him. "Something you want to tell me?"

"Not until you tell me everything you know about this supposed bride."

"Just that Louis had a mistress, his only one, from what I understand. She bore him a daughter, then died of a fever shortly afterward. On her deathbed, she made Louis swear to look after the child, for she knew that the Queen was furious over the entire affair. From there, the information about the child turns into speculation. Some say the King had her spirited away to a convent, others claim that the Queen's mother, Marie Theresa, got rid of the infant to save her daughter the embarrassment of having a bastard at court." Colin shrugged. "For some reason, these fellows you've encountered believe she was brought here."

"Pymm knew all this, didn't he?"

"Of course he did," Colin said. "And you would have as

well, if you hadn't gone charging out of White's like a mad-man." He grinned at his cousin.

Temple ignored him, pacing a few steps back and forth. "None of this makes sense."

Colin walked over to the sideboard and poured out a cup of coffee for his cousin. "It does when you consider Louis's mistress was Scottish."

"Scottish?" He took a sip of the strong brew, choking it down like the bitter truth that was staring him in the eyes.

"Yes. Her parents had settled in France after Culloden. Relations of the Bonnie Prince. Royal relations."

"It can't be," Temple said, backing away, shaking his head, despite the gnawing truth that had stared him in the eye this morning. "It can't be Diana. She's Lamden's daughter. Everyone knows that," he said, more to convince himself than Colin.

"Is she?" Colin asked. "Who was Lady Lamden? Have you ever heard mention of her? I haven't. And neither has Lady Finch."

"Lady Finch?" Temple asked. The woman was a terrible busybody, but if there was anyone who could rival Pymm in uncovering the secrets of the *ton*, Lady Finch was the one to do the job. But the mere fact that Colin had sought her assis-tance told Temple that his cousin was coming to the same conclusion as he was.

Without the damning evidence that Temple had seen.

"What did she say?"

"That she understood Lamden married some Scottish cousin while he was in France, and that the poor girl died in childbirth. He was recalled shortly afterward and came home with his infant daughter and a wet nurse who spoke no English."

Temple shook his head and backed toward a large chair in

the corner of the room. He collapsed into the wide leather expanse and stared straight ahead. "Coincidence," he muttered. "It's all bloody coincidence."

But even to his own ears, he didn't sound convinced.

Colin's brows rose. "Anything you'd like to tell me?"

"No." Temple frowned at his cousin. "Well, yes." He took a deep breath. "I saw something. On Diana. On her shoulder, specifically. She was wearing only her chemise and—"

Colin's brow arched, then he started to grin.

Temple groaned. "It wasn't like that."

"If you say so." Colin glanced away, obviously attempting to hide his amusement.

"Oh, stifle it," he told him. "She has a mark on her shoulder. You wouldn't notice it that much, for it looks like a birthmark, but when Marden spotted it, you'd have thought he'd found the Holy Grail."

"Marden was there, when she was wearing her chemise?" Colin shook his head. "Now that must have been an interesting evening."

"Pay attention," Temple told him. "Diana came to the Assembly Rooms in Buxton wearing her chemise."

"Her what?" Colin coughed a bit and then shook his head. "And I thought Georgie had the corner on scandal." He caught up another chair and dragged it over beside Temple's. Sitting, he asked, "What was it that Marden spotted?"

"A birthmark. But I don't think it is one. It appears to be a brand."

Colin eyed him. "What does it look like?"

From his cousin's tone, Temple had the feeling he was afraid to ask. Just about as much as Temple was afraid to tell him.

"A fleur-de-lis. She has a small fleur-de-lis burned into her shoulder."

Colin's mouth fell open, and he stammered something Temple couldn't make out.

"Yes, quite so," he told his flabbergasted cousin, reaching over to pound him on the back. "Very much the reaction I had."

Colin held up his hand to stave off any more of Temple's assistance. Then he shot his cousin a very serious look. "If this is true, you know what it means? Can you imagine the groups who would use an Englishwoman in France as an opportunity to foment revolution here?"

"Yes, I can." Temple shook his head. "I fear I've brought terrible danger to your doorstep. I apologize, but I didn't know who else to go to for help."

"Rubbish," Colin said, clapping his cousin on the back. "Georgie will be in alt. She'll start arming the footmen and upstairs maids and drilling them in the driveway." Then Colin turned more sober. "Pymm was right about one thing."

"And that would be?" Temple asked.

"Diana must be wed. Immediately." Colin rose, hands behind his back, and rocked on his heels.

Temple well imagined this was the stance Colin often took on the rolling deck of his ship, the *Sybaris*.

"Yes, I know she must be," he agreed. "It is the only way to safeguard her."

"You are going to make me a rich man," his cousin said, now grinning from ear to ear.

"Rich? How so?"

Colin cringed and then had the good manners to look embarrassed. "After you left White's, there was a bit of speculation, and I fear I got a little caught up in it."

Temple arched a brow. "About what?"

Hemming and hawing, Colin shuffled his feet. "You know I'm not one for betting or rash stakes, but I just wanted to see those smug, lazy bastards humbled just once at their own game."

"What did you bet?"

"Two thousand pounds."

"Two thousand?" Temple choked out. He knew Colin was a man of means, but he was also a cautious man who would never bet unless he knew he was certain to win.

What the devil could Colin have been so sure of to risk so much?

"Tell me exactly what you wrote in the book that got you into this muddle."

"That you'd succeed in finding and marrying Lady Diana before any other man."

"Marry Diana?" Temple stammered. "Me? You know that isn't possible."

"Oh, not this again," Colin said.

"Here me well, cousin," Temple said, "Two thousand pounds or not, I'll never marry her."

"Lady Diana," a voice called down the stairs.

Diana whirled around from the door of Colin's study, her face red with shame.

It wasn't for the fact that she had just been caught eavesdropping, because she'd only just pressed her ear to the door. No, what brought the color to her cheeks were the only words she'd managed to overhear.

I'll never marry her.

Temple's adamant tone tore down every hope she'd ever held that he would eventually come to his senses.

She'd been a fool all these years to think otherwise.

"Lady Diana, are you well?"

Diana took a deep breath, hoping to still her quivering

lips, the racking shudders in her chest. Of all the people who had to see her thusly, it had to be Colin's wife.

Inside the study, the men's voices began to rise, but their words, fast and heated, melded together into a cacophony.

Lady Danvers shook her head and held out her hand. "Come along. From the sound of it, they'll be at it for hours." She offered a small, tentative smile to Diana. "Besides, I think we have much to discuss. And plan."

In that moment, Diana knew she'd found a friend, and a determined ally.

Chapter 12

"**I** know you love her," Colin said, meeting his cousin's inscrutable gaze with a challenging one of his own. "How can you even consider such a choice?"

Temple shook his head. "Don't you see, *this* is the only choice I have."

"I don't see that, not at all," Colin told him, stalking over to his desk and throwing Pymm's special license down on top of it. "You love her. And for some ridiculous reason, she loves you . . . still," he added, hoping to make a point. "How can you even think of asking me to marry her off to someone else?"

Temple flinched and looked away. The idea of Diana being another man's wife cut him to the core.

He supposed it always would have, but in the last few days, being in her constant company had only renewed the heartache that he thought he'd banished years ago.

Colin caught him by the shoulder and spun him around. "The luckiest day of my life wasn't the day I met Georgie, it was the day she became my wife. Marry Diana. Don't live the rest of your life with regrets."

"But what about Diana? How can I say she won't come to rue her choice?"

"Don't you think if she was of such limited character, she'd have given up on waiting for you and married someone else by now?"

"Nonsense. She hasn't an inkling what being my wife would entail." Temple ran a hand through his hair. "You of all people should have some idea of what I'm saying."

Colin had heard this argument too many times. Temple's fears were ridiculous. If it were any other woman, Colin might have agreed, but this was Diana Fordham they were discussing.

She possessed a tenacity of spirit and will that Colin had seen in only one other woman. And he'd had the good sense to marry that one.

"I'm doing this for Diana," Temple said with a resignation that sent Colin's frustrations through the roof.

Especially because he knew that once Temple set his heels, it was next to impossible to change his cousin's stubborn stance. If he continued to argue the point, his obstinate relation would only dig in harder.

He and their grandfather had much in common, as much as they both would disagree on the point.

Only Temple possessed one thing their grandfather never would—a heart. As much as he disavowed it, Temple only needed to bridge the divide between him and Diana, and it would quell the fears that seemed to lock his cousin in a lonely exile from life.

"Discreetly send out word," Temple told him in a voice devoid of emotion. "Whoever arrives first, wed Diana to him without delay." He paused for a moment, and Colin held out hope that he was reconsidering, but it wasn't to be.

"Elton and I will continue on toward Scotland as if we are still making a dash for Gretna. Hopefully Marden will take the bait and follow us, while Diana remains here safe with you."

Colin gave it one more chance. "What if I can keep her out of sight, at least until you get to Scotland and determine if these rumors of a French tangle are true or not. Then you can return and marry her."

Temple shook his head. "It matters not who her father is. Not to me. But if she is Louis's daughter, she'll only be safe once she is wedded and bedded."

He turned and shot a look of pure challenge at his cousin that seemed to say, *And not by me*.

"Diana, there is no reason why we can't straighten all this out." Georgie smiled, then glanced at the door. "Though I do wish my sister were here. No one can set a man on his ear like Kit."

"If only I could convince Temple that he doesn't need to protect me from his life. I'm hardly the wide-eyed innocent I was when we first met."

Georgie waved her hand at Diana. "After all these years, Colin still requires constant persuading that he needs me. And Temple . . . I well imagine he is twice as stubborn." She took a sip from her cup of tea. "Do you love him?"

Diana nodded.

"Have you told him?"

"I've tried. But it doesn't matter. It's as if the more right it seems, the more he pushes me away. Why, I truly think he would have let me marry Colin."

"Well, thank goodness that never happened," Georgie said.

Both women burst into companionable laughter. After but a few moments in Georgie's company, Diana felt as if she'd known the other woman all her life.

But Diana's humor didn't last long. "Oh, Georgie, what am I to do? I've waited so long for him. I thought I could accept his change of heart. King and country and all that honor rubbish. But not any longer. Can't anyone see that he is tired? That he's given his country everything but his life? He's lost, and I'm not going to wait idly by for the day when he doesn't come back."

Georgie nodded in complete understanding.

"His work for the Foreign Office is going to kill him."

"You know about that?" she asked, her eyes wide with shock.

"Yes, but don't tell him."

"Oh, never. Temple is quite proud of his deception." Georgie grinned. "How long have you known?"

Diana blushed. "Since the day I was to marry Colin. But it matters not how. I only knew then that I couldn't marry anyone but Temple."

"Then I'm glad you discovered the truth in time," Georgie said, patting her swollen midsection.

"So am I."

Georgie leaned over and refilled Diana's cup.

Diana nodded her thanks, and continued, "Before I found out, I could never understand Temple's sudden change of heart, his wretched indifference. Once I knew, I told myself that he just didn't want to embroil me in such dastardly affairs."

The door to the salon came flying open, and in dashed a young girl. "Mother? Mother?"

"Here, Chloe," Georgie said.

Chloe let out a long, anxious sigh, as if the end of the world was coming. "I can't find Sarah. She's supposed to be taking her lessons with me and she's gone missing. *Again*."

Diana hid a smile behind her hand. She knew that Chloe was supposedly Georgie's daughter from a previous marriage, and that Colin had adopted her, but if Diana didn't know better, she would swear that the little girl's inky locks and riveting eyes were the exact image of Lord Danvers.

And if Chloe was close to nine years old that would mean . . . Diana gave up on the math that placed the child's arrival within nine months of her broken engagement to Lord Danvers.

Obviously Colin's heart hadn't been torn asunder for very long.

"Never mind about your sister," Georgie was saying. "I sent Sarah on a little errand."

Chloe's mouth pursed, and then she glanced over at their guest. "Are you Lady Diana?"

"Yes, I am."

The little girl eyed her up and down. "Aren't you supposed to marry Cousin Temple?"

"Chloe!" Georgie said. "That isn't something you ask a lady."

"Well, I would think she would know," the little girl replied. The child crossed the space between them and sat down beside Diana. "How did you meet him?"

She smiled down into the rapt face looking up at her and reached back to those treasured memories, the ones that had held her in good stead all these years. She'd never told anyone about her affair with Temple, but now seemed as good a time as any.

"It was by chance that we first met . . ." Diana began.

Sussex, 1796

The carriage skidded to a clattering and unearthly halt on the moonless and pitch-black road.

Inside, Lady Diana Fordham, a recent student of Miss Emery's Establishment for the Education of Genteel Young Ladies, tumbled from her seat and landed in a heap on the floor, uttering a ripe phrase that was most unlikely to have been learned at her very proper school.

And from the deep intake of breath, her hired companion, who had landed beside her in much the same fashion, didn't approve much more than Miss Emery would have of the oath Diana had chosen.

"Lady Diana," Mrs. Foston began in a voice that harbingered another lecture on the propriety of young ladies. "I hardly think—" she began as she started to right herself. "Oh dear. Oh my. Oh, I believe I have injured myself."

Diana thought Mrs. Foston would be better served if she just came out and cursed.

"Let me lend you a hand," she suggested instead. Diana helped the lady back up to her seat and then fumbled in the darkness for the window and pulled open the shade. "Gribbens? Gribbens? Are you well?" she asked their driver.

"I'm fine, milady," came the gruff reply. "And you and the missus?"

"Mrs. Foston is hurt, but I am unharmed. What happened?" she asked, feeling around for her bonnet, which had flown off in the tumult.

Besides frowning on cursing, Mrs. Foston was loath to see her without a bonnet. Her companion took her duties very seriously, seeing to her young charge with the utmost care and strictest of rules. Diana imagined that was because the lady had no family or income beyond the little her army sergeant husband had left her before he'd died.

Since Lord Lamden had hired Mrs. Foston as a favor to her husband's colonel, an old family friend, the lady was determined to discharge her duties with almost a military fervor—much to Diana's chagrin.

After some more frantic searching, her fingers closed over the bonnet's silk ribbons, tugging it loose from beneath the seat, and then plopping it back over her curls.

"There's a bit of a problem, milady. Now, you stay inside there, and Michaels and Wilson will have . . . um, will have . . . *it* cleared away right quick."

From behind the carriage, the two footmen leapt down from their posts. The flicker of a lantern passed by, as they brought the light from the rear of the carriage forward to survey the situation.

Diana waited silently inside, the only sounds their boots crunching in the gravel on the roadway, and then the deep intake of breath as one of them stepped around the front of the horses.

One of the beasts nickered and then balked, rattling its bridle and bit, and lurching the carriage back a few feet.

"Is it alive?" she heard Wilson mutter to Michaels.

"Could be a highwayman's trick. I heard tell they used one in Dorset until it stank too much for them to carry about."

"One what?" she called after them suspicious of the man's uneasy tones. "What exactly is in the road?"

"Oh, milady, don't you fret a moment about this. Just do as Gribbens tells ye and stay inside the carriage." Michaels, another longtime family retainer, sounded as uneasy as Gribbens.

And like Gribbens, knew their mistress wouldn't stay put for very long.

Diana's hand was already on the latch. "Whatever is *it* that you don't want me to see?"

"Really, miss, it ain't a sight for yer eyes."

That was enough for Diana. She bounded out of the carriage, deliberately ignoring Mrs. Foston's protests, for she knew the lady's injury prevented her from doing much other than complaining—vehemently.

Better to ask forgiveness than permission, Diana thought.

She followed the shaft of light knifing through the darkness until she came to the wall presented by the backs of Gribbens, Michaels, and Wilson.

"What is it that has us waylaid and the three of you so flummoxed?" she asked, prodding her way between them.

"Oh no, miss. Don't," Gribbens warned.

And then Diana saw it.

A man facedown in the road before them. His body lay at an unnatural angle.

"Is he dead?" she whispered.

"Don't rightly know, miss," Michaels said. "Like Wilson was saying, it could be a trick."

Then she noticed that both Wilson and Michaels had their pistols drawn.

"Oh, botheration," she muttered, reaching over and snatching the lantern from Gribbens. Ignoring his protests much as she had ignored Mrs. Foston's, she stalked over to the body. "If it were a trick, don't you think it would have been sprung by now?"

Setting the lamp down, she knelt beside the man and put her fingers on his neck. His skin was still warm, and there was a faint pulse beneath her fingers.

She let out a deep breath, one she hadn't realized she was holding.

"He's alive," she said over her shoulder. *Barely.*

She caught up the lamp again and tried to discern who he might be. By the expensive cut of his coat and the sheen of his boots, he wasn't some mere ruffian.

"Wilson, Michaels, be quick and turn him so we can see who he is."

In all likelihood it was one of their neighbors thrown from his horse while coming home from the squire's dance.

The footman caught the man and rolled him over, the poor fellow groaning at the movement. But his identity remained a mystery, for he wasn't anyone Diana had ever met.

Dark hair framed a young, handsome face. A strong jaw, carved features, and a hawkish look made him seem almost like a fallen angel. A most unholy one.

She put her hand on his shoulder, and shook him slightly. "Sir, sir, what has happened to you?"

He did not reply, but instead a warm, wet feeling crept through her gloves. When she pulled her fingers back, a dark red stain spread over the once white kid leather.

Blood. His blood.

"He's been shot," Michaels said.

"Highwaymen," Wilson muttered, in a tone that hinted that he'd been right all along. "Best we be getting you home, milady."

"Then load him into the carriage quickly," Diana instructed.

"Miss?" Gribbens said, as if he swore he hadn't heard her correctly.

"I said, load this man in the carriage. We certainly can't leave him here. He'll perish."

"But miss, your father is in London. He's not likely to be pleased about having a stranger in the house when he's not home."

"Botheration, Gribbens, you sound like Mrs. Foston. I am

not about to leave this man to die in the road like a stray dog. Get him in the carriage."

Her stance told all three that she wasn't going to yield.

And if their protests were bad enough, nothing surprised Diana more than when Mrs. Foston cursed roundly at having a bleeding, unconscious man heaped onto her lap.

Danvers Hall, 1809

"And so you saved Cousin Temple?" Chloe asked.

"Yes," Diana told her. "I suppose I did."

"That's almost as wonderful as how Aunt Kit met her husband," Chloe said with a sigh, as only romantically inclined little girls could. She leaned forward and whispered loudly, "She met her husband when she was sent to jail for stealing."

"Chloe!" her mother scolded. "That isn't to be repeated."

Diana resisted the urge to laugh, for she didn't know what was more amusing, Chloe's feigned innocence at having let slip a family secret or Georgie's lack of denial of the story's veracity.

Considering the tales Diana had heard bandied about concerning Lady Danvers, her sister being in jail seemed a most likely escapade for one of the Escott sisters.

"Your secret is safe with me," Diana told Chloe.

Chloe smirked over her shoulder at her mother. Then her inquiring gaze turned back to Diana. "If Cousin Temple wasn't awake, how could he fall in love with you?"

"He wasn't asleep for long," Diana said.

The door to the study opened, and a harried-looking young woman, who Diana assumed was the governess, entered the room. "There you are, Miss Chloe. Come along, it's time for your luncheon." She glanced up at Lady Danvers. "Ma'am, the twins are demanding your attention on a matter of a knot. I haven't the faintest idea how to tie something called a Spanish bowline and they believe you know how."

Georgie rose and excused herself. "I won't be long," she told Diana.

Chloe left reluctantly, towed along by her governess. She stopped at the door, tugging her hand free. "Lady Diana, will you tell me the rest of your story later?"

Diana smiled and nodded.

But the story she'd tell the little girl would be a more respectable version than the one that played in her memories.

Sussex, 1796

"Is he going to live?" Diana asked Mrs. Foston.

"Aye. He's young enough. As long as it doesn't get infected." She sat on a chair beside the bed, with her ankle propped up. Despite her own injuries, Mrs. Foston had tended the man's grievous wound as if she were able to stand on her own two feet.

Diana glanced at the wad of padding on the man's bare shoulder, thankful that her companion was not just some ordinary widow, but the widow of an army sergeant. Mrs. Foston had followed her husband on campaigns in India and the West Indies and probably knew more than the local surgeon about removing a bullet. While the lady had only hinted at the grim reality of being an army wife, Diana suddenly realized that Mrs. Foston's life hadn't always been adventure and fine travels.

"We got the ball out," the lady said, glancing over at the bloodstained bowl and the offending piece of lead she'd managed to dig out of the young man's shoulder. "That bodes well for him. Now you should get to bed," she told Diana. "Your father would sack me if he knew I'd allowed you in here."

Diana couldn't take her eyes from the man before her. "I'm not about to tell Papa, and no one else will either," she said, shooting a significant glance at the wide-eyed maids and the cook standing beside the bed. They all nodded in agreement, for none of them would breathe a word of it to the master.

It would implicate them as well.

The only naysayer was Michaels, who stayed at the door with a pistol in his hand.

"Is that necessary?" Diana asked him.

"We don't know who he is, miss."

"He's a young gentleman who was held up. What more is there to know?" She shook her head. "Besides, I hardly think he is in any condition to pillage the house, Michaels. Go get some rest."

The footman glanced at Mrs. Foston for confirmation.

"With the amount of laudanum I poured down his throat, he'll be out till tomorrow."

"If you don't mind, I'll just wait outside the door, milady," the loyal Michaels said.

Diana nodded. "The rest of you can go and seek your beds."

The servants seemed to breathe a sigh of relief and filed out quickly.

One of the maids, Lucy, stopped and turned to say, "I'll send up Mary to watch over him, milady. She's a dab hand with sick lambs."

Diana smiled her appreciation, though in her opinion, the man sleeping in the bed appeared anything but a lamb.

What's more, when she peered closer at his devilish features, she felt her life inexplicably tied to his. There was neither rhyme nor reason to it, but his life was now hers. And she meant to see him healed.

She glanced up to find her hired companion watching her. "Mrs. Foston, I insist you go as well," she told her. "You need to mend that ankle. I'll stay with him until Mary comes up."

The lady frowned and appeared likely to argue.

Diana quickly added, "You'll be of no use to him or me tomorrow if we still can't locate the doctor and you're laid up in bed."

The lady's lips pressed together in firm resolution, but when she shifted in her seat to find a more comfortable position, her face took on a pained expression that appeared to surprise even her.

"Yes, perhaps I should," she said. "Tell Mary that if he gets a fever, she should come and get me. I have some powders that may help."

"Michaels?" Diana called out. The man sprang into the room as if he were ready to battle an invading army. "Could you please lend Mrs. Foston your assistance? I don't think she'll be able to walk unaided."

The man offered his arm to the lady, and they left.

Finally, Diana was alone with him.

Glancing around to make sure she was just that, alone, she reached down and brushed the back of her hand across the stranger's cheek, letting the dark stubble rake her skin. There was such a quiet strength to his features that she knew he was going to live. He just had to.

She smoothed his brow and knelt to whisper quiet words of encouragement to him. Even as she drew closer, she found her gaze fixed on his lips and wondered if she dared.

Better to ask forgiveness . . . she thought, leaning closer and letting her lips touch his.

And when they did, his lashes fluttered, and his lips moved against hers, his mouth opening and responding to her tentative touch.

So much for Mrs. Foston's assurances regarding her dosage of laudanum.

She didn't know what to do, but he certainly did. His lips teased hers to open up from their stiff, puckered pose. His teeth nipped at her bottom lip and pulled her closer. Her mouth opened just as his tongue swept over her lips.

A burning, hot and liquid, ran through her veins and down to places so private she dared not believe what was happening to her.

"Oh my," she whispered as she wrenched back from the bed, her hands covering her lips as if to hide the evidence.

His eyes sprang open and he gazed at her, a gamut of confusion running across his face.

His eyes mesmerized her, surprised her with their mysterious, velvety black depths. She didn't know what she'd expected, but certainly not this gaze which held so many secrets.

Dark ones.

Why she thought such a thing, she couldn't fathom. She just knew this man wasn't any ordinary young gentleman.

The thought sent a shiver of fear down her spine.

For him. And for her.

"Who are you?" he croaked in a voice hoarse and deep. His lips moved again, but this time barely any sound managed to come out.

She reached over for the pitcher and poured a small amount of water in a cup. Holding it to his lips, she let him take a few sips.

Once he'd drunk, he glanced back up at her. Shakily he raised one hand and touched a loose strand of her hair, his fingers toying with it, while his eyes took on a dreamy cast. "Am I dead?" he whispered.

She shook her head, suddenly finding her usual bravado had deserted her utterly.

"Then you aren't an angel?"

"Certainly not," she told him, finally mustering the courage to speak. Imagine, someone thinking her an angel! Miss Emery wouldn't have sent her home early from school if that were the case.

"Then I'm not in heaven?" he asked, glancing around the shadowy room.

"No," she told him, reaching down to smooth the blanket. "You're in Sussex."

"Some would say that is as good as dead," he managed to jest. "But still, how is it that I have been commended into the care of a goddess, if I am not dead?"

"I'm hardly that," she said, feeling her cheeks flame and that fluttering in her stomach begin anew.

"I beg to differ," he told her. "And I'm a good judge of these things. What is your name then, oh goddess?"

She was almost loath to admit it. "Diana."

His mouth turned into a lopsided grin before he leaned back into his pillow, closing his eyes. "I was right. I am in the care of a goddess," he mumbled before succumbing to the effects of the laudanum.

Just then the door opened ever so slightly.

"Milady?" Lucy poked her head in. "Mary's gone home for the night. Her sister's time has come, and Mary was set on being there when the babe arrives. Should I find someone else to sit with the gentleman?"

Diana shook her head. "No, Lucy, that will be fine. I'll sit with him, and Mrs. Foston will relieve me in a few hours."

The girl glanced at the bed, her lips pursed into a frown. "Do you think you should, milady?"

"Yes, I will be fine. Besides, Michaels will be right outside once he returns from seeing Mrs. Foston upstairs. Now go to bed."

The girl bobbed her head and left.

And Diana slumped down into the chair beside the bed. It had been her decision to bring him here, and now it was her responsibility to see him recovered.

A few hours later, she wasn't as convinced of her abilities.

Her patient struggled to rise from the bed, but stopped halfway up, whether it was from her placing her hands on his chest or the pain from his injuries, she didn't know.

"You must stay still or you'll open your wound," she told him, pressing him back into the comfortable confines of the feather mattress.

"Wound?" he said, looking one way, then the other, until his gaze fixed on the thick wad of linen cloths bound around his shoulder. He cursed and tried again to rise from the bed.

"I won't let you leave," Diana said, blocking his way. "You are in no condition to get out of bed."

The blanket fell away, and for the first time, Diana saw the full expanse of his muscled chest, the raw masculinity of his body. She'd been banned from the room when the footmen and Mrs. Foston had stripped him and cleaned his injuries. Apparently they had removed *all* his clothes.

With one sweeping glance, she understood exactly why young ladies weren't supposed to see men unclad.

"Oh my!" she sputtered, looking away because she knew she was supposed to, not because she wanted to.

The young man cursed. "What have you done with my clothes?" He continued to struggle to get out of the bed. "I must be away. I must get to . . ." His hand went to his forehead, while his words faltered to a halt.

Peeking through her fingers, she saw him wavering. His face had gone so pale, she thought he was going to get his wish and leave Sussex, and England for that matter, permanently.

"I must be away," he managed to say one more time before he fell back into bed, this time in a dead faint.

"Oh, botheration," she whispered, peering down at his prone form on the bed. "I've killed him." And she hadn't even managed to ask him his name.

She would have liked to have known his name, since he was the first man to kiss her.

Then she noticed that his chest was still moving up and down. His face was regaining some color, not much, but enough to cheer her that he wasn't going to die.

At least not yet.

An hour later he began to shiver and shake as if he were caught in a snowdrift, so she piled on every blanket, coverlet, and sheet in the room.

Taking his icy hand, she brought it to her cheek. The warmth of her skin seemed to shake him from his ravings, and he caught hold of her as if she were his savior. With strength she wondered how he could possibly still possess, he yanked her in beside him and curled up against her slight body, clinging to her as if she were a child's beloved toy.

Diana started to protest, but suddenly his body heaved in a great sigh, and his struggles faded away. Even his breathing took on a regular, even keel, so much more soothing than the rasping, heaving gasps that had racked his body but a few moments ago.

"Sleep, my fair goddess," he whispered, his fingers once again toying with a strand of her hair.

"I . . . I . . . shouldn't be here," she stammered. But her protest went unheard, for he was once again asleep.

Fearing waking him or taking away the comfort he found nestled against her body, Diana lay as still as possible, awed by the delicious sensation of being held by a man.

A naked one at that. Oh, if anyone saw them, she'd be ruined.

Glancing over her shoulder at his face, she peered lovingly at the dark stubble starting to grace the strong curve of his jaw, the dark lashes that hid eyes rich and tempting.

Ruination seemed a small price to pay.

Diana sighed. She'd stay this way until just before the servants arose and then assume a more proper distance.

Yes, that was the perfect solution, she thought drowsily. But before she drifted off to sleep, she wondered if she might, by chance, be able to steal one more kiss . . .

Danvers Hall, 1809

The door to the salon opened and Georgie returned, but before she could settle into her seat, the door burst open yet again, and a lithe whirlwind with dark curls and brilliant blue eyes came dashing into the salon.

"Mama, I did as you asked. I listened to Papa and Cousin Temple."

This, Diana decided, must be the elusive Sarah.

Georgie looked neither apologetic nor embarrassed. "I

would have wheedled the truth out of Colin eventually, but this seemed the more direct route." She paused. "You probably think I'm horrid."

"No, inspired," Diana said. Then she turned to Sarah. "What did your Cousin Temple say?"

The girl glanced at her mother, who nodded for her to proceed. "He said he is going to Scotland."

"Oh, Diana, this is good news." Georgie clapped her hands together. "Colin convinced him to marry you."

"Oh no, Mama, Cousin Temple isn't going to marry her. He told Papa to marry her to the first bastard who shows up."

"Sarah!"

Her daughter appeared as unapologetic as her mother had been moments before. "That's *what* Cousin Temple said."

Georgie blew out a disgusted sigh. "Men! It would serve that dunderheaded fool right if you did marry someone else."

Sarah shook her head. "It isn't like that, Mama. Cousin Temple didn't sound all that happy about it. Not in the least. He said it was the only way to see Lady Diana safeguarded."

"Safeguarded!" Diana bounded up from her chair and started to pace furiously from one side of the room to the other. "I am sick to death of that man trying to protect me! Can't he see that it is the other way around? I am trying to save *him*."

She paused in her hysterics for just a moment to look at the mother and daughter who sat side by side, both calmly staring at her.

Sarah turned to her mother. "I rather like her."

"So do I," Georgie said. "So do I."

Diana threw up her hands. "Oh, what am I to do? He's determined to leave me behind."

Georgie stood and made her way to Diana's side as

gracefully as a woman nearing her term could move. She wound her arm around Diana's shoulders and gave her a tight squeeze. "Never fear, I have some experience in these matters."

Chapter 13

The next morning, Colin's voice rang out from his study, echoing through the house like the sharp retort of cannon fire. "Georgie! Blast it, Georgie, where is it?"

In the dining room, Lady Danvers serenely enjoyed her morning repast while the footmen cringed as the master of the house continued his tirade.

"You may go," she told the relieved servants.

They scurried from the dining room knowing full well the mistress and master were going to have one of their "discussions."

There would be no need to lurk about hoping to overhear what was being said. When Lord and Lady Danvers discussed something, it was surprising it wasn't heard in Mayfair.

"Georgie," Colin hollered again. "Drat it, I know you are about. Come out and tell me what you've done."

Georgie smiled and continued buttering her toast.

Colin came barreling into the dining room as if the house were afire and the French were sailing up Lake Windermere, the waters of which sparkled and lapped at the grassy promenade that ran from the shore to the nearby doors. "Where the devil is *it*?"

"Where is what?" she asked, as calmly and innocently as she could muster.

"You know damned well what," Colin said, standing at the head of the table as if he were on the quarterdeck of his ship and shouting orders at his crew.

"Colin, you'll have a fit of apoplexy if you continue in this fashion. That and you'll wake the children, that is, if you haven't already," she scolded. "Now please sit and have some breakfast and we can discuss whatever it is that has you in such a vexing state."

When Colin continued to stand his ground, Georgie's brow cocked and she nodded for him to take a seat.

"Yes, well, sorry for the shouting," he finally muttered, before pulling out his chair and settling into it.

She continued spreading another layer of butter on her piece of toast. "Now what is this all about?"

"I placed some papers in my strongbox last night and this morning they are missing."

Georgie fixed her gaze on her toast. "And you believe I took them. Colin, you know I haven't the skills necessary to open your strongbox. Picking locks is Kit's forte, not mine."

"Yes, well, if your sister were in the house I would be heaping this upon her head, but I still suspect you know where they are."

"And why is that?" she asked.

"Because you have buttered that poor piece of bread three times since I arrived."

Georgie looked down at the pile bending her toast in half and cringed.

"Now do you want to tell me how you got that special license out of my strongbox and where it is?"

Georgie wasn't about to confess that Kit had taught her how to pick locks on her last visit to Danvers Hall. Instead she launched a swift counterattack. "You certainly didn't think I'd stand idly by while you married poor Lady Diana off to one of those nobcocks, did you? How could you even consider such a notion?"

Colin threw his hands in the air. "Georgie Danvers, I'll not be drawn into another argument by letting you taunt me with false colors. Now where is that special license?"

"I gave it to Lady Diana. I thought she should have it. If a woman is going to be married off in some hideous bride sale, then at least she should have some say in the matter."

"She'll have plenty of say. I have no intention of seeing her wed to anyone but Temple." Colin glanced around the room. "By the way, where is Lady Diana?"

"The poor dear was so worn out yesterday after her travels, I fear she went to bed quite exhausted."

It hadn't answered Colin's question, but at least it was the truth.

"Well, good. The longer she stays asleep, the better off she is. And she must stay out of sight, Georgie. I need your help on this. If we are to keep her safe for Temple, she needs to remain out of sight. The servants need to be instructed to tell anyone who asks that the marquis and Lady Diana left at first light for Gretna."

Something in his grave tone tweaked at Georgie's conscience. "Colin, whatever for? You sound so serious."

"I am. I fear Diana is in terrible danger."

Georgie chewed on her lip for a moment. "As bad as all that? Are you certain?"

Colin cocked his head and stared at his wife. "What have you done? Georgie, tell me immediately. What have you done?"

The great clock in the hall struck the hour and Georgie sighed in relief. She'd promised Diana she wouldn't say a word until after ten, lest Colin try to stop their plan.

Now she was free to tell the entire story. So she did.

Colin sat in his chair for a few moments, shaking his head, as if he couldn't believe this, his wife's latest scandal. "Georgie," he said, his voice ominous in its tone. "How could you?"

"She loves him," Georgie rushed to say. "And you know he loves her. Oh Colin, can you forgive me?"

Then her husband surprised her and laughed. "Forgive you? I'm just dumbfounded I didn't think of it myself." He rose from his chair and held out his arms. "Come here, Georgie girl. Have I told you how much I love you?"

"Not today," she said, falling into the warm embrace of the man she loved so very much. Casting a glance out the window at the road beyond, she said a little prayer that Lady Diana would be as lucky.

Temple drove the carriage northward along the shore of Lake Windermere as if the devil were nipping at their heels. Elton sat beside him grumbling.

With no one about, Elton wasn't about to let Temple off lightly, heir to a dukedom or not.

"Don't see why you don't just marry the gel," his servant said. "Then we wouldn't have to drive all the way to Scotland on some fool's errand." He spat over the side, as if to punctuate his displeasure.

"I cannot marry Lady Diana," Temple told him.

"Don't see why not." Elton crossed his arms over his chest and nodded at a pothole up ahead. "She's not bad looking and she'll come with a passel of money."

Temple drove around the hole that could have swallowed

a pony cart or at least one of their wheels. "I'm not going to discuss the matter, Elton, so you might as well leave off."

"Harrumph," the man snorted and closed his eyes. "Got to marry one day, lad. No two ways around that. Can't figure what ye're waiting for." Elton leaned back in his seat and pretended to sleep.

Temple wasn't fooled. He knew it worried the man to distraction when he decided to drive. Elton was convinced that Temple would put them into the ditch one day.

But he needed to be in control of something. Lord knew he had little control over his own life.

Once, for a few glorious days, years ago, he'd lived the life he'd always wanted. With Diana.

But even now, when he looked back on those precious days at Lamden House, he often wondered if it had been naught but a dream. For by the time he'd returned to London, he had been rudely reawakened to the life that lay ahead for him.

London, 1796

The Foster ball was one of the premier opening events each Season, and it appeared this year was going to be no different.

The Marquis of Templeton stood near the door watching the arriving guests. He dismissed one young lady after another, for he was waiting for the arrival of a certain miss.

Lady Diana Fordham.

It had been over two months since he'd last seen her, kissed her, and he was anxious to renew his suit.

When Temple had woken up that first morning at Lamden Hall, it was to a throbbing shoulder and memories of a beautiful young woman whispering encouragement to him, offering him her lips as a balm to the hell he was feeling.

And over the fortnight that he spent recuperating there,

Diana had been a constant figure in his sickroom, despite Mrs. Foston's best efforts to keep her impetuous charge well away from him.

Obviously the lady knew what was behind her young charge's flushed cheeks and starry-eyed gaze.

And though he hadn't done anything too dishonorable, he wasn't about to let anyone else have the chance.

Lady Diana Fordham wouldn't be available for very long this Season. He intended to call on her father first thing tomorrow morning.

He continued his sentry's watch of the door, when to his dismay, he heard his grandfather's voice behind him.

"That you, boy?" the duke called out.

Temple flinched. He couldn't help himself. He'd be one-and-twenty soon and still he found himself cringing each time the duke crossed his path.

While other men took great pride in their heirs, Temple knew he was a miserable disappointment. His grandfather made sure to remind him of that fact each time they met.

"There you are, boy," his grandfather said, coming to stand beside him. There was no handshake exchanged, no words of good wishes. The duke found such displays nothing more than weak-minded falderal.

"Heard you were shot," His Grace said, in a matter-of-fact tone that would have been more appropriate if he'd been asking Temple how he liked the cattle offered at Tatt's the previous week. "I won't stand for it, boy. Won't have you throwing your life away."

Temple tamped down the anger welling up inside him. He might be his grandfather's heir, but that didn't give the duke the right to dictate his life. "I have no intention of ending my work for the Foreign Office just because of my recent inconvenience."

"Inconvenience!" the old man snorted. "You damned near died."

Temple glanced at his grandfather. From anyone else that might have sounded like genuine concern, but he knew that such feelings were impossible coming from the duke.

At least she cared, a small voice whispered. *She loves you.*

At the doorway, a bevy of young ladies was entering. Temple did his best to glance nonchalantly in their direction. The last thing he wanted to do was to alert his grandfather as to his feelings for one certain miss.

He shouldn't have worried; his grandfather was lecturing him once again and hadn't an inkling of the rebellion Temple was considering.

Outright anarchy, the duke would call it.

". . . I'll not have it. Mark my words. You are my heir and as such you will do as I say."

"And that is, Your Grace?" he murmured.

His grandfather's face colored darker than his favorite claret. "Demmit boy, listen to me. You will cease these common heroics and settle down. Why, I'd rather see you turn into one of these featherbrained popinjays that all the town considers fashionable than continue risking *my* dukedom for some ill-conceived idea of nobility." To emphasize his point, he waved his hand in dismissal at a young rake dressed to the nines and turning heads with his outlandish fashions and exaggerated manners. "True nobility is knowing when to send your inferiors to do the job."

Just then Diana entered the room. She paused for a second at the doorway, and glanced about the room until her gaze met his. Then her starry eyes sparkled just as he remembered.

He felt as if they were the only two people in the room, but unfortunately they weren't. Worse yet, his grandfather noticed.

"She's a right fetching gel. A bit lively though, but that could be *improved*."

Temple spoke before he considered his words. "I wouldn't want to see her improved."

"Bah!" the duke sputtered. "You'll change your mind soon enough after you marry her." Before Temple could utter a word to the contrary, the duke stopped him, holding up his aristocratic hand in a gesture that was known to silence the House of Lords. "I've heard the rumors. I know you fancy her. So go ahead and marry the girl. Bring a good dowry, and we might even get the King to join Lamden's earldom into the Setchfield title." The man puffed out his chest and rubbed his hands together as if it was all settled. "Oh, I have my reservations about the match. Lamden's been too lenient with the chit. But a few weeks at Setchfield Place and she'll understand what nobility means. I'll see to that."

Chills ran down the length of Temple's limbs at the thought of Diana being subjected to the duke's heartless definition of nobility.

He knew it only too well. It had been beaten into him every day since his own parents had drawn their last breaths and the duke had taken charge of his young heir with a ruthless ambition.

"Your Grace," he said in the best civil tone he could manage, "when I marry I have no intention of living at Setchfield Place."

The duke laughed, chortling guffaws that held no humor, only mockery. "You don't, do you? And where do you propose you'll live, boy?"

When Temple didn't answer, standing moot and ramrod-straight, the duke only laughed harder.

His grandfather continued. "You'll live where I say and when I say. As long as I'm alive, you haven't anything to your credit but what *I* give you." His eyes narrowed and his voice lowered to tones meaner than a badger. "Don't you ever forget that."

Even then, Diana flashed a smile in his direction, a smile capable of inspiring mutiny. Make a man believe that he could slay dragons. Even the ducal kind.

But his grandfather was a shrewd man and most likely saw the insurrection brewing in his heir.

"Don't you get any foolish notions like your father did. He thought he could marry against my wishes and live on your mother's money, live on their love for each other. Live on love! Bah! We know what came of that, now don't we?"

His great gray brows drew together in a stormy line. "Once your mother's money ran out they had no choice but to come crawling back to Setchfield Place begging like a pair of ragtag gypsies." The duke shot another glance over in Diana's direction. "Love destroyed your father. Took his pride. Made him weak to your mother's demands. I won't see you make his mistakes."

Temple wanted to tell the duke that it wasn't true, that love hadn't made his father anything but happy, but in some ways what his grandfather was saying was true, and that in itself was enough to terrify him.

Setchfield rubbed his hands together as if they'd reached some sort of accord. "There now, I'll send my man around to gather up your things and have them installed in my town house. In the meantime, I'll see to the settlement and all. I won't have Lamden thinking he can send her off with less than our due."

The duke's machinations chilled Temple to the core. This was exactly why he'd disavowed his grandfather's money in the first place, why he chose to live in near poverty.

What had he been thinking? It was bad enough that he

was ensnared by his grandfather's ill will, but he couldn't ask Diana to share such a prison.

He tried to hold on to the memories of his fortnight with her, the joy of her kiss, the brilliant sparkle in her eyes. But in the face of his grandfather's scorn, he felt his grasp on those precious memories slip away.

For he would never come crawling to Setchfield Place as his father and mother had. In humiliation, subjecting themselves to the duke's control, his scorn.

"Sir, I'm not moving back into your house." Temple glanced once again at Diana, this time seeing her as if she were some far away dream. He wasn't going to make his father's mistake . . . to follow his heart and live to regret his folly. "You've made a mistake. I have no intention of marrying the chit."

His grandfather's eyes narrowed. "Don't think you can cut a better deal with Lamden behind my back. I've already spoken to him, and he's not all that fond of the union. Thinks I'll bedevil his precious girl. The only way you'll win his approval is with my help, and I won't give it unless you agree to my conditions."

"That, sir, will never happen," Temple told him. And he meant it, with every ounce of fortitude he possessed.

"Hmm. Don't want to live on foolish pride, eh?" The duke eyed him once again. "Got more sense than I thought. Perhaps we are cut from the same cloth." He cocked his nose in the air and glanced over the crowded room, like a lion eyeing its dinner. "Upon my honor, there's Fellerby. 'Bout time someone informed him what an idiot he is." He stomped off, his next victim well in his sights.

Temple's heart cracked.

Yet what could he do? He had no income other than the nominal salary Pymm paid him—which was barely enough for him to live on without having to take a farthing from his grandfather. But to ask Diana to share his poverty? He couldn't do that.

One day he might inherit his grandfather's title and riches, but Temple knew better than to cling to that hopeful thought—the Setchfield dukes were a wretchedly long-lived lot, and his grandfather showed no signs of doing anyone the favor of dying.

Live on love, some long-lost voice seemed to urge him. *Go ahead, my boy.*

Temple shook his head. What had it gained his parents? A life spent at the whim and mercy of the duke. He tried to remember that they'd been miserable, unhappy, but he couldn't. His parents' love had been like a blindness to everything but themselves. He couldn't fathom how they had done it, for they'd lived in their own world, despite the duke, spoke their own language, and in the end, died within days of each other rather than be apart.

Leaving him alone. So very alone.

Yes, he'd seen the results of that futile dream and the anguish it left in its wake.

Temple closed his eyes and took a deep breath. And when he looked again he spied the overly fashionable young man who'd paraded by earlier and earned the duke's complete and utter disdain.

Suddenly he saw a new way to ensure that he and his grandfather weren't cut from the same cloth.

"I do say, sir," Temple asked. "Who is your tailor?"

"Me, sir?" the man asked, holding up a lorgnette and striking a particularly foolish pose. "Say, aren't you Templeton, Setchfield's heir?"

"I am. But Temple is the address my friends use. And you, sir?"

The man preened anew. "Lord Stewart Hodges. But to

you, Stewie. Now, sir, you were asking about my tailor. I was just about to head to White's for a meal. Join me and we could discuss the matter in some detail. Besides, not much of account here. I was hoping to pay my addresses to a certain young lady tonight, but it appears she wasn't invited. An heiress, mind you." He sighed. "Bit on the thin side since my father died, and my brother isn't so generous. Second son, and all. So I've got to find a bride this year. Suppose I'll have to suffer Almack's for that."

Temple forced a laugh and followed Stewie to the door.

But only too quickly Diana was in his path, her sweet lips parted in a broad smile, her eyes full of love for him.

The chattering words from his newfound friend fell silent. In fact, the entire room seemed to still.

Faltering only for a second, he ignored the hammering in his heart, the joy of being so close to her again, and stepped around her, continuing toward the door.

"Temple," Diana cried out.

He kept walking.

"Temple!" she called out, a rising tide of panic and pain filling her voice.

Not even he could ignore that. He came to a halt.

And now, to his annoyance, the room did grow quiet at the prospect of some scandalous display about to be played out.

Stewie glanced over his shoulder. "I say, do you know that bossy chit?"

Temple turned and looked at her, sweeping his gaze from the top of her head to the tips of her satin slippers as if he were searching for some remarkable feature with which to revive his memory.

Mrs. Foston stood behind her, her hand on Diana's shoulder restraining her charge from bolting forward and making a further spectacle of herself.

"Do you know her, Temple?" Stewie asked again, stepping up to his side like a second, as if they had been boon companions for years rather than mere moments.

He shook his head, looking directly at the woman he loved so very much, and said, "No, I can't say as I do. Deplorable manners, don't you agree, Stewie?"

Diana gasped, the blast of it like an icy wind cleaving his heart in two.

And yet even as the chill of her anguish seemed to cut him off from life itself, hope held on to a tiny spark, and sent up one last prayer, before Temple locked his love away forever.

Wait for me, goddess.

Lake District, 1809

The first jolt brought Temple's attention back to the road. The second one threw him from his perch.

For those infinitely long seconds as he catapulted through the air, he knew he should be having some inspired moment of insight before he died, but the only thing he could think of was Elton's admonishment.

Marry the gel.

Fine words indeed to end one's life with, he thought wryly, especially when he realized that his servant was right.

Diana will never know the truth. I love her with all my heart.

He landed in a hedge, the thorns shredding his coat, cutting him in a hundred different places, but much to his chagrin he lived.

Behind him he heard the carriage come to a crashing halt,

the horses screaming in protest at the tangled mess behind them.

He tore himself free from his barbed snare and staggered to where the toppled carriage had come to rest.

"Elton!" he yelled. "Where are you?"

His driver clung to the seat atop the carriage, the wily man having somehow managed to ride out the storm.

"Last time I let him drive," he was promising the frantic horses as he scrambled down from the wreckage. Elton calmed them with soft words and a gentle touch here and there. Once he was satisfied the beasts were fine, he shot an assessing glance at Temple and smirked.

"Landed in the briars, eh?" Elton chuckled at his own joke.

Temple didn't find anything at all amusing about their situation, since it seemed that half the thorns were still stuck in his coat.

Besides, he was supposed to be the decoy to lead the French away from Diana, not the sitting duck for them to swoop down and discover.

"Can we continue?" he asked.

Elton held up his hands, then walked around the carriage to survey the damage.

On the far side, they found their problem. One of the wheels lay cracked and tilted to one side.

Elton eyed it critically and then announced, "Not as bad as it seems. We can probably mend it well enough to get us to Ambleside. I'll get my tools."

Temple followed him, divesting himself of his jacket and rolling up his shirtsleeves. If his grandfather could see him now, he'd probably be more ashamed of his heir for lowering himself to common work than for being London's premier fool.

This was no time, however, for aristocratic privileges.

At the back of the carriage, Elton was having trouble getting the trunk open. The accident had left the lid wedged tight.

As Temple and Elton started to shove it open, there came from within a frantic pounding.

They stepped back from the trunk and stared at it in shock.

"Botheration," a voice called out. "I'm stuck in here. Get me out!"

Diana.

Temple ignored her, and instead turned to Elton. "Did you know about this?"

His servant shook his head. "We'd better get her out of there."

"I say we leave her inside," Temple said. "Serve the little baggage right."

"I heard that," Diana called out. This was followed by more pounding and cursing.

With a particularly hearty kick, the lid came wrenching open. A rumpled and rattled Lady Diana sat up. She frowned at the pair of them, then turned her ire toward Temple. "I suppose *you* were driving."

It wasn't a question but an accusation, one that pricked at Temple's anger more so than the discovery of her presence.

He should be furious with her, but a tiny part of him sent up a mighty "huzzah."

For if Diana wasn't at Danvers Hall, she wasn't about to be married to another man.

But as much as Temple wanted to celebrate that fact, Diana's arrival in their midst only meant she was now in more danger than before.

Not that it seemed to matter to the lady.

Diana took a deep breath and began to climb out of the trunk. She didn't dare ask for help, for Temple looked mad enough to be on the verge of ordering Elton to shut her back in.

"What the devil are you doing in there?" he finally said.

"What does it look like," she shot back, realizing that helpless and innocent were no longer going to work to her advantage. "I'm coming with you."

"I don't recall inviting you along."

She caught hold of the edge of the trunk and threw herself over the side and into the dusty road. "Yes, well, you have a bad habit of not consulting me before you make decisions regarding my life." She brushed off her skirt and then placed her hands on her hips.

"What were you thinking, hiding in there?" he asked. "You might have been killed."

"I wouldn't have had that problem if you would let Elton drive. Really, Temple, you're a terrible whip."

She bustled past the two of them and tipped her head to survey the damage. "I think I heard you say you could fix it?" She directed this question at Elton, deliberately ignoring Temple.

"Aye, miss, I could have," Elton replied, as he glanced up from her hiding spot. "But it doesn't look like we'll be getting very far now."

"Why not?" This came from Temple.

"Because the tool case is missing."

Diana bit her lip and glanced back inside the box. "Do you mean that rather heavy sack that was inside there?"

"Aye."

"I fear it was in the way," she said, backing up a few steps. "I had to leave it behind so I would fit."

Temple reached inside the trunk and pulled out her valise. "But I suppose *this* was necessary?"

She plucked it from his hands, for fear he would cast it into the lake. "Of course. You couldn't expect me to travel without my belongings."

Temple groaned and started stalking toward her.

Diana suspected her valise wasn't the only thing Temple was considering tossing into the dappled water.

"Sssh." Elton hushed them both as if they were a pair of noisy, errant children. "Someone is coming."

Temple caught her by the arm. "Back inside you go."

"I don't hear a thing," Diana said, shaking at Temple's uncompromising grasp and digging her heels into the gravel. "Now let me go."

"If someone is coming, then the only way to see you safe is to see you hidden away."

"If you think you can stuff me back inside that trunk on such a flimsy claim, make no mistake, you'll find yourself back in the thorns."

And even as Diana was about to make good on her threat, the distinctive *clip-clop* of horses's hooves and the grinding turn of wheels echoed down the road.

Diana and Temple froze, while Elton shot them both a look of pure redemption.

"Goodness, you were right," Diana whispered. "We are being followed."

Temple let go of her abruptly and strode over to the carriage, ripping and pulling at the jumbled contents inside the wreckage in search of something. Elton had gone to the front and was doing the same, rummaging about under the driver's seat.

For a moment, Diana stood rooted in place, her gaze fixed on the bend in the road some hundred or so yards away. Then she remembered the gift that Georgie had given her before the lady had helped Diana stow herself away in the carriage.

She ran over to her forgotten valise, thankful that it hadn't gone flying into the lake.

Temple came around the side, a pistol in his hand. "Get in the trunk," he told her.

"No," she said, still rummaging in her valise. Her fingers closed around Lady Danvers' gift.

"Do as I say," he said in a steely voice that surprised even Diana. "I won't have you taken. And I won't have you harmed."

"If they think I'm the King's daughter, they won't harm me." She rose up from the ground, brandishing Georgie's pistol. "And I have no intention of being stolen by anyone."

Chapter 14

Temple had been faced with many adversaries in his life, but never had he seen such a look of fear and shock as was on the face of the poor farmer who rounded the bend in the road and discovered three armed people pointing weapons at his poor load.

The man dropped his reins as his hands went flying up in the air. The tired plow horse gave out a great sigh of relief, thinking that his journey was over and came to a happy, plodding halt.

A black-and-white wiry-haired dog, the size of a well-fed cat, sat up in the seat beside the driver, his paws in the air.

"Yes, he appears quite the dangerous French agent," Diana said, tossing a disgusted glance at Temple and Elton. "Especially his well-trained partner."

"Our sincerest apologies, sir," Diana called out, handing Temple her pistol, and approaching the man with that enchanting smile of hers that always made Temple say yes even when he'd vowed to say otherwise.

"Gave me quite a start, you did," the man said, his hands

still in the air. He shot a nervous glance over her shoulder at Temple and Elton.

Diana waved her hand at both of them, and then glared until they put their weapons down. "I fear we were set upon earlier in the day and thought the brigands were returning." She sniffed and made a delicate little shudder, as if the memory of the experience was about to put her into a state of vapors.

"Oh miss, that sounds right terrible."

"Yes, it was," Diana readily agreed. "I fear I will never be the same."

Temple thought she was starting to put on the brown a bit thick, even for this simple fellow, but Diana had the man eating out of her hand.

"And your carriage?" the man asked.

"Ruined," she said, an air of desperation clinging to her words. She leaned forward and whispered loudly. "Our man let my husband drive, and he hasn't much skill." She hung her head and shook it, as if it were her greatest embarrassment to have such a spouse.

Husband?

Temple decided to take over before she had him wrapped in wool and pushing into his dotage. He stepped in front of Diana. "Sir, could we ask your assistance? Our tool chest was waylaid, and we have a broken wheel that needs mending."

The man nodded his head, appearing all too relieved not to have to be dealing with a potentially hysterical lady. "Aye, sir, that I can. I've lost my fair share of wheels on this road." With that, the man climbed down from his wagon and joined Elton and Temple in examining the carriage.

"Temple, I'd have a word with you," she said, catching him by the arm.

He shook her free. "It will have to wait."

Thus dismissed, Diana went over to her valise and fetched

the bag of food Georgie had sent with her and settled on a nearby rock for a few biscuits and a tin of cold tea.

The farmer's dog, a quick creature with a patch of white over one eye, jumped down from the seat and dashed over to Diana's side, settling in at her feet. His paw scratched at her shoe and he tipped his head just so, as if to let her know he wasn't averse to sharing.

"I wouldn't be feeding him, missus," the farmer said. "I made that mistake a few weeks ago when he wandered onto me farm, and he moved right in."

"What type of dog is he?" she asked, ignoring his warning and tossing the fellow a bite of biscuit.

The dog caught the piece and then bowed his head.

"I think the better question would be what kind of dog isn't he," Temple said.

The farmer scratched his head. "I think he's just a regular dog, missus. Nothing fancy."

"Does he have a name?" she asked, tossing the little charmer another piece of biscuit.

"None that I know of. And don't say I dinna warn you. You'll never be rid of him now. I was taking him into town for me mum. She don't like dogs, but I can't keep him. My best collie has been put out and won't herd since His Majesty there arrived, full of tricks and stunts, he is."

Diana didn't care. The little fellow tipped his head again and grinned at her. She gave him another piece.

By the time they had managed to wrestle the carriage upright and get the wheel back on, the dog was happily snoring at her feet.

Temple came over to her side. "The wheel isn't safe to carry a load, so Mr. Maguire has offered to bring us along in his wagon, while Elton follows with the carriage."

Diana nodded and rose. "Come along, Tullius," she said,

and immediately the dog sprang awake and trotted along at the very edge of her skirt, casting an admiring glance up at her every few steps.

"Tullius?" Temple asked. "Isn't that a little formal for someone of his, shall we say, questionable breeding."

She smiled down at the little fellow. "Then I shall call him Tully. Come along, Tully."

The farmer's wagon was loaded with a stack of firewood, crates of chickens, and buckets of milk.

"For me mum," he said, pushing the load aside, to make room for Temple and Diana. "She likes living in town now, so I bring her in some supplies once a month." He turned to Temple. "Not a good idea to have your mother live with you when you decide to take a wife."

Temple nodded, as if the two men were in perfect accord on the subject. He turned to Diana and held out his hand. "Your carriage, my lady." He eyed the open back of the wagon, and then caught her by the waist and swung her up. For a moment, he found himself staring into her eyes.

The recrimination and the questions there tore at his gut.

"You shouldn't have left me."

"I had to," he said without even thinking.

"You had to? Leave me for another man to claim? Ridiculous. Did you ever consider asking me what I thought about that notion?"

Before Temple could respond, Mr. Maguire called back, "Are you both settled?"

"Yes, sir," Diana called up to him sweetly, smiling as Temple went to scramble into the empty space beside her.

But he wasn't fast enough. Tully bounced up from the road as if he were made of springs and sat himself down next to Diana.

"Away, mutt," Temple said, now trotting behind the wagon.

Tully looked once at Diana, then growled fiercely at Temple.

Diana smiled and wrapped her arm around the little dog.

Temple made one last frantic leap up onto the wagon and plopped down beside his new rival. "You do have a way of collecting the more discerning beaux."

"I doubt he'd leave me behind."

"At least not until you run out of those biscuits."

"That doesn't explain why you left me with Colin."

"'Tis complicated."

"Because you think I'm Louis's bastard daughter?" she whispered.

He nearly toppled out the back of the wagon. "How did you—" Temple stopped himself. Staged elopements, stealing away in trunks, and now eavesdropping? He made a note to himself to keep Diana and Georgie well separated in the future. Colin's wife had probably chronicled his entire conversation as to Diana's likely parentage. And wasted no time in sharing her discovery with Diana.

Pymm would be hard-pressed to find two better spies for England.

"It's not true," she was saying, her voice lowered to an urgent hiss.

Temple shot a glance over his shoulder at the farmer. Satisfied the man wasn't listening, nor could he hear over the cackle of the chickens and the creaking of the wagon, he still lowered his voice. "Whether you are or aren't his daughter matters not to me."

"Well, I'm not his daughter. The notion is ridiculous."

"Not to Marden."

She looked at him. "Or you. You think I am. How can you believe such a thing?"

"The mark on your shoulder, for one thing."

" 'Tis nothing but an accident of birth."

"That mark is no accident, Diana. It's a brand. It was put there on purpose."

Her brow furrowed, and she crossed her arms over her chest. "Oh, hang that mark. If you were a gentleman you wouldn't have mentioned it. And not to Colin."

"If you were a lady I wouldn't even know you possessed it."

She colored and looked away. The wagon rattled and shook its way down the road at a wretchedly slow pace.

After a time, Diana spoke again. "Don't you think I have as much right, nay more so, to discover the truth of all this? If it were you, would you have stayed behind to let others discover the truth?"

He couldn't deny that.

"I'm coming with you," she said with quiet resolution.

Temple was caught. It wasn't as if he could turn around and take her back to Colin's. They'd most likely run right into Marden and his murderous lot.

"I'm going with you, Temple," she repeated. "I won't be wed without knowing who I am."

"Aye, Diana. As you wish."

Now with her added to their party, Temple considered his best course of action to see them to Scotland quickly. If they could get to Ambleside before midday, there was a fair chance that they could hire a new carriage and be on their way before Marden caught up with them.

For now that she was making this quest hers, he was resolved to help her find her identity.

And then he would see her married.

Temple's plan seemed sound until they arrived on the outskirts of Ambleside. Set at the head of Lake Windermere, the city appeared a serene haunt for those who loved the tranquil waters of the lake and the misty mountains beneath which the hamlet sat nestled.

As they drew near the city, Diana fished out her beloved travelogue.

To his chagrin, she began to read aloud.

" 'It is believed that the quaint village we now know as Ambleside was originally the Roman fort of Galava, built in the first century of our Lord. The Roman fortifications along Lake Windermere acted as vital link between the port city of Ravenglass to the west and extending all the way north to Hadrian's Wall.' "

Temple eyed the distance to the lake and considered if he could possibly throw that wretched volume far enough out into the waters so that not even Diana would dare venture out to save it.

Diana, on the other hand, was eyeing the mountains around them and then glanced back at Temple. "I would so like to see Hadrian's Wall. Will we be going near it?"

"Need I remind you that this is not a sightseeing trip?"

She shrugged. "Yes, I know that time is of the essence, but if we just happen to be passing that way . . ."

Temple's reply was saved by the shuddering halt of the wagon as it stopped before a neat little cottage. The stone house was covered with ivy, while a yellow rose bush tumbled over the doorway. The instant the wagon came to rest, a woman bustled outside, her arms wide and her face not all that dissimilar from Mr. Maguire's.

"Johnny," she called out. "I've been expecting you for hours."

"Aye, Mum," he replied, climbing down from his wagon and letting himself be enveloped by his mother's embrace. "There now, that's enough, Mum," he told her, shaking himself free. "I had to help these poor people, so it delayed me. You weren't worried, now were you?"

The woman tousled her son's hair as if he were a youngster returning from an afternoon lark. "Not in the least." She glanced over at the wagon and frowned. "I had hoped that you'd bring Jane. I have so much to tell her, why I'll never remember all the talk next month." She shook her finger at her son. "That wife of yers is sure to be vexed that she's missed all the excitement."

Mr. Maguire seemed unimpressed with the idea of excitement. Perhaps finding three armed strangers on the road was enough for him in one day.

"Just the same, who have ye brought along with ye?" his mother was asking. "Perhaps they've an ear for gossip." She cast a curious gaze at Temple and Diana, her eyes narrowing as she looked over at Diana. "You wouldn't be that bride everyone is talking about, now would you?" Before Diana could stammer a denial, the lady marched over until her nose practically touched Diana's. She squinted and cocked her head. "No, I can see it now. You're too old to be this heiress."

Nudging Temple, Mrs. Maguire leaned toward him. "From what I hear, these heiresses are young, innocent things. This one has a sharp-eyed look about her. Probably keeps you in line. Harrumph! Though I imagine she has her work cut out for her in that task," she said, giving him a saucy glance that had probably worked much better fifty years earlier.

"She has her ways," Temple confided.

"Good for you, gel," the lady told Diana, winding her arm with Diana's and pulling her down from the wagon. As she led her along the path toward the open door, Mrs. Maguire said, "Marriage works best when a man knows his place.

Some said I kept my John laced too tight, but he didn't come home drunk and he never raised a hand to me. And that's what's important."

Diana smiled at the woman. "Perhaps we should find this heiress and see to it that she starts her married life off on the right foot."

Mrs. Maguire laughed heartily. "Gel, if I was to give that heiress my advice it would be this: Don't get married. Keep the money for yourself."

Both women laughed, though Temple didn't think Mrs. Maguire's advice was all that amusing. Still, the lady obviously knew about their plight, and if so, that meant that Penham and Nettlestone were nearby, or worse, Marden had cast his net in a wider circle than Temple had suspected.

"Mrs. Maguire," Temple called out. "Who is this heiress?"

The lady stopped, turned and cocked a brow. "What would ye be needing with an heiress?"

"One never knows," Temple said, offering her a wicked gleam and a wink.

Mrs. Maguire let out a whoop. She turned to Diana. "Oh, gel, you've picked a rare one." She chuckled some more, then smiled. "Well, since Jane isn't here, I might as well share my news with you folks. Johnny hasn't the inclination for a good tattle."

Johnny snorted and continued to unload the supplies he'd brought his mother. "Some of us have work to do rather than spending our days gabbing over the fence."

"Bah!" she said, waving her hand at him. "I've done my years of work, let an old woman have her fun." She turned to Temple, "Now where was I?"

"This heiress?"

"Ah yes. Ran away with one man and then killed him when she decided to set off with another."

Temple cast a sly glance at Diana and spied the shock on her face.

"I hardly think the lady would kill her own betrothed," Diana said, rather defensively to Temple's ears.

The lady shook her head. "The ruin of money, I tell you."

Temple nodded in agreement, only to find Diana shooting him a hot glance. "Is there more?" he asked, doing his best to ignore her murderous gaze. If he wasn't careful, Mrs. Maguire would be adding his name to the list of Diana's alleged victims. "I can't imagine why this young lady hasn't been apprehended."

Mrs. Maguire edged closer to him, having found an eager audience. "From what I heard just this morning, she's a sly, wicked thing."

"Indeed!" Temple said. "How so?"

"They almost had her in Buxton not but a few days ago. But she used her wiles to escape."

"Wiles?" he asked, feigning an innocence that sent Diana into a choking fit.

Mrs. Maguire shot her an annoyed look for interrupting her tale.

"Dust from the road," Temple explained.

"The well is out back," Mrs. Maguire told her. "Go fetch yerself a drink."

"No, I'll be fine," Diana muttered through gritted teeth. "Pray, do go on."

"Where was I?" Mrs. Maguire asked.

"Wiles," Temple and Diana said at the same time.

"Ah, yes. As I was saying, this gel used her wiles to escape the authorities in Buxton when she . . . when she"—the lady shot a glance over at her son, who wasn't paying them any heed, but still she leaned forward and whispered—"went naked to a fancy assembly."

"Wha-a-at?" Diana sputtered. "I never—"

"—heard such a thing," Temple said, finishing her outraged response, and placing his arm around her protectively, as if he were shielding her from such shocking information.

In truth, he gave her a warning squeeze, and she heeded his advice by keeping any further protests to herself.

Their benefactress shook her head. "I never heard such a thing either. But it's the honest truth, it is. I had it from a peddler just this morning."

"A fine source, I would estimate," Temple said.

"He is, he is indeed," Mrs. Maguire replied.

To this, her son muttered something under his breath about "idle tongues."

They ignored him, and Mrs. Maguire retook her audience with the next of the heiress's adventures.

"After this heiress gave the good people of Buxton such a turn, she went on to force a seamstress, at gunpoint mind you, to make her a new wardrobe, one of them *trousseaus*, I hear tell about. French nonsense, to be sure. Just the same, the poor seamstress has been in a fit of vapors ever since."

"Utter nonsense," Diana muttered.

Mrs. Maguire missed the point of Diana's words, saying, "Isn't it though? New clothes because ye're getting wed. Let me tell you, if yer old ones were good enough to catch him, they should be good enough to keep him."

"You're a sensible woman, Mrs. Maguire," Temple told her.

"Well, thank you, sir," she said, preening under his praise. "Some folks don't see that," she said, shooting a gaze at her son.

"Amazing," Temple said. "Don't you think so?" he asked Diana, giving her a squeeze.

She wiggled out of his embrace, and began smoothing her

rumpled cloak. "Yes, quite so," she managed to reply. "Now about this heiress, you were saying she gained a new set of clothes, but what sort of man is this she's gone to such lengths to share her misdeeds with? Perhaps it is his evil influence that has led her to this life of discontent."

The lady snapped her fingers. "I knew you were a smart one the moment I saw you. That was my first thought exactly. This fellow was to blame for all of it, but sadly that isn't true."

Temple shot a knowing look at Diana. But his superiority didn't last too long.

"You'd expect that it would be all his fault, her fall into disgrace, but from what I heard from the peddler, her latest betrothed is nothing but one of those town fellows, a regular idler." Mrs. Maguire tapped her finger to her skull as if she were checking a melon in the marketplace. "Daft upstairs, if you know what I mean. Hasn't got the wits to tie his own laces, let alone mastermind half these capers. Obviously this gel found herself a cabbage-head for a groom so she can gain her inheritance without the hindrance of some smart fellow stealing what's rightfully hers."

"Mrs. Maguire," Diana said, beaming from ear to ear, "that sounds like the closest thing to the truth I've heard in ages."

Diana paced across the short expanse of Mrs. Maguire's garden. Temple sat on the bench before her, his brows creased into a worried line.

The lady had gone to see that her son didn't spill the milk down the cellar steps, "like he's done the last two times," she said.

They were alone now that Elton had driven on to the wheelwright's, and they sat trying to come up with a plan in the face of the additional information that the talkative lady had provided.

"The two lords she spoke of must be Penham and Nettle-stone," Diana said aloud. "Who else would want to set up a trap to stop us?"

Temple glanced at her, his eyes widening.

"Yes, well, and the authorities from Geddington," she added. "But to set up roadblocks between here and Penrith, that seems a bit excessive, don't you think?"

"You heard Mrs. Maguire, you're worth twenty thousand a year, it would make a man do just about anything to have such a bride."

Diana glanced heavenward and sighed. "Such an exaggeration. Twenty thousand a year. Really! 'Tis only fifteen."

"Fifteen thousand?" Temple sputtered. "Why, even that's a fortune."

"Yes, I suppose so," Diana said.

"And here I thought you were only worth two, maybe three thousand a year. But fifteen? If I were Penham and Nettlestone, I'd have a net spread from here to the border to make sure you didn't slip through my grasp." He let out an exasperated sigh.

"There has got to be another way around Penrith, Temple. If we could just slip past these roadblocks, then we'd gain ourselves enough time to cross the border." She knelt before him. "Do you really believe that my answers lay in Scotland?"

"Yes. I have a cousin there. He's done some work for Pymm, and his knowledge of the clans and their secrets is astounding." He nodded toward the high fells surrounding the town. "But unless we can grow wings and fly, there is no other way to Penrith but along the roads on which Penham and Nettlestone, and most likely Marden, have their eyes and ears firmly placed."

Diana wasn't listening to the rest of what he was saying,

for the first part of his statement had tripped something in the back of her mind.

Grow wings and fly. She'd heard those words before.

"Grow wings and fly," she repeated. "Temple, that's it! That's exactly how we'll slip past them." She rose up and kissed him and then raced over to the wagon. Flinging open her valise, she caught up her guidebook, frantically thumbing through it until she got to the passages she recalled reading not a few days earlier.

"No, not that," Temple groaned. "I'll be as addlepated as Mrs. Maguire contends I am if I have to listen to any more of that drivel."

"This is hardly drivel," she told him. "And for once you are going to listen."

Chapter 15

By nightfall, Temple knew he should have stuck to his original plan and grown wings.

It would have been more practical.

"I can't imagine where we went wrong," Diana said, chewing on a slice of bread from the loaf that Mrs. Maguire had given them to save them from "starving of their own folly."

Their folly, as Temple was starting to call it as well, had been to take a route that hadn't been used in centuries. Diana's infamous Billingsworth had sent them up into the fells of Cumbria with a paragraph that began:

Long since the echoing tramp of Roman sandals have faded into history, the once famous road known as High Street is now merely a track over the high fells of Cumbria. Only fools and outlaws still dare to traverse its dangerous heights . . .

He shook his head. Since he was now wanted for a spate of crimes in half the counties between London and Ambleside, Temple decided to count himself amongst the outlaws in Billingsworth's description, rather than the other category of High Street wayfarers.

According to the guidebook, High Street would lead them twenty miles from Ambleside, up over the peaks and back down onto the far side of Penrith. And most importantly, past all the traps set to catch them.

For truly, who would ever think that Lady Diana Fordham and the luxury-loving Marquis of Templeton would even consider crossing such a stretch of open country on foot?

So they decided to set out on in just that fashion while Elton drove the newly repaired berline through the traps that awaited them on the road. If he failed to make it past Nettlestone and Penham, a notion that left Elton highly insulted, they would hire a chaise and four and make a final mad dash for Scotland.

The usually loquacious Billingsworth had offered a sketchy set of directions on how to follow the legendary Roman road that they had traveled faithfully until the weather had turned from a bright sunny day into something that resembled a January tempest.

The clouds gathered quickly overhead and then unleashed a torrent of rain. The pleasant enough path immediately turned into a slick, treacherous track, and it was then that Temple decided they should set out cross-country in hopes of finding a farmhouse or other form of shelter.

Diana had wanted to stay on Billingsworth's course, convinced that another hour would see them into Penrith.

Another hour, Temple surmised, would see them both drowned.

Three hours after his assertion that shelter would be better sought by leaving the trail, they stumbled, drenched and exhausted, upon a small stone cottage. The ceiling, what was left of it, let in rain in spots, and one wall was partially collapsed, but the fireplace still worked, and he'd been able to get a blaze going in it.

"Mr. Billingsworth's guidebook has been so accurate thus far, I find it impossible to believe he failed us now." She glanced over at Temple, her gaze filled with accusations.

"What do you want me to say?" he asked her. "That you were right and I was wrong?"

She nodded. "That would be a good start. I found the directions quite clear." Opening the book, she held it up for him to see, reading aloud, " 'Once you get past the ruins at the brook, you need to follow the track precisely.' " Pausing, she glanced up at him. "I doubt Mr. Billingsworth wrote the word 'precisely' with the intention of his readers taking shortcuts." She set the book aside and took another bite of bread.

"If we hadn't gone off course, we'd probably still be out there," he offered in his defense, though even to his own ears his argument sounded rather hollow.

For some reason, when Diana looked at him, he didn't want to appear anything but the hero he saw reflected in her eyes.

And heroes definitely didn't leave ladies stranded in the middle of the Cumbria wilds. Then again, heroes probably didn't entertain the thoughts that Diana's wild array of fair curls and the pink of her lips had him considering.

"Truly this isn't so bad," he said, waving his hand at their shelter, a decrepit cottage that had most likely been abandoned since the Black Plague, if the cobwebs and dust were any indication.

Diana stared at him, her lips pinched together. Instead of offering a tart reply, she cast a significant glance about their surroundings, as if she were silently comparing them to the comfy inn and fine meal they would be sharing right now if it hadn't been for his "shortcut."

"Considering my financial state, this may well be the best I can afford at the present," he joked, hoping to tease a smile from her lips.

Her mouth didn't even twitch with a hint of amusement. Instead she tossed a piece of bread toward Tully.

Tully let out a sharp bark and then deftly caught the offering in midair. The cheeky little mutt whirled around a few times on his back legs, as if dancing for his supper.

Diana laughed and tossed the dog another piece.

Oh, for him she laughs, he thought. Outdone by a dog of indiscriminate breeding.

Temple shot a glare down at the beastly mongrel. "By the way, who invited you along?"

Tully growled his reply, then planted himself in front of Diana, resting his heads on his paws.

"I don't think he realizes the importance of an invitation," Diana said. "Rather like your friend Stewie." Her mouth might still be set in a steady line, but at least her eyes were sparkling with a bit of humor.

He reached for a slice of bread. "Then Tully is a good lesson indeed. I shall make it a rule never to feed Stewie. Elton would probably quit if the fellow wouldn't go home."

Diana laughed at this, and Temple smiled. He loved to hear her laugh.

When he went to take a bite of bread, he felt a delicate scratching on his knee. When he glanced down, a pair of soulful eyes gazed up at him, begging for a morsel.

Diana was once again occupied with Billingsworth, so he slipped the dog a piece of his meal.

"I saw that," she said, not even bothering to look up. "What will Elton say about your new dog?"

"Oh no, I think Tully is all yours," he told her.

Trying to get rid of the dog had truly been like having

Stewie back in their midst. When Diana and Temple had started down the road in Ambleside, the little dog had dashed after them, trotting along at the hem of Diana's skirt as if he'd always been at her side.

No matter how they tried to shoo him back, Tully was of one mind. He was going with them whether they liked it or not.

Diana had been delighted. Mr. Maguire's wry grin suggested the farmer was only too thrilled to be rid of the mutt. And Mrs. Maguire bestowed upon them a bone to take along for the little fellow.

"You do have a way of attracting the most endearing champions." Temple cocked his head and eyed the dog. "Who does he remind you of? Nettlestone or Penham? I think with those crooked teeth, he's a dead-on ringer for Penham."

Diana laughed. "Oh, stop it. Tully is much more handsome than Lord Harry."

"Now, now. The day isn't over, you could still be the gentleman's bride yet. It wouldn't do for your bridegroom to know he came in second to that ugly mutt."

Tully growled.

She shook her head. "I have no intention of marrying Lord Harry. Or that infuriating Nettlesome, either."

Temple wasn't done. He rather liked vexing her. It brought her color up, and right now her cheeks were a lively shade. "Why shouldn't you marry one of them? Your father approves of the match, so you won't run the risk of disinheritance."

She leveled her gaze on him. "How many times do I have to tell you, I don't care about the money?"

"Oh, you'd care if you had to make do without it." Of this, Temple knew only too well. For a man it was an easy thing, to set aside pride and honor and all that, but for someone like Diana, raised in the luxurious world her immensely rich father could provide, it would be a tremendous hardship.

Then she said something that rather stopped him.

"Have I cared the last few days? Do I appear to care right now?"

Temple opened his mouth to reply, to offer a hundred different instances when she'd protested the method and means of their travels. Like being rousted from bed at an ungodly hour, tossed out a window, riding practically naked across the countryside. Not to mention the sporadic meals, sleeping in hayricks, and being the subject of a malicious tide of gossip.

She should be complaining about the state of her tattered and dirty hem, her lack of a maid, a chaperone, a proper cup of tea. Her slippers, sensible though they were, would be ruined by the time they reached Penrith. Between them they hadn't the coins for a decent room, let alone a good meal—having spent most of her money on new clothes and posting fees to get to Danvers Hall.

She was miles from a decent bed, a hot meal, or even the vaguest form of shelter, and had yet to utter a complaint other than a few well-earned comments about his "shortcut."

No, in truth, he realized he didn't know the Diana before him. All his images of her perfect innocence had been chipped away in the last few days. And in their place he found an enticingly different woman.

Her blond hair, instead of being bound in the latest modish yet restrained fashion or covered with a bonnet, tumbled free in lazy, tempting tendrils from a haphazard chignon. Her cheeks and lips were pinked from the fresh air and a hint of sun.

She'd taken off her wet stockings and sodden slippers, and her bare toes wiggled before the fire in the hearth.

The patronesses of Almack's and all the other arbiters of fashion and manners back in London would be horrified at her natural state.

Temple would never be able to look at her again without remembering how she looked this night—like the most beautiful woman he'd ever seen. And it tore at his heart that he was about to lose her.

If only . . .

He drove his heart back into those lonely reaches and did his best to ignore the way his feelings for her were starting to overtake his carefully measured reason.

"You'll have to marry someone," he said, doing his best to steer the topic back to the most important issue—and ignoring the fact that Elton had said the exact same thing to him earlier in the day. "You can't return to London unwed."

Her brow rose into a regal arch. "And whyever not?"

"Your father announced to White's that you'd eloped with Cordell. He might as well have taken out an advertisement in the *Morning Post* with the headline: *My daughter is utterly ruined.*"

"Have you forgotten, the viscount is no longer with us. That ought to stave off the worst of it," she said.

Temple groaned. "He was murdered, Diana. It isn't like he fell off his horse in a drunken stupor. The man was shot in cold blood."

She pursed her lips. "I didn't kill him. That honor is yours until you can prove otherwise."

He hung his head in his hands. She could jest all she wanted, but this was a terrible muddle.

"And besides," she said, "I was never alone with Cordell. Mrs. Foston can attest to that. The only man I've been alone with is *you.*"

Yes, he was well aware they were alone. Too alone.

He glanced up at her. "I don't think anyone is going to look upon Tully there as a suitable chaperone. No matter how much he sets up growling. The only way to save yourself from complete ruination is to be wed. You must see that?"

She didn't appear to be listening. She stared into the flames with a gleam in her eye that seemed to Temple to be nothing more than a harbinger of trouble.

"Ruined," she was saying under her breath and with such pride. "I am, aren't I?"

"Most decidedly," he told her.

Her lips curved into a smile, and she sat up a little straighter.

Well, she needn't look so proud of herself.

"Haven't you a care for your reputation?" he asked.

"None."

Temple wanted to argue the matter with her, but in truth, he'd always been a little envious of Diana's disregard for Society. Her status as the Earl of Lamden's daughter offered her some margin for eccentricity, and as such, she had pushed the restraints of her position to the limits time and time again.

And then it struck him. "You've done all this not to *get* married, but to keep from being married. And I don't mean this ridiculous elopement with Cordell, but that scene at Almack's the Season before last, and the incident on Rotten Row last summer."

She looked at him as if he'd just discovered how to add pence together.

But it made no sense. Of course she wanted to be wed. It wasn't as if she hadn't been betrothed.

"You accepted Colin's offer," he pointed out.

Diana tossed the rest of her piece of bread to Tully. "I would never have been in the position to accept Colin's proposal if it hadn't been for you." Her words trembled with a bevy of emotions.

In the fireplace, a piece of wood snapped and cracked.

Smoke caught in a down draft blew into the room.

Something about the old cottage, lost in time as it was, pulled up their past, wrenching it to life as gaping as the holes in the roof, as tempestuous as the storm outside.

The question he'd studiously avoided asking her for all these years came issuing past his lips as if pulled by forces unknown.

"Why, Diana? Why did you agree to marry my cousin?"

Her eyes crinkled at the corners. He could see that she had an answer ready to spill out, an accusation really, but something held her back.

"If you don't want to say—" he began.

"Oh no," she said. "I'm more than happy to tell you. It's just that you've never asked."

"Perhaps I didn't want to hear your reply."

"And now?"

He braced himself. "Go ahead."

"I only agreed to marry Lord Danvers because you were so changed when I came up to London for my Season."

As he'd always suspected. "So you thought to punish me?"

Her answer surprised him.

"No, I don't think I thought that at all. In truth, he reminded me of you. Not the Temple I found in London, but you, the man I fell in love with in Sussex. Honorable, brave, steadfast."

"That boring?" he tried teasing.

She ignored him. "Colin would never have forsaken me. Not for any reason."

Temple flinched but couldn't help adding, "No, my cousin wouldn't have. You could say Colin's steadfast nature is rather like Tully."

"Oh bah!" she sputtered, crossing her arms over her chest.

"I should have known you would make a joke of this. And imagine, fool that I was, I held out a ridiculous belief that you would never let me marry him." She paused for a second. "Or any other man, for that matter."

Temple glanced away, shame filling his gut in a cold coil. He should have been honest with her. Told her the truth. But coward that he was, he feared that if he'd gone to her, he would have fallen prey once again to her soft, stealing glances and her unflagging belief that together they had a chance at happiness.

"I suppose Colin did you a favor then, turning treasonous and giving you an excuse to toss him over," Temple said.

She shook her head. "It wasn't Colin's court-martial that made me change my mind." She paused for a second. "It was you."

"*Me?*" Now it was Temple's turn to shake his head. "I never gave you any indication that I was willing to marry you."

But the look on Diana's face suggested otherwise. "I know who you are. I know what you've been hiding all these years. I know everything." She leaned forward. "Temple, you are no more a fool than I."

"Eloping with Cordell belies that statement, madame," he said in his best Corinthian manner.

"Oh, just stop," she told him, rising to her feet. "Stop that wretched act. I hate you when you wear that idiot's mask."

He'd like to tell her that his "idiot's mask," as she called it, had saved his life more times than he could recall and given him access to conversations that the holders thought far above his witless abilities.

Now he clung to it because it was safe, a wall to hide behind in the face of her outrage. It was far safer than letting her discover the truth.

That he was a coward.

"Oh, botheration. I had no intention of marrying Cordell, anymore than I would the likes of Penham or Nettlesome."

"Nettlestone," Temple corrected, still grasping the comfortable vestiges of his masquerade. But suddenly he felt it slipping away, and for the first time in years, he couldn't find a way to tighten his grip and wrestle it back into place.

Because for some reason, one he was sure he didn't want to know, he didn't want to be that Temple any longer. Nor did he want to be cut from the same cloth as his grandfather.

"The baron matters not," she told him, chipping away at his perfectly constructed role. "I spent three years of my life trying to determine why you turned from me, what had possessed you to change in only a few short months from the brave and heroic man who professed to love me to the vapid fool I found in town."

"Why didn't you just ask me?" Knowing Diana's forthright manner, it was rather unbelievable that she hadn't.

"Would you have told me the truth?" she asked. Her voice lowered to almost a whisper. "Would you have changed your mind?"

His silence was her answer.

"I thought not." Her bitter words cut him to the quick.

"You shouldn't have waited for me," he said, as if he didn't really want to say the words.

She stared him straight in the eye. "I'm not. Not anymore. You made your desires quite clear yesterday."

Temple flinched.

"Yes," she said. "I was eavesdropping on you and Colin."

"You weren't supposed to hear that."

"Whyever not?" She sighed. "Of all the people you should be saying that to, don't you think I deserve to be the first to hear it? I've waited for years, Temple, for you to set me free."

"You should never have waited. You should have married someone else."

Please, he pleaded silently as he had for so many years, *find someone who can give you the happiness you so deserve.* And even as he said the words, he cursed the lucky bastard who caught her heart and stole it away from him.

And at the same time, his original prayer always broke in. *Wait for me, goddess.*

She reached for another slice of bread, holding it in her hand, as if toying with eating it or giving it to Tully. After a pause, she tossed it to the dog, just as she had tossed away so many years waiting for him. "I had my reasons."

"I can hardly see that I gave you any indication that I would ever marry you."

"No, you made your feelings quite clear at the Fosters' ball. And I was heartbroken. Heartbroken enough to stop believing in the magic we shared that fortnight in Sussex. Then I discovered the truth of the matter, at least what I once believed was the real reason for your reluctance."

"And what would that be?"

"Your work for the Foreign Office."

He had been staring at the flames, unwilling to face her, but her quiet statement brought his gaze rocketing up to meet hers.

"*My what?*" he sputtered.

"The Foreign Office," she replied as calmly and as matter-of-factly as if she were referring to some country gentleman's hobby, like growing roses or breeding prize hounds. "You know exactly what I mean. The work you do for that awful Mr. Pymm."

Temple felt as if he'd been stripped bare. There were only a few people who knew about his work. Colin, their grandfather, Elton, and of course Pymm. But he'd never thought, never suspected that anyone else had discovered his secret life.

"Who have you told of this? Who else knows?" he demanded, suddenly seeing his charade coming to a stunningly inglorious end. He caught hold of her wrist. "Tell me."

Tully growled, but Temple shot a hot glare at the beast and snarled back, "Be still" with such ferocity that the dog turned tail and hid his head behind Diana.

She tried to pull her hand free, but he held on tight, as if he held on to his very career. Finally she gave up her struggles. "No one else. I have told no one." Then she paused. "Except Lady Danvers. But she already knew." She tugged at her hand again, and this time he released it.

Temple frowned and kicked at a loose stone on the dirt floor. "Georgie would know," he muttered. "That woman can unearth state secrets as easily as buy a new hat."

The same could be said, he thought, of Diana, but he wasn't going to give her the credit. It would only give credence to that smug look on her face.

"How?" he asked. "How did you find out?"

She bit her lip, staring into the flames. He thought for a time she wasn't going to tell him. Then she glanced up and met his gaze.

And answered his question by telling him about a certain day on Bond Street when she'd gone to buy a hat, and in less time than it took Mrs. Foston to purchase three yards of green cording, Diana's life changed utterly and completely.

Chapter 16

They sat in silence long after Diana finished her story.

Sliding her slipper across the dirt floor, she nudged his boot. "Did you love her?"

The question caught Temple unaware. "Love who?"

"Mademoiselle de Vessay?" Diana plucked at her skirt, her gaze focused on her lap, as if she didn't dare look at him for fear of the answer. "You risked much to save her. Twice."

Aha, so that was what was bothering her.

Temple suspected the frown creasing Diana's brow had more to do with Lucette's effusive French manners and less with the fact that he'd almost lost his life dispatching two French agents.

Up until a few minutes ago, he hadn't thought of the encounter in ages. It had only been another day in his work for Pymm. He'd been assigned to collect information from the socially prominent young lady. Welcomed everywhere—amongst the *ton* and the close-knit *émigré* society—Mademoiselle de Vessay had been recruited by Pymm to collect information on French activities in England, Royalist and otherwise. It had only been a matter of dancing with the popular chit once a week or so, or offering to escort her to dinner at a supper ball, during which she'd fill his ear with the bits of news she'd gathered. It wasn't Pymm's policy to hire ladies, for he was of the opinion they weren't reliable, but Lucette proved her worth time and time again.

Temple knew why the girl worked so hard. The money Pymm provided kept her and her mother out of the utter poverty that swallowed up so many of their homeless compatriots. The money wasn't much, for Pymm was as parsimonious as he was distrustful, but the modest income allowed the comtesse and her daughter to move freely amongst the *ton*.

"Did you?" Diana asked again. "Did you love her?"

He shook his head. "No."

"You could have died in that alley."

At this he grinned. So she did care about his life. Not that she should, he tried telling himself, but that she was worried thrilled him. "Lucette was an excellent informant who found herself in trouble. I did nothing more than repay the service she'd given so unselfishly to England."

"I don't think she felt that way," Diana muttered. "Besides, you were the one who saved her and her mother in Paris. Their mysterious benefactor who plucked them from the tumbrel at the very foot of the guillotine."

Her words came out more of an accusation—evidence presented that he'd held an affection for Lucette that went beyond their dangerous profession.

Yet what could he tell her? The truth?

That there had only ever been one woman to hold his heart.

"It was hardly as dramatic as all that." Temple attempted to brush off the grandiose images of a mythic hero that the de

Vessays had allowed to grow in the wake of their arrival in London. "The comtesse and her daughter are French. They tend to add a liberal measure of drama and fabrication to their tales. I simply helped them escape their prison and brought them here after the comte was murdered."

"You make it sound as if you merely escorted them to a house party."

Temple ran a hand through his hair. He wasn't a modest man by nature, but he hardly deserved any sort of admiration for his feats. He'd done what was necessary. What any man would do. "Diana, there were many more people who died during the Terror than were saved. In that respect, I hardly consider my work worthy of such regard or adulation."

"You've done far more than anyone else would have considered," she said with quiet resolution. "Risked far more than you should."

"How would you know?" he asked.

She just looked at him, with one brow cocked.

From her smug expression, he had the feeling she could recount the exploits of his career better than he could. He didn't know how she knew, but whatever she thought of his deeds, or misdeeds as Pymm might say, he didn't want this misplaced praise.

"I do what is necessary," he said, using the same words he'd thrown at his grandfather countless times when the old duke railed against his reckless disregard for familial obligations.

Family first, boy, his grandfather always replied. *Family first*.

Temple continued, lest she heap any more tributes on his less than worthy shoulders, "Before you start giving me credit for being a hero, might I remind you that Pymm pays me for my services. I just like to keep my landlady from locking me out and to see to it that Elton is well fed."

"Bah," she said with a wave of her hand, sounding more like his grandfather than he cared to consider. "You do it because you couldn't live your life any other way. And it's the only reason I don't hate you. I can understand that you do what needs to be done, but Temple, can't you see that we could do it together?"

"*Together?*" he managed to sputter forth. "Are you dicked in nob? 'Tis a dangerous world out there and certainly no place for a lady."

She should never have to see the sights he'd witnessed. No lady should. That she'd watched two men die at his hand was bad enough, but what if she were to have seen thousands die, as he had in Paris, one after another until he thought he would never erase the blood from his memories?

"Diana, this mad chase to the border of yours is nothing compared to the chaos of a continent at war."

She sat on the edge of her seat. "Yes, yes. I don't relish the idea of men dying or observing such horrors, but there are other things I can do—such as uncover secrets." She paused for a second, then jumped up and opened his valise. Before he protested, her hand plunged inside and moments later plucked out a piece of paper. "Like this special license you left in Colin's care. I thought you might have more need for it than Lord Danvers so I returned it to that secret flap in the bottom of your bag."

She held up the paper as if it were undeniable evidence of her worth.

He wondered if there was anything left in his life that she didn't already know.

Incorrigible, wretched little minx.

"I think we are well matched, you and I. Think of what we could accomplish together."

Despite himself, he saw what she suggested. A life with Diana at his side. It was a tempting fantasy. One that enticed him with visions of daring deeds and even more rewarding nights.

No matter how sincere she might be, he knew the right of this, and so he said again, "No, Diana. I won't take you with me."

"Colin takes Georgie," she pointed out.

"My cousin takes his wife because she has the uncanny ability to stow away on his ship. She hardly travels with him invited, because Colin knows as well as I that war is no place for a woman."

"And why not? Do you think I stay behind blithely ignorant of what is happening? I follow all the accounts in my father's newspapers. I've cheered victories, cried over defeats and mourned for men whose names I never knew until I saw them listed among the dead. For I know that until this war is won, you won't come back to me. I go to bed every night cursing that wretched little man in France and in the same breath praying fervently for your safety. There isn't a woman in England, who loves a man determined to do his part, who doesn't do the same, every day and night."

She rose and walked over to the fire, tending it with a quiet fortitude, much as generations of women had tended hearths while waiting endlessly for a loved one to come home.

After prodding the coals into a fine bed, she added another piece of wood. She waited for a moment until it caught, and then, satisfied with her task, swept her hands over her skirt.

Finally, she turned to him. "How would you like to attend ridiculous balls and endless parties pretending to be happy and secure while you knew your beloved was in danger from a threat that you could not protect him from? Not knowing if you will ever see him again? Ever feel his lips press against yours?"

Temple was taken aback in the face of her vehemence, her determination, her passion. She was right. The sitting and waiting and inability to help—why, it would drive him crazy.

But protecting her from the war had hardly been his true reason for disavowing her. He had sought to protect her from a far worse fate than the French.

No, he shielded Diana from the menace of his grandfather's machinations. For in truth, they had killed Temple's gentle mother, then broken his father's heart.

No, the foe he sought to keep Diana safe from could not be vanquished any more easily than Napoleon, and that meant he only had to strive harder to see that she never suffered his mother's lot.

Lost in his own thoughts, he didn't realize she'd come to kneel before him until she took his face in her hands. The warm, steady fingers cradling him soothed his fears.

"Temple, I won't let you decide my fate," she said in a whisper of a voice. "I cast my lot with you a lifetime ago. And I won't live apart from you any longer."

Her earnest gaze locked with his. He felt himself lost in those marvelous eyes of hers, in the cream of her cheeks, the soft pink of her lips. Her every nuance reminded him of a gentle English rose, to be protected and cherished. Except of course her heart. There Diana reminded him of the true miracle of a rose . . . its unflagging renewal year after year, despite summer's drought or winter's icy hand.

She refused to stop blooming and growing, no matter the adversity.

"Kiss me, Temple." It was no cloying request, no flirtish tease, but an order from a woman determined to change the course of his heart.

What she didn't realize was that his heart didn't need changing.

"Kiss me," she repeated, this time her breath, sweet and tempting, drifted and mingled with his own. She tipped her head and parted her lips, moving ever closer to his. "Kiss me and tell me you don't love me."

He couldn't. He couldn't kiss her and deny his love. He'd be betrayed by his own desire for her.

And yet while he knew he should set her aside, set her straight, he couldn't. Not when those eyes held him in her thrall.

Tired of waiting, tired of being second, Diana threw what was left of her tattered reputation to the stormy winds outside and pressed her lips to those of the man she loved.

Yes, they'd kissed several times over the last few days, searching, questioning explorations, passionate moments that had only teased their memories of the past.

Lawd sakes, she wasn't going to spend the rest of her years wishing she'd known the love of a man. For when she'd tossed aside her betrothal to Lord Danvers, she'd sworn right there and then, she wouldn't marry unless it was to Temple.

If he wanted to cling to his feigned indifference, that was well and good, but right now she wasn't going to be put off. And if all she could do was steal a small piece of Temple's heart, then she was willing to live as a thief.

So she stole a kiss, a kiss meant to taste his soul, purloin some hint of the love she knew he held for her in some dark, unreachable place in his inexplicable heart of stone.

How she had hungered over the years for his kiss, for his embrace. More so than was probably proper.

But why shouldn't a woman hunger as much as a man?

His lips were firm and unyielding at first. But that was Temple. The Jericho inspired walls he'd built around himself only needed the blare of trumpets to tear them down, and Diana believed with all her heart that she knew the notes to that trembling, triumphant song.

Bold and unrepentant, she defied his tightly reined indifference and teased his lips with her tongue.

"Open your heart for me," she whispered, her lips brushing against his. "Let me in, Temple. Just this once."

Just this once, let me in, my love.

His lips opened to her assault; his tongue welcomed her caress.

Come with me. Come with me, her thoughts sang, hoping in some way he would hear her siren call.

The passion she'd held for him, carried for oh so long, sparked once again, the coals never having had a chance to grow cold. Her fingers wound in his hair, curving around the back of his neck.

As they continued to kiss, an ache so keen and familiar unwound within her, leaving Diana's knees weak. His lips, the taste of him, the way his tongue swept over hers, possessing her as if she belonged only to him, left her breathless, left her aching to do more than just this . . . this teasing, haunting dance.

Grow bold, my love, and deliver me from this need . . .

The line from one of his poems echoed through her thoughts, urging her to take matters into her own hands.

Literally.

Her fingers plied at his jacket, pushing it off his shoulders, plucking at his cravat until the usually elegantly tied cloth was in an ignoble pile on the floor. Under the wool, the lace, and the linen lay a wall of muscled strength.

And a heart.

It beat beneath her fingertips in a wild rhythm, as ragged

as his breathing, as deep and true as the growl that rose up from his throat when her hands delved further down to wrestle with the buttons on his breeches.

She remembered only too well what he'd felt like that morning she'd awakened nestled in his arms. What she'd rediscovered in Nottingham. That what lay under all his layers was strong and hard.

No longer sixteen, she didn't have any fears of what that hardness could do.

No, she welcomed it. She wanted it. To touch it, to feel it. For it to drive into that heated place between her thighs and take away the aching need he'd started so many years ago with just one kiss.

And when her hands found him, the length of him, hidden and trapped inside his breeches, she stroked him, teasing him, enticing his manhood, as she'd done when she'd begged him to kiss her.

Come to me, Temple. Take me.

"No!" he said in a ragged shudder, setting her aside so violently, she fell back on the floor, landing in a whoosh of tangled petticoats and muslin.

"Botheration!" she sputtered. "Have you gone mad?"

"I will if I continue this course," he told her as he dodged out of his chair and shoved the ramshackle piece of furniture between them. "No, Diana, I cannot do this."

She glanced at his breeches. "I would say otherwise."

He snatched up his discarded jacket and shrugged it on, drawing the coat over the undeniable evidence she'd wrought.

"This is wrong. I can't," he said again vehemently, more to convince himself, she supposed.

"Can't?" she asked. "Or won't?"

"If we were to . . . were to . . ." He stammered over the

words as if he were speaking to some ingénue bride on her wedding night.

"Make love," she offered.

"Yes, that," he said, waving his hand at her as if trying to catch a lifeline. "If we were to . . . to . . ."

"Make love."

"Demmit, yes, make love," he finally said. "I'd dishonor you. I can't and I won't do that. Do you know what it would mean if we were to succumb to this foolishness?" He ran a hand through his hair, letting out a long, ragged sigh and shudder. "I'd have no choice but to offer for you."

She cast the chair aside, sending it skittering across the room.

Tully let out a yelp and then, looking from one glaring human to another, chose the chair, hiding beneath the overturned shelter.

Temple backed up, and Diana followed, stalking him across the room until she had him trapped against the wall.

She prodded her finger into his chest. "You mean to say that you won't make love to me because if you did, you'd have to marry me?"

Temple nodded. Gads, he'd faced down enemies before, men with death in their eyes and hatred blazing in their hearts, but he'd never seen the likes of Diana at this moment.

The woman was possessed. A determined goddess in her full wrath.

"Diana, I won't do this," he said, praying silently that he sounded convincing.

She laughed at him. "Lawd, Temple, if I'd known that all it would take to get you before the parson was to gain your bed, I'd have bribed Elton to let me into your bachelor rooms long ago."

He didn't doubt she would have. Nor did he doubt that Elton would have taken the coins.

"But I don't want marriage. Not if it means you are forced by pistols to the church and compelled against your will to take me to bride." Her hand reached out, and once again she touched his face, her fingers running along his jaw. Her touch sent a raft of traitorous tremors through his limbs, ending in the most traitorous one of all. "I don't want anything less than your heart—given freely and willingly."

He closed his eyes and reached up to pull her hand from his face, then he drew her into his embrace. He tipped his mouth down to her ear, marveling at the scent of roses that always seemed to surround her.

He wanted to start nibbling and not stop. To kiss her neck, to bare shoulders, to bare her further and love every inch of her flesh.

But he couldn't.

His fingers twined in her hair, as if of their own volition, sliding through the silken strands, taking their time so as to memorize every moment.

Then, with the dread of a man who knew no way to avoid the inevitable course of fate, he whispered into her ear, "Diana, I beg you, leave me be. I will not do this. I cannot do this."

She shook her head, "Temple, we can—"

"No," he told her. "What you want from me, I cannot give you."

"Grow bold, my love, and deliver me from this need," she whispered, as a hot tear spilled onto his shirt, soaking through the linen like a brand to his heart.

The familiar words left him stunned.

As she whispered the rest of the stanza in a voice filled

with emotion, he felt as if he were hearing the lines for the first time.

> With your heart entwined with mine,
> 'Tis all I will ever need.
> Your ragged cry, your trusting lips,
> Your tears are mine,
> Until we are together again,
> Until the end of time.

Temple pushed her away from him. "How do you know this?" Did he really have to ask? The minx had rifled his possessions on more than one occasion from what he'd gathered. And even this, his most private of possessions, she'd dared to invade. "You shouldn't have read that. It wasn't yours to see."

Her lips curved into a trembling smile, a droplet still glistening on her cheek. "I didn't know you wrote poetry."

"I don't."

She swiped at her tears with the back of her hand. "Once again, I beg to differ. Your poems are beautiful. I think they should be published. Like the exploits you keep hidden from the world, you should share your accomplishments with Society, instead of playing their fool."

"What have you done to it? Where is it?" he asked, not listening to her pleas, instead storming past her and catching up his valise. Yanking it open, he began foraging inside, plucking out his extra clothes, his belongings, and tossing them hither and yon. Finally, he closed his fingers over the only thing that really mattered. His only legacy. His fingers wound around the familiar leather of the binding. It soothed his soul without his having to read even a line.

She stood silently beside him. "I'm sorry if my reading your work upsets you."

"They aren't my poems. And they weren't meant to be read."

"Not yours, indeed, of course they are. It has your name on the inside page and at the end of every poem are your initials." She reached over and plucked the book out of his tight grip and opened it, pointing confidently to the telltale byline.

He glanced over at Diana. Her brows knit together as she looked from the book back up at him.

He had no choice but to answer the question about to spring to her lips. "The poems were written by the Marquis of Templeton, but not this marquis." He took a deep breath. "They are my father's verses."

"Your father?" she said, her brows still arched in a puzzled line. "I know this sounds odd, but I never thought of you as having a father. Or a mother, for that matter."

"Not many people remember my parents. They were married for a very short time, and they disavowed Society in general, preferring their own circle of friends."

"Just the more reason you should see these published, so your father's work will live on as he didn't have the chance to."

"Grandfather would have a fit of apoplexy if these were to be printed. He has an unholy aversion to those with literary aspirations."

"Then I don't suppose he was fond of your father's work."

Temple laughed, a short, bitter sound. "When my father lay dying, the duke arrived at Setchfield Park just in time for the doctor to give him the news that my father wouldn't live through the night, he was too far gone with fever. Instead of going up to sit beside his only son and heir in his final hours, to find some forgiveness between them, he took the news as his opportunity to start burning my father's journals and books before any mourners might arrive and discover his son's unholy tendencies."

Diana gasped, her hand covering her open mouth.

Rather than the pity that Temple thought he might see, he saw only the horror in her eyes at such sacrilege.

"I never thought your grandfather as bad as all that."

"It would be like calling Boney a nice chap."

"How did this one survive?" she asked gazing upon it with a rare regard.

"My father had it with him at his sickbed, and he gave it to me just before he died." Temple sighed. "I wasn't even supposed to be there, but against my grandfather's wishes, I snuck in. The duke was convinced I was the sickly type and would quickly succumb to the same illness. I knew he planned on sending me away on the morrow, and though only six at the time, I was determined to see my father one last time."

Diana smiled.

Temple remembered walking the long, dark halls of Setchfield Place, the great, rambling family seat. The original house had been an Elizabethan manor house, and over the centuries had been added to and changed, until it was the great sprawling palace the Setchfield dukes smugly called home.

The ghastly place always left him petrified with terror, especially the long, dark halls lined with the portraits of his ancestors. His grim relations frowned down from their heavy frames and hangers like a line of dead men on the gibbet.

But determined he was, and not even an entire gallery of disapproving Setchfields could have deterred his steps as he padded his way from the vast nursery to his father's sickroom on the opposite side of the house.

"There was a footman in the room, and one of the maids. When I came in, my father waved them away." Temple paused. "They knew the duke would be furious, and if I was discovered there, they'd both lose their positions. Yet they also knew this was the last time I'd see my father."

"So they let you stay."

He nodded. "I sat on that immense bed and held his hand until he died a few hours later."

Great, glistening tears welled up in the corners of Diana's eyes. "I imagine that was a comfort to him to have you close."

"You would think so, but all he would do was urge me to go before I was discovered." Temple cast his gaze up at the ceiling, trying to still the tears stinging his eyes. "I think he hastened dying so I wouldn't be caught."

Diana took his hand and squeezed it. She guided him over to the edge of the stone hearth. Sitting down before the flames, she tugged on his hand and bid him to join her. Once he'd settled beside her, she curled into the crook of his arm and lay her head on his chest, staring into the flames. "Tell me about him. And your mother, as well."

Temple's memories of his parents seemed almost as elusive as the fire before them, flickering and wavering, never lingering in one spot for very long, and in an instant consumed by the vagaries of time.

But still, he clung to the precious few he'd dared hold.

"My mother was beautiful. She had long black hair and dark eyes. I thought she'd been born a raven."

Diana giggled.

"Yes, well, laugh all you want, for you will also find it amusing that I believed my father to be a dragon slayer."

She struggled to sit up and craned her head to look at him directly. "A dragon slayer?"

"Oh yes. For whenever my grandfather came for one of his interminable visits, my mother always said we would survive because my father knew a spell to dispatch the old fire breather."

At this, her earlier giggles dissolved into a hearty laugh. "I'm sure there are plenty in the *ton* who would like to know that spell. Your grandfather can be quite intimidating."

At this, Temple nodded. "Try being his heir. It killed my father, and it would have killed me if I hadn't also inherited a measure of the old goat's stubbornness."

Her voice fell to a soft hush. "How was your grandfather responsible for your father's death?"

"My mother was nearing her confinement for another child and my grandfather ordered us all to attend him at Setchfield Place. He despised how close my parents were, that they lived a happy, simple life in the country and thought nothing of Society. If my father would have had his way, he would have lived his entire life in the country and never gone to London."

"I don't suppose your grandfather approved of that. He's rather fond of his prominent position."

"Too proud," Temple said. "When my father eloped with my mother, the duke was outraged, and for a time, my parents just ignored him and lived off a small inheritance my mother had received from a distant uncle. But unfortunately, neither of them was very good with money, and it ran out. My father swallowed what little pride he had, and they went and sought my grandfather's help."

"And did the duke help them?"

"Oh yes, in a manner of speaking. By then, I'd been born, another Setchfield heir, so he decided to relent. He let them have use of a small manor house and property. I think he feared that if he let them into Setchfield Place, their literary friends would arrive in droves, like ants to a picnic."

Diana laughed. "So they got their way."

"In a sense. It was fine for a time, but then my mother started increasing, and the duke heard about it. As much as he despised my mother, he was insistent that this child be born at Setchfield Place. I hadn't been, the first Setchfield heir not to be born within those hallowed walls, and he considered it one of my many failings."

Temple paused for a moment, drawing a deep breath, and then continued. "They put him off as long as they could. I think they hoped to delay him long enough so they could avoid the pomp and ceremony of a birth at Setchfield Place. But the duke was insistent. He sent his carriage and an ultimatum. Come or be cut off."

"So what did they do?"

"We went. Over fifty miles of bad road in the middle of winter, with my mother so great with child, she took up one side of the carriage."

He stopped and turned away, the rest of the memories too hard to face.

But Diana seemed to understand, and moved closer, taking his hand in hers. "What happened next?"

"What do you think happened? The babe came early, there in the middle of a snowstorm. The drift was so deep it seemed to envelop us. The driver and my father had to lead the horses on foot, clearing a path as we went. We made it to a poor inn, not ten miles from Setchfield Place, but we couldn't get any farther. It was there that she and the child died, before help or a midwife could be summoned. My father was inconsolable. He was overwrought with grief."

Diana's fingers tightened around his. "Oh, how terrible for him. For you."

"For all of us." Temple paused. "He came down with a fever almost immediately and perished a few days later. The doctor said it was the chill, but I know he died of a broken heart. He couldn't see spending the rest of his life without her."

"But he had you," she said. "He should have persevered for your sake."

"I thought that as well. For years, I resented that he just

gave up. But I look back now and realize he hadn't the strength to do it. With my mother at his side, he was a dragon slayer, but without her . . . well, he was merely my grandfather's inept and imperfect heir."

"So he thought it was better that he left you in your grandfather's clutches?" Diana's quick temper rose in defense of the child left orphaned.

Temple smiled and reached down to smooth her hair, still her passionate fires. "My father lived his life through his poetry and basking in the glow of appreciation in my mother's eyes. She loved him not because he was the heir to a dukedom, but because he cherished her and she him. They were kindred spirits. I think my grandfather resented her so much because she spoke my father's language—poetry, literature, the joy in beautiful things, in quiet contemplation—mind you, none of which His Grace will ever comprehend."

"Still, how could he leave you alone? He left you to fend for yourself."

"Not entirely," Temple said. "Before he died, just as the sun was starting to spur hints of dawn across the horizon, he opened his eyes and smiled at me. Then he made me promise that I'd never forget his example, or forget my mother's gentle influence. That I wasn't just the heir presumptive to the Setchfield duchy, but the dragon slayer's heir. That I had his and my mother's legacy to continue."

She swiped at the tears in her eyes, and the ones still lingering on her cheeks. For a time they sat silently watching the flames in the hearth, each lost in their own memories.

Then Diana let out a long sigh. " 'Tis too bad you haven't kept your word to him."

"Kept my word?" Temple sputtered, setting her aside once again. "I have done nothing but honor his request."

Diana sat up on her knees. "And how would that be? In this childish game you and your grandfather play of seeing who can vex the other more? Your father didn't live to annoy your grandfather, he lived for love. Unlike you, he married the woman who caught his heart, no matter the consequences. He wrote his poetry and spent his time happily away from town."

"Yes, but don't you see what it cost him? Cost my mother?"

"Their deaths were but accidents of life. Yes it was partly your grandfather's doing, but your father lived his own life."

"I hardly see how I am not living my own life," Temple said in his defense, though something inside him nudged him in the gut that this passionate woman before him was more likely to understand his father's vow than he had.

"Is this how your father would want you to live? Alone? Constantly risking your life? And to what end? Don't give me that 'For King and country' folly. You think by refusing to marry me you can spare me from the dragon. Keep me safe from the perils of the world? Bah!" she scoffed, her temper now rising above the storm, wild and full of fury. "You do it to protect your own heart. You safeguard yourself, you selfish bastard. You're as bad as your grandfather in that you don't believe in love."

Diana stalked over to the table and grabbed up his father's book of verse and thumbed through it. Her eyes sparkled for a brief moment as she found the lines she searched for.

> *By the light of your eyes,*
> *the taste of your lips, I live.*
> *You are my endless sanctuary,*
> *my life and hope.*

She snapped the book closed and shoved it into his hands. "The man who wrote those words would be appalled by your example. And so am I."

Then in one last defiant act, she caught up the special license and threw it into the flames—well rid of an unwanted marriage. Well rid of any desire to marry him.

Chapter 17

Temple sat in one of the dry, dark corners of the cottage, Diana's accusation weighing heavily on his thoughts. His back up against the wall, he nudged at the loose stones in the dirt with the toe of his once immaculate boot. More than once, he looked up and cast a furtive glance at the sleeping beauty curled up on his cloak before the fire.

Could he have been wrong all these years? Temple suspected that his grandfather's scorn and distrust had wheedled their way into his heart until they had become part of his very soul.

Could Diana be right that the best use of his father's command wouldn't be to avoid love, but to live in its reckless joy and uncertain future?

To find his own lady for which to slay dragons.

Irritating his grandfather was easy. Slipping in and out of France, a challenge to relish. Loving someone, letting one's heart open up? It terrified him more than he could imagine.

For once you loved someone, truly gave her your heart, you risked everything.

As he looked down at her still figure, her soft features, he realized the disquieting truth of the matter. The one he'd done his damnedest to ignore for so long.

Words echoed through his thoughts, urging him to renew his life, his destiny.

Grow bold, my love, and deliver me from this need.

It struck him as ironic that the only truth he could find at this very moment, the only words he could recall, was a single line of poetry from his father.

They rang with a legitimacy that urged him to be honest. Honest with himself and with Diana.

Yes, he lived his own life, but he had disavowed his heart. And of all his sins, that was the worst.

He pushed off from the wall, rising to the challenge of the vow he'd made so many years ago. The one he'd made to Diana and been unwilling to acknowledge until she'd opened his eyes. And his heart. Suddenly everything that he'd held dear, the independence of his work for Pymm, vexing his grandfather, living by his wits and Fate's capricious call, seemed meaningless compared to one thing.

Diana.

As if she heard his silent plea, she stirred.

Her movement startled him. What was he going to do? Fall down before her and declare his heart?

Knowing Diana, she'd accuse him of having imbibed the contents of the flask Mrs. Maguire had sent along in the bottom of the sack.

She moved again, this time her head turning toward him, her lips parting slightly, as if she were offering them to some unseen lover.

Temple grinned. Those sweet lips had always been his downfall, his never-ending temptation.

Now they would be his salvation.

Crossing the space between them, he knelt before her.

From the other end of the hearth, Tully glanced up from where he slept and eyed Temple, as if trying to decide to challenge this interloper, or allow the indiscretion.

"Careful, you mutt," he whispered. "I'm about to do the right thing."

Tully let out a low growl.

"Listen well, my friend," Temple told him, "look the other way this time and it will be beef bones and a warm fire for you for the rest of your days."

Sensible little beggar that he was, Tully picked himself up and trotted to the other side of the cottage, curling up in a ball and politely putting his back to the couple.

Temple nodded his thanks and turned back to Diana. And when he did, for one panicked moment his mind revolted.

Don't do this. Are you mad? He took a deep breath, his gut clenched with fear. *Don't succumb to her.*

Temple glanced upward, holding his hands over his ears to still the voices within. He'd listened to that coward's voice, his grandfather's words, for too long.

What would his father's advice be?

The howling wind outside filled his ears, followed by the haphazard beat of the rain as it pelted the slate roof overhead. Yet none of it could drown out the loud, commanding answer that rose from his heart and pushed him forward.

Slay the dragon, and steal the bride.

The lips teasing Diana's were as familiar as they were wanted.

So very wanted.

Yet hadn't she suffered this haunting dream so many times before, awakening only to find herself alone?

She tossed and turned and tried to shake away the lazy

warmth spreading through her veins, the wretched, aching need that seemed permanently coiled between her legs.

"No," she murmured. "Leave me be."

"Never again," whispered her tormentor. His lips nibbled at hers, then covered her forehead, her cheeks, her neck, and her ear with little teasing kisses.

His heated breath tickled her senses, his lips ignited a hot trail of passionate promises.

Then the kisses became more insistent, the whispered words in her ear more fervent.

"I need you, goddess. I won't be complete without you."

"Temple?" she whispered. "I don't believe you. You always leave."

"Never again. I'm yours forever. That is, if you'll have me." When he ended his ardent appeal, his lips covered hers in a kiss that took her breath away.

Diana's eyes sprang open.

"Temple!" she managed to say, that is, once he'd finished his kiss.

Diana was no fool. She'd never interrupt one of Temple's mesmerizing kisses, dreamed or real.

"Temple, what are you doing?" she whispered. Truly, she shouldn't ask, but just take hold of him with both hands and never let go.

"Slaying dragons," he said, his fingers toying with a strand of her hair. His gaze, so full of need, locked with hers.

"And in the morning?" she asked, doing her best to ignore the way her heart hammered in a wild tattoo.

"In the morning?" he asked, his voice taking a deep, passionate tenor and sending shivers down her spine. "After we do this again, I'm going to hie you across the border and make you my bride."

Diana frowned. All this was naught but another dream. Or there was one other explanation. "You've gone mad."

"Mad? Yes. Ramshackle and around the bend not to have done this long ago."

She matched his grin with one of her own. Did she dare believe him?

How could she not when he captured her lips with his, sealing the offer he'd made with a rapturous kiss.

Diana answered him the only way she'd ever wanted to— she wound her fingers around his head, his neck, and pulled him closer.

This time she wouldn't let go.

And it appeared, neither would Temple. His hand swept away the cloak covering her, then returned without even a heartbeat between, to tug at the ribbon holding up her bodice. The palm of his hand covered one breast, leaving her nipple tingling beneath his heated touch.

As his fingers worked the ribbon loose, his kiss deepened, his tongue sweeping over hers, with a deep, anxious plea.

She opened herself to him, tasting him, teasing him, imploring him—especially when his fingers dipped beneath the edge of her neckline and began to caress her.

He'd touched her thus in Nottingham—that reckless, heated tussle that had given her a tantalizing and torturous hint of the heaven awaiting her in his arms.

As they had before, his fingers seemed capable of lighting fire beneath her skin as he cradled her breast and then found the raised, pebbled firmness of her nipple, leaving her willing to toss aside her reputation, throw away her virtue.

In Temple's arms she could almost believe she was his goddess.

His goddess. The words sent shivers down her spine. They

also emboldened her. That, and years of frustrated waiting for him to come to his senses.

She arched her back, reaching up and pulling at her own bodice to free herself for his attentions. Her breasts ached for his skillful ministrations, ached and burned.

Diana loved his touch, craved it, for it sent her senses reeling, filling her with a careless, ravenous hunger for more.

His mouth tore from hers, the cold air biting greedily at her heated lips.

"No!" she gasped. "Don't stop."

"I must," he said.

Her gaze must have reflected the murderous intentions in her heart, for Temple only laughed at her.

"No thunderbolts, goddess. I just haven't heard you say yes."

"Yes. Yes. Yes, to anything," she told him, catching hold of his shirt and yanking him back against her.

He caught her wrists, pinning them over her head, while the weight of his body held her hips and legs securely in place. "No, no more protests, not until I know that you will consent to be my wife."

"Oh, for mercy's sake, Temple." She squirmed and wiggled in his grasp. "Do you really need to ask?"

"Aye," he said, his voice smoky with emotion. "I need to hear you say it."

Diana knew what he was really asking. If she forgave him. How could she not? As he'd described his childhood, the loss of his parents, she saw only the small, frightened, lonely boy lost in his grandfather's exacting world.

What had Temple's examples of love been? His father's broken heart and his grandfather's heartless example. No wonder love and all its powerful mysteries left the man terrified.

That he'd crossed this tiny cottage to declare his heart meant more to her than if he'd crossed oceans—for it meant he'd conquered and slain all the fears that had bound his heart, held him hostage.

And kept them apart.

"Yes, Temple, I consent to be your bride."

He leaned down and kissed her, tenderly and completely.

Then he went to release her, loosening his grip slightly, but changed his mind, holding her fast. His features shifted with a wolfish delight. "I rather like you like this . . ." He eyed her open bodice and winked.

Given this was Diana, her eyes lit with a wicked appreciation. "I rather like *you* like *this* . . ." She struggled a bit more. "Is that wicked of me to enjoy this?"

"Terribly," he told her, nipping gently at her earlobe.

"Good. Now let me go so I can be truly wicked."

"With pleasure," he drawled. Temple released her, but only enough to capture her once again, this time with his lips as he devoured her in a voracious and hungry kiss.

"Love me, Temple," she whispered. "Love me."

"For the rest of my life, goddess. For all my days."

She sighed happily and let him claim her heart, her body. His mouth blazed a trail of one steamy kiss after another from her lips down her neck, until it wound its way to one of her breasts, eagerly lavishing the nipple with scorching laps from his tongue.

Her hips rose of their own volition to meet his, and what she found there made her sigh with delight.

Straining beneath his breeches, his manhood tempted her with its stiff, enticing welcome.

Diana was only too glad not to be some young, naïve bride. Over the years she'd overheard enough of married women's conversations to know she should either be terrified or would face the world in the morning with a deliriously happy blush.

As Temple's fingers began to draw up the hem of her skirt, brushing over her legs, her thighs, over the curls in that very private place, she knew which type of married lady she would be.

She opened her mouth to say something, to say anything, but at that moment Temple once again covered her mouth with his, and between the way his tongue teased hers and his fingers slowly stoked the fires below, she felt herself floating toward the heavens.

Her body rose to meet his touch, her legs opening to him.

She'd never imagined anything so glorious, that is, until his fingers delved a little deeper and he pushed her past the clouds.

"Oh my," she gasped, her eyes opening wide. "Do that again."

He grinned at her. "Bossy chit."

"On this I insist," she said, her hips swaying in an urgent cadence. "Do that again."

And when he did, stroking the swollen and heated nub, liquid fire bolted into her veins.

Diana heaved a sigh of relief. She hadn't been dreaming.

"Oh, again," she whispered.

"As you wish," he said into her ear, nibbling a path from her neck to her bare shoulders and back to her nipples.

Yet even as Temple heated her senses into a molten delight, she realized she needed more. She needed to feel *him*.

It was her turn to propel him to the clouds.

And she knew just where to start.

The moment Diana's fingers ran over the length of his hardness, Temple wondered if he'd ever again remember

how to breathe. Instead of the tentative explorations one
would expect from one's virgin bride, Diana reached for him
as she did everything in her life—with a bold, demanding
statement.

Her hand started at the root and ran up his length until her
fingers closed over the sensitive tip, rubbing it until he made
the same appreciative moan she'd issued not moments before
when he'd touched her so intimately.

"I thought as much," she whispered.

He smiled to himself. So she was going on an exploration
of her own.

And it didn't appear she needed Billingsworth for this
journey.

Her fingers fumbled for just a moment over the buttons at
his waistband, but what they lacked in experience, they made
up for in pure, unadulterated enthusiasm. Before he knew it,
she had his breeches undone and was kneeling before him,
tugging his boots off.

She made quite a delicious sight, her hair tumbling down
in a disarray of curls and tousled strands, her bodice open, allowing him to see the delightful curves of her breasts, her
rosy nipples hard and peeking through the thin muslin of her
chemise.

Her face was a study of serious intent, her brows furrowed, her mouth in a taut line as she faced the enemies
standing in her path to passion.

His boots and breeches.

She would have put the best valet to shame in her effi-
ciency and tenacity.

And he was rewarded with the sound of a breathless, anxious sigh of delight when she vanquished her foes and spied
her reward.

Her eyes widened at the sight of him, then a wicked, sly

smile tipped her lips. No maidenly fears in Diana, only appreciation and determination.

She shrugged off her own gown with a slow, deliberate movement that left Temple's mouth dry. With the fire behind her, her thin chemise gave him a teasing glimpse of the woman he'd loved for so long. While at sixteen she'd been a tempting little minx, now at nine-and-twenty, he could appreciate the woman grown.

She reached up and plucked the remaining pins from her hair. As he gazed at her full, firm breasts, the nip of her waist giving way to the round, womanly curves of her hips, the long, supple length of her legs, he saw her in the years to come—her stomach round and lush with their children, her arms curved around a babe, children at her feet.

And her arms, her welcoming arms, always open to him, her eyes aglow for him and only him.

It was a breathless wonder that made him realize what it meant to be a dragon slayer.

The moment he'd lost his heart to her, his course in life had been set—to give and discover with Diana the love that only two people, kindred spirits, as his mother would have called them, could find.

"What are you thinking?" she whispered, as if she feared to break the spell around them.

"I'm considering all the ways I intend to tell you that I love you."

She smiled. "And those would be?"

He shook his head. "I have no intention of telling you."

Her pretty mouth opened in an outraged moue.

Instead, he caught her by the hand and tugged her closer. "I have no intention of telling you, goddess. I have every intention of showing you."

Diana's eyes shone. "And where would you start? We goddesses are demanding types."

"As well I know," he said, starting to tease her lips with a kiss.

She grinned and then pressed her lips to his, clamoring for more.

As their mouths fused together, their bodies also tangled, their hips meeting in a heated brush, her legs twining with his.

Temple had never known such a feeling of completeness, a melding of emotion and flesh into a fevered, shared need.

He rolled her on her back, so his body covered hers, and contemplated all the ways he was going to show her the love he'd denied her so long.

Diana gazed up into Temple's smoky gaze and felt the depth of his love for her reach all the way to her toes.

His body seemed tensed and waiting, ready to devour her with endless kisses, with delirious passions. His hardness pressed into her, burying its silken head into the apex of her thighs, insistent and seeking at the same time.

Her body opened to him, eagerly bidding him welcome, her legs wrapping around him, pulling him closer.

Diana gasped at the intimacy of his maleness as it penetrated her wet, heated core. He continued to ease into her, slowly, carefully.

She should be frightened by this invasion, by the unknown before her. Yet all she felt was the welcome relief of having him inside her.

Gazing into Temple's eyes, so full of love and need for her, she knew she was his goddess, his stolen bride.

"Love me, Temple," she told him.

His manhood stroked her, stretching her as he continued his sensual possession.

She moaned as he pressed deeper into her, bringing with him that tantalizing ache that left her coiled and tense, knotted and tangled. She wanted him so very badly, her heart beating wildly, and the need for something she didn't understand drove her headlong into a mindless state.

"Love me, Temple," she told him fiercely. "I'll not wait any longer."

With that, she caught hold of his hips and held him fast as she rose up to meet him. She let her body rock back and forth to ease him in and out, with each stroke going just a little further.

This was what had been missing from her dreams, from her desires, this masculine hardness sparking her fires into a raging blaze.

But his progress became impeded and she cried out in frustration.

"'Tis your barrier." He smoothed her hair, and kissed her brow. "It may hurt to breach it, but 'twill only last but a moment."

Hurt? What was pain to this wild, craving need that begged to be answered.

"Be done with it," she begged him. "Take me, claim me, Temple."

"Mine forevermore," he told her, as he thrust into her and broke past her virginal wall.

Yes, it was as he had said, painful, but not for long. He kissed her past those hasty moments, whispering words of love in her ear, suckling at her breasts until that current of lightning raced down her limbs like a winged messenger heralding the passion yet to come. Her hips danced upward, begging him, nay, demanding him to stroke her anew.

And he did. He filled her, and she wondered that her body could contain him.

He rocked inside her, in and out with slow, tortured strokes, and when she thought she'd go mad, he quickened his pace, carrying her upward to the clouds yet again.

She cried out, wantonly and shamelessly, with her need. "Oh, Temple, don't ever stop."

His body covered hers in a fevered heat, and she clung to his back, to his hips, hanging on as his thrusts became fiercer, striving to go even further into her needy depths.

She felt the first hints of something start to take over her senses as he continued to drive into her. She couldn't see, she couldn't hear—at least anything beyond the roar of her heart and Temple's ragged breathing.

The night spun out of control, as if swallowed up in the storm outside, by the tempest within.

Her hands grappled to find something to hold on to, clinging to his shoulders, while her heels dug into the ground, her legs pushing her up to meet his reckless pace.

Temple drove into her one more time, a powerful thrust, a claiming like none other, and she felt as if he'd toppled her into a giant chasm.

Her world exploded, sending racking waves of pleasure through her, releasing her from her former prison and at the same time capturing her in a magical spell.

How could this be true? How had he wrought this enchantment?

Above her, Temple stilled and shuddered, his manhood continuing to seek her depths as if he couldn't get enough, driving deeper and deeper until he completely filled her, emptying himself into her.

She understood his madness—for she was still writhing and dancing on his hardness, searching for every last echo, every last vestige of this trembling bliss.

As it finally started to drift away, on ebbs and tides, her

eyes fluttered open. His features held the same enraptured picture of contentment that must have been echoed on her own.

Diana reached up to cup his face, stroke the line of his jaw. She needed to know that this was real. She wanted to reassure herself this wasn't just another teasing, taunting dream. So when she touched him, sliding her fingers over his lips, the ones that gave her so much pleasure, and he whispered the words she'd longed to hear, she knew that her dreams had come to live in her heart for always.

"I love you, goddess," he said, placing little kisses on her forehead, her nose, her lips. Rolling slightly, he carried her with him, so she faced him, with her back to the warmth of the fire.

"And I you, Temple," she whispered. "I love you so very much."

They kissed again, then they lay nestled together for some time, savoring the wonderment they'd found in each other's arms.

Eventually Diana sighed.

"What was that for?" he asked.

"I'm finally and truly ruined," she said with a glee that only Diana could find in such a statement.

He sighed and then laughed a bit. "Yes, I fear so. If I wasn't inclined to marry you, your father would see to it."

"Then I'm glad you are inclined, because I fear my father would shoot you before he'd allow you to become his son-in-law."

"Then I'll send the duke over with the good tidings. That ought to solve all our problems."

Diana swatted his shoulder. "You wretched beast. How can you jest about all this?"

"Because I care not what anyone says, not your father, not my grandsire."

She nodded in agreement, then laid her head on his shoulder.

After a few moments, Diana whispered, "What changed your mind? What made you come to me?"

He brushed a hand through her errant hair. "That line from my father's poetry. The one you found so compelling."

"I'd say you were bold indeed," she teased. "I can see why your grandfather doesn't want your father's work published."

"And why is that?"

"Because it would probably cause a riot of passion amongst the *ton*."

"I hardly think it would do all that," Temple replied.

"Would you care to wager?" she asked, lifting her lips to his and winding her legs around him once again.

"Bold minx," he said.

"I've only just started."

Chapter 18

"Temple! Temple!"

Diana's urgent cries wrenched Temple from the heavenly dream he was lost within.

He woke up with a smile on his face, having heard her call out like that several times during the night.

He rolled over to cradle her in his arms, but discovered the pallet beside him empty.

As his eyes now wrenched open from their sleepy slits, he blinked at the slash of sunlight pouring through the open door of the cottage.

Outside, Tully barked and complained with a frantic pitch.

"Shut up, you mongrel," came an angry voice, then a horrible yelp as Tully cried out in pain.

Then there was a terrible silence, broken by Diana's angry voice. "You beast! How dare you harm that poor little creature."

This followed a *thump* and a man cursing out in pain.

Temple bolted upright and scrambled for the door, catching up his breeches as he went.

Outside, the brilliant morning sunshine blinded him, but only momentarily. He tugged his pants on and surveyed the scene before him.

On the ground nearby lay Tully. He couldn't tell if the dog was dead or alive, but he didn't have time to check.

"Temple!" Diana called out.

"Templeton?" came the surprised responses from the pair on either side of her.

Penham and Nettlestone.

They started at his state of undress, then turned and glanced purposefully at Diana.

"So you thought to steal her for yourself, eh, Templeton?" Nettlestone said.

"Yes, for yourself," Lord Harry repeated. "Tired of living on your grandfather's benevolence, eh?" Penham laughed and turned to his former rival, now turned partner-in-crime. "Did you hear that? Quite a joke, eh? Benevolent—Setchfield?"

"Yes, yes, immensely funny," Nettlestone said, smiling.

The man had every right to be grinning, Temple thought. He was holding a pistol.

Beyond the pair stood a gig. How they had found them, Temple couldn't guess, but apparently they were closer to the road than even he'd thought.

"She's ours now," Nettlestone said, jerking his head in the direction of the carriage.

In the backseat, the one usually reserved for a tiger, Diana sat bound and tied.

They truly had a tiger by the tail, for the lady was fighting them every bit of the way. She kicked and struggled and cursed them in such a rough manner, Lord Harry blushed.

And sported the makings of a hell of a shiner.

No wonder they'd put her back there, Temple thought.

Somehow she'd managed to slip free of the gag they'd

tied around her mouth. "They surprised me this morning when I went outside to . . . to . . . oh, never mind that part. They grabbed me and put this rag in my mouth so I couldn't warn you." She shook her head again, this time working the cloth completely off her mouth. "Is Tully . . . is he . . . ?"

Temple went to take a step toward the poor little fellow, but Nettlestone cocked the pistol and shook it. "Don't move, my lord. I'd hate to have this end in such a fashion."

Temple froze, for in addition to being a dab hand with horses, Nettlestone was also a deadly shot.

And considering his less than stately stature, if he leveled his aim, Temple didn't want to consider where the bullet would lodge.

Instead he tried to discern Tully's state, but couldn't see if the mutt was breathing. He glanced back at Diana, ashamed not to have better news for her. Ashamed that he'd fallen into such a deep and sated sleep.

"I can't tell," he told her.

Tears filled her eyes as she stared across the space toward him. *Don't let this happen.*

He could almost hear her pleas. Gads, how was it that he finally came to his senses, and then *this* happened. He should never have left his post at the wall to come to her bed, he should never have . . .

Nettlestone puffed out his bandy chest, "Only you would leave a mutt to do a man's job. Mark my words, this lady won't be out of my sight until she is lawfully my wife."

"I do say," Lord Harry interrupted, "she may well choose me."

Nettlestone smiled indulgently at his young partner.

Temple had news for them, the only man Diana was going to marry was the one standing before them.

His fierce determination must have shown on his face, for

Lord Harry, bold with Nettlestone at his side, and far enough away from his mother to have gained a little backbone, said, "Don't think we can't guess what's gone on here. But Nettle and I are willing to look the other way. She's still got her fortune even if she might not have the rest of what should be ours."

"As if it could have been yours, you spineless—" Diana would have continued if Nettlestone hadn't raised the gun and pointed it—not at Temple, but at Tully. "Be quiet there, Lady Diana. For if my boot didn't finish off that little blighter, this bullet will."

Diana's mouth opened further, but then it closed with a decided snap.

"Now if you'd be so kind to turn around, Templeton," Nettlestone told him, "And let Penham here tie you up a bit, we've got a wedding to plan." The man shrugged. "Sorry, old fellow, but you aren't invited."

Temple turned around slowly. One of the first rules of espionage was never to allow oneself to be tied up.

And he had no intention of violating that rule today.

He also knew his foe. Though new to town, Lord Harry had quickly become a regular at Gentleman Jim's, and a favorite sparring partner among the sporting set. It was said that what young Penham lacked in spine to stand up to his overbearing mother, he vented with full force in the boxing ring.

No, Penham was a viable and dangerous adversary.

But all Temple had to do was get him into a position where he could use the other man as a shield.

Penham approached slowly. "Don't want to hurt you, Temple. Always considered you a friend, but mind you, I've a bit of a reputation around town, and I'm not afraid to land a facer on you."

"Similar to the one the lady landed on you?" Temple said over his shoulder.

Penham frowned. "Wasn't very sporting of her."

"You'll be wearing one for the rest of your life if you make that harridan your wife. Consider this fair warning."

Penham shot a nervous glance back at Lady Diana. "She's just overwrought, is all. My mother said she'd be a handful when I started courting her, but she'd see her put in her place right enough." A length of rope dangled in his hand. "Now give me your right hand there, and we'll get this nasty business over with."

Temple extended his left hand, and when Penham reached down to grab it, Temple swung his other fist.

He connected, but to his chagrin, Penham's reputation as a tough fighter appeared well deserved.

The younger man reeled back, but remained standing. As he rose to his full height, he met Temple with a dead-eyed gaze.

Temple gulped. This wasn't going to be easy.

Not wanting to give Harry an inch, Temple dove at him, hitting him in the gut and driving them both into the dust. He had the advantage of not being encumbered by a waistcoat and jacket as Harry was, but that was his only advantage.

Apparently Penham had also practiced a fair measure of street brawling, for he fought back with the same disregard for gentlemanly rules that Temple showed.

They rolled about in the dirt, gouging and kicking and punching at each other like a pair of street urchins, while Nettlestone shouted, "Stop this! Stop it, I say!"

Then the inevitable happened. The dueling pistol, with its touchy trigger, discharged, sending a wild shot in the air.

The fight came to a wrenching halt, Temple having pinned

Harry to the ground and about to deliver a punishing and finishing hook into his face.

But it was all for naught.

Nettlestone stood beside them, staring foolishly at the smoking pistol in his hand and then down at the scene before him.

His nimble little mind must have realized that once Temple finished off Penham, he'd be next.

So the baron did the only thing he could. He whirled the gun around in his hand and smashed the butt into Temple's forehead.

Stars exploded before his eyes, and the last thing he remembered as he fell beside the vanquished Tully was the look of utter surprise on Nettlestone's face.

When Temple awoke, the sun had climbed well past midday.

His face was being washed by some wretchedly smelly wet cloth, and when he tried to swipe it away, it growled at him.

"Tully," he whispered, never before so glad to see the little dog up and alive. He reached over and gave a tousled swipe at the mutt's floppy ears. "Not about to let the likes of Nettlestone stop you, eh?"

The mutt barked twice, then sat down beside him, as if in complete agreement and awaiting their next course of action.

Temple imagined if the dog had his say, the first thing he'd want to do is take a piece out of Nettlestone's ankle.

Not that Temple wasn't opposed to holding the baron down and letting the dog chew the overbearing lord a good reminder to be kind to animals.

He grappled his way up from the rocky ground, one hand

on his aching head, the other steadying himself as he struggled to his feet.

Around him, the Cumbrian countryside sprawled like a sparkling gem. While yesterday it had stormed like January, today it reflected only the joys of June, with blooming flowers poking up around the edges of protruding rocks and the ground sparkling with drops of rain left over from the night's torrents.

He scanned the horizon, searching for a road or track. There must be one nearby, since Penham and Nettlestone had managed to bring a gig all the way to the cottage's craggy doorstep.

But nothing greeted his sight except the endless fells.

He'd never felt so alone in all his life. He who was so well versed in solitude and loneliness.

That was, until Diana had come into his life. Even after he'd disavowed her, so many years ago, he'd always sought her out—across the room of a crowded ball, a glance at her father's box at the opera. Catching a glimpse of her had always brought a measure of comfort to his heart, though at the time he'd chided himself into believing that he sought her out so as better to avoid her.

Now he knew differently. He'd watched for her because the sight of her replenished his heart. Left him with an inkling of hope for a future with her.

How many times had he lied to himself by saying that he didn't want her?

Now that he'd lost her, his only thoughts were how much he wanted her. In truth, needed her.

And most importantly, how to find her.

"Do you know which way they went?" he asked Tully, willing to stoop to begging favors from a mutt.

The little dog stood up on his hind legs and danced his beggar's revue.

"That may find us a meal, but hardly a road," Temple told him.

Undeterred, Tully dropped to all fours and started trotting away, his pointy tail wagging high and confidently.

Temple started to follow, realizing that perhaps there was a track there that he hadn't been able to discern before. However, the first sharp rock that bit into his bare foot stopped him cold.

In his haste to find Diana, he'd forgotten that he still wore only his breeches. He hoped his shirt, boots, and jacket remained where they'd been discarded in pleasure and haste the night before.

"Just a moment," he told the dog as he picked his way back inside.

His boots and shirt remained where Diana had tossed them, though his waistcoat and jacket were gone.

No doubt Penham had taken them to replace his own ruined costume. Given the thrashing he'd bestowed on the young man, Temple supposed he should be thankful for his boots . . . or anything else they'd left that would aid him in following them.

Shrugging on his shirt, he discovered that everything else they'd brought along was gone.

Diana's traveling case, his valise.

His gaze shot to the table, which now stood empty.

His father's book of verse. *Gone.*

"Wretched thieves," he muttered as he stared at the blank spot. Temple felt the loss keenly. He'd had that book with him every day since his father's passing.

Apart from Diana, it was his most prized possession. It

had brought him comfort and solace through so many difficult times.

Now only anger coursed through his veins.

But to his surprise, they hadn't necessarily robbed him blind. Mrs. Maguire's sack of provisions remained, probably overlooked because the battered bag looked as if it had once belonged to the cottage's last occupants.

Temple pounced on it, his stomach growling in delight. He caught hold of the last of the lady's heavenly bread, the loaf that Diana had taken so much delight last night in devouring, and savored each bite—with a few tossed in Tully's grateful direction.

"We have to find her, fellow," Temple said. "Before they get her to the border." Though he'd been furious with her last night, he was glad Diana had burned the special license before Penham and Nettlestone arrived. In their hands it would have meant sure disaster. Without it, it made their task of marrying her all that much more problematic.

He could well imagine they'd have a difficult enough time of it carting a bound and gagged woman in an open gig over thirty-five miles of open road—in plain sight for anyone to see.

Anyone to see.

The piece of food in his throat nearly choked him. Temple sputtered and coughed over his chilling revelation.

Anyone would be able to see her. Including Marden.

How could he have forgotten?

He cursed loudly and roundly, Tully adding his own howling refrain. He swore not only for the danger represented to Diana, but if Marden found her with Nettlestone and Penham, the deadly French agent would have no qualms about seeing both of them left in the road—dead where they stood.

Temple yanked on his boots and then glanced down at himself. Coatless, hatless, and horseless, he would be hard-pressed to get anyone to believe he was the Marquis of Templeton, the heir to the Setchfield duchy.

As he turned to leave, the toe of his boot nudged something. He looked down to find a small book. His father's verse, he thought at first.

But as he picked it up and turned it over, he discovered much to his chagrin that Diana's captors were more discerning than he had given them credit for.

They'd left behind her wretched volume of Billingsworth.

He was about to cast the toady little travelogue into the hearth when he stopped.

He glanced at the book, recalling something Diana had said days earlier. Frantically, he started thumbing through the pages until he found the entry he was looking for.

Outside Penrith stands the ancestral home of the Net-tlestone barons. A great pile of medieval architecture, it reflects what was once a noble and imposing castle. For those interested in seeing such a sight, it is recommended to call upon the home only when the current baron is in town.

Temple grinned. No wonder Nettlestone had found them. They must be close if not already on his lands. And if the baron was smart, he'd have gone straight home and tossed Diana into a traveling coach before making the final dash to the border.

If he knew his goddess, she'd have Pins and Needles dancing in circles, either with her antics or by turning them to bickering.

She had a talent for sowing strife, his goddess.

And for once, he was happy she did.

Temple wasn't too far from the mark regarding Diana's manipulation of her erstwhile suitors. She'd set them against each other before the gig had jolted its way down to the main road.

She sat back in her seat. "I'll have you know I'm being chased by a French agent who will think nothing of killing you both in order to steal me away."

Both men glanced over their shoulders, and then burst out laughing at her statement.

"Lady Diana, who would have thought at your age that you would be capable of such a tarradiddle," Nettlestone said.

"French agents, indeed!" Lord Harry scoffed. Then the pair of nitwits began laughing again as if they'd never heard such a jest.

Vexed, Diana didn't say anything more. Serve them right to run into Marden and find themselves with their toes up in the dust. Especially after what they'd done to Temple and Tully.

"What makes you think I'll marry either of you?" she asked. "I won't, you know. I won't marry either of you."

Nettlestone and Penham exchanged looks that said they hadn't considered that option.

But the baron, used as he was to the scorn of Society, came up with a solution. "You'll be married. With or without your consent. I've a cousin in Gretna who'll do the job. No questions asked. He owes me a favor or two, for all I've done for him."

Diana doubted the tightfisted Nettlestone had done anything for this cousin, but she had no illusions that the baron wasn't capable of bullying someone into granting him this boon.

But Harry didn't appear so convinced, and at this, Diana smiled.

"Lord Harry, would you force me to marry? Marry another man?"

The young man blushed and sputtered. "I-I-I hadn't looked at it, I mean to say, I-I-I never thought of it, my lady."

She let him muse on those thoughts for a few miles. She was furious with both of them for leaving Temple unconscious in the middle of the countryside. She knew he lived, as well as Tully, for she'd set up a huge ruckus after Temple had fallen and refused to stop her caterwauling until Penham had checked both the marquis and the dog to assure her of their welfare.

That Temple lived had given her reason to hope.

After a time, they came upon a farmer with a wagonload of goods. Diana started in the moment they got within earshot.

"Help, please sir, help me," she cried as plaintively as she could. She tried for tears, but had never been much of a thespian. Instead she held up her bound hands and begged further. "These villains have stolen me from my husband and children, please sir, call the magistrate, call for the local guard."

Instead of being rightly horrified, the man ignored her, respectfully doffing his hat at Nettlestone and moving his wagon aside to let them pass.

"Well, of all the . . ." she muttered after they'd passed and she'd cast a scorching glance back at the farmer.

"You won't find much help from my tenants," Nettlestone said. "The families on my land go back generations, most since before the plague. That's because while the sickness raged all around these parts, none of the Nettlestone villeins suffered."

Diana held her tongue as to her theory on that supposed miracle. Much hadn't changed for the Nettlestone family since the fourteenth century—like the *ton* of today, not even the plague sought out their company.

"Aye, our loyal tenants come in quite handy," he continued, his chest puffed out and his nose in the air. "Yes, indeed. In fact, it was one of my good fellows who spotted smoke coming out of that deserted cottage and sent word that someone was encroaching on my lands."

That explained how Penham and Nettlestone had been able to find them so easily, Diana realized. They'd had the entire population of Nettlestone tenants working for them. In truth, it had rather shaken her faith in their general incompetence to think that they'd come across her and Temple by use of their own wits.

Now she needed to put their arrogance and unfailing inanity to work for her.

"Oh, help," she called out to no one in particular. "Someone do help me! I've been kidnapped, despoiled, ruined. Oh, help!" She set up a racket that had even the horses turning their heads to see what the fuss was.

"We can't take her all the way to Gretna like this," Penham pointed out. "Listen to her. The first town we pass through, she'll have everyone in the village turned out."

"More so," Diana added gleefully.

"Then tie her gag back on," Nettlestone said testily.

Diana leaned forward. "I'll bite the first hand that dares." She smiled, letting them both get a good look at her white teeth.

Penham shrank away from her. "She has us, Nettlestone. She'll not do this willingly."

"She's not so clever, Harry." The baron clucked at the horses and turned them from the road to a nondescript and overgrown drive that most would miss if they didn't know it was there. After a few moments, a looming heap of stone came into view. Nettlestone nodded toward the pile. "Nettlestone Castle. Just awaiting its next baroness."

"You haven't won her yet," Penham grumbled.

"Then we'll settle this matter right here and now." He nodded back at Diana. "We can lock her in the bridal suite and have a bit of luncheon in peace."

Penham didn't look convinced; he glanced first at Diana and then at Nettlestone. "Is the room secure? I mean, secure enough for *her*?"

Diana grinned.

"Quite," the puffy little baron said. "You may find this surprising, but on occasion the Nettlestone brides have exhibited an inexplicable amount of reluctance at the idea of marrying into our esteemed family."

Both men chose to ignore the inelegant snort that issued from the tiger's seat.

"Let me assure you," Nettlestone said, "the room can withstand any female's trickery. Without it, our lineage wouldn't have continued for nigh on these past eight hundred years."

Such an illustrious and productive history seemed to satisfy Penham's reluctance. "Then shall it be dice or cards?"

"Dice," the baron declared. "I feel quite lucky today."

Diana's mouth fell open. "You mean to *dice* for my hand?"

Nettlestone glanced over his shoulder at her. "What would you have us do? Duel for you? I think not. Shabby waste of Penham's life, you know. I'd kill him for certain."

"I think we already decided I was the better shot," Penham

said. "Don't you recall, we had that contest outside Buxton?"

"Ah, yes," Nettlestone said. "I forget. My apologies, sir."

"Of course," the young man replied. He turned around to Diana. "That has been the vexing part of all this. Trying to find a competition where one of us doesn't excel. Both of us are far too competent for just your average gentlemen's wager."

Diana glanced up at the sky and counted to a hundred. "Competent" was not a word she'd use to describe either of these lordlings, but she held her tongue.

As they rode closer to the castle, a monstrous hulk of stone and ivy, Diana viewed it with an eye for escape. But as Nettlestone had boasted, the place appeared a regular fortress. Though in truth it held none of the majesty of a great castle, no craggy heights, no great tower. Rather, it looked as if it had tumbled over a few centuries ago, and none of the Nettlestones had bothered to notice.

Penham and Nettlestone began a full-blown argument as to the rules for their dice match.

Diana considered pointing out that neither of them had the game correct, but said nothing. As long as they were occupied in their bickering over her hand, they wouldn't be taking her any farther north.

"I'll find a way to escape them, Temple," she whispered to the wind. "Mark my words."

Temple and Tully reached Nettlestone Castle by nightfall after four wrong turns and a sketchy set of directions from one of the locals. He stormed up the drive having come to three conclusions.

He'd find them still there and he'd retrieve Diana from their clutches by whatever means necessary.

Or, if they had already fled for the border, he'd steal one of the baron's best piece of cattle and ride like the devil to beat them to Gretna Green.

But the one option that kept him walking with a stride full of purpose and frustration was that if anything had happened to Diana while she was under their unwanted protection, he'd kill them both outright.

That is, if Marden hadn't already done him the favor.

The stable yard and front court of the castle were deserted. Temple guessed the servants were all at their evening meal, which meant he had little time to find Diana before the household set out to complete their final chores of the day. The front of the house was dark, no torches or lanterns to greet a visitor or cheery candles in the window to offer a beacon of welcome.

Moving around the house, lurking like a common thief, Temple tried one window after the other, as well as all the doors, only to find them barred.

"A trusting sort, eh, Nettlestone," he muttered after once again finding his way impeded. Then from an open window just off to his left he heard two men arguing.

"I hardly say that toss was fair, milord," Penham was complaining. "It wasn't on the green at all."

"'Twas so," Nettlestone shot back. "Why, it was a fair throw and I'll not listen to another word. Might I remind you it was your choice to dice for her hand?"

Temple stood stark still, waiting for Diana's voice to chime in—he knew her well enough to know the lady would have her own opinion on the matter.

But her voice was remarkably absent as the bickering continued. Temple crept forward and surveyed the scene within.

Nettlestone and Penham sat opposite each other at a great

oaken table, engaged in a game of chance. The large, sparsely furnished chamber echoed with their vocal rivalry. A few threadbare tapestries hung from the walls, and the sconces dripped and smoked with tallow candles.

Temple could see why Nettlestone was so determined to win a wealthy bride—his property needed the care and restoration that Diana's fortune would surely provide.

As for Diana, she was nowhere in sight.

Hidden away, he surmised. Considering Nettlestone's desire for her fortune and the lady's nature, the pair had probably locked her up until they'd decided her marital fate.

And if they were smart, she'd be in either the castle dungeon or the tallest tower.

Temple glanced upward, scanning the rooms on the tower corners, thankful the Nettlestone fortunes had never been so great as to afford more than three floors.

And not far away, there was a room that glowed with a brace of candles. The only room illuminated on any of the upper floors.

It had to be where they were holding her.

Temple crept past the open window, where Penham was pouring the baron another measure of some potent liquor, as well as one for himself, and muttering a slurred comment about "double or nothing."

If he was lucky, the two fools would be at it—drinking and gambling—all night. In the meantime, all he had to do was to find a way up to Diana.

As he crept closer to the window, Temple discovered his route.

Buried under the ivy, an old trellis leaned against the wall. Ivy and an ancient rose competed for the rungs that ended well past the window above.

As he tested whether it could hold his weight, the first rung crumbled in his hand. Cursing, Temple glanced upward once again. Since he couldn't find an open door, he was running out of options.

So he prayed the next rung would hold him. It did. As did the next. The third one cracked and crumbled in his hands, but the next one only creaked. And so he climbed to the rescue of his ladylove, one rotten step at a time.

"Diana?" he whispered as he reached the illuminated pane of glass. He clung to the wretched trellis as it groaned and wavered under his weight. "Diana?"

Demmit, where was she? If she didn't hurry up, the Nettlestone gardener would find him in a heap. There'd be no need for flowers or greenery for his funeral; he'd probably bring half the wall along with him.

"Diana, do you hear me?"

"Yes," came the bemused reply.

His heart leapt at the sound of her voice. He'd found her. For a moment he forgot he was forty feet in the air and clinging for dear life.

Gads, he was good at this rescuing damsels in distress business. Perhaps if Pymm tossed him out of the Foreign Office, he could consider it as his new form of employment.

"Come to the window," he whispered as loudly as he dared. "I'm here to rescue you."

"I daresay that trellis won't hold both of us." Her reply came from someplace other than within the room beyond. "Besides, I already ruled out that method of escape as decidedly unsound. It was much easier to bribe the maid and make my escape down the backstairs."

Temple glanced downward. Diana stood on the ragged grass below him, a grin from ear to ear, and in her hands the reins to two saddled mounts. His valise was tied to one saddle, her traveling bag to the other. Tully, his pointed tail wagging merrily, stood at her hem.

Instead of being vexed that she'd once again outsmarted everyone, including him, he nearly lost his grip. Besides, the sight of her filled his heart with joy, a completeness that he'd never known.

A gift he now understood was the blessing of love.

"If you are quite done playing the fairy tale hero," she said, "you might consider getting down from there before you break your neck and leave me with no choice but to have to actually marry one of those nitwits."

He held his position. Now that he thought about it, perhaps he was a little put out that he hadn't been able to save her properly. "What are you doing down there? Get back up here and let me rescue you," he said, nodding toward her prison window. "Some story this will make for our grandchildren if you steal all the glory."

The trellis groaned and swayed, the rung in his hand cracking and threatening to give way.

"Tell whatever version you like," she said, "just get down from there."

He decided that the better part of valor would be to live to tell the tale, even if he couldn't figure prominently as the hero, so he started to climb down.

She tipped her head and smiled up at him as he made his careful descent. "You want children?"

"Scads of them," he said. "I understand you need the little nippers if you want to eventually have grandchildren."

If it was possible, she grinned even wider.

The trellis lasted until Temple was nearly to the bottom, then the poor thing gave way and he toppled the last eight feet. As he'd predicted, he was buried in a bower of vines and blossoms.

Diana rushed to his side, plucking off the stray bits of ivy and the wayward thorns from the roses.

"Temple, you great idiot. What were you doing up there?"

"I would have climbed twice that to reach you," he said, pulling her down into the grass with him and kissing her soundly.

"Only twice?" she teased.

"To the stars if I'd had to," he told her. For it was true. He might have discovered his heart last night, but he hadn't learned the depth of it until today. The miles he'd walked not knowing her fate—he'd never felt so lost and alone.

She made a delicious little sound of contentment as he kissed her soundly and thoroughly.

"Do you think it would be proper if we—" She winked, her eyes sparkling with an indecent invitation.

"You mean here and now?"

She nodded.

Temple considered what was before them. All they had to do was to ride the thirty-odd miles to Gretna Green and get married without incident.

Too bad, he thought, it would never be as easy as all that. Especially considering his body was already hardening at the thought of being inside her, of feeling her bare skin against his.

No, no. It would never do. He shook his head.

"Why not, Temple?" she whispered, her eager hands straying to the inside of his shirt.

He knew a thousand reasons that he should set her aside and tell her no. They needed every minute they could muster to put as much distance between them and their enemies as possible.

Temple didn't relish going another round with Penham and had the bruises to prove it, even as his blood started thrumming wildly in his veins, his body hard with need.

"Please, can't we just . . ." Her lips nibbled at his ear and whispered a request into it that made his throat go dry.

It wasn't some languid joining that she was asking for, but a hot, greedy moment in which to slake her thirst, sate some measure of her long-restrained passions.

She was mad with desire for him, and he for her.

And besides, who was he to refuse a damsel in such obvious distress?

Chapter 19

They made love in the overgrown grass of Lord Nettlestone's gardens, quickly and fiercely, before they set
the rest of his horses loose and rode hell-bent for Gretna
Green. While the night before had stormed and rained, this
evening the moon lit their way, the stars twinkling guides as
they finished their quest for the border.

Diana rode in a state of dizzy wonder. Whether it was the
heady rush of making love with Temple again or the thought
that on the morrow they would be man and wife, she didn't
know. Almost afraid the starry night was just another teasing,
taunting dream, she didn't dare pinch herself, but clung to
each moment so she would never forget the romance of it all.

They crossed the River Sark and rode into Scotland, stopping only for the old man who collected the tolls. The ruddy-
faced Scot gave them a sly smile.

"Let me guess," he said to Diana in his broad accent.
"You're that London heiress, eh?"

Before Temple could offer one of his poorly conceived
lies, Diana nodded enthusiastically. "Oh, aye. But unfortu-

339

nately, my father is quite opposed to our match. We'll be beggars."

The old man laughed sticking out his hand out for the toll, which Diana paid with the last of her stash of coins. He eyed her anew, then cast a speculative glance at Temple. After he spat on the ground, he said to Temple, "Best to warn ye, I've had three of them heiresses this week. Half the spinsters in the countryside are claiming to be her just to catch all the fools out searching for the lassie."

Temple laughed. "Never fear, I promised the chit I'd make her a duchess one day, so I believe we are even on that score."

The man laughed as if he'd never heard such a jest and was still blowing his nose and wiping at his tears as he pulled the barricade out of their way.

Diana shot one last smile at the toll collector. "I *am* the heiress, I'll have you know."

"Lassie, you're the best one I've seen so far," he replied with a broad wink to Temple.

They arrived in Gretna just before dawn, exhausted and famished.

The entire town still slept, except for a stray cat or two roaming about the streets.

"Let's find an inn and get a bit of rest," Temple suggested. "Then when the vicar awakens, we'll get married."

They'd already agreed that a handclasp ceremony might be fine for some, but neither was willing to leave to chance that between her father and his grandfather they'd find some way to have such an unorthodox ceremony nullified.

Diana nodded, too tired to argue, and soon found herself being shown to a room by a sleepy but understanding inn-keeper.

Apparently the good people of Gretna Green were used to

strange arrivals at all hours and welcomed the exhausted yet determined lovers with open arms.

It was their business, after all.

But on one point the innkeeper's wife was adamant. "I won't have ye sharing rooms in my establishment until ye are married, right and proper."

And so Diana was shown to a comfortable room at the end of the hall. Temple and Tully were pointed toward one on the opposite end.

"Sleep well, sweet goddess," Temple bid her, under the watchful eye of their Scottish hostess. "In a few hours we marry."

The heavyset woman snorted and shook her apron at him, shooing him off to his room, while she hustled Diana into the safety of the bridal suite. "Och, doesn't he have a fine way with words." The lady frowned and shook her finger at Diana. "He'd better have more than a glib tongue and fancy manners or you'll find yourself with a houseful of bairns and an empty larder. I've seen too many of his kind pass through and the sorrow they leave in their wake. That's the sort of man who can talk a woman into believing anything."

But Diana barely heard the woman's stern warning, for she'd discovered the comforts of the bed, and was nearly asleep, drifting happily into a dreamy world where such dreary predictions never came true.

Diana awoke some hours later, when a fresh-faced maid arrived. The girl carried a pitcher of water in one hand and a tray of food in the other. As she set out the food on a small table, she kept casting curious glances in Diana's direction.

"Is there something the matter?" she asked the girl.

"Oh no," the girl said, her face turning a rosy shade of pink. "It's just that I've never met an heiress before, that's all.

First a duke and an earl, then that handsome marquis of yours, and you being an heiress." She shook her head and sighed. "Me mum is never going to believe the day I'm having."

A duke? An earl?

"What duke?" Diana asked, a pit in her stomach growing icy cold. "What earl?"

The girl's eyes grew wide. "Real fancy ones, milady. The duke's got a huge carriage outside. And you know the earl, I 'spect since he's yer father."

"My father?" The pit widened into a veritable chasm.

The girl nodded again. "Come to see you married, I imagine." She glanced toward the door, where from somewhere beyond Diana heard a rising cacophony of voices.

Her father's included.

Making herself busy, the girl tried to appear nonplussed about the contentious situation. "It will be all right, miss, once he calms down and you're wed proper-like."

Diana flinched. "Wed proper" would not be her father's definition of a marriage to Temple.

She was about to ask the girl to help her dress, but realized she'd been so tired she'd slept in her clothes.

As she ran a hand through her hair, something caught in her fingers and she pulled it free.

A bit of ivy from Nettlestone Castle. Then she glanced in the mirror and realized a little more than a hasty repair would be necessary.

She looked, as she'd once heard in a play, "well tumbled."

The last thing she needed was her father to suspect she was no longer an innocent. He'd probably shoot Temple without a second thought.

She stared at the mirror and tried to decide what to do first.

"Let me, milady," the girl said. "I've got five younger sisters and have had quite a bit of practice. Besides, can't have you going down looking like this. Not on your wedding day."

The girl proved to be a dab hand, and had Diana's blond hair brushed, twisted, and pinned up in a simple country fashion.

"Hmm," she mused. "You'd look much better with a wreath of gillyflowers, but I suppose you don't have time for that."

Most decidedly not, Diana thought, when from downstairs came a thundering outburst.

"Marry my daughter? You? Why, I'd rather see her wed to Nettlestone."

Diana bolted up from the chair. "Thank you—"

"Martha, milady."

"Thank you, Martha. You should come to London, you'd make a fine lady's maid."

"Me?" the girl blushed a rosy hue. "Oh, go on with you."

"If you ever need a job, you come to London."

"But I don't know your name, milady," the girl said.

"In a few hours I'll be Diana, Marchioness of Templeton." *If my father doesn't kill the groom.*

Temple weathered the Earl of Lamden's initial outburst like a seasoned sailor bracing for the first winds of a storm.

He hadn't borne his grandfather's blustering for all these years not to know how to buckle down for a real tempest.

Speaking of his grandfather, Temple hadn't been surprised when the innkeeper had summoned him downstairs for an audience with the earl and found his grandfather, as well, standing before the fireplace.

The duke had always kept close tabs on his whereabouts,

despite Temple's best efforts. Apparently having learned that he'd been sent after Diana, his grandfather and the earl had joined forces to find their wayward heirs.

His grandfather hadn't bothered to greet him, other than to nod once, a grim look on his face.

None of this boded well for his and Diana's plans.

"I won't have it," Lamden was saying. "You're a wastrel, and an idiot, and—"

The door to the private room swung open, stopping Lamden in mid sentence. Temple expected to see Diana coming in, but to his surprise, it was another all-too-familiar and decidedly unwanted face who entered the room.

"Pymm," Temple said. No wonder the duke and Lamden had been able to find them so quickly.

The man grinned, a rare sight on his pinched face. It made him look like a rat who'd just escaped the cat with a wedge of Stilton.

"Temple! I knew I'd enlisted the right man for the job when I sent you after Lamden's gel." He nodded to Lamden and the duke as if they were just servants to be politely acknowledged. "Setchfield," he murmured as he bustled past the duke and held out his hands to the fire.

"Pymm," the duke replied tersely.

Temple thought his grandfather, a man who exacted his due deference from all, would be outraged at this snub, but to Pymm he remained vaguely polite, which was as uncommon as Pymm's smile. He'd have to ask Pymm one day what secrets he held over the duke's head.

Pymm rubbed his hands together. "Now the innkeeper tells me Lady Diana isn't married. How is this? I gave you that special license so any delay could be avoided. But never mind, I've taken care of matters. Nettlestone and Lord Harry are outside." He glanced at Temple. "I'd suggest you leave by the back door. Both men seem to be under the impression that you have wronged them rather dearly."

"Pymm, it's not like that," Temple told him. "I've made a change to your orders."

The Foreign Office spymaster waved his hand at his best agent. "When haven't you? I'm used to your insubordination. But what is important now is that the gel be married posthaste." He walked toward the door, as if about to see to the task himself.

Temple caught him by the shoulder and held him fast. "And why is that, Pymm? You know, I'm still not sure why you of all people have so much interest in Lady Diana's marriage. You hate to travel, and for you to come all the way up here, this seems an uncommon favor for a friend."

"Ah, Templeton, you are just overtired. Always looking for secrets where there aren't any. Good man, though," Pymm said, shaking himself free and casting an uneasy glance around the room.

Pymm turned to Lamden. "Told him to use any means possible to see her wed, and it sounds like he's done a fine job of coaxing the chit up across the border." He paused and said to Temple. "Of course *you* don't have to wed her. I've got two willing grooms outside, though I do say they are just as eager to settle a debt or two with you, Templeton, something about horse stealing and some improprieties that I don't think should be discussed here." He nodded toward Diana's father and then shook his finger at Temple as if he were reprimanding him for stealing tarts. "If I know you, you used every trick in the book to bring her to heel. Good for you. You've earned your assignment to Constantinople. I'll make a full recommendation to the Secretary for you to be sent to the Ottoman Empire when I return. Excellent job, my lord, excellent work."

"Because I outwitted Marden? Because I discovered that she's not Lamden's issue, but the natural daughter of Louis Bourbon?"

Pymm paled.

His grandfather glanced up from his glowering stance, his mouth falling open.

Temple caught Pymm by his badly tied cravat and hoisted him up until his feet pedaled in the air. "I've had my fill of your high-handed ways. You lying bastard, you threatened me with expulsion from service and tossed me without warning into Marden's path. She's the daughter of a king. Did it ever cross your mind to tell me?" He shook him for good measure. "What have you to say for yourself?"

"I-I-I—" the man sputtered and choked.

The only person who did manage to say anything was Lamden. "There's only one way you could have discovered that secret, you cur, and if I thought for a minute you had—"

His outraged response was cut off by a small cough from the door.

"It matters not how Temple discovered it, Papa," Diana said, rooted in the doorway, one hand holding the door frame for support. "The only thing I want to know is, is it true?"

Temple released Pymm, shoving him aside, and going toward her. He was cut off by Lamden, who rushed to his daughter's side.

"Diana," he said, clasping her in his arms and placing a fatherly kiss on her brow. "Dear girl, thank God you are unharmed. You've given me a time of it this past sennight."

"And you haven't answered my question," Diana said, stepping out of his embrace. "Am I your daughter? Or is it as Temple says, that I'm Louis's bastard."

Temple felt everyone in the room hold their breath—with the exception of Lamden and Pymm.

From Pymm's expression it was obvious he'd known all along—exactly as Temple suspected. He wasn't angry that he'd been sent after Diana, for what would have become of her if he hadn't gone chasing her up the Manchester road? Temple shuddered at the thought of it. She'd be trussed up like a Christmas goose and on her way to France right now.

And he would have lost her forever.

As much as Temple wanted to continue throttling Pymm, it now seemed he'd probably have to ask him to stand up for him at their wedding. After all, their wedding was to his credit.

Pymm, the matchmaker.

The better revenge would be to let that moniker bandy its way through the clerks at Whitehall.

"Diana, I had hoped you would never learn the truth," Lamden said.

"So it is true?" she whispered.

Lamden nodded.

She sucked in a deep breath. "Didn't you think I had the right to know this?"

"No. Never," Lamden told her, pulling her into the room and closing the door. "Telling you would have been tantamount to putting your life in danger."

"I think that has already come to pass, my lord," Temple said, coming to stand behind Diana.

Instead of the smile he expected on her face at his support, she glared at him.

What the devil had he done now?

Before he had time to ask, Lamden continued.

"Your mother came to me after she discovered she was with child. She was the daughter of a Scottish nobleman, a cousin to the exiled prince. Her father and Louis both claimed a passion for engineering. The King found it delightful that Arabella shared her father's talent for inventing, so she was often at the King's workshop. His Majesty was intrigued by her, as most of us were. I was just a young adjunct with the English ambassador, hardly a match for the sophisticated men who swirled in her wake." Lamden closed his eyes for a moment, as if he were recalling those days in his mind.

"She was such a beautiful woman," he said, continuing his story. "So lively and fair, just as you are. Every man sought her company, but she knew the vagaries of the French court too well to give in to some mild flirtation." He let out a long breath. "But obviously one doesn't say no to a king. How it happened, I know not, only that afterward, Louis sent her away before the Queen heard the rumors."

Diana shook her head. Temple could see that as much as she wanted to know the truth, it was a devastating moment. Everything she knew about her life was a lie.

Lamden must have seen her anguish as well. "I loved your mother with all my heart, and married her in secret so you'd have the protection of my name. Before you even arrived, wee little thing that you were, I never thought of you being anything but *my* child."

She sniffed at the tears welling up in her eyes. "Oh, Papa," she whispered. She rushed to his arms and hugged the man who was in truth, though not deed, her father. After a few moments, Diana tipped her head back and looked at him. "How is it that I bear the King's mark?"

"Louis knew the child Arabella carried was his, and when she went into labor, he arrived in secret at our Paris rooms. He had with him his confessor and a young novice as witnesses. I believe you have met his novice."

There was a tense moment of silence, before Temple interjected, "Marden."

Pymm nodded. "He left the church before he was ordained, just as the Revolution was beginning. He's been a
thorn ever since."

"Still, Papa," Diana said. "Why did you let him mark me?"

"It was your mother's wish. The midwife had given up
hope that she'd live, and she was in so much pain and so desperate to see you safeguarded. She thought that there might
be a day when you would need the King's favor and that
mark would be your savior."

"Who would have thought it would almost lead to your
demise, my lady?" Pymm had the poor sense to add. "And
now it will mean a wedding for you. So who is the lucky
groom to be, Lord Harry or Baron Nettlestone?" He rubbed
his hands together, oblivious to her devastation, solely focused on seeing England protected.

She glared at the man and looked about to finish what
Temple had started earlier.

Temple took her hand in his and answered for her. "Neither of them. As I was saying before, Diana will be *my* bride."

She spun on him, her face drawn, her mouth set in a hard
line. Snatching her hand free of his grasp, she said, "Please,
no more of your false offers. I heard you quite clearly at the
door. *A fool's errand.* That's what this all was to you. And
fool that I am, I thought you came after me to save *me*, not to
save your position with *him*." She pointed her finger at
Pymm as one might an unwanted and undistinguishable pile
left by an ailing cat.

"Diana," he began, "it wasn't like that—"

"Like what? I heard what was said. You came after me because you had to. Because you wanted an assignment to the
Ottoman Empire. Learning the language so you can hire a
Persian servant indeed! You lying, conniving, wretched
louse. I never want to see you ever again."

She whirled from the room and left in a flash of muslin.

Temple tried to follow her, but his grandfather stepped in his path. "Bad business, this. We should be away. Let Lamden see her married off. Think of our legacy. You'll be the Duke of Setchfield one day. You can't have a bastard for a wife." The duke dismissed it all as if he'd just sent back a plate of beef that tasted off. "Consider yourself saved by this turn of events."

"Saved from what?" Temple said, his voice rising above even the duke's infamous roar. "Living the rest of my life with the woman I love? I think not, sir." He pushed past his grandfather and headed for the door.

"If you marry her, I'll . . . I'll . . ." the duke began to threaten.

Temple whirled around. "You'll what? Cut me off? You've already done that, and I have yet to starve. Cut me off from your affections? You haven't any. If I don't marry Diana, I stand to end up as lonely and empty as you. And that is one deficiency the Setchfield legacy will not endure."

"I won't hear of it," Lamden complained. "I won't have an idiot for a son-in-law."

"Glad to hear that Nettlestone is out of the running then," Temple replied. "I'd hate to have to kill both him and Penham." He strode from the room, determined to make things right with Diana. Yet as he entered the common room, about to ask which way she'd gone, a round whirl in orange came dashing up to him.

"Temple! I do say, Temple!"

"Stewie!" Temple said, stunned at the sight him. If this continued, next he'd find Prinny walking through the door to wish him merry.

"My good friend," Stewie effused, clapping Temple on the back and grinning profusely. "How could I live with myself if I missed your nuptials? Couldn't let you come all this way, suffer so many deprivations, not to have a credible witness at your side. For who in their right mind would ever believe the Marquis of Templeton capable of stealing himself a bride. And a rich one to boot." He bowed, his hand wavering in a grand flourish. "Consider me here to lend you the protection of my good regard if matters take a difficult turn. I am at your service."

"Really, Stewie, you needn't have bothered," Temple said, meaning every word of it.

"Bother? Bother? Tut, tut! Not another word. We are the best of friends. I would have crossed the seven seas to stand up at this blessed event." He pulled Temple aside, then rose up on his tiptoes to whisper, "I do hate to be the bearer of bad news, but the other reason I came is because I fear there is a sheriff looking for you."

Temple was almost afraid to ask. "A sheriff?"

"Oh, aye. The Sheriff of Nottingham. It would be quite a lark, you being chased like some nefarious criminal by the Sheriff of Nottingham, if the man wasn't so determined to find you. Some bad business about you assaulting him and murdering Cordell." Stewie shook his head. "Not that Cordell didn't deserve a bad end, but by your hand? Ridiculous! I told him straight out he was mistaken. My friend Templeton, I said, is no more capable of committing murder than he is of wearing last year's waistcoat. Imagine, you murdering anyone?" Stewie blew out a loud sigh.

"Stewie, thank you for the warning, but I must be—"

"Nay, listen. There is more." Stewie blocked his path. "I fear the good sheriff was quite insistent on finding you and I told him you had other business to attend to, what with eloping with the heiress to Gretna and all—"

"You told him I was here?"

Stewie cringed. "I fear so. He tricked it out of me, knavish fellow that he is. And I think you might want to consider getting on with your wedding and perhaps taking a long trip abroad, for he's searching the town as we speak."

"Here? In Gretna?" Temple asked.

The man nodded his head quite emphatically, threatening to send his tall, beaver hat toppling over. "I'll do my best to keep him out of your way, but you might want to get on with the business at hand."

"I intend to, Stewie. I have every intention of doing just that."

"Oh, and Temple?" he asked.

"Yes, Stewie?"

"I hope the gel isn't having second thoughts. I've got a lot wagered on her becoming your marchioness."

First Colin, now Stewie. Temple wanted to groan. If he did pull off this marriage, he was going to make them both very rich men and beggar a good portion of the *ton*.

"I only ask," Stewie was saying, "because I saw your bride leaving in quite a huff. Nerves, I suppose, but it wouldn't do for her to call it all off now, you know what I mean?"

Temple ignored the financial motivation behind Stewie's concerns and latched on to the real gem of information the man held.

"Which way did she go? Which way, Stewie?"

"A man in love, I do declare!" Stewie grinned and clapped Temple again on the back.

"Which way, Stewie?" he said, nearly rattling the mushroom out of his Hessians.

He pointed toward the door. "Out. She ran out the door and turned right, I believe."

Temple followed his directions without a glance back, leaving Stewie to straighten his coat and fluff his ruffled cravat. "A man in love, and with an heiress to boot! I've always said there was more to Templeton than met the eye. I've always said it."

And so he did to the empty room around him.

Chapter 20

Diana had stumbled out of the inn into the brilliant sunshine of a lovely June morning. The perfect day to be wed.

Yet all she could hear, instead of the chirping of birds and the greetings of passersby, were the stern words of the innkeeper's wife.

I've seen too many of his kind pass through and the sorrow they leave in their wake. That's the sort of man who can talk a woman into believing anything.

And Temple had. He'd talked her into coming to Gretna by a means most foul.

Her heart didn't want to believe it, but everything Pymm had said made more sense than the tarradiddle Temple had been feeding her.

He'd traded her heart for Pymm's mission to the sultan's court.

Well, she knew where she'd like to send the pair of them, and it was a fair shade hotter than some distant Eastern land.

Though in truth, he hadn't lied to her. He hadn't come after her because he didn't want to see her wed to another man. He'd come after her because he'd been forced.

Oh, as much as he had told her true, that he hadn't come after her because he cared, she'd never quite believed his denials.

Not until now.

Diana felt sixteen all over again, standing at the Fosters' ball, tears streaming unchecked down her cheeks as Temple denied her the first time.

Botheration, her dangerous gamble had failed. Failed horribly.

She continued her tear-blinded course down the street until a pair of strong arms caught her.

"Lady Diana, are you well?"

The concerned voice came from none other than Lord Harry Penham. Boring Harry. Harry with the harridan mother.

True Harry.

It mattered not. Not anymore.

"My lady, I'm sorry for the way we stole you away yesterday. Believe me, it was all Nettlestone's idea. I would never have harmed Templeton intentionally. I was taught to respect my elders, not brawl with them." He pulled a handkerchief out of his jacket pocket and pressed it into her hand. "Is there anything I can do for you?"

Diana laughed, a little hiccup of a sound. "Yes, Lord Harry, there is. Marry me."

His mouth fell open. "But I fear Nettlestone won that honor. Trounced me soundly."

"Nettlestone cheats. Besides, I want him not. I want you." She caught his hand and began towing him toward the church that Temple had pointed out as they'd ridden into town just a few hours earlier.

Had it been just this morning? It felt like weeks ago.

"But . . . but . . ." Penham stammered in protest.

"Oh, do be still, Harry," she snapped at him.

Harry wasn't the second son of a domineering woman not to know when to shut his mouth and do what he was told.

So off they went, hand in hand toward the church.

But neither of them noticed the dark, scowling man following in their wake.

Temple's search for Diana ended at the inn's front door. He barreled into Nettlestone, and for the moment he forgot his vow to kill the baron.

"Templeton, glad to see you," Nettlestone breathed. "You've got to come with me. That knave Penham has got her. Saw him with my own eyes stealing her away to the church. Should have known he'd never honor our agreement. I won the lady, fair and square, I did. Now I'll have to demand satisfaction. I'd be glad to have you as my second."

"Your what?"

"My second. I'm going to kill Penham and then take his widow. I suppose I'll have to let her mourn him. What would be an appropriate amount of time in these circumstances, an hour? Mayhap two?"

Temple wasn't listening. "Where are they?" he thundered.

"Why, in the church," Nettlestone told him. "He took that annoying Frenchie with him as a witness. And after all our days of friendship, I would have thought he'd at least ask me."

Temple's blood ran cold. "Frenchman?"

"Yes, the one from Buxton."

Temple uttered an ugly curse. "A Frenchman? With Penham and Diana?"

Nettlestone took a step back and nodded. "Well, if you want to stand up for Harry, you can have the spot, no need to lose one's temper over such a trifling matter."

Temple caught hold of the baron. "Do you still have my pistols?"

Nettlestone paled in the face of Temple's uncharacteristic fury. "Now, there's no need for violence, Templeton. If you want the chit, she's yours."

"Give me my pistols," Temple ground out.

The baron reached inside his jacket and produced the pair. "Demmed twitchy things. Not at all reliable."

Temple wasn't really listening, he was checking to see that they were loaded, and then glanced once at the church. He took the baron by the arm and shoved him toward the inn. "Go inside and fetch a man named Pymm. He'll be with Lord Lamden. Tell him Marden is here."

"Martin, yes, indeed. I'll convey the message," Nettlestone said, his teeth practically rattling as he tried to steady himself.

"Not Martin. The man's name is *Marden*." Temple let out an exasperated sigh. "Make haste, man; there isn't a moment to lose."

Nettlestone frowned. "Templeton, you make this Marden fellow sound as if he is attempting to single-handedly topple England."

"He is," Temple said. "But not with my bride."

Diana stood before the vicar knowing she was making the worst mistake of her life. It was one thing in a fit of anger to drag a willing man to the altar, but quite another to utter the words that would bind her to him for the rest of her life.

Lady Harry. Diana shivered. Oh, wouldn't Temple be laughing up his sleeve. Oh, truly, she didn't care a fig what that double-dealing bafflehead cared or said.

Oh, but she did.

"Do you, Lady Diana Fordham, take Lord Harry Penham to be your lawfully wedded husband—"

The door of the church flung open, a ray of sunshine racing up the dark aisle.

Diana turned, a blazing smile on her lips.

Temple! He'd come to stop her. He'd come to tell her it was all a great misunderstanding.

"Sir?" the vicar called out. "Can I help you?"

The tall, dark figure strode into the church, closing the door behind him. Once again he was cast into shadows until he began walking up the aisle, his arm outstretched.

Diana continued to smile until she saw what he held.

A pistol.

"Temple!" she hissed. "Don't shoot him."

Then she looked again, and realized the man there to stop her wedding wasn't Temple.

"So sorry, mademoiselle. But I can't let this travesty continue. Not when your true groom awaits you in France." Then he nodded his head, and two men slipped from behind the altar, one catching hold of the vicar, and the other, Lord Harry.

"I do say," Diana's momentary groom muttered. "I won her fair and square."

"Bah, you English," Marden scoffed. "Your sense of honor and love makes me ill." The man raised the pistol and pointed it at Harry.

Diana stepped in front of Marden's next victim.

"You'll have to kill me to kill him, sir."

Marden smiled. "If you serve France with half as much heart, mademoiselle, you will have made my exile here in England worth every loathsome moment."

* * *

Marden's men had tied up Penham and the wide-eyed vicar quickly and efficiently, then begun the arduous task of dragging a protesting Diana down the aisle.

"Your Highness," Marden said to her, "quit struggling. When you are Empress of France and the world is at your disposal, you will thank us."

"I'll not marry that bandy-legged toady of yours anymore than I would have Lord Harry."

Penham made a muffled protest from behind his gag.

Marden ignored them both. "You'll enjoy being an empress. You were born to the role. You may not be legitimate, but I have a cousin in Rome working on that issue right now. I believe there is some ancient precedent that we may be able to use to see you declared a rightful heir."

"I believe the word you mean is 'coercion.' I've no more a right to the French throne than you."

"I beg to differ," Marden said, his mouth narrowing to a ratlike smile. "That mark on your back was left there by your father, Louis. He wouldn't have put it there unless he intended to ensure that you rose to a place of preeminence at his court. You are of noble blood. French blood."

"My father is the Earl of Lamden," she shot back defiantly. "And I am English."

Marden caught her by the forearm and twisted her limb until a shock of pain ran through it. "I won't mark you, Your Highness, but I do have some persuasive means by which to gain your cooperation, which I intend to have."

Tears filled her eyes, but she refused to give in to him. *Never.* Never would she be drawn into this man's insane plan.

The door to the church bounded open, and a single figure stepped into the shaft of light.

"Let go of her, Marden, and I'll let you live."

Temple!

Diana's heart thrummed to life. As much as she was thrilled to see him, she also realized he was no match for three armed men. He was resourceful and capable, but three armed men were too much even for a dragon slayer.

"Let her go," Temple repeated, a deadly calm filling his words, his order drifting up to the saintly choir above.

Marden laughed, a wicked howl that rose into the rafters of the church like a devil's keen. "I think not. I've chased her this far, and as you well know, I'm not averse to killing for my prize."

The man's confidence brimmed over as he pointed his pistol at Temple. "Monsieur, I believe we have met before, and I don't mean at that wretched assembly in Buxton." His eyes narrowed. "Yes, I remember now. You called yourself Verdier and were bandied about court as Josephine's long-lost cousin."

Temple nodded. "You have a good memory, monsieur."

"I would not suggest returning," Marden told him. "For I fear your reception would be quite different."

Glancing down at his fingernails, Temple said in a droll voice, "Lawd, sir, why would I want to do that? In truth, I found the company in Paris quite an ignorant and unrefined lot. But what do you expect of a people who agree to be led by an upstart peasant?"

Marden growled something low and menacing as he aimed the pistol at Temple's heart.

"I wouldn't recommend that," a deep voice said from behind Temple.

Diana glanced up to see the doorway filled with others, crowding in behind Temple—his grandfather leading the charge. The duke shouldered an ancient musket, probably a leftover from the Jacobite rebellions and borrowed from the innkeeper. Her father claimed a large, deadly-looking pistol.

At either side of her, Marden's wily cohorts loosened their grips as they were obviously losing interest in their portion of whatever reward they had hoped to gain by taking her to France.

Diana shook free of them.

But Marden was not so easily deterred. He caught her by the wrist and yanked her in front of him, using her as a shield, then laid the muzzle of his pistol against her forehead. "I'll not leave without her. She is intended for France. Are you all fools? She will be an empress. The mother of emperors."

To her surprise, Stewie, of all people, poked his head around the duke. "I do say, don't you think she's a little long in the tooth to be casting off as Boney's bride? Surely there's some young Italian bird who would suit quite nicely rather than some London spinster?"

Everyone turned and glared at the little interloper, and he shrugged and retook his position well hidden behind the duke's towering figure.

Diana cringed. Though he made her sound as ancient as Methuselah, right now she'd be willing to claim she was the devil's twin sister if only to convince Marden to let her go.

"Her age is a concern, but she has other attributes," Marden admitted, hauling her deeper into the church. Diana knew he was going to try to effect his escape out the back door. He probably had horses and more men at the ready. "Besides, the priest who was at her birth is willing to remember the year a little more favorably." He smiled at Diana. "You are now only two-and-twenty."

There was a whistle in the back of the room, probably from Stewie, that mocked such an attempt to deny her age.

Deny her age . . . Deny her age . . .

Diana realized her age was one thing, but there was something else not even Marden would be able to undo.

"The day of my birth may be easy to change, but the fact that I'm not a virgin can't. I doubt your emperor will be all that pleased with any of you for bringing him a despoiled bride."

"Not a virgin?" stammered one of his henchmen.

She shook her head.

That was enough for Marden's compatriots. They shot out the back of the church, the sound of the door being nearly ripped off its hinges echoing like the toll of a church bell in their hasty scramble to distance themselves from this debacle.

"It cannot be." Marden shifted from one foot to the other, his eyes glancing wildly about the room as his brilliant plan crumbled before him.

"Oh yes," Diana said quite cheerfully over her shoulder to him. "I'm ruined. Utterly and completely."

"You worthless bitch," he said, seething with anger. "Don't you see what you've thrown away?"

"Yes. Marriage to a man I despise. And I would do it again and again. And I intend to. With the man I love with all my heart."

Her gaze met Temple's, but instead of an acknowledgment of their shared heart, she saw only horror in his eyes. Then she realized why.

In taunting Marden to gain her freedom, she'd gone too far.

But what she hadn't foreseen, Temple had. And with instincts honed from years of service, he leapt forward, even as the Frenchman began to pull the trigger. Temple caught his arm and wrenched it upward, just as the gun fired. The bullet went aimlessly into the ceiling, sending down a shower of plaster and splinters.

Without a moment's hesitation, Temple slammed his other fist into Marden's face, sending the man careening into the aisle, out cold before he hit the stone floor.

The sheriff rushed forward.

Temple pointed at Marden. "Sir, there is the man you seek. This is the man who murdered Viscount Cordell." He bowed slightly. "And please accept my sincerest apologies for our earlier encounter."

"No need to apologize, my lord," the sheriff said. "Mr. Pymm explained it. Honored to help you. Deeply honored." He nodded to two other fellows, obviously his assistants, who began to cart the unconscious Marden out of the church.

Temple then turned and caught Diana in his arms, pulling her close. She collapsed against the familiar strength of his chest. His arms wound around her and she knew, just knew, she'd been a fool not to listen to him earlier.

He held her as if he would never let her go.

Then he bent his head down and kissed her soundly, scattering any further doubts that Pymm's words might have cast onto her heart.

When he finished, she glanced over his shoulder to find Nettlestone untying Penham, while Stewie assisted the pale and shaky vicar.

"Aren't you going after the others?" she asked Temple, prodding him to follow their enemies.

"No," he said, kissing the top of her head, brushing her cheek with his fingers as if this were nothing more than another lazy morning.

"Why not?" she bristled. "They were about to kidnap me and make me the Empress of France."

Temple ruffled her hair. "Only you would complain of such a fate."

"Have you met the groom?"

He grinned. "Actually I have."

"I still think you should go after them." She pointed at the door with one hand, her other balled into a fist and planted on her hip.

Temple shook his head, affecting his Corinthian stance. "No need, my lady. Pymm and a band of ruffians he brought along with him are outside. I would gather by now they have it all well in hand, not to mention the able services of our good friend, the Sheriff of Nottingham. Besides, I have business here that needs attending." He nodded to the white-faced vicar who stood shakily before the altar. Stewie lent the man of God a steady hand, confident in his place as Temple's groomsman.

Diana grinned and nodded and started to walk hand-in-hand with Temple toward their future.

Only their path was blocked by Nettlestone and Penham.

To her surprise, the pair bowed respectfully and conceded their previous claims to Temple.

"No hard feelings, eh, my lord?" Penham said, offering his hand.

"None, sir," Temple told him.

Nettlestone made his apologies as well, and the three shook hands. Then the baron and Lord Harry dodged past them, headed for the door as if they were late to their own weddings.

"Where are you going?" Diana asked. "Aren't you going to stay?"

Nettlestone shook his head. "Would love to, but the Earl of Kingswell lives not twenty miles from here. Rumor has it he has two daughters of a marriageable age. Penham and I have decided to go have a gander at the chits."

"Twins," Penham said with a wink, then a nudge into the baron's ribs. "And well dowered."

"Couldn't get to town this Season because their mother fell ill." Nettlestone shook his head as if the tragedy was more than he could bear. "Terrible luck that, but it means we'd best nab the birds before the countess makes a recovery or knocks off and they go into mourning."

But they didn't make it very far before they were collared by Diana's father and dragged back up the aisle.

"Diana!" the Earl of Lamden said. "Don't take another step."

Diana held her ground, hands on her hips. "Father, there is no need to shout. I am safe."

"That's not the problem," the earl said, his voice shaking with anger. "Who was it?" He rattled Nettlestone and Penham like a terrier might a pair of rabbits.

"Who was what?" she asked.

Her father's mouth set in a hard line. His brow furrowed, and then he spoke. "Penham, you'll not be running out on my daughter."

Diana realized what had her father so upset. She rushed over to the young man's side before her father strangled him with his iron grasp on the poor boy's collar. "Papa, it wasn't Lord Harry."

Her father grimaced. He leaned forward and whispered. "Not Nettlestone, gel. Tell me it wasn't him."

She shuddered and shook her head.

The earl let out a deep sigh of relief, dropping his two prisoners. "Then who did this?" he bellowed.

As for Penham and Nettlestone, they scurried out of the

church and out of sight for fear the earl might change his mind.

"Who did this to you?" Lamden shouted.

The answer came from the front of the church. "I did," Temple declared.

Lamden's gaze swung from him back to his daughter. "That idiot?"

She nodded, grinning from ear to ear.

"You want that horse's ass to be my son-in-law?"

"Oh yes, Papa. I do."

Being a man faced with a ruined daughter and the likelihood of having the *ton*'s biggest idiot for a son-in-law, Lamden did what any right-minded father would have done.

He raised his pistol and pointed it at Temple.

Epilogue

Setchfield Park
Devonshire, 1817

The fast-riding messenger who arrived at the house was shown to the duke's private study immediately, where the important missive he carried was handed over directly to Setchfield, as it had been the courier's instructions that no one else was to see it.

Such occurrences were a rarity at the duke's home, at least they had become such since Napoleon had been sent to his lonely exile on St. Helena. But this was the third dusty and exhausted rider to arrive at Setchfield Park in the past week, and he provoked a flurry of speculation amongst the staff as to what these obviously important missives could contain.

Government pleas for the duke's opinion? Tidings from the Foreign Office? England was now at peace; what could warrant so many hasty entreaties?

Then again, this was the Duke of Setchfield . . . it could be anything. As it was, the servants didn't know what to think of their master and mistress. Hardly ducal, they lived life with a rare joy and country simplicity, transforming their once gloomy palace of a house into a welcome home to any and all.

It hadn't always been thus; there were rumors that the duchess's father had been opposed to the match, and the duke's grandfather, the previous duke, had also been dead set against the marriage. But for some reason, they wed, despite the protests and proved all the naysayers wrong with their happiness.

Not that the old duke's opinion had mattered for very long. Angered at Temple's choice of bride and furious at the world's disregard for his opinions, the duke and his general ill-temper at everything had been overcome by a fit of apoplexy that took his life. He fell dead in the House of Lords, just as he finished calling Lord Fellerby a "horse's ass." And though he was greatly lauded and buried with all the pomp and ceremony due his rank, no one mourned the loss.

"What is it that Rafe wants now?" Diana asked from the doorway of Temple's study. Though her husband had held the title of Duke of Setchfield for nearly the entire length of their marriage, Temple he was to her, and Temple he would always be. She entered the room with a familiar shadow trotting happily at her heels, Tully.

"Vouchers," Temple told her, then he grinned. "To Almack's."

She cringed.

"Obviously," he said, handing the letter to her, "he doesn't know of your long-standing exile, or he wouldn't be asking."

She glanced over the quick, hastily written missive and shook her head. "What would Rafe be doing at Almack's?"

Temple shrugged. "I haven't the vaguest notion. This latest assignment is surely going to be his death. I much prefer it when he is investigating a murder or a theft from a house party. It sounds much safer than entering those hallowed walls."

"Why do you say that?" Diana asked. Her husband's cousin, Raphael Danvers, had returned to England after the war, and since he had neither title nor money, had sought to make his own way in the world.

"Because if he is willing to enter Almack's, that could only mean he's involved with a woman." Temple shuddered. "I predict he'll be leg-shackled by the end of the Season."

"Leg-shackled?" Diana said, crossing the space between them, her fair brow arched.

Her husband grinned. "Leg-shackled," he told her, opening his arms to her and drawing her into his lap. "A tenant for life. The fate that awaits all of us unsuspecting and unwitting men. Next thing you know, Pymm will be parsoned. Oh, what is the world coming to?"

"Oh, go on with you," Diana said. "Are you telling me you regret being married?"

He gazed up into her eyes, a wicked gleam glowing there. "Well . . ."

She pushed away from him and crossed the room. Tully followed her, only too aware of his mistress's moods. He dashed past her and out into the hallway before she pushed the door shut, then turned the lock, trapping her and her husband inside.

Tully was more than happy to give them their privacy. Besides, there was always his second favorite person in Setchfield Park to visit, the cook.

Within the study, Diana shot her husband a slanted glance. "Shall we discuss these regrets?"

"Diana, I have work to do," Temple protested, rising from

his cluttered desk and crossing the room, leaving his accounts and reports in a forgotten pile.

"You're right, you do," she murmured as she met him halfway. For a moment they stood before each other. "Starting with this word 'leg-shackled.'"

He reached out and caught her by the wrist, pulling her quickly into his arms as if he couldn't manage another moment without feeling her. His mouth covered hers in a deep, hungry kiss. Eight years of marriage, and he still couldn't get enough of his stolen bride. His tongue swept past her lips, dared her to come meet him in passion's embrace.

Diana moaned, low and throaty, pressing her body against his. Her hips rose instinctively to his, feeling the taut hardness of his manhood, already eager to fill her.

"Goddess," Temple whispered into her ear, while his hands skillfully divested her of her gown and chemise. "How will I ever get enough of you?"

"Let me show you where to start," she whispered, plucking at his shirt and breeches until they were both naked, their hands claiming and loving the familiar curves and hidden secrets of the other.

Temple swept her up into his arms and carried her over to the large settee in one corner of the room. He laid her down on the velvety chaise and gazed with adoration at the beautiful woman who was his wife.

His goddess.

She held her hands up to him. "Love me, Temple."

It was an urgent plea, a tender command.

His lips sought hers as he covered her, tasting her sweet mouth, running kisses down over her breasts, pausing only for a minute or two to tease her nipples into hard, puckered declarations of passion.

She writhed and arched toward him, and his path went

lower. First his fingers, delving between the sweet folds, opening them up so his lips could follow.

At first he lapped slowly, teasing both the bud hidden within and her into a frenzy of passion. As her breathing grew more fitful her body more insistent, he went faster, devouring her sex, until her fingers dug into his shoulders and his name came out in a ragged cry from her lips.

"Oh Temple! Oh yes!"

Diana's joy burst forth in an intoxicating delirium. She said his name again and again as waves of longing faded into utter rapture.

Temple glanced up at her sated features and grinned. He crawled back up her, kissing her here and there, enjoying the taste of her silken skin, her fevered flesh.

For he knew that despite her having found her completion, Diana was never sated for very long, and she'd want to see that he found his desires conquered as well.

And so it was that as her own last, trembling quakes started to flee, Diana caught hold of him and pulled him into a fiery kiss, her thighs opening to welcome his hardness.

Temple needed no help to find that treasured cleft. He filled her quickly, and soon the room echoed with not one ragged cry, but two voices raised together in unison and pleasure.

"Leg-shackled?" Diana asked, now that the fires within him had been quenched.

"Happily so," he told her. "Why, I'd marry you again, even without your father's pistol pointed at my head."

"He apologized." Diana sighed and nestled closer to her beloved husband. "I miss him."

"I do as well."

The Earl of Lamden had eventually come to see his daughter's choice of husband in a new light. With Pymm's assurances that Temple wasn't quite the fool he appeared, the earl discovered a son-in-law with whom he could share his love of politics and intrigues. And when the earl was sent with the English delegation to the Congress of Vienna for the peace talks, he insisted Temple be included in the party, as a voice of reason and experience, as well as to keep an eye on the wily French diplomat Talleyrand.

Before the earl died, he'd made one other last gesture of goodwill to his beloved family. Rather than see his title revert to the crown upon his death, he'd petitioned the Prince-Regent to see it continued by having the earldom pass to Diana's second son. And the Prince, well aware of Lamden's long service to his country and the family's historic loyalty to the crown, granted the boon, amending the original medieval writ of summons and issuing a new Letters Patent.

And so it was that under their roof lived the Duke and Duchess of Setchfield; their seven-year-old heir, the Marquis of Templeton; the five-year-old Earl of Lamden; and Lady Arabella Devinn, their three-year-old daughter.

Setchfield Park had finally become a happy, loving home.

Diana pressed one more kiss to her husband's lips, then bounded up from settee, hastily donning her clothes and heading for the door.

"Where are you going?" Temple waggled his brows at her. "I've much more I could tell you about the joys of being leg-shackled."

"It'll have to wait," she said. "I must start packing. I do so hate packing, but it is necessary."

"Packing? For what?"

"To go to town. I'm dying of curiosity to discover who has that rapscallion cousin of yours up in the boughs. She must be something to send *him* in search of vouchers." Pausing for a second, Diana then said, "I must write Georgie immediately and see if she'll meet us there to help this girl."

Temple groaned. "I suppose I'd better go as well. Can't let you go racing off on this fool's errand without my help." Then he suddenly brightened. "I'll drive."

Diana shook her head. "Oh heavens no, Temple. I'd like to get there in one piece. Besides, I won't leave the children, and I won't have you risking their lives with your driving."

"But Diana—"

"No, Temple. You're a terrible whip. Not every man is born a dab hand with horses. Your talents are elsewhere."

"And those would be?"

The Duchess of Setchfield glanced once at the closed door, then back at her naked husband. He winked at her, and she happily shrugged off her gown and rejoined him, only too delighted to oblige Temple in showing him just exactly where his talents lay—in love and passion.

And in the process, put off packing for another hour or so.

Author's Note

While Louis XV, the Sun King, was known for his mistresses and passionate affairs, his grandson and heir, Louis XVI, was not a very successful ladies' man. For the sake of fiction, I gave the rather shy and awkward king his own moment of glory in the form of Arabella, a fiery Scottish lass with a passion for tinkering and kings.

The other half of Diana's story, the search for Napoleon's bride after he set aside Josephine, did indeed have agents scurrying all over the royal houses of Europe, each one bent on finding the perfect bride for their temperamental emperor. Luckily for Temple, he got to Diana first, and happily for me, I got the pleasure of bringing you their madcap adventures in *Stealing the Bride*.

As for my next Regency adventure with the Danvers clan, if you read the epilogue, you know that Raphael Danvers is now back in England and up to his neck in trouble. I think it's high time he went out and found himself a bride. Don't you? Watch for news of his return on my website, *www.elizabethboyle.com*.

Best wishes always,

Elizabeth Boyle

A romance from Avon Books is always a welcome addition at the
❀   beach, the park, the barbecue . . .   ❀

Look for these enchanting love stories in August.

TO LOVE A SCOTTISH LORD by Karen Ranney
An Avon Romantic Treasure

The proud and brooding Hamish MacRae has returned to his
beloved Scotland wanting nothing more than to be left alone.
But Mary Gilly has invaded his lonely castle, and while it's true
that this pretty healer is beyond compare, it will take more than
her miraculous potions to awaken his heart.

TALK OF THE TOWN by Suzanne Macpherson
An Avon Contemporary Romance

Nothing puts a damper on a wedding day quite like discover-
ing your Mr. Right is *Mr. Totally Beyond Wrong*, which is why
Kelly Atwood knocks him flat and boards a bus to tiny
Paradise, Washington. One look at the gorgeous outsider and
attorney Sam Grayson gets hot around his too-tight collar,
because this runaway bride is definitely disturbing his peace.

ONCE A SCOUNDREL by Candice Hern
An Avon Romance

It was bad enough when Anthony Morehouse thought he had
won a piece of furniture in a card game, but when he discovers
that *The Ladies' Fashionable Cabinet* is actually a women's
magazine, he can't wait to get rid of it. Then he sees beautiful
Edwina Parrish behind the editor's desk, and Tony is about to
make the biggest gamble of all.

ALL MEN ARE ROGUES, by Sari Robins
An Avon Romance

When Evelyn Amherst agrees to her father's dying request, she
can scarcely imagine the world of danger she is about to enter—
or that it will bring her tantalizingly close to Lord Justin
Barclay. Here is a man to turn a young lady's head, but Evelyn
refuses to be diverted from her mission, especially not by this
passionate yearning for Justin's embrace.